IN FOR A RUBLE

ALSO BY DAVID DUFFY

Last to Fold

IN FOR A RUBLE

★ DAVID DUFFY ★

THOMAS DUNNE BOOKS
ST. MARTIN'S PRESS
NEW YORK

THOMAS DUNNE BOOKS.
An imprint of St. Martin's Press.

IN FOR A RUBLE. Copyright © 2012 by David Duffy. All rights reserved. Printed in the United States of America. For information, address St. Martin's Press, 175 Fifth Avenue, New York, N.Y. 10010.

www.thomasdunnebooks.com
www.stmartins.com

ISBN 978-0-312-62191-9 (hardcover)
ISBN 978-1-250-01244-9 (e-book)

First Edition: July 2012

10 9 8 7 6 5 4 3 2 1

For my parents

WEEK ONE: THE DEAL

★ CHAPTER 1 ★

Everything about Sebastian Leitz was big. The man himself was six foot four and weighed two-eighty easy. A tractor tire wrapped his midsection, he wore size fourteen shoes, and nobody made gloves to fit his hands. The out-size head, with its fat pear nose, kidney-pool blue eyes and inflated inner-tube lips, made him seem larger still. The head was topped by a bushy, orange Afro that had last seen the barber when Brezhnev was general secretary of the Communist Party of the Soviet Union. A circus clown on steroids. His voice—a foghorn bass—could've filled a big top.

Leitz needed the big head to hold the brain. He'd earned two doctorates, mathematics and economics, from Harvard and MIT. He'd written count-less papers and a half dozen books. He was a full professor at Columbia by twenty-six. People were talking Nobel Prize by thirty. That was before he quit academics and went to Wall Street to make big money.

Leitz was worth several billion, and he'd made it all himself—in little more than a decade. His hedge funds regularly ranked high on the perfor-mance charts, and Leitz himself consistently topped the compensation tables.

He had a blowback laugh and a blow-up temper. Both blew with the force of a saboteur's bomb—unseen, unexpected, until they knocked every-body in range off their feet. As I came to find out, not everyone got back up.

He had strong opinions and was willing to state them loudly and longly if he thought there was reason to do so. Otherwise he didn't waste breath. He ignored anyone he pegged as foolish or stupid. He didn't give a damn what they thought of him.

Leitz had a big penchant for secrecy. No one at his firm (other than him-self, of course) was allowed to take anything home from the office. An idle comment in the elevator, if it involved the company's business, was a firing offense. He hated losing—big time. He was known to throw whatever was in reach at whomever put him on the wrong end of a trade. When I met him, he was working on the biggest deal of his life—buying and merging two of America's TV networks, thereby taking hold of a big chunk of the media landscape. His bid had dominated the financial press and the tabloids for weeks.

Leitz was a force of nature—one of those people God or whoever is in charge put here from time to time to shake things up, make life interesting. I suppose, despite everything, that's why I liked him. But all the size and smarts, money and privilege in the world are no guarantee you won't fuck it up.

★ CHAPTER 2 ★

I didn't know any of this the first time we met. I didn't know much beyond what the press told me about his TV bid—BOLD! BIG TIME! BIG BET ON THE NEW FUTURE OF OLD MEDIA!—and his wealth. The New York papers were more forthcoming than Leitz's friend and my partner, Foster Klaus Helix, known as Foos, who arranged the meeting.

"How successful is he?" I asked.

"Leitz does okay," Foos said.

"What's okay?"

"Pretty good."

"S&P was up twelve percent last year. He do better than that?"

"Some."

"How much some?"

"Enough."

"He's a quantitative hedge fund manager, why's he trying to buy TV networks?"

"Thinks he'll make money."

"Their current owners think they don't make enough money. What's Leitz going to do different?"

"Make more money."

I let it go. I didn't really want the meeting. I didn't want the client. Leitz sounded like a bigger, richer, more opinionated pain in the ass than my last client, and he and his family turned out to be big trouble. But that was just an excuse. Truth be told, I didn't feel like doing much of anything, I hadn't in months. I was still thinking, unsuccessfully, about the woman who'd turned my life upside down before she walked out of it without even a kiss good-bye. She'd warned me she'd do that, twice, and she'd been true to her word. I couldn't blame her. I'd done my part to show her the door. I hadn't meant to, I'd had no choice. We're all our own best friend and enemy, as one of our proverbs puts it.

I kept hoping against hope she'd change her mind and come back. That carried me through the first few weeks. Then I heard she'd left her job—a high-profile appointment as United States Attorney for the Southern District of New York, something she'd worked hard to get—and blown town. After two weeks of not wanting to get out bed, I tried to convince Foos to let me use the Basilisk to find her. Maybe if I followed wherever she'd gone, pleaded my case, recanted, promised to change, she'd see the error of her ways. I didn't really believe it, but I had to try. Not that it mattered—Foos refused flat out.

"Who's side are you on?" I asked.

"What makes you think I'm dumb enough to choose sides?"

"She got to you, didn't she? Before she left. Made you promise not to help. What was the bribe? I'll double it."

He smiled and went back to banging on his computer keyboard. I don't know which was worse, the depression or the frustration. I knew the Basilisk could find her. That beast can find anyone. But its master wasn't cooperating.

"Don't believe everything you read in the papers," Foos said. I was doing more research in preparation for our meeting.

I ignored him on the grounds he was making me do my own homework—and I was still pissed off. I told myself Foos was right, I needed something to occupy my mind. I didn't really believe that either, but the alternatives for the day—vodka, beer, more vodka and beer—worked in his favor.

Even before he strode upon the media stage, Leitz cut a big swath, not that hard to do in New York if you've got the funds. He donated his way onto the boards of the Guggenheim Museum, Carnegie Hall and his teaching alma mater, Columbia. He bought expensive pictures at Sotheby's and Christie's, often bidding for himself instead of hiding behind a dealer or auction house functionary. He threw high-profile parties at his East Side mansion, packed with celebrities who invested in his hedge funds. He wasn't afraid to tell any reporter who'd listen that the government should stay the hell out of the hedge fund business. He might have been giving second thought to some of those comments, since the government—in the form of the SEC, FTC, FCC and Department of Justice—could have a lot to say about whether he was allowed to pursue the current objects of his desire. Still, not bad for a second-generation immigrant kid from Austria via Astoria.

Leitz came from a big family—a brother and two sisters, four kids in all. He lived in a double-fronted brick town house on East Sixty-second Street, to which he'd added the brownstones on either side, giving him twelve windows across the front—a ton of real estate anywhere, an enormity in Manhattan. I guess he needed room for *his* two kids (from two wives), housekeeper, nanny, and pair of Bernese mountain dogs, which I initially mistook for small Saint Bernards and was quickly corrected.

Foos had known Leitz before he became rich, when they were both ordinary, working-stiff, academic geniuses. They'd met at some conference of eggheads while Foos was at the Institute for Advanced Study in Princeton and Leitz at Columbia. Probably struck up a friendship over the lunch buffet—the two biggest brains and bodies in the room. Both left academics soon afterward, Leitz to Wall Street and Foos to move modern data mining forward several decades in as many years.

After Foos sold his company, he gave Leitz some of his fortune to invest along with a chunk of the assets of the foundation he endowed and runs—STOP, short for "Stop Terrorizing Our Privacy." I'd read Leitz required a minimum investment of $5 million and regularly racked up returns north of 30 percent a year, after fees of 3 percent of assets under management and the first 30 percent of profits earned. Fees were another big thing about him.

When I asked Foos about that, I got the usual, "Leitz does okay."

I gave up. I checked STOP's records, which I'm entitled to do since I'm the other member of the board, although Foos neglects to send me financial reports—or any other reports for that matter. I don't know how much of STOP's money Leitz invested, since the assets could be spread among multiple managers. STOP's most recent tax return, which I downloaded from the Internet, showed total assets of $208 million. It started with $50 million five years ago. The markets had tanked in the interim. Leitz indeed appeared to be doing okay.

On our way uptown, I again pressed Foos about his friend.

"What happened to the first Mrs. Leitz?"

"Bad scene."

"You know her?"

"A little."

"How bad?"

"The worst."

"And wife number two?"

"Jenny. She's cute. Smart too."

"Bad? Cute? Smart? Care to add a little color?"

"Not my business."

He looked out the window, and we rode in silence the rest of the way. In the twenty years I'd spent with the KGB, I'd never heard of anyone standing up against a full-bore Cheka interrogation. Given the chance, Foos could've been the first.

Someone had left the *Post* on the cab's backseat. NEW BIDDERS EXPECTED IN TV WAR, the headline read. The story cited Wall Street sources, all unnamed, stating that several consortia, involving everyone from Warren Buffet to Bill Gates to a couple of Chinese billionaires, were in the process of putting together offers to rival Leitz's. Wall Street was in full M&A—merger and acquisition—frenzy. The fees alone were expected to run into the hundreds of millions. The ensuing battle could last months.

Normally, I'm as caught up as the next guy in stories like this one, events that promise change and upheaval in the landscape—economic, social and cultural—of my adopted country. My natural curiosity (a character trait I've never tried hard to tame) would be working overtime at the prospect of meeting the man who'd set it in motion. But today as I read the story, noted the names, registered the humongous amounts of cash involved, I felt no spark. Whatever Leitz wanted didn't matter much. He might occupy my time, perhaps a bit of my attention, for a day, a week or a month, but he and his bidding war wouldn't do a damned thing to alter the fucked-up mess that had become my life.

At the corner of Madison and Sixty-second, Foos paid the driver. We walked half a block east. The morning was bright and crisp, not too cold for the second week of January. The remnants of a New Year's storm lined the sidewalks, mostly frozen slush now, covered with a coat of city grime, nothing compared with the three feet of black encrusted snow I'd left in Moscow back before Christmas.

Leitz's spread was almost precisely midblock, on the north side of the street. A handsome six-story brick house at the center, with cream-colored trim. Half the façade was flat-fronted, half formed a graceful bay, as if the architect had tried to make one house look like two. Avoiding ostentation perhaps. The rest of the expanded mansion comprised two traditional New York brownstones on either side. Foos pushed a brass button by the black door, and a Filipina answered. She smiled hello, ushered us inside, and offered to take our coats.

We stood in a stone-floored, chandeliered entrance hall that occupied the full width and half the depth of the double brick house. An elliptical staircase swirled upward at the center. The hall was hung as a portrait gallery—nineteenth century European, maybe a few American, paintings covered three of four walls. One picture caught my eye, a handsome, bearded man in his late thirties. I went over for a closer look. It was what I thought—a self-portrait by Ilya Repin, probably painted in the 1880s. I'd seen one like it at the Tretyakov in Moscow. The Met has a couple of Repin's works, but they're hard to find outside Russia. Leitz was becoming a little more interesting.

Foos came up beside me. "Nice picture."

"We've got some good painters. He's one."

"Not surprised. Leitz knows his stuff."

"Please, gentlemen, upstairs. Mr. Sebastian waits." The maid stood by the staircase pointing. We followed her direction.

Carpeted wood steps, painted balusters and a smooth mahogany banister climbed all six stories. On the second floor, two sets of double doors opened off the central hall into a high-ceilinged, paneled room in the front. I got off to take a look. It ran the width of the brick house—six windows—with a marble fireplace at each end. The furniture was a mixture of English and French antiques. A Picasso cubist still life hung over one fireplace in refined revolutionary conversation with a Braque over the other. Matisse, Cézanne and Manet graced the other walls.

"One more flight, boys, the inner sanctum," a loud voice called, and I returned to the stairs to see a large head of curly reddish-blond hair flopping over the railing from above. Foos was already halfway up. I followed, regretting not being able to spend more time with the paintings in the drawing room. But I didn't know what was to come.

On the third floor, off the stairs, I came face-to-face with a huge Rothko color field—blue and red and purple. The closeness and intensity took me aback, until I realized that beside me was another one of the same size—yellow, orange, and red. I turned slowly around the hall. There were four of them, one for each wall, and the impact was overwhelming, a whirling cocoon of color, too close and too bright, and much too deep, to take in all at once.

Foos passed through unaffected. He'd been here before. I spun in my spot, trying to establish myself and get some perspective. It wasn't possible. Three-dimensional hypnosis. I had to fight to break the spell and pull my eyes from the color, infinite in its intensity. I turned to the red-haired man in the doorway.

9

He was smiling. "People say it's over the top, but I like a real kick in the ass."

"You got that, all right," I said, extending my hand, head still spinning His paw enveloped mine in a tight grip. "Sebastian Leitz. Come in."

This room was as big as the one on the floor below, also paneled, but in blond wood with clean, contemporary lines. Fireplaces at both ends again, but these had simple, limestone mantels with no frills or decoration. Wood fires burned in both. The paintings were contemporary too—Franz Kline held down one end, Robert Motherwell the other, two more heavyweights thrashing out their own generation of abstraction. But it was the top right corner, above the desk, that caught my eye. A smallish canvas, compared with the others, eighteen inches by three feet, highlighted by a single spot. A collection of blue, yellow, red, green, and brown rectangles floating on a white background.

I remembered the painting—and where I'd first seen it. Kasimir Malevich, *Suprematist Composition,* painted in 1916. I'd gone to look at it at Sotheby's a few years ago, right before it sold for $80 million. I raised an eyebrow at the buyer. He nodded.

"Not many people get that. But you're Russian, right? Not *Black Square,* but the best I could do."

"You did well. It's . . . You know as well as I do—words are hard to come by."

For my money, Malevich is the greatest of Russian painters, one of the greatest of all painters, and along with Kandinsky, perhaps, the first real abstractionist anywhere. Leitz had placed the picture in the traditional position of an icon in a Russian house, just as Malevich himself had done with his most famous painting, *Black Square,* when he showed it for the first time in 1915, declaring, none too subtly, a thousand years of representational painting passé.

"Thank you. It's my favorite picture."

"I like the Repin downstairs too."

He gave me a look that indicated I'd passed some kind of test. "You're the first to recognize that. Come sit by the fire."

Leitz led the way to a group of black leather Le Corbusier club chairs under the Motherwell. Foos lounged in one. At the other end of the room, under Kline's big, brutal, black brushstrokes, two flat screens sat on a desk and a row of monitors were embedded in the paneled wall. They flickered with red and green and blue, too far away to see the actual numbers.

Foos poured himself a cup of coffee from a chrome thermos without waiting to be asked and lifted an eyebrow at me. I shook my head. Leitz already had a cup in front of him.

I looked from one to the other while I waited to see who would speak first. Since I was a guest, and wasn't sure I even wanted to be here, I had no reason to get the ball rolling.

Leitz was wearing an XXL cashmere sweater, dark green, suede patches on the elbows, over a gray T-shirt, along with baggy brown corduroys that hadn't seen an iron or press in weeks. His shoes stood out. Elegant, dark brown wingtips, English or Italian, I couldn't tell which, well worn but freshly shined and in great shape. Foos was dressed as Foos always dresses—black sweater, black jeans, black boots. His mane of black curly hair was a little frizzed in the cold air and showing a bit of gray. He'd had a few inches trimmed for the New Year, one of his few concessions to the calendar, but it still hung thickly well past his shoulders. His black eyes looked at me from behind black, chunky glasses. His big pointed nose ran left to right from my position, and since his mouth opens mostly on the right side, it makes his whole face lopsided. He was as tall as Leitz and a few pounds lighter. Leitz's weight settled around his middle, while Foos's hung evenly from his shoulders, which I've never understood since I've never seen him do anything remotely resembling exercise.

I was wearing my winter uniform—black turtleneck and dark gray flannel trousers. I'd handed in my black leather jacket downstairs. I had a comfortable pair of English-made loafers on my feet that probably cost less than Leitz's socks. In the spring I trade the turtleneck for a T-shirt, the leather and flannel for linen, and I don't have to worry about what to put on for another six months. The injuries I'd suffered last June—some at the hands of my old friend and nemesis, Lachko Barsukov, some at my own—had healed, and I'd worked myself back into pretty good shape, despite too much vodka and beer. I was showing no flab on my six-foot, two-hundred pound frame. Since Victoria left, no one was around to complain if I was carrying extra weight, but staying in shape is a vanity like any other—and one of mine, the result of a half-starved youth when making it through the day was no better than a fifty-fifty bet. Victoria said she liked my brown eyes—they had a curious sparkle—straight-ahead nose and squared-off triangle of a chin. My hair, once bushy and black, had thinned to the point of a sixty-year-old by my late twenties, in my mind the result of the same youthful malnourishment. I'd shaved my scalp and kept it that way. Today, it was probably showing some red from the cold air outside. I hadn't worn a hat.

Nobody said anything for several minutes, an unusual occurrence in

America—or anywhere. Leitz looked at me, I looked at the paintings. Foos might have taken a cat nap. Three men, content to take silent stock. Nine times out of ten—ninety-nine times out of a hundred—someone has to fill the void. Not today. I'm used to this treatment from Foos—we can go days without much more than grunting at each other—but Leitz intrigued me by saying nothing. When he was ready, he broke the silence.

"Thank you for coming to visit. Foos told me a little of your background. You've had an interesting life."

"Sounds like he's told you more than he's told me." I smiled to show I meant no offense. Leitz smiled back.

"I require all of my clients to sign confidentiality agreements which my lawyers drafted expressly to prohibit people from talking about me or my business. Foos is one of the few who abides by his word."

"With him, you didn't need the agreement."

Leitz chuckled. "I told my lawyers the same thing."

Foos said, "You guys going to talk business or shall I go hang with Jenny while you get acquainted?"

"Patient too," Leitz said. "How much do you really know about me, Mr. Vlost?"

"Call me Turbo. Only what I read in the papers, which Foos tells me not to believe."

Leitz chuckled again.

I took the bait, maybe because the pictures had me interested. "You run a hedge fund, a family of funds, actually, with assets of some twenty billion. You're very successful. So successful that a few years ago, you returned half the money you manage to your clients, whether they wanted it back or not. You said you couldn't keep earning the kind of returns you and they were used to. I'm guessing that also meant you couldn't keep charging the fees you and they were used to, which are supposed to be the highest in the industry."

He nodded but said nothing.

"That pissed a bunch of them off, which must be a peculiarly American irony—wealthy people getting angry because someone gave them their money back."

He smiled and nodded again. "So far, you're very well informed."

"You have a reputation for secrecy. Your investors have no idea what you're doing with their money. You're known for being mercurial, I've seen less complimentary terms used too. You get away with it because of the returns you generate. You're what Wall Street calls a rocket scientist. You use your mathematical skills to make big bets in the financial markets and you're right more often than you're wrong."

"That's essentially correct, except the word 'bets' connotes gambling. I don't gamble, not with my clients' money. The markets are highly efficient, but they're not perfect. I develop mathematical models that identify small inefficiencies. My investments count on these inefficiencies correcting themselves in time, which they almost always do. The investments are market neutral—I might go long in a convertible bond and short the underlying stock, for example—so I don't care whether the market goes up or down."

I heard this before. I'd also heard there's no such thing as a free lunch. "Care to explain that little collapse back in 2008?"

He sighed the sigh of someone who's been asked the same question too many times.

"In the early days, we and a few others had the playing field mostly to ourselves, and we did quite well. Imitation being the purest form of flattery, it didn't take too long before other smart people figured out what we were up to and piled into the game. Some tried to copy us, either by imitating our moves or developing their own models and software, and a number pursued other strategies. Too much money chasing not enough deals. Made finding new inefficiencies harder and less profitable, the reason, as you say, we reduced the size of the funds we manage. There was also too much leverage. Cheap credit's like an addictive drug—the users keep taking more and more to achieve the same high. Eventually they OD. Cut off the supply, same thing happens. When the shakeout came, a lot of people got hurt. We actually made money. We were up twelve percent in 2008 and forty-three percent in 2009, thirty-five percent last year."

"Sounds like competition to me."

"I have no problem with competition. It makes my job more difficult, but that's the nature of capitalism. My problem is theft."

Foos grunted his approval—we were finally somewhere.

"My business is all computers," Leitz said. "They run the models, access the markets for information, crunch the numbers, identify opportunities. Everybody works this way. The amount of information to be gathered and processed is way more than any individual or group of individuals could handle. The competitive advantage therefore is in the modeling and the software—and the cost of capital."

"Somebody has to provide the modeling and software. Or have the computers learned to do that themselves?"

He laughed. "No, that's where we mortals still add value, at least for the time being. But we're hostage to the electronic executioners of the strategies we develop. We can't operate without them. So we go to substantial lengths to make sure they're secure. A few months ago, we were subjected to an attempted break-in, electronic."

"Brute-force attack," Foos said. "Somebody used their own computer to run the possible password combinations for one of Sebastian's employees. Could've worked, but fortunately he changes passwords every week and the bad guy's computer was a little slow. Whoever it was tried again, twice, but I suggested some improvements in encryption and a few other areas, and they didn't get very far. Things should stay copasetic in the near term, but there ain't no panaceas in this business."

"This related to the TV bid?"

"I'm assuming it is."

"Anything like this happen before?"

"No.

"Any idea who'd try it?"

"Another bidder, or prospective bidder. Lots of rumors out there. Competitor, maybe. Disgruntled investor. Someone with a grudge against hedge funds. Plenty of those out there too. Maybe just a hacker."

"No hackers anymore who aren't in it for profit," Foos said.

"You do anything recently to piss anyone off?" I asked.

"Like make them take their money back? No." He laughed.

"Tell me about the TV bid."

His face darkened. "What do you mean?"

"Why you're in it. This is hardly a bet—sorry, trade—based on market inefficiencies."

The darkness lifted, replaced by inquisitiveness. "Don't take this the wrong way, but how much do you know about capital markets?"

"Marx identified three essential elements of capitalism—capital, labor, and markets. I've studied their interrelationships, albeit perhaps from a different perspective than yours."

He chuckled. "Fair enough. But Marx left one element out—cash."

"I appreciate cash. It's why I don't keep much money in the markets."

He laughed again. "Good for you. Then you'll understand where I'm coming from. A different perspective, as you say. Everyone focuses on TV networks as businesses in long-term decline. Competition from cable channels, the Internet, video games, not to mention good old evolving demographics. No question about it, long-term outlook sucks. That's a technical term. Not a business most companies, especially growth-oriented public companies, want to be in anymore."

"So?"

"Cash. It's still a cash-rich business. You have any idea how much cash one network throws off in a year? Billions. Now think about two. Then think about two, merged, redundancies and overlaps removed, market share enhanced, if only because there are now three where there were four. In cash flow terms, one plus one equals three, maybe three and a half. You got cash like that, you got options, in a capitalist way of thinking, of course."

"In any way of thinking. I'm still keeping most of my money in the mattress. How come nobody else figured this out?"

"I'm sure they have, especially now that I've shown a spotlight on it. That's why I expect competition. Cash flow is a commodity, like any other. The difference between success and failure in this deal is price, how much you pay to acquire that cash flow. I think my analysis is better, more productive, than anyone else's is likely to be. If you were getting into the game, it would be helpful to know what the other guy's planning to do, wouldn't it?"

"So you think that's what's going on?"

"Timing suggests it is. So does the amount of money involved. It's enough to attract someone with the kind of resources this guy seems to have."

"And you want me to find this guy?"

"That would be ideal, of course, but I'm not naïve. I'm more concerned about security. Foos says we're secure, and I believe him. He also says, no panaceas, as you just heard. I want you to put yourself in this guy's shoes and see if you can find a way in."

★ CHAPTER 3 ★

I still didn't want the job. Foos was staring straight at me, all but imploring—take it, you need something to do. He was trying to kill two birds with one stone—help Leitz and give me something to occupy a troubled mind. Well-meaning friends can be a real pain in the ass.

Nowhere near the pain I'd been in since Moscow, though. I'd gone in December hoping it would change my mood. Not much traction before the family roof caved in once again.

I got reacquainted—more accurately, acquainted—with my son, Aleksei, as we started to fill in the thirty years since the time I'd left him and my ex-wife. "Abandoned" is his word, "thrown out" is mine, but we've agreed to disagree. That we found each other was fate at work, especially since Polina and I didn't talk after the split, and I'd moved to New York back in 1992. There was a price to be paid, of course—if you're Russian there's always a price—in this case, the death of his mother. I didn't feel guilt or sadness. She was a tortured soul, and she'd done more than her share of harm—mostly to me. I didn't see why he should either, since she truly had abandoned him, but try telling that to a son about his mother.

This was all maybe manageable, although Aleksei wasn't making it easy. My attempts to find some kind of roadmap to rapport were running into a major roadblock—the Cheka, known today as the FSB, known to most as the KGB (its longest running incarnation), known previously by multiple names and acronyms, but all anyone needs to know is that they all stand for state security. The specific problem was my connection to the Cheka, my employer for twenty years, which my son presumed was as strong as ever, despite ample evidence to the contrary. That made the kick in the gut Sasha delivered, the one I was still trying to work through, all the more devastating.

I've been doing long-distance research for years into an unknown past—wondering if it was truly unknowable. The Gulag, where I'd grown up, did a few things well. One was eviscerate its victims' lives. Another was keep records. The records still exist, in the archives of the Cheka. I've been working, in secret, with an archivist I know only as Sasha, who's helped many people uncover their pasts. My mother's history was relatively easy to reconstruct, from what I'd been told as a child and from Gulag documents. There was a brief period in the chaos of the early 1990s when things opened up, even at Lubyanka, and Sasha was able to unearth a little information about my presumed father, then the Cheka flexed its still considerable muscle, and the doors to the archives slammed shut. Numerous questions about my parentage remained unanswered. Sasha had managed a breakthrough last summer, but he and the new information ran afoul of Lachko Barsukov. Before I figured out that Lachko wasn't my only Barsukov nemesis, Sasha had to go underground. When he surfaced and felt safe, I booked a flight to Moscow. I had a bad feeling about what awaited me there, and I wasn't wrong, but I wanted out of New York, away from Victoria's memory. For some reason, I keep thinking distance can dull the pain of the past.

Sasha met me for dinner a few days after I arrived.

"I never should be telling you this," he said. "You're not ready, nobody could be. There's a chance I'm not right, but I can't follow up. It's a new world at Lubyanka since I got back. Everything's locked up tighter than ever. You need special clearance. Orders from the Kremlin. Some say from the man himself."

The man would be Comrade Putin, whose positions in the New Russia have included president and prime minister, but whose power is more akin to that of general secretary of the Communist Party in the old days. Even after he entered politics, Putin remained first and foremost a Chekist.

Sasha slid a piece of paper across the table and stared into his glass. "It looks like we were wrong, and this is your father, your real father." He didn't want to say it. I can't blame him.

I unfolded the paper.

Two initials and a name.

L. P. Beria.

I spent Christmas back in New York, researching what I could about Lavrenty Pavlovich Beria, thinking about Aleksei and trying not to think about Victoria. Not necessarily in that order. It's funny—growing up in the

Gulag, there weren't any holidays to celebrate. When I was an adult in the Soviet Union, Christmas wasn't observed. When I moved to New York, I lived alone, and I didn't pay much attention. But this year, for the first time, as I walked the streets amid the holiday decorations and preparations, I felt lonely. I wasn't sure what to make of that. For all I knew, Victoria didn't even like Christmas. She'd lived alone much of her life too. All I wanted was to be able to ask her.

Progress with Aleksei might have cut the blues, but he'd walked out on our second dinner together when he found out how deeply the Cheka runs in his lineage and declined to meet again. I couldn't fault him. The Cheka was the one Soviet institution to make the transition to so-called Russian democracy with little loss of power. What was once known as the state within the state became in many ways the state itself once Putin took power, and it ruled with the same tools it had long used so successfully—fear, intimidation, violence, and making absolutely certain its own interests came first. As an officer with the Russian Criminal Prosecution Service, which wages a form of David-and-Goliath institutional warfare against its much more powerful rival, Aleksei viewed all Chekists as enemies for life. Like many, he also blamed the Cheka for the problems with the New Russia, and he wasn't entirely wrong. Or even mostly. I kept trying to demonstrate that my departure from the organization was complete and total and twenty years earlier, but he inherited my stubborn streak, at least on that subject.

All of which meant it was going to take time for him to figure out what he really thought of me—I understood that—but I wasn't prepared to wait another couple of decades for the result. I understood equally well that to push it would shove him in the wrong direction. One more situation whose outcome I couldn't do a damned thing about, which just added to the general depression.

Then there was Beria—the Soviet Union's most brutal butcher, head of the Cheka from 1938 to 1953, serial rapist, Stalin's favorite executioner—and the idea that he could be my father. He doesn't look like a bad man—ski-jump nose, receding hair line, cleft chin, and rimless spectacles. Looks can be deceiving. But did *I* look like *him*?

Since Sasha's revelation, Lavrenty Pavlovich has taken to putting in periodic appearances in my consciousness, showing up unannounced, often in uniform, usually wearing a mocking grin. I'm not that familiar with apparitions, although lots of my fellow *zeks* saw them all the time in the camps. Murdered sons, daughters, or parents. Loved ones left behind. Relatives who'd vanished, just as they themselves had done. Sometimes the visions

19

were causes of comfort, other times, fear. Beria didn't comfort, he didn't scare either. There was a time when the mere mention of his name could cause unchecked terror, but he'd been dead for sixty years. Old ghosts aren't that scary. Mostly he mocked—with well-chosen words and that grin. The first few times, I was mildly concerned with my state of mind, but I put the visions down to too much vodka and the head injury I'd given myself last summer when, a day after being beaten senseless, I'd cracked my skull on a glass coffee table. After the first few appearances, Lavrenty Pavlovich and I reached our own détente—he showed up when he chose, and he mostly left when I told him to.

Information on Beria the man was hard to come by, beyond the essential facts of his career. Head of the Georgian secret police, secretary of the Communist Party in Georgia, then for the Transcaucasian region, member of the Central Committee of the Communist Party, deputy head of the People's Commissariat for Internal Affairs (NKVD), member of the Politburo, commissar general of state security, overseer of purges, murders, and crimes too numerous to count. Stalin is supposed to have introduced him to Roosevelt at Yalta as "our Himmler."

Beria hasn't received the attention most mass murderers get, and what was out there wasn't necessarily reliable. A couple of biographies (one overly florid, the other too dry), some academic papers, but not much that told me about the man. I could have gone back to Russia, but I'd find less information there. The current powers are schizophrenic in their treatment of history, particularly the Stalin era. On the one hand, they want it remembered as a great patriotic age—the time when the Soviet Union became a major twentieth-century power and, at enormous sacrifice, turned the tide of the Great Patriotic War. This is true, so far as it goes. But buying into Stalin as icon requires turning a blind eye to the greatest crimes against humanity this side of Nazi Germany, crimes that Russia as a nation—Russians as a people—have never come to terms with. So we try, with the active participation of our leaders, to sweep them under the rug, hoping in time, I suppose, that the world will forget. One reason there's little information available about the perpetrators, including Comrade Beria, and much of what there is has been locked away.

I badgered Sasha periodically by phone and e-mail, but the answer was the same—no clearance, no access. I was stuck in genealogical limbo, hoping for the opposite of a smoking gun. No way to move things forward with Aleksei until I found it—or didn't. Unable even to look, I got more and more gloomy.

Seeking diversion, I pestered Foos about the Basilisk and Victoria. He just shook his curly mane and ignored me. He's good at that. But I got on his nerves and that's one reason he took me to see Leitz.

"I'm not a computer expert," I said to Leitz.

"I got that end covered," Foos said.

"A bunch of firms do this kind of thing for a living," I argued. "Network protection, cyber-security, hackers for hire. This is right up their line."

"I don't know them and I don't trust them. There's also the issue of publicity. I don't want any. Foos says I can trust you."

" 'Trust' and 'qualifications' have different definitions in the dictionary."

Leitz shook his head. "Foos knows everything anyone needs to know about computers. He tells me you've been in jail and you used to be a spy. You have a shot at knowing how someone like this thinks. That's the most important qualification I can think of."

I looked at Foos. "How much did you tell him?"

"The basics."

Leitz said, "He told me you have what we call a checkered past—in and out of jail in the Soviet Union until you caught the attention of the KGB. You speak half a dozen languages, a valuable skill. You served twenty years in the most elite department of one of the world's most successful espionage organizations, including several tours here in the States. He says you have an unconventional mind and you're choosy about your clients. He hinted he might have some leverage in that regard."

I was still looking at Foos. "That mean what I think it means?"

"Maybe."

"When?"

"Soon."

Leitz's summary was accurate as far as it went. The jail he referred to was the Gulag, the network of prison, forced labor, and death camps established by the Bolsheviks, expanded beyond comprehension under Stalin and maintained by his successors up until the end. I was born in the Dalstroi camps, in Siberia, my mother having been sent away twice, the first time for doing nothing, the second time for being arrested the first time. I'd worked hard to overcome my past, including having the official record of my birth and subsequent arrest and imprisonment erased, but I still know I'm a *zek*—the most shameful thing a Russian can be. Unless he's also the son of Lavrenty Beria.

Keep things in the present. "Foos tell you what I charge?"

"He was vague about that."

"Normally, I get hired to find things—people, valuables, money. I take a third of their value as my fee."

Leitz laughed. It filled the room, pushing at the walls. "I can't argue with that. I more or less charge the same thing. But if we assume this is about the TV deal, we're talking about a sixty-five-billion-dollar transaction. A third of that . . ."

"Could be real money."

Leitz laughed some more. Maybe it was his brains, maybe it was his success, but I could tell I was dealing with someone totally comfortable in his own skin. You don't meet many people like that.

"You said you appreciate cash," he said. "Tell me how much you want—within reason."

I shook my head. If this was meant as a way to take my mind off my troubles, I might as well have some fun with it.

"I don't get paid unless I'm successful. But if I am—that is to say, if I find a way in and access your data—I'll take a painting as my fee."

He looked skeptical. "You know the value of some of these works . . ."

"Is more than twenty billion?"

He laughed again, quietly this time. "Point taken. Which painting?"

His eyes went to the Malevich, mine followed, but I knew that was a nonstarter. I thought about the Rothkos outside, but it would be a shame to break up that quartet. I like both Kline and Motherwell, but while I don't work cheap, I'm not a gouger.

"I'll take the Repin."

He didn't hide his surprise. "There are many more valuable works . . ."

"It's an arbitrage opportunity. I figure the market will catch up."

He grinned at that. "That was my assumption when I bought it—six years ago. So far, it hasn't worked out."

"You made a bad trade. Here's your chance to get out."

"I wouldn't say bad. I happen to enjoy the picture. But if that's what you want . . ."

"Done."

Foos was chuckling, shaking his head as we walked down the block.

"What's funny?" I asked.

"You, man. What else? You mope around for months—no focus, no energy.

You say you're depressed. Can't get it up for anything. You go home to the old country, come back in worse shape than ever. You're a total pain in the ass, not to put too fine a point on it. So I set you up with the smartest guy on Wall Street, and it takes you maybe ten minutes to size him up and play him for a sucker. They teach this in spy school?"

"Your friend Leitz is looking at the issue from the wrong perspective. A common problem, as he pointed out."

"I wouldn't remind him about the common part, if I were you. He's already gonna be plenty pissed and he's got a big-ass temper."

"I always follow your advice. When are you going to let me at the Basilisk?"

"Soon, like I said. How long you going to take to do this job?"

I shrugged. "You got me into this. How long you want me to take?"

Foos grinned. "He's let this TV deal go to his head. Thinks he's a big shot. Go for maximum impact."

"In that case, we should be in sometime tomorrow."

★ CHAPTER 4 ★

The Sam Ash musical instrument empire anchors the Times Square end of West Forty-eighth Street between Seventh and Sixth and evokes, in a cramped quarter block, New York of a different era. Low-rise brick and stone buildings, coated with decades of grit and grime, windows jammed with guitars, amps, drums and horns—all carrying SALE! signs screaming about deals beyond belief. I could imagine A. J. Liebling and his telephone-booth Indians hanging out in the neighborhood, as they had a half century earlier, hustling tourists, eating at cheap luncheonettes, drinking in seedy bars, hitting the occasional nightclub when they wanted to strut their stuff. If I worked the imagination harder, Miles and Bird and Diz played the "52nd Street Theme" in the background. I could even hear Symphony Sid's midnight radio broadcasts from the original Birdland—the Metropolitan Bopera House, as he called it—just four blocks up Broadway. The streets would have been full of men in wide-striped suits and fedoras, their women wearing tight dresses with flared skirts and heels. At least that's how I saw it, from the records of the bop era, the writings of Liebling and others, and movies of the period. By the first time I arrived in New York, 1977, that era was long over, and a sea of sex shops drowned the area in sleaze.

It took a few decades, but the city drove the sex emporia away (or at least to other neighborhoods) and the developers moved in, toting tax incentives and architectural plans for new skyscrapers, each bigger and uglier than the last. Once built, they pulled off the dubious accomplishment of evoking nostalgia for the strip joints and peep shows. My destination was one of those office towers, but it was only 6:30 P.M., and I had time to kill before one New York work day came to an end and another began. I could have spent a wistful hour in a bar, but one vodka led too easily to another these days, and I told myself I was working, which required a clear mind. So I strolled the streets, thinking about the past—near and far—and reminding myself jobs are not all that easy to come by, and I should be grateful I had one. I'm good at rationalizing, less so at listening to myself when I do. I tried to focus on the Repin portrait and where I was going to hang it. That made me feel a little bit better.

I walked around a crowded Times Square, half the people on the street heading home after work, the other beginning their evening out. I heard at least a dozen languages, tourists enjoying the bright lights of the Great White Way—one of New York's enduring sights. Except the lights left me cold these days, partly because of my frame of mind, but mostly because the heart of the place had been gutted. The old Times Square neon had character and seedy charm. These lights were as soulless and airbrushed as the buildings they were mounted on.

An enormous baritone saxophone, five vertical feet of tangled brass, a shiny relic of Liebling's bygone era, caught my eye in the Sam Ash window. It carried a SALE! tag of $4799! I stopped to contemplate the economics of the musical instrument business. Not much call for baritone sax players these days, or any days, yet to get in the game required an upfront investment of nearly five grand, not to mention the cost of learning to play the thing. This was one of those instances when capitalism didn't add up, at least not to an ex-socialist. In the Soviet Union, the instrument would have been owned by the state and used by an individual of appropriate interest and skill. There would have been a perceived benefit to society, justifying the expense, of having well-trained and -equipped baritone saxophone players—if only because the West had them too, and we had to keep up. Here the cost was borne entirely by the misguided person who fell in love with the baritone sax—as opposed to, say, the piano, violin or, better yet, electric guitar—with little hope of recouping his investment, at least through use of the instrument. But maybe, as Leitz said, I was looking at the issue from the wrong perspective. I'd have to ask him.

I continued along the block to the east. The height of the buildings rose as I approached Sixth Avenue, from five stories to fifty. The materials changed too, from dirty brick to steel and glass and shiny marble. I stopped across from number 140, half a billion dollars worth of concrete, steel, stone, and glass—and no aesthetic merit whatsoever. The lobby was gray and white and blue marble. The directory told me Leitz Ahead Investments—my client appeared to share my view that any pun was better than none—occupied the forty-second and forty-third floors. The lobby guard was checking IDs and issuing passes. I might have bluffed my way past, but I didn't need to. I returned to the opposite side of Forty-eighth Street, found a wall to lean against, put my cell phone to my ear and pretended to be deep in conversation while I watched the door.

Around 7:30, small groups of Hispanic men and women started to form on the sidewalk. They arrived in twos and threes, from the subway stations east and west, some still carrying their unfinished evening meal. They talked quietly among themselves. By 7:50, there were more than twenty, and if there was a single green card among them, I was ready to buy the whole bunch dinner. These were the cleaning crews for the building, workers for a contract company that paid minimum wage with no benefits, but asked no questions about place of birth, legal residence, or Social Security. That made them easy prey.

I wasn't looking to exploit vulnerability. When I was in the spy business, I always found incentives bought better cooperation than threats—one of many reasons I'm an ex-socialist. I crossed the street and moved quickly from group to group, speaking Spanish, repeating the same speech. "Good evening. I apologize for disturbing you. I am not from the police or government. I have a five-hundred-dollar offer for the person who cleans floors forty-two and forty-three and a hundred dollars for the man or woman who introduces me. I will return here tomorrow night at this time. That is the last time any of you will need to see me. Thank you for your assistance. Good night."

It took less than five minutes, by which time they were starting to drift inside. Work started at 8:00 P.M. I walked off to the east without looking back. They would be suspicious, a few even frightened. But six hundred dollars was a lot of money. I was all but certain to have the man or woman I needed tomorrow night.

I arrived back at 140 West 48th Street at 7:15 P.M., Wednesday. The cleaners started to gather around 7:30, just like the night before. I waited in the same spot, not bothering with the fake phone call. At 7:40, one of them broke away from his group and went to talk to a man in another. The body language of the second man said he wanted nothing to do with his coworker and, I assumed, by extension with me. The first man was whispering fiercely, gesturing with his arms, getting more and more animated. He was an excitable type. He wanted his hundred-dollar bounty. The other guy just shook his head. The rest of the cleaners moved away. I gave brief thought to crossing the street and intervening, but I had no idea why the second man was hesitant, and I'd more than likely queer the deal, assuming there was a deal to queer.

After a few more minutes the first man broke away and, looking up and down the block, walked across to me.

"I am sorry, señor," he said in Spanish as he approached. "My friend is the man you want but . . . he is a timid soul, he is frightened. I have tried to persuade him you are an honorable man who means no harm, but he says it is too big a risk. The money . . ." He looked me straight in the eye and shrugged.

I stifled a chuckle. The supposed argument across the street was an act—a charade for my benefit—with the sole purpose of setting up a negotiation. These twenty-first-century telephone-booth Indians were true to the spirit of their predecessors.

"I understand perfectly," I said, holding the man's eye. "But my patience is not infinite. Seven hundred for your friend. Two hundred for you. I'm leaving in two minutes."

The man nodded quickly and trotted back across the street.

This time there was no argument, just thirty seconds of quiet conversation before the two men came to me. The first man was smiling. The second still looked fearful. His eyes darted up and down the block. I shook hands with both of them but didn't ask their names. They didn't inquire after mine. I dubbed them Bold and Timid.

I asked Timid how many floors Leitz Ahead Investments occupied. He looked up and down the block again before answering, "Two." I asked him to describe them. He depicted a double-height, glassed-in trading room with workstations and computer screens around the perimeter of an enormous table and surrounded by offices and conference rooms on both levels. I asked about the computers. That stumped him. The best I could get was lots of screens connected to boxes under the big table. Good enough for me. Leitz would have the trading floor outfitted with high-powered workstations, networked to servers and data storage that could be on another floor or in another location altogether. I took a small device from my pocket. It looked like a black electronic tollbooth tag, about two inches square, two-sided tape on the back.

"I want you to pick one of the computer boxes in the middle of the big table," I said. "Not close to the edge, further underneath, you understand?" We were speaking Spanish, and he nodded, hanging on my every word. "Peel off these strips and stick this to the back of the box, out of sight, okay?" He nodded again.

"That's it," I said, reaching for my wallet. A new look came into Timid's eyes, not fear this time, but uncertainty.

"Something wrong?" I asked as gently as I could. "Do you want to go over it again?"

He shook his head and looked up and down the block once more.

"What then?" I said.

"It's just . . ." He paused, unsure. The bold one, impatient, told him to spit it out. I smiled to show I was in no hurry.

Timid gathered up his courage. "I am sorry, señor, but I am confused. Do you want me to put this on the same machine as the other one?"

★ CHAPTER 5 ★

I got to Grand Central and thought about turning left or right. Right meant downtown and either back to the office or home alone and another night of vodka and takeout food and fruitless research into my past. I turned left, took the subway up to Eighty-sixth Street and walked over to Trastevere. Giancarlo greeted me as he always does, putting his hand to his cheek and smiling, a reminder of the first night I had dinner there with Victoria, and she walloped me when I let her know how deeply the Basilisk had dug into her private life. Like Leitz, Victoria has an explosive temper. After the second wallop—that same night—I'd learned to see hers coming and get out of the way.

Trastevere was her favorite restaurant, and she was one of Giancarlo's best customers. Her absence had to be putting a dent in his profits, although he never appears to be hurting for business, probably because he's a genial host, his food is among the best in town, and the clientele in the East Eighties can afford his prices, which I politely describe as astronomical. I'd gone back there a few times after she left, hoping to bump into her casually, but she was much too smart not to anticipate my amateurish efforts. I continued to show up once or twice a week because it was a pleasantly melancholy place for a good meal. She probably held that against me, exiling her from her favorite place to eat.

Tonight, the room was busy, as usual, but my regular barstool was free, and I headed that way after handing over my jacket.

"Signore Turbo, you know you are always welcome at a table," Giancarlo said.

I thanked him, but went to the bar all the same. It feels less like you're eating alone when you have the bartender to exchange small talk with.

I ordered a martini with Russian vodka and Giancarlo came over to tell me the specials. It occurred to me I've never looked at his regular menu. He was pushing a wild boar stew, which I ordered with a grilled octopus salad to start. He recommended a glass of a Barbera he'd just got in. I said that would be fine. The first night, he and Victoria conspired to stick me with a $475 bottle of Barolo, but since then, he and I have reached a more reasonable understanding about wine. The octopus was delicious, the stew even more so. The wine was good, not in a league with the Barolo, but neither, I assumed, was the price. I enjoyed my meal while I replayed the events of West Forty-eighth Street.

Leitz was right to be concerned. Someone was after his secrets. They'd tried the brute-force electronic attack; when that didn't work they'd resorted to an old-fashioned approach, just as I'd done. These were sophisticated, high-tech crooks—but crooks first. Early November, Timid had told me, he'd been approached. He hadn't wanted to describe the men who'd threatened, then bribed, him to install the first computer bug. He was deliberately vague on height, hair color, girth, dress, accent. His friend, Bold, professed not to have seen them. I wondered where they'd learned the tricks of their trade, and secured the descriptions with another two hundred dollars.

One was an ordinary-looking man, medium height, brown hair, plain features—anglo, of course—wearing a puffy, dark blue jacket over khaki pants and running shoes. He did all the talking—he described the trading room layout and told Timid exactly where to place the device. That suggested an inside connection—Leitz had more problems than he knew. The other man scared both of them. Also anglo, very tall, ugly, mean. He didn't say a word, but they could tell. Buckteeth, fading hair, pockmarked skin, and a look that conveyed how he'd happily eat their entrails while he raped their wives and daughters. Timid had been quick to agree to their proposition.

As I rethought it now, however, over stew and red wine, I realized I'd sized it up wrong, too quick to jump to conclusions. Ninety minutes earlier, back on West Forty-eighth Street, they had confirmed my belief about carrots over sticks. I knew better than that. Timid and Bold were double-dipping—take my money, sell out the first guys, then extract another fee from the first guys by selling me out as well, ratting how I was interested in the same setup. The price of the Repin had gone up. Time to watch my back.

The restaurant crowd had thinned when I finished my dinner. The city may never sleep, but Upper East Siders who can afford Trastevere have Wall Street battles to fight in the morning. Giancarlo came over to chat. He asked, as always, if I'd heard anything from Victoria. I shook my head.

"Don't worry, my friend, she'll be back."

"I keep hoping you're right."

"Only a matter of time. You'll see. What you and she had—no woman can stay away from that."

"It was that obvious?"

"Signore, I'm Italian. And I am not blind."

He filled my glass. "On me." He went to help some departing diners with their coats.

I sipped my wine and thought about what he had said and whether what we had was indeed stronger than her need, as she put it, not to have her heart broken. A restaurateur as successful as Giancarlo learned to be a shrewd judge of character. Better than I was, I hoped. Of course, he didn't know I'd all but driven her out the door.

She had lots of reasons, she kept saying, for not getting too close. I focused too much on all the reasons *I* was giving *her*. In retrospect, maybe she was sending a signal that had more to do with her than me. Maybe it wasn't my doing after all, her abrupt departure. I thought again, for the hundredth time, whether if given the chance, I could change my ways.

What goddamned difference did it make? I was still dining alone.

I paid the bill, wincing slightly. Barolo or Barbera, Giancarlo didn't serve up any bargains. Victoria was extracting revenge on the wallet as well as the heart.

Outside the temperature had dropped into the twenties. The wind had a sharp edge. I decided to walk a few blocks anyway, work off the stew. Traffic on Second Avenue was sporadic, the sidewalks mostly empty.

I made it to the mid-Seventies and was thinking about hailing a cab when a tall man in a long overcoat fell into step next to me. At least six foot seven, with thinning hair and a sharp, pockmarked face, pulled forward by a long nose and buckteeth. I couldn't judge his age. His collar was turned up around his neck.

The man the cleaners had described. He oozed creep. Nosferatu, I thought, the impossibly tall vampire played by Max Schreck in the German silent movie from the 1920s. I looked for a coffin under his arm. It wasn't there, but that could have been the lights playing tricks. Vampires can do those sorts of things. There were now two men in lockstep twenty feet head ahead. A glance back saw two more, the same distance behind.

Nosferatu said, "Keep walking, *zek*."

How the hell could he know that? He spoke Russian with a Belarusian accent. I answered in flat American English.

"Sorry. I don't understand."

"Bullshit. You understand fine. Keep walking."

"Is there some kind of problem?"

"For you."

I kept walking. So much for watching my back. But if they wanted to kill me, I'd already be dead. The *zek* reference bore into my brain.

"I'm going to explain the situation," Nosferatu said in Russian.

"You'll have to speak English," I said in English.

"Shut the fuck up and listen." He stayed with Russian. "I know who you are. I know who you used to be. I know everything. You know nothing, not about me, not about anything. That is the way it's going to remain. Do you understand?"

No point in answering that.

"I said, do you understand?"

"I understand I have no idea what you're talking about," I said, still in English.

"You will learn the spirit of cooperation. Sooner than you think. What were you doing on West Forty-eighth Street? Remember what I said and think very carefully before you answer."

There were a handful of replies, none of which was going to satisfy him. I thought carefully, as instructed. The key question was whether he'd seen me pass the computer bug to Timid.

"Trying to find a way in," I said.

He grunted. Sometimes honesty is the best policy.

"Who for?"

"Myself. Who's your boss?"

"None of your fucking business. That's my point. None of this is your fucking business."

"We're all interested in the same thing."

"What's that?"

"You don't know? You'd better ask your boss."

The right hand came around so fast I had no chance. It hit me square in the stomach with the force of a hydraulic hammer. Boar stew and red wine erupted into my mouth as I doubled over, gasping for air. I stayed that way for a minute, collecting my breath and my wits. He didn't look like he should have that kind of strength.

I glanced up and around. Nobody on the street, except the four men front and back who had closed in, ready to assist. Nosferatu grabbed the back of my collar and pulled me upright.

"Keep moving."

Easier said than done, but I spat sour stew and tried to put one foot in front of the other.

"Who are you working for?" he asked.

"My own job," I coughed.

"What do you want, once you get in?"

"Information, what else?"

He hit me again. Same force, same place. This time, stew spewed onto the sidewalk as I went to my knees.

Kneeling, retching, I sensed a few onlookers starting to gather. I took hope in that. Nosferatu jerked me up again and pushed me forward. The other guys moved too, staying in formation, but closer now. The onlookers remained where they were.

"One more chance, *zek*. What kind of information?"

I had the dim idea that I was better off if he thought I was hired to find him than if I was trying to compete with him.

"Whatever you left behind."

He considered that for a moment before he slugged me once more. This time, stew splattered a parked car before I fell to my knees and vomited more stew onto the sidewalk. His strength was superhuman. I couldn't take much more of this. No one could.

The other four guys moved in close. They were looking around. More onlookers stopped to see what was happening.

Nosferatu was impervious. He pulled me upright. His eyes bored into mine. "If you have one ounce of intelligence, and your Cheka file indicates you used to, you will stay the fuck away from things that are none of your fucking business." Two steel fingers stabbed my chest, punctuating each word with enough force to crack ribs. "That way, you might live out the week. I will tell you one more thing—if you see me again, it will be the last time."

My back exploded in pain as one of his cohorts hit me in the kidney. Nosferatu's fist came around once more—into the right side of my face. The left side bounced off the cold concrete of the sidewalk.

I didn't try to get up.

A good Samaritan rolled me over and offered to call an ambulance. I told him I was fine. He looked dubious. He was surely right. I didn't want the help he was going to call. I made it to my knees without retching. Nosferatu and his friends were nowhere to be seen.

"Fight over a girlfriend," I murmured. The Samaritan still looked dubious. I took his hand and he pulled me to my feet. Everything spun. I was surrounded by five or six people, all wanting to help, none quite sure how.

"I'm okay," I croaked. "I'll be fine." None of them believed me.

"I called nine-one-one," another Samaritan shouted, holding up his cell phone. "Ambulance on the way."

I took a step toward the curb, scanning the street for a cab, before my knees buckled.

The first Samaritan held me up. "Easy," he said. "Help's coming."

"Thanks." I was still scanning the street. "Let me lean on this car."

He released his grip and I stumbled against a parked SUV. A free cab sped down the avenue, three lanes over. I took a breath and stepped halfway into the street, hand raised as high as I could. Every muscle screamed. The cab hit the breaks, cut across traffic and screeched to a stop a foot away. I might have been safer with Nosferatu. I should have thanked the Samaritans, but I was bound for freedom. I yanked the door open, causing more muscle protest, fell into the backseat, and croaked, "Downtown."

I all but passed out as the driver pressed the pedal to the floor.

I pulled myself upright around Thirty-fourth Street, causing shooting pains in my chest, back and head. I told the driver to drop me at Pine and Water. His look in the rearview mirror was more dubious than the ones from the Samaritans. He wore a turban and the name on the license was Indian. He said, "Excuse me, sir, not my business, but you want hospital, maybe?"

"Pine and Water," I repeated.

"But, sir, you look . . ."

"Pine and Water!"

"Yes, sir."

He still didn't appear happy when we got there, but he took the twenty I pushed through the divider, let me get out, which I managed without falling, and sped away at the one speed he seemed familiar with. I nodded feebly to the night guard in the lobby, who's used to comings and goings at all hours in all conditions, and took the elevator up to the office.

Foos and I rent the twenty-eighth floor of a boring tower with stunning views. We have a reception area nobody uses—it was left by the previous tenants—that has chairs and a sofa. I stretched out on the latter for a rest.

I might have passed out, I'm not sure. When I felt up to moving again, I stumbled down one of the Basilisk's twelve server corridors, which took time because they're all forty feet long, and I had to stop once or twice, leaning against a floor-to-ceiling wall of electronic brainpower, to rest. I finally emerged into the large open area in the back. The lights were off except in a few outer offices. The smell of marijuana floated in the air. Pig Pen heard me and squawked, "Russky! Tiramisu?"

We've had this conversation before. Foos's African gray parrot used to be obsessed with pizza. But he bonded with one of his master's Ralph Lauren model girlfriends, two iterations ago. Veronica was her name. She ordered tiramisu every time Foos took her to dinner, ate two bites and brought the rest to Pig Pen in a parrot bag. When Foos moved on to the next girl, as he inevitably does, Pig Pen went into a funk. He's still not completely over her—or the tiramisu.

"No luck, Pig Pen," I told him the first time he asked. "Do I look Italian?"

"Russky," he agreed.

"Do I look like Veronica?"

"No cutie. Russky."

"That's right. So what makes you think I have tiramisu?"

He considered that. "Cross Bronx. Accident cleared."

Resorting to the traffic reports, which he listens to constantly on 1010 WINS, is his concession whenever logic overwhelms desire. That hasn't stopped him from continuing to try on subsequent occasions, however.

Tonight, he took a closer look at me, and said, "Ouch."

"You got that right. Boss here?"

"Boss man!" Pig Pen squawked at full volume, which is a lot louder than seems possible. "Russky help!"

Foos emerged from his office. "Jesus, who ran you over?"

"Leitz's fault," I said, stretching out on a sofa. The open area is divided into two seating arrangements—one organized like a living room, the other a big conference table with a dozen chairs. Around the perimeter are a dozen glassed-in offices and conference rooms.

"Hang on," he said. He went to the kitchen and returned with rubbing alcohol, disinfectant, and a bag of ice. "Can you do this, or you want me to?" he asked.

"I can manage. Take a look at my back, though." I could just shrug off my jacket and lift my turtleneck.

He whistled. "That's gonna be a pepperoni and eggplant pizza in a couple of hours. You sure you don't want the hospital?"

"I'm sure. Better have more ice, though."

He went back to the kitchen. I closed my eyes and used alcohol and disinfectant on my face where Nosferatu and the sidewalk had broken the skin. My gut was uncut, but turning its own shades of pizza color. Foos returned with more ice and the vodka bottle.

"Drink?"

"What do you think?"

He poured two glasses as I tried to arrange ice bags. Pig Pen was holding on to the cage wire across his office door, watching with evident concern. His radio played in the background, forgotten for the moment. But I think they were on sports, in which he has no interest.

The vodka burned going down but felt therapeutic. I held out my glass for more. Foos poured, but said, "Better take it easy. I'm guessing your head's as rattled as the rest of you."

He had a point. I took another small sip, put down the glass, and shifted a couple of the ice bags.

"So what happened?"

I told him about West Forty-eighth Street, the cleaners, and Nosferatu and his friends. He listened without interruption, then said, "And you got no idea who this guy is?"

"None. But he's got Basilisk-like information about me. That says he knew my name, who I am."

"If the first bug's his, he's had access to my e-mail exchanges with Leitz. You okay for the moment?"

"I can manage."

He went to his office and I could hear him banging on his keyboard. I think I dozed again until he came back.

"Your bug's working like a charm. We've got access to Leitz's entire network, including servers and data storage. I can see the other bug, but I had to look hard to find it. Whoever it belongs to has sophisticated technology. I can also see some other weird shit, which I'll check out as soon as I call Leitz."

"Hold on." I pulled myself upright, which got everything that had calmed down angry again. "We're dealing with shrewd customers. Leitz has a big temper. You tell him he's been invaded not once, but twice, by persons unknown, he's likely to go ape and do something stupid, like yank out both bugs. Better we're there when he learns the bad news. Set up a meeting for tomorrow morning."

"He's not going to like it."

"A few hours' delay? The bad guys' bug's been there for weeks. They already know everything they want to know. My bug isn't harming anyone, except maybe me."

"You gonna be able to make it uptown in the morning?"

"I made it downtown tonight."

"That was more luck than skill. You're gonna be hurtin' tomorrow."

"Tell Leitz we'll meet him first thing at his office. That way I only have to make it to Midtown." I hoped Nosferatu didn't have a 24-7 watch on the place. But if he did, he was watching East Sixty-second Street too. He could have had someone follow me yesterday. Regardless, we were going to meet again sooner or later, despite his admonition.

"You look like hell, but I think you're feeling better," Foos said.

"Does that mean I can use the Basilisk?"

"Patience."

"I can blame both you and Leitz for the way I look. I'm not sure getting pummeled by a guy who takes obvious pride in his work is on the AMA-recommended heartache recovery program."

"What are we going to tell Leitz?"

"Deliver the Repin. My job was to show how to get access to his computers. Not my fault someone else got there first."

"If I know you, you're not leaving it there. Not after the beating you took. You could've told the vampire look-alike the truth about what you were doing and walked away."

As usual, he was right. I wasn't leaving it there. But, equally, I wasn't certain how far I wanted to take it. I'd completed the job, and Leitz's hedge fund and TV bid were his problems. That said, Nosferatu tugged as hard as he punched. I didn't like being beat up in my adopted town. I liked less the idea that it could be done with impunity. I liked less still the idea there was someone out there with ready access to what should be either classified or well-buried information about my past.

"What's Leitz going to want to do?" I asked.

"His first impulse will be to protect his data."

"He's behind the curve."

"Yeah. But he's gonna be plenty pissed, so you're applying logic to an irrational situation."

"So?"

"Once he calms down, I think we can convince him to chase the fox, if that's what we want to do, and we send the fox in an unexpected direction."

"Maybe, except I think this fox is a bear."

★ CHAPTER 6 ★

I took the subway, which was a mistake. The rush hour train was fish-can jammed. Every jostle and bump felt as though Nosferatu had hit me again.

Force of habit, I suppose. The Moscow Metro is the only transport I use when I'm there. It's efficient (not a ubiquitous Russian trait), and the stations contain better art than most museums. I used public transportation wherever I was stationed with the Cheka—New York, San Francisco, Washington, London—because it was one way to connect with the local populace. I've always tried to fit in, a legacy from the camps where one lived among multiple factions who didn't always get along. I was a kid without formal allegiance—getting along was one way to make it through the day. I happen to like cars—I own two—but they do cut you off from your surroundings. They also provide cushioned seats and a steel wall of protection—more to the point this morning.

I'd awoken aching all over. Shots of pain stabbed my back and chest when I moved. I get up at six, a lifelong habit, and I have an exercise regimen I follow most mornings—either a five-mile run or three miles followed by a half hour of weights at the gym. I spent my childhood deprived of just about everything, food included, and I eat more than my share now to make up for lost time. I stay in shape on the theory that the average life expectancy of a Russian male is only sixty-five years at last count, and my upbringing already took its toll on mine. Pain trumped theory this morning.

My torso was painted purple and blue. My face was red, blood clotting along crisscrossing scratches on one side, black-and-blue bruises on the other, a shiner around the right eye. The colors extended well above the hairline I didn't have. Overall, it wasn't as bad as the beating Lachko's thug had given me six months earlier, but I didn't want to run into Nosferatu again anytime soon. Unless I was carrying a shotgun.

I made breakfast with extra coffee and logged on to Ibansk.com, the creation of a man known only as Ivan Ivanovich Ivanov, a muckraking impresario with a fondness for breathless hyperbole, who produces the most widely read blog in Russia. His supercharged collection of fact, insider rumor, speculation and high-heat opinion (his) gives readers—denizens, in his parlance—a seat at everything from top-secret Kremlin conferences to oligarch's private rooms at the latest, hottest Moscow (or London or Paris or New York) nightclubs, as well as more intimate settings. He's fun to follow and, more to the point, accurate in his barbs. I know because I know the list of people who'd like to see him executed. It starts at the top of the Kremlin and includes many of the men I used to work with.

I'd been keeping a close eye on Ivanov because I'd been a firsthand witness in December to what bore all the signs of the outbreak of Ibanskian gang warfare. After dinner with Sasha, I'd left him at the Pushkin Square metro station and decided to walk the mile or so down Tverskaya, one of the city's oldest thoroughfares, known as Gorky Street in Soviet Times, to my hotel. I stay at the Metropole, a marvelous old place halfway between the Kremlin and Lubyanka, where many of the original Bolsheviks lived in the early days of the revolution. A mosaic on the façade still calls on the proletariat of the world to unite. The restaurant may be the most opulent room in Moscow. The ironies of Russian history captured in a single building.

A clear evening, not too cold. I was enjoying the winter air as I came up on one of the many restaurants/nightclubs/casinos that cater to the desires of the newly rich by giving them flashy, overpriced venues to show off their leggy girlfriends while trying to spend more on Champagne and caviar than the oligarch at the next table. A phalanx of Mercedes roared down the wide avenue and pulled into the Ibanskian equivalent of the VIP parking lot— the sidewalk in front of the club. Not the easiest thing because the sidewalk was already crowded with a dozen other Mercedes, BMWs, Bentleys, and Range Rovers. Several bodyguards, not bothering to hide their weapons, emerged from the new arrivals. Some rules are just common sense—never try to break up a dog fight, never walk voluntarily into a group of drawn weapons. I waited for a break in the traffic to cross to the far sidewalk.

About the time I got there, two more Mercedes roared up Tverskaya from the opposite direction, traveling too fast, not uncommon in Moscow, but something about them flashed trouble. I ducked behind a parked Lada as they screeched to a stop. Four men leapt out, fire spurting from the muzzles of their machine guns.

The bodyguards were slow. Three fell in the first barrage. Others got their guns up, and a firefight was on. I heard more than I saw as I knelt behind the parked car, hoping thin Russian steel was up to the task of stopping lead Russian bullets. The *RATTA-TAT-TATTA-TAT-TATTA* of gunfire filled the night. Slugs ricocheted off stone. The street shook as a car exploded. Flaming metal flew overhead and bounced off the building behind. Cars skidded and crashed. The gunfire ebbed, then resumed in intensity. When it finally stopped, as suddenly as it had started, I didn't move for a minute before peeking through the Lada's blown-out windows.

Carnage everywhere. A dozen cars sprawled across the avenue at all angles, riddled with bullet holes. Few had window glass left. The bodies of three drivers lay collapsed over their steering wheels. A lone horn blared under the weight of one, a heavyset woman in a blue coat. She could no longer hear it. She was missing the back of her head. On the far sidewalk, where I'd been walking a few minutes before, fallen fighters sprawled across pockmarked metal and concrete. I counted six, there were probably more. The exploded car burned full bore. The first police sirens whined in the distance.

In the center of the slaughter sat one Mercedes, fatter and heavier than the rest, the paint peppered but the glass intact. Armored. As I came around, the back door opened. A dark-haired young woman in a backless dress emerged from the car, as if stepping out. Except she wasn't stepping. She wasn't moving. She was supported by the man behind her. Three ugly red holes perforated her pretty skin. Her torso straightened for a moment before he let her drop on the pavement. She'd been attractive in life—fine skin, good figure—but the heavy makeup she'd applied for her evening out now functioned as a death mask, freezing her last instant of fear and pain. It also froze her age, which couldn't have been more than fifteen.

The man who dropped the corpse climbed out after her. He was tall, in his fifties. He wore a suit and was the only person or thing unmarked by the attack. They must have just been exiting the car when it started. She'd been first and taken the bullets meant for him.

The man looked straight at me as I approached. He blinked once, and I had the sense of a mental photograph being recorded.

"Who the fuck are you?" he said, the voice calm, annoyed and full of authority, as if I were trespassing on his property.

"A passerby. I saw . . ."

"What did you see?"

I pointed around. "Hard to miss."

"Forget all about it," he said. "Walk away and forget it."

"But there may be wounded . . ."

"Everyone will be taken care of. I will make sure of that. Go now."

The next question was a mistake, but curiosity is a lifelong affliction. "Who are you?"

He blinked again, another photo taken, before reaching inside his jacket. I thought he was going for a gun. Instead he came out with a wallet and held out a wad of ruble notes.

"Beat it."

"I don't need money."

I left him there and picked my way through the wreckage still looking for anyone who needed help. I found only corpses. The body count pushed a dozen.

The sirens grew louder. Another rule—don't get involved with Russian police unless you're still an active Chekist. I hustled down Tverskaya, passing a posse of police cars headed to the scene. At the bottom of the street, the cops sealed off the street at Manege Square. No one stopped me, no one tried to ask questions. As horrific as the massacre had been, it was far from a rarity in the New Russia—Ivanov's Ibansk. It would be dealt with accordingly.

I walked the last block to the Metropole and went up to my room, where I logged on to Ibansk.com. Not half an hour had passed since the shooting. The sirens still whined. Ivanov was on the case. And he had the name of the target of the attack, the one man left standing, the man I had spoken to.

Efim Konychev.

Tverskaya Terror

Ibansk Alert! Warfare erupts! A calculated attack this very night outside Tverskaya's White Nights Club. The target? One of Ibansk's biggest oligarchs and one of the powers—some say, *the power*—behind the Baltic Enterprise Commission, the scourge of the Internet, the hoster of choice for evil online.

Efim Konychev survived. How is surely an Ibanskian miracle. A dozen others did not. Who organized the hit? What was the reason? Who's the shapely number who bought the agricultural cooperative someone had picked out for Konychev to purchase?

Rumors have reached Ivanov in recent weeks of dissention in the ranks of BEC management. It's never been a comfortable partnership, more an amalgamation of headstrong hoods. The riches that rolled in during the boom years helped paper over differences and dislikes. Setbacks in recent months—Ivanov hears rumors of system crashes, cash flow interruptions and client defections—may have turned up the heat under already simmering tensions. Accusations of cheating and double-cross ensued. *Surprise!* This is Ibansk. Ivanov surmises one BEC power decides another is to blame—and goes about settling the score in the one way Ibansk knows best.

It appeared I'd witnessed an opening salvo in a battle over the future of the Baltic Enterprise Commission, a shadowy network of Web-hosting servers across the old Soviet Bloc, the go-to resource for anyone looking for a safe place on the Net from which to spam, scam, phish, hack, steal, or purvey porn, especially porn featuring kids.

Konychev was a favorite subject for the chronicler of Ibansk, probably because he was as good a personification as one could find of the unbridled capitalism, Kremlin control, and often crooked undertakings that define the New Russia. I'd been following the news via Ivanov's posts since returning to New York, which mostly dealt with growing clashes within the BEC and the unknown whereabouts of its boss. According to the latest post, earlier today:

Once thought impregnable, the BEC is in disarray. Disagreements over expansion into new, higher risk lines of business—hacking for hire, industrial espionage, anyone?—have opened fissures among the already fractured federation. Ivanov hears the premier hoster of hackers has itself been hacked—although whether this was simple vandalism or invaders with more insidious purposes is thus far unclear.

The big question is Efim Konychev. Where has he been fiddling while his empire burns? He hasn't been heard from since the attack on Tverskaya. Reports of infighting among the bosses and beneficiaries of web sleaze abound. That's one reason he may be lying low. Another could be the identity of the young—and Ivanov does mean *young*—lovely who was with Konychev the night of the Tverskaya attack. She took three slugs in the back, cut down in her pre-prime. Her identity is a mystery even Ivanov cannot unravel. He can only presume that's because Konychev wants it that way.

Foos called just as I was finishing breakfast.

"That weird shit on Leitz's network I saw last night? I spent some more time looking around after you went home. He's got someone inside working something outside. Guy, maybe gal, goes out through a couple of zombies, accesses data, brings it back, but only to his hard drive, doesn't touch the servers, and he covers the route pretty well—though not quite well enough."

Zombies are sleeping computers left online that cyber-crooks borrow when they don't want to leave a trail, usually for spamming or denial of service attacks, but no reason they can't obscure other trails.

"This connected or unconnected to Nosferatu's bug?"

"Unconnected, it appears. Only happens a few times. Three in August. Then again in November. Then December thirtieth. That's it."

"How much should we tell Leitz?"

"He's your client," he said and hung up. That's Foos.

If Nosferatu had anyone watching 140 West Forty-eighth Street, I wasn't going to spot him or her in the morning crowd that filled the block, so I walked straight to the door of Leitz's building, head down. The lobby guard asked my destination, checked my New York driver's license, grimaced at my battered face and dispatched me to the forty-second floor. A pretty twenty-something receptionist sent me up a staircase to conference room A. She didn't do any better job of disguising her unease.

The conference room overlooked the trading floor, which at a few minutes after nine, appeared fully staffed by some forty men and women with an average age of thirty-two, all in various stages of undress. Midwinter, but they were all wearing T-shirts, tank tops, capri pants, some in gym shorts. A few wore shoes. The Gillette company wasn't making much money on razor blades. Paper plates holding the remains of breakfast, more fruit and bran than bacon and eggs, littered the desks. The heat was on high. I took off my jacket as the door opened behind me.

"I know what you're thinking," Leitz's voice boomed from behind. "Everybody does. Fact is, there's more pure brain power on that floor than eight Manhattan projects combined."

"Brain or bran?"

He laughed his big laugh. "Both. I hire brains not suits. I feed 'em, I don't care what they eat. Coffee?"

"Black."

I turned as he went to the sideboard to pour. He was dressed in the same

46

cashmere sweater, corduroys, and handmade shoes as the other day. Foos leaned against the door jam, grinning. He'd got there early to soften up his friend, I hoped.

Leitz handed me a mug. "Foos said you took some heat at my expense. I see he wasn't exaggerating. I'm sorry. I wasn't expecting anything like that."

I shrugged. "Neither of us were."

"I'm sorry, in any event. Foos also says you have news."

Foos and I had discussed how to break this news last night, before I stumbled the two blocks home to my apartment. We agreed the direct approach was best—or least worst. I was still prepared to go with the plan but, remembering the warnings about the temper, I took my coffee to a chair on the far side of the table.

I said, "I bugged your computers last night. We've had access to your entire network for the last twelve hours."

The big face turned red. "Not possible."

"Not only possible, but easy."

Two big hands balled themselves into fists the size of cantaloupes. Eruption was a spark away.

"NO! You've only had . . . I don't believe it!"

I tossed some pages across the table. "Here are e-mails you sent this morning. Behind those are the spreadsheets one of your branny brains was working on at seven fifteen. You've got some interesting trading positions too. I printed it all for easy reference."

"He's telling it straight," Foos said.

Leitz glanced at the papers just long enough to see they were what I said. He threw them aside, and the fists pounded the table, which was granite and had to weigh several hundred pounds. It shifted on its stand. He turned to Foos.

"GODDAMMIT! You told me . . ."

"I told you the perimeter was secure and it is," Foos said. "You weren't hacked."

"Then . . . WHAT?" Leitz swung his glare back to me. The jowls shook, the eyes fired. I wouldn't have wanted to be one of the half-clothed mathematical geniuses reporting a losing trade to this boss. Something about the needlessness of the rage made me want to rub it in, but that also could have been getting beat up, not to mention my overall frame of mind.

"Pedestrian. I bribed a member of your cleaning crew. He put a wireless recording device on a box on your trading floor. That gave us access to everything."

"Cleaning crew?"

"Simplest way in. I could have used a half-dozen others." Leitz's fists rose again but stopped in midair. He stood and went to the phone on the sideboard. Foos was looking unusually uncomfortable.

"Don't," I said.

"DON'T WHAT?"

"Don't call whomever you're calling to tell them to fire the cleaning crew. The next one will be just as easy to penetrate. All it took was a thousand dollars—and I probably overpaid since it was your money."

The phone flew straight at my head until the cord jerked it back and it clattered onto the tabletop. That didn't stop me from ducking.

"Leitz! Chill!" Foos said.

Leitz looked at the phone, then at his empty hand. He shook his big head. "Sorry."

So far the direct approach was working like a charm. I looked around to see what else he could throw. Foos read my mind.

"Sebastian, sit down. We're on your side. There's more."

Leitz took his seat. He appeared deflated, almost like a punctured balloon. He'd been broken into, and as anyone would, he felt violated.

"What more?" he said.

Nosferatu's blows ached. I thought about whether I needed this. I looked across at Foos. His face was impassive. But he was out of the line of fire.

"Someone else planted a bug just like mine—eight weeks ago."

The red face turned purple. The outsized cheeks blew out like Dizzy Gillespie's chops, except there was no joy in this visage. The fists disappeared beneath the tabletop. I planted my feet on the carpet.

Leitz started to stand. Muscles stressed beneath the sweater as the tabletop rose. Coffee cups, coffee, pads and pencils, staplers and paper clips slid in my direction. I pushed the wheels of my chair back to the glass wall before three hundred pounds of granite slab flipped in slow motion, teetered at the top of the arc, and landed at my feet with a thump. It missed my knees by inches.

Foos vacated the doorway as Leitz stomped out.

"I warned you about the temper," he said.

"You also told me to go for maximum impact."

I stood, mainly to make sure I still could. No one on the trading floor below paid the least attention to any of us.

———

We waited about ten minutes, giving Leitz time to cool off, before going down to his office on the floor below. Foos seemed to know his way around. I asked him if he still advocated the direct approach. He grunted in response.

The office was all glass. Two large windows looked south and east over Manhattan and on to Queens. Interior panes faced the trading floor. Leitz was at his desk, another stone table, on the phone. He hit a switch as we walked in and the inside glass turned frosty opaque. I stopped by the door, keeping my distance. He noted where I was standing and shook his head. His voice was tight and tense. He was fighting the temper and winning, for the moment.

"All right, yes, dammit, I'll call him," he said into the receiver. "As soon as I finish this meeting. . . . No, I have no idea. . . . Yes, I know, but . . . Not like this, not now."

He put down the phone. "Sorry. Some issues with my son at his school. I owe you an apology," he said to me. "I've always had a bad temper. Sometimes it gets the better of me."

"Damned near got the better of me," I said.

"You're right. I have no excuse. I'm a very competitive person. I hate to lose. I hate the idea of being compromised. Especially by someone who cheats."

"I didn't cheat. You asked me to find a way into your system."

"I didn't mean it the way it sounded. I was referring to the other guy. Our agreement stands, of course. I'll have the Repin delivered."

"Fine. I've got a question about something on your trading floor."

"What . . . ?"

"Out here."

Leitz and Foos followed me out the door. There was a healthy buzz of activity. After 9:30, the market was open, and the underdressed legions were going about their daily battle.

"Wait here," I said and went back into the office.

Nosferatu, if it was Nosferatu, had used the cleaners on the computers. That said he was opportunistic, he'd employed available talent. Unlikely, then, that he'd have an expert crew work the office. That didn't mean his bug was the only one. I went over the furniture with my hands, feeling for anything out of place. Foos and Leitz watched from the door, Foos wearing a quizzical grin, Leitz an angry frown. I was on my hands and knees under his desk, which was pissing off my bruised muscles, when I found it. An electronic doodad, the size of a raisin, tucked in the crease where the frame met

49

the tabletop. I peeled it off the stone, stood, and placed it on top of the desk. Leitz looked ready to blow. I put a finger to my lips and pointed outside. The two big men backed away.

"Let's go to a conference room," I said.

I thought Leitz was going to take a swing at me, but he turned and led the way to a small room on the side of the trading floor. I held up a hand as we entered and went through the search routine again. I didn't expect to find anything and didn't.

"I think we're okay here," I said.

"JESUS FUCKING CHRIST!" Leitz exploded. "WHAT THE FUCK IS GOING ON?"

"I could ask you that," I said. "You've got somebody's attention."

He deflated again as he fell into a chair.

"Serves me right. Arrogance . . . Well, let's just say arrogance is dangerous."

Foos and I stayed by the door.

"Let me ask you this," Leitz said. "Foos told me about the men who beat you up, including the tall man, what do you call him?"

"Nosferatu. Silent movie character, first vampire on film."

"I'll have to rent it. You think he planted both bugs?"

"The tap on the computers, certainly. The one on your desk, I'm not so sure. The cleaners didn't say anything about that. Could have been someone else, like the guy who gave them the layout of your trading floor."

"You asked them?"

"Yes."

"SHIT. How many goddamned problems do I have?"

"You should have your entire office swept, to state the obvious."

"GODDAMMIT!" Leitz swung back and forth between the two of us, face red, fists balled. He was halfway out of his chair. "I knew something . . . I should have . . . SHIT!" I waited for another explosion, but it didn't come. Instead, he froze in midrise, eyes closed tight, for thirty seconds or more.

"Options," he said, as he lowered himself slowly back into his chair. "What are my options?"

Foos said, "I can tag a piece of data and we can follow it. But if these are sophisticated crooks, they'll run us up and down a bunch of blind alleys."

"Nosferatu had a Belarusian accent," I said. "A lot of tech thieves are based in the former Soviet countries. They're smart, tough, and well protected. Even if we tracked them down, probably not much you could do. Legally, I mean."

"Illegally?" Leitz asked.

"I didn't mean it that way. Not much you could do, period."

"So I'm a powerless victim of some shady guys in Belarus? I refuse to accept that."

Americans like to believe they are masters of their fate and the rest of the world is irrelevant. No percentage in pointing out that brand of arrogance. I was thinking about whether to broach the other anomaly in his computer network when a middle-aged woman leaned in the door. "Your sister's on line two. Third time she's called. Says it's—"

"I know, urgent," Leitz said. He punched a button on the phone. "Hello, Julia. I'm warning you, this is already a bad day. And watch your language. I have company."

A nasal twang blew out of the speaker. "Where the hell have you been? I've been trying to get through for an hour. Haven't you heard? New bidder. Sixty-seven-point-five billion. Stock of both companies are up. Street's looking for a bidding war. We need to get out a statement—right away. I sent you a draft. Check your e-mail."

Leitz pushed another button on the phone and looked at me. "I suppose my e-mail is compromised along with everything else."

"Afraid so."

I thought he was going to punch the phone, but he held back. The voice from the speaker became increasingly agitated.

"Sebastian!? Are you there? What's going on? We need to do something, dammit! The stocks are trading . . . Sebastian? SEBASTIAN?!"

Leitz pushed a button gently. "I'm here, Julia. I've got some other issues at the moment."

"What other issues? What are you talking about? We've got to respond. We can't give them the whole day. The press will—"

"I've called a meeting for eleven thirty, here. Bankers, lawyers, you too. We'll review where we stand."

"Eleven thirty? Where we stand? That's two hours from now. We can't wait. We can't—"

"Eleven thirty." Leitz's tone cut off further argument. "I assume you can make it?"

"I . . . Shit. I've got . . . Dammit. There's . . . Hold on."

The phone went quiet. Leitz said to us, "My sister, who is also my PR adviser on this deal, lives life in a permanent state of high anxiety and overcommitment." He pulled a paper from the shirt pocket under his sweater and held it out to me. "This happened just before you arrived."

I took the paper and retreated back to a safe distance. It was a Dow Jones story, timed at 7:48 A.M.

$67.5 Billion Bid for TV Networks

A new consortium has offered $67.5 billion for two TV networks, topping a $62 billion offer from a group led by hedge fund manager Sebastian Leitz.

A spokeswoman for the Leitz group declined to comment and Leitz himself did not return calls to his office.

Wall Street sources, who have been following the situation, say they expect a full-scale bidding war to develop.

"They're not making any more TV networks," one institutional shareholder said. "We haven't seen the end of this. I expect the price to go sky high."

The market appears to agree. Shares of both networks' parent companies were sharply higher in premarket trading.

Julia Leitz came back on the line, shattering the brief silence.

"I can do eleven thirty. I may be a few minutes late. But I still think—"

"Good. See you then," Leitz said and disconnected. He looked at the two of us.

"I can't operate this way."

"They already know about your eleven-thirty meeting," I said. "They'll be looking to see what you do after that."

"I'll tag something coming out of the meeting," Foos said. "Give them the afternoon to pick it up, we'll see where it goes."

"You could try spreading some misinformation," I said. "Although my altercation last night says they'll be on the lookout for that."

Leitz shook his head. "Too many people involved in this thing. Let's just get back to normal so I can function."

I handed back the Dow Jones story. "I take it this wasn't a knockout punch."

He shook his head. "The margins got thinner, but no, not a knockout. Which begs the question of what they're up to." He looked at me. "This is the deal of a lifetime for me. I never dreamed I'd be in this position. I'm not going to go down easily, in fact, I don't plan to go down at all."

"I hesitate to say this, but you've made an assumption there's no evidence to support."

"What? What are you talking about?"

"You assume that whoever placed the bug is working for a rival bidder."

"That seems obvious, doesn't it?"

"Possible, maybe even probable. But, as I said, no evidence."

"What else, then?"

"You're looking at this from your perspective. That's not where the bad guy's coming from. He—or she—is doing what he's doing for his own reasons. His perspective, hers maybe, not yours, is the one that's relevant."

"What are you suggesting?"

"Only what I said. Be careful about assumptions."

"IT'S AN OPPOSING BIDDER!"

I shrugged. I wasn't going to win the argument, and I didn't really care much whether I did.

"I need your help," Leitz said.

"I've done what we agreed."

"I know. But you can find the bastards. I'll take it from there."

"Not that easy."

Foos felt my ambivalence. "That wasn't the agreement, Sebastian."

"Find the bastards," he said. "Just tell me who they are. Give me a name."

"Arrogance talking," I said.

I expected fire but I got a hard, level stare from the kidney pools.

"A good trader always knows what he can get from a deal," Leitz said.

"A good card player knows when the price of seeing the next card is too high."

"I'm prepared to pay for the help I'm asking. State your price."

I don't know why I did it. Maybe because I was already in. Maybe because I knew I wasn't going to allow Nosferatu to get away with beating me up. Maybe because a guy like Leitz gets the competitive juices flowing. I was in the game, and I wasn't about to fold, especially when I held a couple of aces, including one up the sleeve. Maybe just because I finally was intrigued and didn't have anything better to do for the next few days. Or maybe because I too, found myself in a position to get something I never dreamed of. I might have told Leitz those are good times to think twice, go home and sleep it over.

I put down my next bet. "One million dollars. And the Malevich."

That caught him by surprise. The kidney pools widened. He started to shake his head.

I said, "Hear me out."

He stopped.

"One million dollars, cash—if I'm successful. Plus, the Malevich—four months, one third of the year, on loan, in perpetuity. You own it, I get to enjoy it, part of the time. You sell it, that's your prerogative, but I get ten percent as compensation for loss of use."

The laugh that exploded across the room almost blew both Foos and me through the frosted glass. Foos steadied his feet and smiled.

When the laugh softened to a chuckle, Leitz said, "You'd make a good trader. You've got creativity—and chutzpah. But you're trying to take advantage of having me over the proverbial barrel."

"And when you're about to clip some guy on the other side, you stop, revisit the Golden Rule, tell yourself that's not the Christian thing to do, and walk away?"

He was still smiling. "Touché. But what you want is too complicated. The insurance alone . . ." He shook his big head. "It'll never work."

Mathematicians are good card players because they can calculate odds. They're not always the best psychologists.

"That's it then. Good luck." I looked at Foos. "See you back downtown."

I was out on the trading floor when Leitz called, "Wait!"

I returned to the door.

"You'd walk out on a million dollars?" he said.

"A prospective million. I have to find the guys who bugged you to earn it. That won't be easy, as I said. But, yes, and here's why: My last client paid me seven hundred thousand to find his daughter, who was never really missing to begin with, and now wishes he never met me. His wife was murdered, the girl's a borderline basket case, and he's got one foot in the slammer, although that's not my fault. It ended badly for everybody—including me. I lost something more valuable than money. The fee wasn't enough. I'm sorry to tell you, this has a similar feel."

I had to hand it to him, he didn't hesitate. I think he was almost smiling. "Okay. But, the Malevich . . . ?"

"You didn't listen to what I just said. I've already been beaten up once on your nickel. I'm going to be compensated on my terms in ways that satisfy me, however difficult and complicated. If that doesn't make sense to you, I'm sorry. One more thing, while we're at it—if you really want my help, I go about things as I see fit. You hire me, I'm in to the finish. I talk to whomever I want. I find whomever bugged your computers, I earn my fee. What happens with your TV bid, or your other affairs—that's your concern."

He hesitated this time. I turned to go.

"Stop," Leitz said.

54

I turned back one more time.

He said, "Tell me this. You charged the last guy seven hundred thousand. You want a million from me, plus the Malevich. What's the difference?"

My turn to smile. "The last guy didn't try to crush my legs under his conference table. You get a hazard premium."

★ CHAPTER 7 ★

I should have kept walking. To think I could find the guys who bugged Leitz was my own brand of hubris. To think I could find them without suffering consequences was hubris squared. Then again, to think I began to understand what I was getting into was blind stupid. We have another proverb—every fox praises his own tail.

Foos said, "You still playing him?"

"Some. This was an inside job. The data trail you found. The guy who bribed the cleaner knew the office layout, told him where to place the bug. Employee, client, family, friend, someone Leitz does business with."

Leitz hadn't wanted to hear any of that. I'd mostly dismissed the employee possibility on the grounds that he or she wouldn't need the risk of involving a third party. Leitz confirmed he'd only lost two staff in the last year, neither on bad terms. Clients rarely, if ever, visited the office. Vendors were a possibility, but Nosferatu would have had to obtain a list from somewhere. I asked about the bankers and lawyers descending at 11:30.

"All trusted advisers," he said.

"All potentially for sale. Put the trading floor and all offices off limits. Have them escorted from the elevator to the conference room and back again."

He didn't like that idea either, but he said he'd follow my advice.

I broached the subject of family.

"IMPOSSIBLE!" he shouted, temperature headed skyward. "Don't even . . . None of my . . ."

"Any of them pissed off at you?"

"OF COURSE NOT!"

That answer came too fast.

"Anybody under pressure, financial, personal or otherwise?"

"NO!"

Much too fast. I shook my head. "You're not being candid. That's not going to help them or me."

"Chill, man," Foos said to his friend. "All in the Big Dick anyway."

Leitz looked from me to him. Big Dick is Foos's nickname for what he calls the Data Intelligence Complex, the network of computers and databases— government and private—that store just about everything we do that involves anything electronic, from our purchases and paydays to our dental records and divorces. It is all there—death and taxes too.

Leitz looked back and forth between us again.

"We are a normal family," he said, spacing every word. "We've had . . . adversities, like any other family, but we've overcome them. Nobody would . . ."

He left the sentence hanging and just shook his head at the impossibility of familial duplicity. Even geniuses have a hard time facing the prospect of betrayal.

"Sometimes, people don't have any choice," I said. "They're forced to do things they don't want to. Anybody have legal troubles, marital problems, need money?"

"NO!"

"I assume they've all been here, to the office, at one time or another?"

"Of course. I mean, I guess so. Why not? Why is this relevant?"

I let it go. Better to have this conversation later, when I had some idea of who might have set him up.

Back downtown, Foos, the Basilisk, and I went to work. Named by its creator after the mythological beast that was supposed to be the most poisonous on the planet, this Basilisk is hardwired into the Big Dick and is for sure the most poisonously invasive data-mining system in captivity. Fortunately, Foos doesn't let many people use it. I grew up in a society that had no privacy. The state—more accurately the Communist Party—had the self-proclaimed right to find out anything it wanted to about anyone it chose, by any means it felt necessary. For twenty years as an officer of the KGB, I served as an instrument of state and party, although most of my time was spent spying on foreigners. Other people looked after the locals. I left Russia after communism collapsed under the weight of its own corruption and incompetence, and I moved to New York in part to live in a place where individual privacy is respected.

Wrong.

I soon found out how easy it is to acquire all kinds of information—phone calls, purchases, financial records, criminal records, mortgage, tax and car payments, salaries, employment histories, almost everything except maybe how someone voted in the last election—just by asking and paying a fee. Companies like ChoicePoint, LexisNexis, and Seisint maintain voluminous files, fifty billion of them, on virtually every one of us, in the name of more effective marketing and occasionally combating crime or terrorism. Foos was one of the czars of the Big Dick for several years, with a company that employed an earlier generation of the Basilisk, until he realized he was propagating evil. He sold his firm, endowed STOP with half the proceeds, and designed the current Basilisk to be more powerful than anything that came before. He now fights a guerilla war against the entire Data Intelligence Complex, which has resulted in several TV and newspaper exposés, Congressional hearings and a couple of laws that strengthened consumers' rights and infuriated his former clients. He laughs out loud whenever he's reminded of how mad he makes them.

A few years ago, when things were slow and I needed to get away for a while, we made a wager—lunch at Peter Luger in Brooklyn where they grill steaks big enough to feed a Russian village. I bet I could leave town with two days' headstart, and the Basilisk couldn't find me. He laughed and said he'd be ordering a porterhouse. In the end, we both won.

I got a lockbox for the trunk of my car, filled it with cash and took off without saying good-bye on the twenty-seventh of September, figuring whatever head start I could get on the Basilisk was worth it. I drove upstate, then west into Pennsylvania and Ohio, sticking to back roads. Highways have tollbooths. Tollbooths have cameras. Those cameras are connected to databases. It's still primitive, but the Basilisk has photo-recognition capability.

I made leisurely progress westward, following Horace Greeley's advice, even if I was no longer young, staying at out-of-the-way motels and eating at diners and mom-and-pop restaurants where nobody takes much interest in who's passing through—unless they stay. I'd done four tours of duty in the States with the KGB, two in New York and one each in Washington and San Francisco. I'd rarely left the coasts during any of them, and when I did, it was to travel to another big city—Chicago, Minneapolis, Houston, Dallas. This was the first time I got to know the rest of the country—the varied landscape, the orderly towns, the warm and welcoming people. For years I'd heard about "Main Street"—now, I saw it firsthand. When I got west of the Rockies, I bought some camping equipment and spent two months in the national parks of Utah and Arizona. You can really get lost there, if you stay away from the tourists. The landscape is vast, awe inspiring, and inhospitable. Siberia with sun.

In December it got cold and I was feeling the need for less motion and more human contact, so I decided to test my fate in a city. I drove into L.A. a week before Christmas, found a motel room I could rent by the week for cash, and got a job washing dishes in a restaurant where they didn't ask about Social Security numbers. I made friends with the Mexicans who worked there—most of them illegal—and we hung out together, drinking beer and playing cards when we weren't working. They sensed I had something to hide, same as they did, and we all respected each other's space. I still keep in touch with several of them, and I've got standing invitations to visit just about every major city south of the border.

February—time to move on. I drove to Texas, down to Donald Judd's lonesome, soulful installation in Marfa, which felt a little like the Vorkuta camps without inmates or snow. There's even one artist's idea of a Soviet era schoolroom left empty for time and decay to take its toll. Back up north to Dallas and Houston, east into Louisiana and up to Memphis, again taking my time. Sitting by the Mississippi on April Fool's Day, I decided I'd had enough. I'd made it six months. I found a pay phone and left a message for Foos, "Game over." I turned on my cell phone for the first time since leaving New York, and it rang a few minutes later. Foos said, "Good thing you got out of L.A. when you did. I have three pictures of your car on the Santa Monica Freeway and two on Wilshire Boulevard. The Basilisk came within two days of having you dragged down to Room 101." That's the existential hell on earth George Orwell cooked up—it holds each person's greatest fear. Funny guy, that Foos.

This is how I knew the beast could find Victoria in a New York minute if I was only allowed to set it loose. No dice, Foos said for the umpteenth time. Stick to business.

With *Suprematist Composition* as an incentive, that's what I did. I started with Pauline Leitz, missus number one. My questions had received polite nonresponses from her ex-husband. She was a "good woman" and a "good mother" whom Leitz had meet while he was in graduate school. She "hadn't liked New York" and moved back to Minnesota after the divorce. I inferred, perhaps unkindly, that Leitz had married his grad school sweetheart, thought better of it after meeting Jenny, and paid well for her to go quietly with a lot of sincere reassurances that this was best for their son. I wondered if she knew about the lifestyle she'd missed out on—or cared if she did.

It didn't take the Basilisk long to fill out a profile. Forty-four years old, living in Minnetonka, Minnesota, an associate professor of English at Hamline College. She'd published two books on Victorian literature, both out of print. She hadn't remarried and had reclaimed her maiden name—Turner. She and Leitz had been married fourteen years and divorced four years ago. Leitz was just beginning to make it big, he was still a budding billionaire. She came out with $55 million that was now close to $255 million. I wondered if he ran her money. Her house was paid up, as was her car, a two-year-old Volvo. Her credit card bills showed a normal pattern of purchasing at the usual supermarkets and department stores. She had one speeding ticket from two years earlier. Hard to tell from her driver's license photo whether she was blond or red haired, attractive or plain. She vacationed at spas like Canyon Ranch and ski resorts like Vail. Three trips to New York in the last five years, staying at the Regency, a block from Leitz's house. Other than that, I guessed her son came to her.

Jenny Leitz, née Jennifer Chao, ABC (American-born Chinese), also from Queens, was thirty-five, ten years younger than Leitz, for whom she'd gone to work after getting her Ph.D. in mathematics from MIT. Not clear when they became an item, but she'd married him a little less than three years ago, and they had one daughter who was eight months old. Jenny had been pulling down a multimillion dollar income at Leitz Ahead, but she'd quit work after the birth of their child to lead the life of a quintessential housewife and new mother, at least according to her credit cards. Her spending patterns were normal in all respects, but in the last few months, they showed a concentration in shops and restaurants in the far East Sixties. She hadn't taken a job. Perhaps she was volunteering—plenty of hospitals and related organizations in that part of town.

Foos programmed the Basilisk to flag anomalies. A person without a gun license who suddenly purchases several boxes of ammunition. Someone, otherwise healthy, who starts charging large quantities of cold remedies. Most times, such breaks from normal patterns indicate a stolen identity. But not always. Two months earlier, four new phone numbers showed up in Jenny Leitz's records. She'd been calling them, and they her, several times a week. Three belonged to doctors specializing in neurological diseases. The fourth was a medical imaging lab. All were located in the East Sixties and Seventies, the neighborhood around New York Hospital.

Unsure what to conclude from that, except that all might not be well with Jenny Leitz, I turned to her husband's siblings.

First up, Marianna, number two after Sebastian in the family line. Plenty of anomalies here. For the last few months, Marianna and her husband appeared to be living separate lives—she at their home in Bedford, with their two kids, a boy and a girl aged fourteen and eleven, he at their apartment on Park Avenue. Jonathan Stern was the CEO of Kallon Corp., a medical device maker. He traveled a great deal. His hotel charges showed a fondness for nighttime Champagne from room service. His non-hotel charges included more than a few lingerie stores. Perhaps he was bringing Marianna a souvenir camisole from Chicago, a negligee from Pittsburgh, and a new lace bra-and-panties set from Dallas. My money was on local usage. I asked the Basilisk to line up the Champagne orders and underwear purchases. Big surprise—every date matched.

Marianna appeared to have her own problems. She was buying more booze than most Russians. Her chosen drop was brandy, Cognac (Rémy Martin) in the good days, but since her husband moved out, less expensive, some would say cheap, fare—Fundador from Spain and Presidente from Mexico. I actually like both, but I've been known to tipple too much cheap vodka. Their joint checking account provided an explanation. The automatic deposits from Kallon Corp.—$27,000 a month—stopped in November. The account had shrunk from $66,000 to less than $15,000 since. Marianna was feeling the pinch, in more ways than one. A trip to Bedford was in order.

Next in line was the middle sister, Julia, who'd kept the Leitz name when she'd married Walter Coryell fifteen years ago. She and her husband and two kids lived in a loft in Chelsea that had set them back $3.6 million in 2004. They'd financed 50 percent and kept current on both mortgage and monthly maintenance. Julia was a wealthy woman, a bank balance of $50,000 and upward of $8 million in savings and investments. Not in her brother's league, but rich by everyone else's standard. She still shopped discount—H&M and Century 21 and the occasional department store when it had a sale, not that she bought that much. Neither did her husband. She had two BlackBerries, both worked overtime. His worked hardly at all. The kids, boys, aged twelve and ten, attended New York City private schools that set the parents back seventy-five Gs a year. They both had cell phones and texted each other and their friends 24-7, including when they were in class. They had PlayStations and Xboxes and iPads, Facebook and Twitter accounts, and all the other accouterments of upper-class life in twenty-first-century America. I'm enormously fond of my adopted country, but as a former member of the CPUSSR, I often think America could benefit from good old Soviet-style centralized discipline, starting with a rule that every kid should not be permitted to have every gadget that Silicon Valley comes up with. I've yet to find anyone who agrees with me.

Julia Leitz owned a financial public relations firm with two partners. Her office was on Third Avenue in the Forties. Her husband had an Internet company, an amalgamator of travel options—hotels, flights, rental cars—called YouGoHere.com. It had weathered the dot-com meltdown and seemed to be holding on, if not setting cyber-tourism afire. His office was just over the East River in Queens. Nothing appeared overtly out of kilter in the Leitz-Coryell household, but looks can be deceiving.

Thomas Leitz was the baby of the family, six years younger than Julia. He was thirty-five now and worked for the New York City Department of Education, as he had since receiving his M.A. from City College where he also got his undergraduate degree. He lived alone in a rent-stabilized one-bedroom apartment in the Village. He ate out most nights and ran up modest tabs at a few saloons with names that suggested a single-sex clientele. He also had a long-running spending problem—repeated patterns of running up huge credit card debt, carrying it for a few months or more, then paying it off—all at once—canceling the cards and starting again. The Basilisk served up a dozen cycles, going back seven years. Every eight to twelve months, he maxed out two, three, four cards at their $10,000 or $15,000 limits. The damage was done at designer boutiques and the Bergdorf Goodman men's store—$500 shirts, $1,200 trousers, $2,400 sweaters, and $4,000 jackets—and Broadway theaters. When he went to a show, which he did once or twice a week, he purchased the premium tickets the theaters began selling a few years ago—at $400 a pop. None of which he was buying on his $42,000 teacher's salary.

Two months earlier, he was carrying $35,000. Debt service alone was running $700 a month. He didn't appear to have any other assets to speak of, but in late November, his balances were paid off and the cards canceled. At the moment, he had new Visa, MasterCard, and AmEx cards, with an aggregate balance of $8,000. The foothills of the next debt mountain. The timing of the last payoff was too close to the bugging of Leitz's computers to ignore. Nosferatu, if it was Nosferatu, had his choice of targets.

I went two for six on phone calls. A standard not-here-right-now message from Pauline Leitz. A harried-sounding secretary at Julia Leitz's office, with the lady in question shrieking in the background. She had no time to talk to me. A high-pitched recording announced Thomas Leitz was "out and about, but don't pout, leave a message, don't be a lout." A slurry-voiced

Marianna Leitz answered her phone but had a hard time grasping who I was and why I was calling, which had more to do with the brandy sloshing around her glass than my attempt to explain. It took a few minutes, but she agreed to see me the next morning at nine thirty. Jonathan Stern's assistant took my name and number without comment. Jenny Leitz had a high, sweet voice. She said, "Sebastian said you might call. He told me I shouldn't talk to you."

"I'm trying to help him, Mrs. Leitz. I told him I have to go about my job as I see fit."

"Yes, he said you said that too. I don't see how I can help."

"I don't either—until we chat."

Several seconds of silence before, "Sebastian can be very . . . Especially these days. Are you free tomorrow?"

I said I was, except first thing.

"Best not come here. Let's see, I have . . . There's a coffee shop on First Avenue and Sixty-sixth Street. I'll meet you there at noon."

I knew the place from her Basilisk file. I told her noon was fine.

It was a start. With a mental nod to Marianna Leitz, I fetched the vodka bottle and two glasses from the kitchen. Foos was tapping away at his keyboard, but he indicated yes when I held up the bottle. I poured two shots.

"Want to get something to eat?" I asked.

"Social invitation? Haven't had one of those in months."

"Just trying to butter you up until you let me sic the Basilisk on Victoria."

"You track her down, she tells you to get lost. What's the rush?"

"Thanks for the vote of confidence. What about dinner?"

"Can't. Date."

"Krisztina?"

"Uh-uh. Izabela."

"What happened to Krisztina?"

"Nothing lasts forever."

Or in his case, more than a couple off months.

"Izabela—let me guess. Czech?"

"Close. Slovakian. Bratislava."

"Six feet, blond, legs up to her ears for a change?"

"Jealous."

Foos is a certified genius, but a decidedly odd-looking guy with a personality to match. Yet he dates an unending series of models, all tall, most blond, most from Eastern Europe, each more drop-dead gorgeous than the last. It's a continuing source of mystery—and envy—how he manages.

"You and your pal Leitz ever discuss his family?"

"Uh-uh."

"They've got a lot of issues, as they say these days."

"Not surprised."

"Why?"

He looked up. "What family doesn't?"

The loud "arrrr-oooo-gahhhh" of our door horn echoed through the office. One of Foos's jokes—he thinks it's hilarious. So does Pig Pen, who squawks "Boss man!" at full volume whenever it goes off. Two men stood outside holding a solid-looking wooden crate. The return address was Leitz's. It took half an hour and another glass of vodka to yank out the nails and get it open. When I unwrapped the painting inside, Pig Pen took one look and said, "Russky."

"That's right, Pig Pen. Famous Russky. Ilya Repin, painter. How did you know?"

He gave me his 'I'm not the dope you think I am' look. "Russky."

"Takes one to know one," I said. "Maybe you're part Russian, Pig Pen."

"Parrot," he said definitively, meaning, I suppose, that he's a citizen of the world.

"You like the painting?"

He took a minute to look it over. "Eldo."

Eldo's the top rank in his hierarchy. I'd taken him for a ride once in my car, a 1975 Cadillac Eldorado convertible I call the Potemkin, with the top down. We'd toured the 1010 WINS "jam cams" around town, and he thought he'd ascended to parrot paradise. Eldo stuck.

"You have a good eye, for a parrot," I said. "I'll hang it here for now, where you can see it."

Pig Pen seemed happy with that arrangement, but I was thinking Repin deserved a better setting than a sterile office wall. I was at the door, headed for 140 West Forty-eighth Street—a fruitless errand to see if Timid and Bold were still around—when something tugged.

Some issues with my son at his school, Leitz had said.

Foos was packing his messenger bag.

"I want to do a little research on the Leitz kid."

"Wondered when you were going to get around to that."

"You know something I don't?"

"That strange computer activity corresponds with school vacations. I told you that."

I was going to point out he'd said nothing of the sort, but he was already halfway across the floor, bidding good night to Pig Pen. Then it occurred to me that in his way, he had. He'd told me August, November, and December—summer, Thanksgiving, Christmas. That's Foos. Like his creation, he connects data—and expects the rest of us to be as quick as he is.

I fired up the Basilisk and fed in Andras Leitz. I don't know what I was looking for, but had I been given any notice of what I'd find—and where it would lead—I'd have shut down the computer, packed up the Repin, sent it back, and sought refuge with one of my Mexican friends south of the border.

It's not a proverb that I know of, but it should be—you can't peel back the layers of an onion without drawing tears.

★ CHAPTER 8 ★

Things started innocently enough. Andras Leitz presented a typical profile of a typical child of wealthy, New York parents—private school, generous allowance, Caribbean Christmases, too many material possessions. Nothing surprising there. Until the beast served up accounts at twelve different banks with balances aggregating $11.2 million.

One account, at Citi, held $2,200 and was the recipient of what appeared to be a regular allowance, a hundred dollars a week, via electronic transfer from his father's account at the same bank. The others were funded by monthly transfers from a corporate account at State Street Bank in Boston. Those had been increasing steadily over time and now averaged about $20,000 each. They stretched back two and a half years. The most recent was a week earlier—$22,887.63. In all, they totaled just over $7 million. The other $4 million had been deposited, again electronically, in two installments, one in August ($1.5 million) and one at Thanksgiving ($2.5 million). The source of these two transfers was a bank in Estonia. And, as Foos said, the timing lined up with school vacations.

Hard to see how a seventeen-year-old came into that kind of money. Hard to guess what he was up to in the Baltics. Perhaps he copied a few of his old man's trades. The Basilisk guffawed at that idea. So did twenty years of Cheka training and experience. But even assuming for the sake of argument that he was as bent as a world-class crook, how was a high school kid pulling down that kind of dough? I wondered, not idly, whether the elder Leitz had any inkling of his offspring's success.

Back to the data. The Boston connection was explained, possibly, by the fact that Andras was a student at a boarding school in Gibbet, Massachusetts, fifty miles west of the capital, with the same name as the town. Tuition, room and board were setting his old man back $48,000 a year. Andras could have easily picked up the tab himself. I brought up the phone records. Calls to his father in New York, mother in Minneapolis, and a handful of what appeared to be friends. Most went to a woman named Irina Lishina. That surname rang a bell, but I couldn't place it.

I sent the beast back with a new assignment. He (I've always assumed he's a he) came back with another profile.

Irina was also a student at the Gibbet School. Like Andras, she lived in New York City, at 22 East Ninety-second Street, with her mother, Alyona, and her stepfather, Taras Batkin. That name rang a bell too.

Google jogged my memory. Batkin was chairman of the Russian-American Trade Council. At the time I left the Cheka, he'd been a fast-rising officer, a comer. We'd never met, but he got talked about a lot. In more recent years, he was rumored to be a Kremlin fixer, one of those people trusted with looking after the government's connections with private enterprise—legal and otherwise. Irina's father was Alexander Lishin, and I remembered why I recognized his name. He was a regular fixture on Ibansk.com—a crook, major league. I could access more information on them at home. I went back to the girl.

She had a BMW 328i registered in her name in New York. She carried three credit cards with aggregate average monthly charges of about $900. Her checking account contained just over $10,000. Typical child of a typical Russian official—if said official is in a position to have his hand in all kinds of extracurricular enterprises.

That was before the savings and brokerage accounts. Like Andras, more than a dozen spread among eight banks as well as Fidelity, Schwab and E-Trade. They totaled more than $11 million and were fed by the same corporate account at State Street Bank. Just like him, she had two deposits from Estonia, $1.5 mil in November and $2.5 million a month later. Russia's producing some very accomplished young women these days, but a self-made high school multimillionaire seemed a reach. Unless she'd joined the family firm. That seemed a bigger reach. And what was Andras doing?

I went home to continue my research, after the detour to West Forty-eighth Street. Timid and Bold were nowhere among the gathering cleaners. None of those getting ready for work professed ever to have heard of them. I wasn't surprised. Having gotten everything they could from both Nosferatu and me, they'd doubtless decided another cleaning job at another building—probably in Pittsburgh—was in order. Their countrymen were quick to forget all about them.

Dinner was a solitary affair—me, takeout Chinese washed down by Russian vodka and Czech beer, Herbie Nichols on the CD player, and Ibansk.com on the computer. Nichols is an overlooked hard-bop pianist who didn't make many records, but the ones he did get down swing harder than Paul Bunyan's ax.

Ivanov swings his own ax, and tonight Efim Konychev was again the target.

Konychev Spotted—in the United States!

Whither Efim Konychev?

New York, Ivanov's told. Washington too. Dallas, Pittsburgh, and Los Angeles as well.

Nothing odd about that, you say? Well, for one thing, Konychev hasn't been seen since the Tverskaya attack. In hiding, Ivanov hears. For another, civil war reigns among the partners of the Baltic Enterprise Commission. A bad time to be out of town, but maybe right now the rest of the world is safer than staying home.

Intriguing to Ivanov—for the last three years the United States has denied Konychev entry. We hear the Kremlin at its highest levels intervened with the U.S. authorities more than once on Konychev's behalf. No dice—repeated visa applications, made through the U.S. Department of State, were returned to Moscow DOA—dead on arrival, as they say in America, "dead" there having a different meaning than here in Ibansk. Alleged involvement in organized crime is the reason given by the U.S. Department of Justice. (For his part, Ivanov, of course, remains shocked—SHOCKED!—at the idea of organized crime in Ibansk.)

So what's changed?

The Department of Homeland Security appears to have taken up his case. Konychev's recent visits have been under special dispensation from DHS—and against the wishes of the State Department. Why DHS wants Konychev in America is a mystery—unless the oligarch had made some kind of a deal.

But, Ivanov asks, what kind of deal could Konychev offer the U.S. government agency charged with protecting American soil?

A question sufficiently stimulating to engage Ivanov's efforts. Don't stray far.

I searched the Ibansk database for mentions of Konychev, Alexander Lishin, and the BEC. It returned more than two hundred posts. Some contained just a mention, in others, Ivanov ran on at his histrionic and long-winded best.

I sent the full lot to the printer while I finished my takeout, rinsed the dishes, and opened another Pilsner Urquell. Then I settled in on the sofa with the beer, a thick stack of printed pages, and a notepad. Two hours and another Pilsner later I had as good a picture of the BEC as one was likely to get.

Konychev and Lishin were the founding partners. Konychev had already made one fortune in TV and radio. He was one of the first to appreciate the Web's potential for criminal enterprise and, more significantly, that criminals would need places—holes in the cyberspace wall, if you will—to run their scams from. Lishin, according to Ivanov, was the technical genius, the man who connected servers spread all over Eastern Europe, and more important, told them what to do when ordered.

The genius of the BEC is that, technically, it does nothing illegal itself. It simply provides services—Web hosting, data storage—to those who need them. Spammers need memory and processing power to send all those billions of e-mails advertising everything from cheap drugs to bigger body parts. Phishers need the same capabilities from which to con unsuspecting recipients—*Danger! Your account is about to be closed!*—into giving up their user names, passwords, and Social Security numbers. Higher-tech crooks have similar requirements—putting together zombie networks to launch distributed denial of service attacks, the basis for their blackmail schemes, aimed at shutting down companies' or countries' Web presences by swamping them with bogus inquiries. Ditto pornographers.

The thing about computers, they don't care what they do. Memory is memory, it can store whatever it's ordered to store. A CPU is a CPU, it can run any app it's given. Having set up the technical infrastructure, the incremental cost to the BEC of expanding into other lines was virtually nil. Konychev built the client contacts, Lishin built out the network and the software. All kinds of Internet scum were only too happy to avail themselves of BEC facilities. The BEC blew through the dot-com crash in 2000, and when the global economy sunk like the *Titanic* in 2008, the BEC kept swimming in a rising sea of cash. The business just kept growing.

That inevitably attracted the Kremlin's attention. In most Western countries—those governed by the rule of law, for instance—the government would have invested money and manpower trying to shut such a network down and prosecute those behind it. In Russia, where rule of force equals rule of law, the Kremlin summoned Konychev and Lishin to a meeting and put a deal on the table. Cut us in or spend the next twenty years in a cell down the hall from Khodorkovsky in Siberia.

They were quick to agree. A third partner joined the firm, Taras Batkin.

His Cheka background and Kremlin contacts gave the BEC another layer of insulation. Business grew faster than ever. Somewhere along the line, Konychev's younger sister, Alyona, who had been married to Lishin for more than a decade, took up with Batkin. The divorce and new marriage, about six months apart, had taken place three years earlier, apparently without incident. Nobody wanted to upset the apple cart carrying the golden goose, or so my cynical mind suggested. I put the mixed metaphor down to too much Pilsner Urquell.

I finished reading and went back to the computer. Ivanov had no pictures of either Lishin or his ex-wife, but he did have one of Konychev, accompanying his latest post. Taken with a long telephoto lens, it showed the same man I'd seen on Tverskaya, wearing an overcoat and scarf, climbing out of the backseat of another armored Mercedes. A bodyguard held the door from behind, another stood in front, partially blocking the camera's view. His hand reached under his overcoat, no doubt wrapped around a large caliber firearm. Konychev looked straight at the camera, unaware of its presence. Handsome face, soft features, intelligent eyes. Hard to read much into them.

Something behind his head caught my attention, and I leaned in for a closer look. The number of the building, large brass digits affixed to a marble façade—140. The same "1" and "4" and "0" that adorned the exterior of 140 West Forty-eighth Street—Leitz's building. That could be coincidence, plenty of buildings with the number "140" in plenty of cities. Maybe even one or two that used the same stencils. The Mercedes had New York plates. Still, Konychev could be going to visit any one of a score of tenants. He could have been going to the building next door. Everything about his presence in New York could have been coincidence, but I was ready to bet my newly acquired Repin that Konychev was paying a visit to Sebastian Leitz.

★ CHAPTER 9 ★

I got up at my usual 6:00 A.M. and ran a half mile downtown until I found a pay phone I hadn't hit in a while. I used a prepaid card to dial Aleksei's office in Moscow.

"Good morning," I said. "Feel like coffee? I'm buying."

A brief pause, then, "Give me forty-five minutes. Usual place?"

"Fine."

I continued my run, five miles through the cold, dark, empty streets, thinking about the Leitzes, Efim Konychev, the honesty of my client, and how far I wanted to take this. A million dollars is a million dollars, I reminded myself more than once, and I still had a clear vision of *Suprematist Composition* on Leitz's wall that I could transfer easily enough to my own. A stiff wind kept me away from the rivers, I ran fast and was early getting back so I reversed direction and trotted up to City Hall where I found another pay phone and dialed another number, this one belonging to a disposable cell phone.

Aleksei answered on the first ring. I wouldn't describe either of us as paranoid, at least not overly so. I spied on the United States for twenty years, and I suspect there are some old members of the U.S. intelligence community who are sufficiently curious about what I'm up to these days to listen in to the occasional phone call. Aleksei has more immediate reasons to worry. He's an honest cop in a system where honesty is not only shunned but feared. That makes him a target, and there's little question that his phone is tapped. We'd agreed on one thing when we saw each other in Moscow—a system for getting in touch, using phones that can't be traced and a fake coffee date to set a time.

"How're you doing?" I said.

"Don't ask."

"Bad day?"

"One more in a sequence."

"Sorry. Work?"

"Among other things."

I didn't want to ask the next question, but I didn't want to appear uncaring either.

"Your mother?"

"Bad subject."

The Cheka stomped in, wearing high leather boots with steep heels, Lavrenty Pavlovich at the head of the column.

"Maybe I should call another day."

"You're on the phone now. You wouldn't have called unless you wanted something."

Ouch. And true. "Aleksei, I . . ."

"Don't. I'm sorry. That wasn't called for. It's been a bad few days, as I said."

"You're right, though. I'm the one who's sorry. I'm just not used to . . ."

"I understand. It's your kopek."

"All right. Efim Konychev."

Pause. "What about him?" His tone had been sour. Now it was sour and on guard.

"I might be bumping up against him."

"Be careful."

"I figured that out. Ivanov says he's been in hiding since the Tverskaya attack."

"I guess so."

Sour, on guard, and evasive.

"Any idea why he's showing himself now, or why the Feds here are letting him into the country, or why he'd want to be let in?"

A pause before he said, "I can't talk about that."

So the CPS was involved. "He causing your string of bad days?"

"You're not listening to me." Annoyance in his voice now.

Change the subject. "You ever run across a very tall Belarusian, maybe six seven, bald, pockmarked face, bad teeth, exceptional strength?"

There was a longer pause this time. "Why?"

"He laid a pretty good thumping on your old man a few nights ago. More than that, he seemed to know all about me, which suggests certain connections."

"That's your department."

I let that go.

His voice softened. "Okay, few nights ago? Where?"

"Here. Second Avenue. He had four guys with him, but they could've been rent-a-thugs."

The voice changed. "What are you working on?"

"Something I can't talk about."

Another pause. "I've heard about a man like that. Knack of appearing out of nowhere. Superhuman strength. Don't know his name, no one does. Lots of stories, though. He likes to tie people up conscious and slit their wrists so they feel themselves die. If he has time. Otherwise, he just breaks their necks—with his hands."

I was starting to look lucky.

"He's supposed to be the chief enforcer of the Baltic Enterprise Commission."

The connection I was looking for. I paused before I played my next card. I told myself I hadn't been sure I wanted to when I placed the call, but that was rationalization.

"That photo of Konychev yesterday on Ibansk—it was taken outside an office building here in New York. One of the tenants is a big-time Wall Street investor, Sebastian Leitz."

I was listening for curiosity, but he kept his voice flat, intentionally or not. "So?"

"Leitz is bidding on two TV networks here. Sixty-five billion dollars. His computers were bugged eight weeks ago. Right after I discovered that, I got a visit from the bucktoothed Belarusian. I call him Nosferatu, by the way."

"More coincidences than you can tolerate?"

"One way to sum it up."

"And what do you want from me?"

"Information. Background. I'm trying to put pieces together, figure out what's going on."

"You working for—what's-his-name?—Leitz?"

"Can't say."

A long pause this time. "You think we'll ever trust each other. I mean, really trust? *Both* of us?"

I started to answer—*I hope so*—but he was asking a two-sided question. His lack of trust was given and warranted. We both understood that. He was also asking if I could overcome a lifetime of cynical calculation and trust anyone—him—based on things as ethereal as blood and love.

Beria put in an appearance behind the public phone, wearing his Cheka uniform, pince-nez balanced on his ski-jump nose. Eyes dark and humorless, but not without curiosity.

Not so simple, is it? he said.

Go away, I said.

That's not so simple, either. I'm here. I've always been here. I've always been part of it. I've always been part of you.

"Hang on," I said to Aleksei. I let the receiver dangle and walked around the phone stand. The vision vanished. I came back and put the receiver to my ear.

"Sorry, bag lady listening in. I can only say, I'm willing to work on it. I can't think of much that's more important."

"I can tell you're trying. I hear it now. Keep at it. That's all I can say. It's going to take a while."

"I understand that." I looked around. Beria was nowhere to be seen.

He said, "I'm still trying to work some things out. You and the Cheka. You and Polina. I can't say how long it will take. Or make any promises."

Aleksei used our given names, as he'd done since we'd become reacquainted. I was his father, she'd been his mother, but neither of us had been there much in those roles. I had the unrealistic goal of someday being called *Nana*—Dad—but I doubted it would ever happen. A price of fate, and my own decisions, which I also understood all too well. I caught another glimpse of Lavrenty Pavlovich, on a park bench, shaking his head. I shook mine. Beria grinned before he evaporated into the cold morning sun.

"I just want to stay in the game. I won't try to tell you how to play your cards," I said.

"You told me that once before, remember? Don't fold, make the other guy go out first."

"I remember. I didn't know who I was talking to at the time."

"Chekists aren't usually so slow on the uptake. Sorry—I didn't mean that the way it sounded."

"No offense taken."

A long pause. "Tell me this, if you can: This man Leitz, he seeing a woman named Alyona Lishina?"

"Where did you hear that?"

"Around. You know who she is?"

"Konychev's sister, ex-wife of Alexander Lishin. Current wife of Taras Batkin. Also the mother of a girl Leitz's son spends a lot of time with. Why?"

"You're well informed. We're interested. But every time we start to ask we run into roadblocks."

"Cheka roadblocks?"

"What do you think?"

No response to that.

"This your case?"

"Uh-huh." Another long pause. "We've been building a case against the BEC for years, under the Kremlin radar. The problem, as you can appreciate, is that it's a totally online business. Everything is done in the ether—or what they call the cloud these days. You're a phisher and you need a base for your phishing expeditions. You have some contacts in the biz, or you visit a few online sites frequented by like-minded crooks. You get checked out, if you pass muster, you get access to a passworded site that's essentially a shopping mall. Everything you need—applications, storage, memory, processing, protection—all available for sale or rent. You put together your package and use a version of PayPal to pay. You've never met anyone, no one's met you. After a few months, the Web site's taken down and another set up somewhere else. You get access if you're still a customer in good standing. Simple, really, and totally anonymous."

"How did you get on to them?"

"Usual way—get a tip, get lucky, bust a warehouse full of servers. Follow the data, apply pressure, work it up the line. BEC is big enough to require organization, so there is a chain of command, and we followed that. We also tracked the money, which is harder to hide, as you know. It was an international effort, us, the Germans, French, Brits, U.S. DoJ. We followed a half-dozen trails. One of the most productive was a child porn operation over there, busted five or six years ago. That led to the company processing the payments, that led to a couple of European banks, that led to shell companies here."

"And you think the BEC's behind them?"

"You asked about Konychev. He runs the BEC, with two partners—Lishin and Batkin. He's one of yours."

I ignored the barb. "I read that on Ibansk. Ivanov got his facts right?"

"Yes. Not Konychev's choice, even if he is his brother-in-law."

"Ivanov says the partnership was Kremlin enforced."

"Cheka wanted one of its own on the inside. Surprised?"

Ivanov confirmed. Putin himself reportedly boasted, not long after becoming president, that thousands of Cheka operatives had been dispatched to take control of every government, business and, no doubt, criminal institution. Except . . .

"Batkin's based here now."

"I know. *Ambassador* Batkin. Russian-American Trade Council. I'm told he sets great store by his title. We're not allowed to go anywhere near RATC, as I call it. I assume it's a front for Chekists making their second career in organized crime." Definitely a bitter edge to his voice now.

"He one of your targets, along with Konychev?"

"Don't ask. Not that it matters. Lid's been slammed on. Right at the time when the BEC leadership's in disarray."

He made no attempt to hide the frustration.

"Who's being protected?"

"Everyone and anyone, as usual. Watch your step. The tall guy who beat you up, he probably still works for Konychev."

"Thanks. I'll do that."

"I hope you do. . . . I mean that."

"I mean it too."

★ CHAPTER 10 ★

I walked home, Beria by my side.

He doesn't trust you.

What do you know?

I'm the Cheka. I know everything.

I let him keep me company. It was his ground we were covering. Nobody stopped to ask, *Who's he? Why are you talking to him?* Nobody paid us any mind.

This morning's conversation with Aleksei had been the longest since dinner in Moscow when he'd walked out. We'd met twice while I was there. I'd gone looking for, if not reconciliation, at least a start down that road. I was prepared to tell him the truth about my past—the Gulag, the Great Disintegration of my marriage to his mother—and was terrified of his reaction. I hoped he wouldn't hold it *all* against me. I was most worried about the shame of the Gulag and how badly Polina had poisoned the well. I found I had bigger problems. I should have seen them coming—he'd been more than clear last summer—but one of the hardest prisons to break out of is your own point of view.

The first meeting took place two nights after I arrived, at a restaurant the hotel concierge recommended. I wouldn't be seeking his advice again. A dark, close cave, carved out of the basement of an old building near the Kremlin walls, with atmosphere to match. The raucous laughter from an American tour group bounced around the subterranean room, growing in volume as the waiter brought more vodka. The food was a jumble of Russian standards and what's called "continental"—a menu of generic dishes that could have been concocted anywhere. Aleksei was in a bad mood, for reasons he wouldn't specify. I suggested we move venues, but he waved with indifference and said this place was fine. I could barely hear, he didn't have much to say, and I failed to find a path to get a conversation moving.

Outside, afterward, in the cold winter air, he apologized. "My fault. Nothing to do with you. It's . . . Just a bad few days. How about we try again Thursday? I'll choose a place."

I walked back to the Metropole, hopefulness over the next meeting tempered by the sense that one opportunity had been wasted and I wouldn't get too many more. I also wondered how often the "bad few days" came around.

The second meeting started well enough. His choice was a small neighborhood café, above ground and airy, even in the winter dark, with a limited, but appetizing menu and good draft beer. His mood seemed better, if still distant. That was to be expected, I supposed. I had suggested meeting at his apartment—I was curious to see where, and how, he lived—but he quickly parried that. I wondered if we were in his neighborhood. In New York, the Basilisk could have told me in an instant. As Foos is fond of pointing out to anyone who'll listen, Europeans—including Russians—are more protective of their data.

Aleksei was at a table by the window when I arrived. He wore a dark jacket over a navy turtleneck and wool trousers. Two inches taller and thirty pounds lighter than I am, his thick black curly hair was close to needing a trim, but still kempt. He'd been described as resembling a young Mark Twain, and it fit. The black eye patch was in place—the result of being in the wrong place at the wrong time when someone gunned down Andrei Kozlov, first deputy chairman of the Russian Central Bank, in 2006. The someone, of course, was widely presumed to be working for the Cheka.

We'd given the waitress our orders—meat for him, fish for me—when he said, "Okay, tell the story."

I was taken aback by the abruptness of the request—or command, hard to tell which.

"What story do you want to hear?"

"You and Polina. You and Iakov. You and the Cheka. Where you came from. Why you left. Why you live in New York. You decide. It's why we're here, isn't it?"

I listened for emotion—anger, bitterness, resentment, curiosity—but heard none. His voice was flat, almost professional in tone. He was a cop—to the extent he wanted to conduct an interrogation, he'd have a plan for how to go about it.

I didn't have a plan. I'd thought about it, tried to develop one—before I left New York, on the plane, over the last few days. I still didn't know where to start.

"What did your mother tell you?"

I assumed, perhaps unfairly, that Polina had imparted the worst. Maybe worse than that, although she wouldn't necessarily have seen a need to exaggerate.

He shook his head. I thought at first he was refusing to answer. "She didn't tell me much of anything. I asked, of course. All she said was, we were a family of the damned—doubly damned, was the way she put it."

"She didn't say why?"

He shook his head. "She believed it though."

She would have, no doubt about that. "So you really don't know anything about me?"

"Only what I learned in New York."

I was looking at a mostly clean slate—with all the temptations such a vessel presents. I told myself to stick to the facts.

"Let's start with the Cheka," I said. "That'll take us to matters closer to home."

"It's your story."

The voice was still flat. I told the tale of my career, from the Foreign Language Institute through the Second Chief Directorate (counterintelligence) to the First Chief Directorate, whose attention in my time was focused almost entirely on the Main Adversary—the United States—and my five assignments abroad.

"Iakov Barsukov was my guide and mentor throughout," I said.

"That explains one thing." Something else crept into his voice—anger or bitterness or both.

"What's that?"

"Why you didn't shoot the bastard when you had the chance, that night at JFK."

"I owed him everything. That's a tough bond to overcome, whatever the provocation."

"He was a mass murderer. He killed Polina. He tried to kill my sister. As it was, he left her shattered."

"I can imagine how you feel."

"Can you?"

The anger flared in his features, then left again, almost as quickly. I didn't want to get further into that argument, at least, not yet. "I can try."

"Sorry," he said. "Pointless death gets under my skin. Who do you think I inherited that from?"

I sidestepped the temptation to give the answer he was expecting—*Certainly not your mother.* Instead, I said, "Since we're onto Iakov, let me tell you what happened next."

The waitress brought the food, and we both ordered another a beer.

While we ate, I took him through the events of the Great Disintegration. In 1988, I was posted in the New York *rezidentura* for the second time. The *resident*—chief of station—Lachko Barsukov, Iakov's eldest son, was fast climbing a ladder to the top of the Cheka. He'd always been greedy and he was running a side business, ordering everything from Champagne to truffles to designer dresses on the consulate's tab, shipping it all home, where his brother sold it on the black market. One of my agents exposed him, I turned him in. Iakov leaned on me hard not to testify. I made the worst decision of my life—and I didn't even know how bad it would turn out to be. Honor versus loyalty. I opted for loyalty. Dumbest thing I've ever done. But I was screwed no matter what.

Lachko got away with a slap on the wrist. He was tainted, though, and his ascent was over. He blamed me and sought revenge. He mounted a nasty campaign of innuendo. The whispers got around to Polina. I didn't realize how much I underestimated the depth of her insecurity. Her alcoholic father had been run out of the GRU (military intelligence) and sent to the camps. She was horrified at the prospect of her life crumbling again—and being married to a *zek,* although I left that part out for the moment. She set out to ruin me by sleeping with my fellow officers, the kind of indiscretion she knew the Cheka could not ignore. I found out what she was up to before the organization did and made a deal with the devil to save all of us. Polina could raise Aleksei, with my support. I wouldn't interfere, I wouldn't even be a known factor. As if I never existed, a *zek*'s destiny. I didn't reckon on her marrying Lachko, but I'm not omniscient. In retrospect, she was grasping for security and still trying to get even. He'd always had a thing for her and he wanted to get even too. Iakov pulled some strings and I was given an assignment in San Francisco. That was a time-buyer. I was back in Moscow in two years, behind a desk, which I hated. When the opportunity presented itself to call it quits, I did, and moved to New York. Start over."

"That's quite a story," Aleksei said as the waitress cleared our plates. His professional tone was back.

"It's straight—or as straight as I can remember. A difficult time. Memory plays tricks, as you know. I made a big mistake, I tried to rectify it as best I could. You were one big casualty of that. I'm sorry."

He nodded, in acknowledgment or acceptance, I wasn't sure which. Neither of us said anything for a few minutes while we sipped our beer. I had a sense what the next question would be—like staring at a gallows, knowing what it's to be used for, with nowhere to run. My pulse picked up speed as I waited. I didn't know for sure how I'd answer.

"How about your childhood? Where'd you grow up?"

Paralysis grabbed my throat. My heart raced, my breath got short.

"You all right?" he asked.

"Aleksei, I . . ."

He had concern on his face, no doubt over the rising panic on mine.

"The . . . the reason your mother said we were damned," I croaked. My voice sounded like it belonged to someone else. It was all but drowned out by the pounding in my chest.

He was waiting, uncertain what to say or do. I fought for control. I told myself to get on with it. It's only a word. A word I couldn't speak.

"G . . . Gulag," I finally managed to whisper.

He looked at me quizzically.

"That's . . . That's where I was born. That's where I grew up. Your mother never knew—until the end. That's the reason everything fell apart."

He didn't jump up. He didn't run. He didn't shout *NO!* He didn't even look that surprised. He just leaned back and nodded. My heart rate slowed a little.

"Why didn't you tell her before?" he said after a minute.

"Shame. Fear. I was ashamed of my past. Still am. I can barely tell you about it, today, five decades later. And I was scared about how she'd react. I wasn't wrong about that."

He nodded again and crossed his arms. "I have friends whose parents were in the camps. They don't talk about it either. I kind of understand it, I guess. But, at the same time, there were millions of victims. All Russians share that history. It's something we need to come to terms with if we're ever able to confront our past. And we can't do that without talking about it—openly."

I could have cried, from tension and relief. My heart rate returned to normal. The shame that haunted me meant nothing to him. I'd spent the last twenty years terrified—for no reason. Maybe there was hope for Russia—if more people of his generation shared his view.

He was watching my reaction. "You were born there, you said. That means your mother . . ."

"That's right. She was arrested with her parents during the Terror in 1938. Your great-grandparents were artists and died in the camps. Your grandmother was released in 1946 and rearrested in a roundup of ex-prisoners in 1948. She was sent to Dalstroi this time—Siberia. I was born there on March 15, 1953—the day Stalin and Prokofiev died. Bad timing for Sergei Sergeyevich. We were released in Beria's amnesty, but she was too weak to make the journey home. She died on the train. I was brought up in an orphanage, got into trouble as a teenager, got sent back to the Gulag. You hate him, I understand that, but it was Iakov Barsukov who identified my language skills and gave me a chance. He got me out of the Gulag and started my career in the Cheka."

He shook his head. He didn't want to hear that about Iakov. "What about your father?"

"That's less clear. The man I'm named after, Electrifikady Turbanevich . . ."

He was taking a sip of beer. He stopped and laughed out loud. "Say that again."

"Electrifikady Turbanevich."

"You're kidding, right?"

"No. You didn't know?"

"She never told me. How did you get saddled with . . . If you don't mind my asking." He was still smiling.

"He was the man I believed to be my father. My mother broke with tradition and gave me the whole name. They didn't have much time together. 'Forty-six to 'forty-eight, then a supposed reunion in Kolyma in 'fifty-two. She wanted a way to remember him, I guess."

"Okay, but how did he get . . ."

"Stalinist zeal. He was born in the thirties. Lots of kids got screwy patriotic names—Ninel, Stalina, Drazdraperma. Apparently Grandpa Turba was a Stalinist with a sense of humor."

"Unlikely combination."

"The czars couldn't kill Russian humor, neither could the Bolsheviks."

"What did he do, your father?"

"He was a Chekist. On Beria's staff."

He started at that.

"He was a *zek* too. Arrested with my mother in forty-six. Rejoined the Cheka sometime after he was released in forty-eight. That wasn't unheard of, by any means."

"And it still took Iakov and your language skills to get you out?"

"I don't think he had any idea I existed."

"The Cheka would have."

I shrugged. "Maybe. I haven't been able to find those records. And I've been looking."

"And your Grandpa Turba—the funny Stalinist—what about him?"

"He worked for Dzerzhinsky."

"*Dzerzhinsky!?* As in Felix, founder of the Cheka, Dzerzhinsky?"

"That's right. Turba helped set it up. He was also an early victim—he was purged and sent to the camps to die in 1937."

"And you *still* believe Iakov just happened to pick you out of a crowd of *zeks?*"

"Yes. Why?"

"You've got Cheka royalty running through your blood, and you can ask that?"

"I didn't know any of this until after my career was over. I learned it all since I moved to New York."

The waitress offered coffee. Aleksei declined. I did as well. He retreated to his thoughts, and I left him there.

A good ten minutes passed before he said, "We joked in New York about you being the first ex-Chekist. I almost believed it at the time. I guess I wanted to believe it, once I figured you were my father. Now I'm not so sure."

"Why not? What's changed?"

Another long wait before he said, "That night at JFK, with Iakov—seems to me, looking back now, the whole thing could've been a setup. I wandered into it, and you improvised."

"I improvised, that's true. To get you out of there."

"Maybe. The Cheka cuts too deeply into all of us, I guess."

"What's that supposed to mean?"

"You didn't tell Polina about your Gulag past. You say you were ashamed, you say you were scared. Now you tell me how each of my ancestors is more deeply wired into the Cheka than the next. What's the motivation this time?"

"I don't see what you're driving at. I spent the last twenty years trying to find out about my past because I hoped . . . I hoped some day to have the chance to tell you where you came from."

"And you thought I'd be as proud of it—the Cheka part—as you are?"

I had no idea how to respond. "I don't see where pride enters into it," I said after a moment.

"Don't you?" His voice was full of feeling now. Anger, bitterness, resentment raced each other to the fore. An explosion was coming, and I was responsible. But what could I have told him differently?

"Aleksei, listen, I'm sorry. I thought . . . I thought you'd want to know."

Did I sound as lame to him as I did to myself?

He answered that question by pulling a bundle of notes out of his pocket. He counted off several and tucked them under his empty beer glass.

"Maybe you thought wrong."

He stood and left, grabbing his overcoat from the rack without stopping. I didn't try to follow.

The waitress approached hesitantly. I held out the dish of money and ordered a vodka. Half an hour later, having ordered and drunk another, I was still trying to figure out what had happened. I'd underestimated whatever was eating at him as badly as I had his mother a lifetime earlier.

I tried calling him several times over the next two days, but he was busy or avoiding me. Then I had dinner with Sasha and he dropped the hammer about Beria. How would I ever explain that—if I got the chance?

★ CHAPTER 11 ★

Beria disappeared at the South Street Seaport. I got home to find my neighbors, Tina and John, loading suitcases into a cab.

"Going skiing," Tina piped in her eternally upbeat way. Tina's very sweet and what Americans unkindly call an airhead. I think it's both sexist and unfair to rank a woman's brains ahead of her other attributes, which Tina has in abundance. Today, her coat was open and her woolly sweater and leather pants stretched tight over her full figure. I tried not to observe too closely since her husband, a former linebacker for the New York Giants, is Foos's size and solid muscle. I told them to have a good trip and went upstairs to shower.

I got the Potemkin out of the garage and drove to Bedford. It's a foolish car, especially in winter when you can't put the top down and a rear-wheel-drive boat is useless in snow and ice. But I don't get a chance to drive much, and I love the feel of a battleship, albeit an American battleship, on the road.

Marianna Leitz lived on East Meadow Road, a winding, empty country lane lined by old maples, white fences, and stone walls demarcating horse farms and big estates. I found her driveway between two large columns with an electronic gate and a security camera. The gate was open.

I stopped outside to check my messages. A gray Toyota Camry rolled past and disappeared around a bend. I listened to a Gatling-gun recording from Julia Leitz recounting all of the important things she was working on, none of which meant anything to me, before she said, "I might be able to do six, if this deal doesn't blow. If that happens, all bets are off. Come here at six, but call first. I could be in crisis mode." Sounded like crisis mode was a perpetual state she rather enjoyed, as her brother said. Nothing from Leitz's ex-wife or brother-in-law or brother.

The Camry came back the other way. The driver turned his head as he passed. A balding man of about my age. Maybe he was lost. Or maybe he was working.

Marianna's driveway was long, and the house, when it finally came into view, grand, white, and handsome. Big, bare-branched trees dotted the wide, snow-covered lawn. A fenced pool area to one side, tennis court nearby, and a large children's jungle gym–swing complex opposite.

It took a few minutes before she answered the door. She would have been attractive on a good day, but good days had been few and far between in recent months. She looked like hell this morning. Deep creases marred an otherwise fine face. Gray-brown bags hung from brown eyes surrounded by roadmap-red whites. She wore jeans and a sweatshirt and had made no attempt at makeup. Her shoulder-length blond hair frizzed in every direction. She didn't remotely resemble a rich woman living in the lap of luxury. She made a meager effort to smile hello, accompanied by an attempt at a limp handshake, which she couldn't quite manage.

She led me through an entrance hall and a dining room that sat twenty into a sprawling kitchen. Dirty dishes filled the double sink and spilled onto the countertop.

"Sorry," she said, waving carelessly in their direction. "I'm a little behind."

That was an opening, but I let it pass. Better to let her decide when to tell her story.

"I appreciate you taking the time to see me."

She tried to smile again. "Distraction is a good thing these days. Coffee?"

I had the uncharitable feeling the coffee might be the same vintage as the dishes. I declined. She went to the counter and poured herself a cup. She kept her back to me as she took a bottle from the cabinet, added a shot and put the bottle back. Self-medicating, the attempt to hide it more form than function. I know the signs, the feeling. I've done it myself.

Marianna pointed to a table with four chairs by the window. It had a view of the swing set and jungle gym.

"Like I said, I appreciate your time."

She waved again. Time was one thing she had in abundance and didn't want.

"I'm wondering if you've been visited by anyone asking about your brother."

"Sebastian called, said you'd be asking. I told him . . . no."

Her voice was tentative, even through the booze.

"I can understand that, but . . ."

"But what?"

"I'm working for your brother, I'm trying to help. I don't have to tell him everything people tell me." I let that sink in. "There was someone, right?"

She looked around and nodded. "I . . . I don't know why I didn't tell him, except with everything else . . . he can be so controlling . . . I just didn't feel like it, you know? He's got his problems, I've got mine."

"Sure. Everybody does. Who were they? What did they ask? This is just between us."

"I don't remember too much. They said it was some kind of background check. Everything . . . Everything's been a bit of a blur."

"That's understandable." The thing about people who withdraw into themselves, their universe of reference draws in with them. They don't think about the rest of us—they assume we're looking at the world from their point of view. Booze helps that process, of course. "What can you remember?"

She took a swallow from her cup. "Two of them, a man and a woman."

"What did they look like?"

Another wave at the air. "Ordinary. Suits. Business looking. Ordinary looking."

"Okay. What did they say?"

"Asked a lot of questions. About Sebastian . . . and the family. Who we were, what we did. It was strange, to tell you the truth. I didn't say much. The questions . . . They seemed . . . intrusive."

"Did they ask about your . . . situation?"

Pause, the brain cells trying to clarify. "What do you mean by that?"

My turn to wave at the dishes. "It's been a rough few weeks, as you said."

The eyes blurred. "Right. They asked about Sebastian, Jenny, Pauline, the kids, a little, and about Thomas and Julia, but no . . . not about Jonathan or our children."

"Did they say who they were?"

"Some law firm. They gave me a card. Not at the beginning. Only when I pressed."

"You still have it?"

"Somewhere . . ."

"It could be helpful."

"Okay."

She stood, took a minute to get her balance and went off rummaging through kitchen drawers. Partway through the search, she returned to the table for her cup, took it to a cabinet and refilled it from the bottle without bothering to add more coffee. I looked at my watch. 10:14. Even money whether she made it to lunch.

"Ah-ha!"

She returned from the far side of the kitchen, victorious. The card read, ELIZABETH ROGERS, LINDLEY & HILL, ATTORNEYS-AT-LAW, with a New York address and phone number, a Web site, and an e-mail address. I made a note of it all for form's sake.

I wanted to ask an intrusive question of my own. Worst thing she could do was decline to answer, but I was banking on her drinking more now than when Elizabeth Rogers visited.

"How close are you all, Sebastian, your siblings, as a family?"

The eyes clarified again and narrowed. Not as soused as I thought. Her voice took a harder edge. "Why do you ask that?"

"Someone's trying to hurt your brother—the same people who came to see you, I think. They found a way into his business and to do that they had help. You didn't give it to them, so I guess I'm asking if there's any bad blood elsewhere or anything else these people could have exploited."

She watched me for a minute, stood and left the room. I could hear her voice from elsewhere in the house, talking on the phone. Checking with Leitz HQ.

She returned after a few minutes, sat, drank from her cup, and said, "Sebastian says you should call him."

"I will, as soon as we're finished. I'm only trying to help, as I said." I hoped I sounded sincere.

Another swallow. "What was your question?"

"How do you all get on, the family? Any quarrels? Bad feelings? Ancient, unresolved feuds?"

"No feuds, no. Tensions, I suppose, like any family."

"What kind of tensions?"

She thought for a moment. "Personality, mainly. We're all pretty strong minded. Sebastian and Julia have their careers. Thomas has his . . . passions. Sometimes they go off in different directions. I've always been the easy-going one, willing to do whatever, if that kept the peace. But then, I always figured I was the one who had it all worked out—the marriage, the family . . ."

She banged her fists on the table in front of her and dropped her head on top of them, facedown. The cup fell on its side, spilling a puddle of brown liquid. She sobbed into balled fingers. I picked up the cup, wiped up the puddle with a well-used dish towel, found the brandy bottle in the cabinet— Presidente—and poured a few fingers. I felt no qualms about aiding and abetting. I wanted her to talk, and she'd be back at the sauce with or without my help. I put the cup on the table, reclaimed my seat, and took a chance.

"I'm sorry, Marianna. I know a little about your husband. Nobody should have to deal with what you're going through."

She kept crying. Two more minutes passed before she looked up, another second and half before she reached for the cup. She took two swallows before she straightened and looked at me, red-eyed.

"I'm sorry. I'm still not . . . It's just so . . . Where were we?"

"You were talking about keeping the peace—in the family."

She nodded, grabbing at something that wasn't her own misery.

"Like I said, we're all strong minded. The result of our parents dying when we were still young, I think. A car accident—you know that, right?"

I didn't, but I'd accomplished getting on the inside of her story.

"Tell me."

"I was fifteen, Sebastian was eighteen, Julia, fourteen, and Thomas, eight. Thomas suffered most, I think, the youngest—and a tough age. Anyway, we were a teenaged immigrant family, and we had to make do. We did, we all stayed in school, we all worked too. Sebastian was the oldest, so he was de facto head of household, and it suited him. He watched out over all of us, he always made sure we were okay, but . . . as we all grew older, became adults, he never backed off. He still treats us as if we're teenagers cast adrift. He can be overprotective, and that can grate. Not his fault, he means well. Just the way it is, with everything that happened."

"How does that manifest, the grating?"

She took a drink and stared out the window at the snow and the swing set.

"He smothers. He tries to control. It's like, he thinks he's still responsible for all of us, whatever happens. He can't understand we all have our own lives now, we've made our own way, we're responsible for our own . . ."

She stopped short, staring into her cup, realizing where she was going. "Anyway, you know what I mean."

"Having a brother like that, who cares, isn't necessarily a bad thing," I said.

She shook her head, as if agreeing and trying to clear her mind at the same time.

"Not bad. But . . . It does lead to . . . tensions."

"How does he get on with your brother and sister?"

"He and Julia spar all the time. They're the most competitive. He's never liked her husband, and he doesn't approve of the way she takes care of their kids. Doesn't take care of them, in his opinion. He tries to tell her, she objects, and they end up in a fight. Thomas . . . Thomas goes his own way, to

91

put it mildly. Sebastian doesn't understand him, and Thomas doesn't want him to. Oil and water."

No way to ask the next question without appearing intrusive, but I hoped she was beyond caring. "Does Thomas have financial problems?"

"What? Why . . . ? How do you know . . . ?" She shook her head. "I'm not going to talk about that."

"I'm sorry. It's a difficult subject, I know. I only ask because money—lack of money, debts—can make someone vulnerable. I think Thomas ran up some big debts. He could be desperate."

She nodded slowly. "He's always said it's impossible to live in New York City on a teacher's salary. And . . . have you met him?"

"Not yet."

"He's something of a clotheshorse—and he doesn't shop discount, like Julia. I . . . I tried to help him out from time to time. But . . ."

I waited.

"I shouldn't tell you this."

Intuition—often a spy's best friend—said don't push it.

"I can't force you."

She took another drink. "I lent him some money, years ago. Fifteen thousand. Six, seven years ago, I don't remember. He was frantic. I had the cash, he needed it. He kept promising to repay, of course, and I chased him for a couple of years without success. My husband was furious when he found out. Threatened to go to Sebastian. I urged him not to. It was family, what could I do? It was my problem, I said I'd deal with it. Eventually, it went the way of all things . . . subsumed by time and other concerns. He came to me one other time. Right around the time . . . I guess it was four years ago. Twenty-five thousand dollars. I was stunned. I had no idea."

"Did you give it to him?"

"No. I didn't have that kind of cash this time. And I realized something was wrong, badly wrong. I urged him to get help."

"How did he react?"

"Badly. We were in the city, at a restaurant. He called me a horrible name, loud enough for the whole place to hear. We fought and he walked out."

"And he hasn't asked again? Recently?" I was thinking of the $35,000 he'd paid off in November.

"No. I don't see Thomas much these days. I've . . . I've had my own problems to worry about."

"Would he have gone to your brother or Julia for a loan?"

"Not Sebastian. They argued over money before. You know about his temper . . ."

I nodded. "What about Julia?"

"Maybe. They're not that close. And he'd have to get her attention."

"Meaning?" Although I knew the answer.

"Julia is what people politely call a workaholic. She never leaves the office. Barely has time for her own family."

"What about her husband? Would he have gone to him?"

"Oh no." The answer came fast, too fast, not as if she were trying to head me off, but a knee-jerk response, as though the idea itself was preposterous.

"Why not?" I said as innocently as I knew how.

She shook her head. "He just wouldn't. That's all."

That wasn't remotely all, but intuition intervened again—don't press it, move on. I took a shot at another question, half expecting it to bring the interview to a close.

"What happened to Sebastian's first marriage?"

She shook her head and looked out the window.

I waited.

She shook her head again and started to cry. I'd lost her.

"You know . . . You think your problems are the worst anyone could have. Then . . ."

She balled her fists and hit the table again, grabbed the cup, and emptied it.

"Maybe I'll join you," I said, and went to the cabinet. I poured her a healthy shot, found a cup that looked clean, and gave myself a finger and half.

I put the cups on the table and she reached for hers hungrily. I took a sip from mine. Presidente burned, not unpleasantly, on the way down.

"We don't talk about it, you know. We never have. Unwritten rule. Forbidden subject. Taboo."

I waited again. Booze versus taboo—I was betting on booze, and the need to unburden.

"It was four years ago now. Sebastian had two kids with his first wife, Pauline—Andras and Daria. Daria was twelve when . . ."

The fists balled once more, and the head fell on top. Her whole body heaved with sobs. She tried to talk in between. I had to lean forward to make out the muffled, tear-and-brandy-soaked voice.

"She . . . she had . . . she had a gun and . . . she shot . . . shot herself . . . in her room. She . . . she laid down a plastic drop cloth first so she wouldn't make a mess. Oh dear God, why? It was so horrible. We were all there. We all saw the body. Thomas . . . poor Thomas he got there first, he was in the upstairs bathroom. He . . . hasn't been the same. None . . . None of us has."

I waited until the sobbing subsided.

"Does anyone know why she did it?"

She looked up, eyes wet and blurred. "No. Daria . . . She was always such a happy girl. Her brother's the moody one, Andras. Daria was always smiling, laughing. I can still see her—those big blue eyes, blond curls . . ."

She broke down sobbing again. I didn't try to intervene. Several minutes passed before she looked up again.

"It devastated Pauline. She suffered some kind of breakdown. Spent time in an institution. Sebastian stuck by her until she announced she had to leave. She moved back to Minnesota, where's she's from."

Had to leave. Does a mother *have to leave* her family, her kids? My mother held me until she died on a train somewhere in the Urals. Polina abandoned Aleksei. But I always figured that was my fault.

"Was there an investigation?"

"The police came, of course, questioned all of us. They ruled it a suicide. She'd taken the gun from a friend's house a few days before."

That indicated some degree of premeditation on the girl's part, but I didn't need to point that out. I said, "I'm very sorry. I didn't mean to dredge up painful memories."

She nodded and looked into her cup. "Like I said, we don't talk about it, but it's always there, you know, like an ache you can't get rid of. Sometimes it's good to acknowledge it, put it out in the open."

"Your brother—Sebastian, I mean—he doesn't agree with you?"

"No. I mentioned Daria once, about six months after it happened. He got so angry, he totally lost it, threw things . . . I thought he was going to hit me. I never tried again. Neither has anyone else, so far as I know."

Her cup was empty. I went to the cabinet and poured another shot. I caught my refection in the window as I returned to the table and turned to ignore it. Aleksei wasn't wrong in his digs—you learn to be a bastard in the Cheka.

"What's Andras like?" I asked.

"What do you mean?"

"As a kid. You said he's moody. He must have been affected by his sister's death."

"Of course he was. But . . ."

I waited once more.

She shook her head. "I don't know. I don't see that much of him. He went away to school."

"You see him at Christmas?"

"Yes . . . I guess so. Sebastian had the usual family get-together. He was there."

"How did he seem?"

"Fine, I guess. I didn't really notice, to tell you the truth."

That was probably true. The booze would have had an impact. But I also sensed there was something she wasn't telling me.

"Have you met his girlfriend?"

She shook her head. "I didn't know he . . ."

"Girl from his school. She lives in New York. Irina's her name."

She shook her head again. The name didn't register. Her eyes blurred again. The booze was working its will.

"I have to ask one more question," I said. "I'm sorry. Your husband. What happened?"

She clutched the cup in both hands and looked up, eyes open wide and angry.

"What happened? WHAT HAPPENED? He fucks every woman he can sweet-talk into bed, that's what. TWAT, TWAT, TWAT! THAT'S ALL HE CARES ABOUT! Not me, not the kids, just . . ."

She threw the cup across the kitchen. Brandy splattered on the wall, but the cup rolled to the floor, unbroken.

"GET OUT!"

I'd found the line and crossed it, in best Cheka fashion.

I picked up the cup and wiped down the wall with another dish towel.

I put the cup in front of her and said good-bye. She was crying again and didn't look up.

When I walked out to the car, I looked back to see her watching me from the door, cup in hand—hers or mine, I wasn't sure. I had the distinct impression she was making sure I really left. But she could have been waiting until I was out of sight to pour another drink.

★ CHAPTER 12 ★

Still feeling like a heel, I found a parking place on First Avenue, a block from Jenny Leitz's coffee shop. I was a few minutes early. I'd taken my time, driving slowly along East Meadow Road until I approached the county highway that would take me to I-684. I pulled over and put my cell phone to my ear. A minute later, the gray Camry appeared in the rearview mirror. I tried again to get a look at the driver but he gave me the back of his balding head a second time. The car went right toward the interstate. I let him get a good head start.

Leitz was on my message machine, shouting orders. "Call me immediately! This harassment of my family has gone far enough!"

I saw no point in engaging his temper, and I had a hunch Jenny hadn't told him we were meeting. Two good reasons not to call him back. By the time I reached the highway, there were no gray Camrys in sight. I didn't see any on the drive back to Manhattan.

The coffee shop was long and narrow. A counter with stools down one side, booths along the opposite wall. The woman I made as Jenny sat in a booth facing the door, halfway down the aisle. She made me too, and stood as I approached. The antithesis of her sister-in-law Marianna—in appearance and feeling. No more than five feet tall, with narrow shoulders, tucked waist, and trim hips. If Leitz rolled over in bed, he'd smother her. Her black hair was cut short, which showed off her big eyes and smooth Oriental features. She wore red-framed glasses, a purple top, rose-pink silk pants, and two rings—a big shiny rock and a gold band—on her left hand.

"You must be Turbo," she said. "I'm Jenny. Nice to meet you."

Something was wrong. The way she moved. She'd been tentative climbing out of the booth, and she was careful to balance herself as she stood, her hand on the table top. Now, she slid deliberately back into her seat. When she got settled, I saw the sadness and worry behind the glasses. Jenny Leitz was making the most of it, but she was not a well woman.

She had a bowl of soup and a glass of water in front of her. I ordered coffee and an English muffin. She waited until the waitress moved away and said, "You've been with Marianna."

News traveled fast in the Leitz family. Not necessarily good, for my purposes.

"That's right. She call you?"

Jenny shook her head. "Sebastian told me, when I said I was meeting you. He wants you to call him."

So much for my hunch. No secrets in the Leitz family. At least, not unimportant ones.

"How is she?" Jenny asked with a concern that was far from perfunctory.

"Not good. Unhappy, depressed, drinking too much. For openers."

Jenny nodded. "Her husband. She told me all about it. It's killing her. She won't let anyone help."

I must have looked perplexed.

"Oh, I know," she said. "She told me, not Sebastian. He thinks everything's fine. It's our secret."

"But . . ."

"Sebastian can be difficult, as you know. He told me what happened at the office. The conference table . . ."

I nodded.

"His intentions are good—he wants to make things better. He doesn't understand that's not always possible—or even desirable. It may not be what the other person wants. Then there's his temper. It's hard for Marianna, or others, to confide in him."

I took a shot. The odds were comparable to holding a four-card straight and hoping to draw the fifth, at either end—not short, not too long either.

"That apply to you as well?"

The straight filled. The black-brown eyes behind the red frames withdrew, just for a moment.

"We have our problems, like any married couple. Tell me what you want you want to know."

"There are people asking about your husband. People who want to do him harm. They went to see Marianna. She didn't help them, at least I don't think she did. But if they went to her, I assume they've been making the rounds of the family."

"Not me," she said.

I nodded. I didn't think they'd be brazen enough to brace the wife. "I'm sorry to ask it this way. But . . . your husband is difficult, as you say, which for me means uncommunicative. I'm trying to determine if anyone in the family might be willing to help these people."

She shook her head. "No one. It's a family, like any other. Well, maybe not exactly like any other, but a family with all the usual jealousies, peeves, and resentments. But I don't believe for a minute anyone wants to do real harm to anyone else, including Sebastian."

"Marianna said your husband can be very controlling . . ."

"That's true, but I still don't believe anyone means him harm."

"Thomas? Marianna says he and Sebastian don't always see eye to eye."

"That's true too, but no, I don't think so."

"Even if he had financial problems?"

"He's had those in the past. He went to Sebastian for help."

"Recently?"

"Not that I'm aware of."

"Would you be?"

She paused a beat, for emphasis, her eyes holding mine, before she said, "Yes."

"What about Julia, or her husband?"

"Julia and Sebastian depend on each other in their own unique way. Walter . . . I can't say for sure. I hardly know him, to tell the truth."

"You don't get along?"

"No, not that. He's . . . He's just never around. I've only met him a few times. Of course, we don't see much of Julia either. She's always working on something. Neither of them were at our wedding, now that I think about it. But I still don't think he'd do anything to hurt Sebastian."

She made each statement calmly and good-naturedly. But Walter Coryell bore looking into.

"I'm sure you're right about no one wanting to hurt your husband. But do you think anyone could be compelled—bribed, blackmailed, pressured—into helping bug your husband's computers?"

"I think if anyone tried to get them to do that, Sebastian would be the first to know." She smiled. "He said you'd ask me to spill the family beans."

"I suppose I am, but I'm only looking for points of exposure."

"That's another way of saying secrets, isn't it?" She smiled again.

"If you say so."

"I'm a relatively recent arrival. Not much help, I'm afraid."

"Tell me this. Anyone in the family really good with computers?"

She smiled once more. "That would be Andras, Sebastian's son. He's a whiz."

"Tell me about him."

"Surely you don't think he's the culprit!"

"No." Though I was tempted to mention eleven million reasons why he could be. "Just trying to get as complete a picture as I can. Marianna says he's moody."

She thought for a moment. "I wouldn't put it that way. Quiet, certainly. Introspective. He keeps to himself. And he spends too much time online, in my opinion."

"Your husband doesn't agree?"

"He eggs him on. He's thrilled Andras has an interest, something he's good at."

She didn't know the half of it. Neither did he.

"So many children today, they just drift," she said. "Andras has focus. He's looking forward to college—computer science, of course. His first two choices are Stanford and Cal Tech. I don't know who will be more thrilled if he gets in—him or his father. I try not to get too involved. I'm very fond of Andras, but I'm not his mother. She's still very much on the scene, even from Minnesota, in a good way. That's her role, not mine."

"Have you met his girlfriend?"

"The Russian girl? What's her name?"

"Irina. Irina Lishina."

"Once. Last summer. She struck me . . . She struck me as much older than he is, much more experienced. I don't know whether that's good or bad. He's quite taken with her, that much was clear. I hope he's not headed for a hard landing."

"How long have they been going out?"

"I'm not exactly sure. Since the summer, I think. She goes to the same school."

I nodded. Time to resume the role of heel. "I only have one more question. You mentioned secrets: What's yours?"

The eyes retreated behind the lenses. The voice took a less friendly tone. "What do you mean by that?"

"You've been spending a lot of time with doctors in this part of town."

"How do you know that?" Her hands clutched her soup bowl. The eyes flashed, angry.

"I know a lot of things I shouldn't. I'm sorry." I hoped I sounded sincere.

"How?"

"I just know."

She thought for moment. "It's Foos, isn't it? That data-mining machine of his."

I nodded.

"Shit. He's told me about it. I never thought about having it turned on me. What did it tell you? I want to know."

"It takes data like credit card and phone records and looks for patterns, discrepancies from patterns, things that constitute behavior, things that indicate a change in behavior. So it told me about the calls back and forth with the neurologists. It identified the imaging lab. It reported you've been spending a fair amount of time here, at the coffee shop, at the bookstore down the street, at the pharmacy on Second and Sixty-eighth, at the nail salon on the next block. The doctors, they're self-explanatory. The rest suggests a lot of time waiting, between appointments, between tests, so I'm inferring you're dealing with some complex medical issues. I'm sorry—both that that's the case and that I had to find out about it."

"But it didn't tell you anything about my exact situation, my diagnosis?"

"No. It has some limitations, fortunately."

"That's something, at least. And Foos didn't say anything?"

She'd confided in him—that surprised me. Then again, maybe not.

"Not a word. And I asked him about you."

She nodded. "He's a good friend."

She raised the soup bowl to her mouth and sipped over the lip. Her eyes stayed on me as she gathered her thoughts. I took a swallow of my coffee. Lukewarm.

"I've been diagnosed with ALS. You probably know it as Lou Gehrig's disease, a degenerative neurological disorder, usually terminal."

"I know what it is. I'm very sorry." I felt worse than ever—about her, about what I'd found out, about the whole family.

She seemed to read my mind. "Thank you. And don't worry—you were doing the job Sebastian asked you to do. I don't hold anything against you. I just found out for sure a few days ago, and I've been keeping it close until I could talk with the doctors about the ramifications and possible treatments. I haven't told anyone, other than a few friends like Foos. Sebastian doesn't even know. I'll tell him tonight, now that I have the full picture. I wanted to know everything I could before . . . They tell me there are drugs now that can slow the progress . . . There's also a chance of remission, a small one. I'm not the usual candidate for this illness either, so . . ."

"If attitude is anything, you've got a great shot." I meant it. A new mother, she was dealing with the worst kind of death sentence with remarkable equanimity. Most people would have been barely functioning.

"I'm trying to stay positive—as positive as I can under the circumstances. We have money, I'll have the best care. I've determined . . . I determined we should all lead as normal a life as possible. For as long as possible." She looked up at the clock on the coffee shop wall. "Speaking of appointments, I've got one in ten minutes."

"Good luck."

"Thanks. I keep telling myself I'm a lucky person. Everything'll be fine."

I watched while she stood carefully and walked down the aisle to the door. She misstepped once ever so slightly, steadying herself on a table before proceeding.

I hoped she was right about being lucky. She was trying hard to believe it.

★ CHAPTER 13 ★

No call back from Thomas Leitz or Jonathan Stern. I bought an hour on my parking meter and trotted down to the black stone and glass behemoth at Third Avenue and Fifty-sixth Street that housed the headquarters of Marianna's husband's company. The lobby guard declined to allow me upstairs. I called Foos for some ammunition, then dialed Stern's number. His secretary said he was unavailable.

"Please ask Mr. Stern whether he would like to talk to me—now—or whether he would like me to post the following purchases on the Internet, linked to his name."

I read her the list of lingerie items, each purchased in a different city, all charged to Stern's corporate American Express card.

"I'm downstairs, I'll hold on," I said helpfully.

The woman gulped and went away. Three and half minutes later the guard handed me a building pass, the elevator whisked me to the thirty-third floor, and a good-looking woman in her forties escorted me to a corner office.

A tall man in a striped suit, with fair hair parted in the center and a jutting chin, stood by the window, some papers in his hand. He didn't offer to introduce himself. The secretary closed the door softly behind her.

"What the hell's this all about?" Stern said. His voice held neither fear nor anger, just authority. I was a unwanted, unimportant interruption in his day. But not so unimportant that he left me continuing to cool my heels in the lobby.

"The answer to that depends on you," I said evenly. "You've been sleeping with lots of women who aren't your wife. That's between you and her, except randy CEOs of public companies make good copy. You've also been charging Champagne and lingerie to your corporate credit card. That's between you and your board of directors. Maybe you've been accurate on your expense reports about those charges and nobody cares."

The hand holding the papers dropped a few inches. Some of the authoritarian veneer fell away. The mood pendulum in the room swung in my direction.

"I don't give a damn about any of it," I continued, "except for the leverage it provides. We haven't been properly introduced, but the one thing you should know is that I was trained by the KGB. We're very good at using leverage." I smiled to show it was nothing personal. "Answer my questions, and I'll leave. Lie, prevaricate, stonewall, and you'll have many more people asking much more difficult questions by this time tomorrow."

"Who the hell are you? What do you want?" His voice indicated I'd succeeded in moving up the food chain—from irritant to menace.

"I'm doing a job for your brother-in-law, Sebastian Leitz. That's all you need to know about me—except that those corporate card charges, they're only the beginning of what I know about you. You invest in your brother-in-law's hedge funds?"

"What? Yes. But what the hell . . . ?"

"Then why'd you help bug his computers?"

I was all but certain he hadn't—he didn't match the cleaners' description—but I wanted him on edge when he answered.

"WHAT? What are you talking about? Sebastian? Bugged computers. I have no idea . . ."

"Okay," I said calmly. "Sit down. Let's have a rational conversation."

He took the chair behind his desk. I sat opposite and made a point of shifting my body, crossing my legs, getting comfortable. The control pendulum kept shifting.

"Leitz's computers are the reason I'm here. Somebody bugged them, like I said. The same somebody's had a team of fake lawyers making the rounds of the family. They visited your wife. They come here? Elizabeth Rogers is the name I have. The firm is called Lindley & Hill."

"Never heard of her or the firm."

"Ask your secretary if this is another meeting you turned down."

He started to respond, thought better, and picked up the phone.

She had no memory of Lindley & Hill either. That was interesting. I would have given long odds on Stern receiving a visit.

"It's not my business," I said, "but your wife was in bad shape when I left her this morning. She'd put away half a bottle before lunchtime."

"I suppose you blame that on me."

"I'm not assigning blame," I said untruthfully as I got prepared to be thrown out. "I'm telling you what I saw."

He stood and returned to the window. He had a view westward across Midtown and north to the Upper East Side.

"You're right," he said turning back to face me, "about not your business. But I don't need any more enemies out there than I already have. I can't get Sebastian or anyone else in the lunatic asylum they call a family to listen. You seem to care—you brought up Marianna and her drinking. Maybe they'll listen to you."

I should have kept my mouth shut and left. I'd already learned what I could.

"I'm not going to explain or apologize," he said. "The credit card charges were stupid, I'll admit that. And I'll reimburse the company for all of them. But the women . . .

"My marriage has been an empty shell for years. Not my doing. I worked hard to get Marianna to look at the cause, to get help, to hold things together—if only for the kids' sake. I got no goddamned help from her family. When all that failed, I tried to bring it to some kind of rational end. I failed at that too. So, yes, in the last couple of years, I have sought . . . call it what you want—solace, companionship, just plain sex—I don't care. I'm not proud, I'm not particularly sorry either."

There are at least two sides to every story—it always pays to remember that. The truth usually lies somewhere in between. It can be difficult to pin down the exact point on the continuum, and often it doesn't matter. This time, something kicked my curiosity into gear.

"What happened, if you don't mind my asking?"

He shook his head. "I wish I knew. It wasn't an all-of-a-sudden thing. I was probably slow to realize we had a problem. I was traveling even more in those days, trying to get the company off the ground. Strictly solo, by the way."

I nodded. He was being truthful, I believed him.

"Anyway, it finally dawned on me that we were growing apart—all of us, Marianna, me, the boys—and about the same time that we were spending a lot of money on booze. I cut back on my schedule, spent more time at home. That just seemed to make it worse—put Marianna on edge. She was drinking more than was good for her. I tried to talk about it. She wouldn't listen. She didn't want to face it. I tried to get Sebastian and the others to help. He made an attempt at least, but she kept him at arm's length. She's good at that. The others? To be honest, they were no help at all."

"How long ago was this?"

He looked out the window for a moment.

"Two years, give or take—when I woke up to something happening, I mean. If I'm honest, I'd say the drift started two years before that."

Right about the time Daria Leitz shot herself.

He said, "It was two years ago when I made my big mistake. I was in Chicago, it had been a bad day, a bad trip, I got to talking to a pretty woman at the hotel, we had dinner, one thing led to another and . . . I saw her a few more times, and she assumed things were more serious than they were. When I tried to explain, she threatened to call my wife. She knew her name and number—she'd done her research. I didn't believe she'd follow through, but I was wrong. Marianna flew off the handle. We had a horrendous fight, I kept telling her to quiet down, but she just kept screaming. No way the kids didn't hear. That's when I decided it was over. I was wrong about that too. You know that expression, 'Takes two to tango'?"

I nodded.

"Also takes two to break up. She refuses to discuss it. But every time I show up in Bedford, she berates me with language no one should have to listen to. Certainly not children. So I've taken to staying in the city. I can't go forward, can't go back. I'm at my wits' end, I don't mind telling you."

"That why you cut off the money?"

"She told you that?"

I shook my head.

"Then how . . . ?"

"I told you, I know lots of things."

"I don't want to hurt her. But it's the only way I can think of to get her to face reality."

The reality I'd witnessed was downgrading from Rémy to Presidente.

"Tell me one thing," I said. "These so-called lawyers who went to see your wife—if they asked her to help with Leitz's computers, if they offered her money, do you think she'd go along—in her current state, I mean?"

He came back to the desk and sat down, head in hands. When he raised his eyes, I could see the emotional exhaustion they held. That's tough to fake. He'd been telling his story straight.

"I wish . . . I wish I could say no, no way. But these days, to be honest, I have no goddamned idea."

It was 2:30 P.M. when I put the Potemkin back in the garage. I stopped at a gourmet deli a block from the office and bought a designer smoked salmon sandwich. They were pushing a new brand of gelato, one of whose flavors was tiramisu, so I took a small container of that too. Upstairs, I put a spoonful in Pig Pen's bowl.

"Try this. Frozen tiramisu."

Pig Pen took a long, skeptical look before sticking his beak into the bowl.

"No tiramisu," he announced.

"It's gelato," I said. "Tiramisu flavor."

"No tiramisu. Gigolo."

"Not gigolo. Gelato. Italian ice cream."

"Gigolo. Russky bull." He retreated to the backmost perch, where he goes when he's pissed off, and gave me his hostile, one-eyed stare.

Foos was in his office, the last bites of a cheeseburger and fries on his desk. My designer salmon seemed less appetizing.

"I bought Pig Pen some gelato. He thinks I tried to trick him with Russian tiramisu."

"Pig Pen has a very discerning palate."

I doubt parrots have palates, but there was no point arguing. I opened my sandwich. Foos eyed it with bemusement. "Diet?"

"You are what you eat."

"Personally, I never aspired to be a fish."

"I spent the morning with Marianna Stern, Jenny Leitz, and Jonathan Stern. That family's got nothing but trouble."

"What did Jenny have to say?"

"She told me about the ALS."

"Life's not fair. She's way too nice a person for that."

"Agree. You didn't think it worth mentioning?"

"She asked me not to talk about it."

And that, of course, for Foos, was the end of it.

"What do you know about Marianna and Stern?"

"Not much. Only met them once or twice."

"Their marriage is all washed up, she's a lush and won't consider divorce, he's chasing other women."

"Shit happens."

"You didn't know?"

"Nope."

"You are aware that Andras is a computer whiz?"

"Kid's pretty swift. I wrote him a couple of college recommendations."

"You didn't think *that* worth mentioning?"

"He's Leitz's son."

"You're the one who pointed out that the strange computer activity corresponded with school vacations."

"Never thought about it that way."

Mathematicians and psychology. There's just a disconnect.

"You know anything about a woman named Alyona Lishina?"

"She's a knockout."

Knockouts were something he had experience with. "You've met her?"

"Sure. She's Russian. Temperamental."

"You suggesting cause and effect?"

"Got a mirror?"

"I don't know who's less forthcoming, you or Leitz. Are they . . . ?"

"Just friends, so far as I know."

"That's not what I hear."

"I told you before, don't believe everything you read in—"

"I didn't read this. Aleksei told me."

He shrugged. "Russian rumor, still a rumor."

True enough, and if this rumor had any kind of traction I would have read about it on Ibansk.com—it's the kind of insider tidbit Ivanov makes a living on.

"Here's some fact." I told him about Andras's multimillion-dollar bank account.

"Huh. I wonder if . . ." He clattered away at his keyboard. "Looks like you're on to something. That strange activity originated at Leitz's house. He's got the home system networked through the firm's."

"What's the kid up to?"

"Can't tell. Hard to avoid concluding that he's ripping someone off, though. Question is, who and why?"

"There's more. His girlfriend's in it with him. She's got the same bank accounts and deposit patterns. Her name's Irina Lishina—Alyona's daughter."

"You're full of surprises."

"So's your pal Leitz. What do we know about the Baltic Enterprise Commission?"

"Bad-ass mofos. Web hosting for hire, if your business is spamming, phishing, or kiddie porn. Premium service, pretty much bulletproof. Everybody thinks they were behind the denial of service attacks on Estonia and Georgia a few years back, working for your former colleagues in the Kremlin. Word is, they've been experiencing a few glitches, but there's been no noticeable decline in spamming, phishing, or kiddie porn. Lowlife online thrives as always. Why?"

"Aleksei thinks the same thing. Says the guy who beat me up on Second Avenue last week is the BEC's chief enforcer."

"He sure about that?"

"That's what he says."

He leaned back in his chair and looked across the desk at me. I had his full attention now.

"They the ones targeting Leitz?"

"Could be. Let me show you something."

I walked around the desk, brought up a Web browser on his computer, logged onto Ibansk.com, and scrolled to the photo of Konychev.

"That's the man behind the BEC. Check out the background."

Foos stared at the screen for a moment, and said, "Huh. See what you mean."

"His sister is Alyona Lishina."

"I'm finished being surprised. You gonna tell Leitz?"

"I'm betting he already knows about Alyona. Andras, I'm not sure. I'd like more information about what the kid is up to first—and whether and how it ties in with his old man's office being bugged. Let's check out that law firm."

Foos worked the Lindley & Hill Web site while I called Elizabeth Rogers. Halfway through the second ring, there was the slightest pause and *click* as the call was transferred from the 212 area code to somewhere else—out of state, probably out of country. Another ring and a female voice answered.

"Lindley & Hill." No discernible accent.

"Elizabeth Rogers, please."

"I'm sorry, she's out of the office. Would you like her voicemail?"

"Do you know when she'll be back?"

"I'm sorry, I don't."

"Does she have an assistant?"

"One moment, please."

The voice came back in ten seconds and announced the assistant was away from her desk. Whoever set this up had covered the bases. I asked for voicemail and listened to another accentless voice announcing herself as Elizabeth Rogers and asking me to leave a message. No point in that. Elizabeth Rogers didn't exist.

Neither did Lindley & Hill. Foos said, "That Web site's no more in New York than I'm in Alaska."

"Can you tell where it is?"

"Locator bug reports Eastern Europe."

"Will they know someone was asking?"

"Did we suddenly enter amateur hour?"

Nosferatu or his boss or someone was going to a lot of trouble. I thought about that and the fact that so far, all the Leitz family had succeeded in doing was heaping their problems on top of my own. I was looking forward to meeting Julia.

The phone rang. Foos answered, listened a moment, rolled his eyes and put the caller on hold.

"You ain't heard nothing yet," he said, handing me the receiver. "Thomas Leitz. If this guy ain't light in his loafers, Pig Pen's a bald eagle."

I released the HOLD button and introduced myself.

"Big Brother Sebastian says I'm supposed to talk to you, and I *always* do what Sebastian says."

Unlike Foos, I try not to jump to stereotypical conclusions, but Thomas Leitz had the same high, tense voice I'd heard on his message machine, with the addition of a pronounced lisp. Foos arched an eyebrow across the desk. I turned away.

"Thank you for returning my call. I'd prefer to talk face to face, if that's all right with you. I can meet at your convenience."

A long pause, as if Thomas Leitz wanted to convey that no meeting would be convenient.

I waited.

Finally, he said, "I teach at P.S. One-forty-six, all the way east on Houston, by the Drive. We're having a conference here tomorrow morning. I'll meet you outside when it's over. Say noon, if you don't mind working Saturday."

He said the last part with a sneer, as if he clearly did mind.

"I'll be there. How will I know you?"

"You can't miss me. I'm the one who looks like a screaming queen."

★ CHAPTER 14 ★

Still plenty of time before I was due in Midtown, so I walked north past City Hall and through Chinatown and Little Italy into eastern SoHo. The overcast sky darkened and a chill wind came up, but it wasn't unpleasant. As I walked, I called a *Wall Street Journal* reporter I know. He and I were both working on an insider trading scam a few years ago, each for his own reasons. We were able to help each other out, so we continue to take each other's calls.

"Julia Leitz," I said, once I'd established he wasn't staring down the barrel of a deadline.

"Jesus. You hiring a PR firm?"

"Just going to talk to her. Family matter. Hers."

"You shouldn't ask a reporter about flacks. We hate 'em. Half the time they're trying to keep us from the story, the other half they're wasting our time with stories that aren't stories. Even when they're helpful, we can't bring ourselves to admit it."

"So you know her?"

"Sure. There're a handful who're pretty damned good at what they do, as much as we hate to say so. She's one. Smart, tough, opinionated. Her approach is all or nothing, takes no prisoners. She works on big corporate deals—mergers, acquisitions, restructurings. Every transaction is either going to remake the entire landscape of corporate America or end capitalism as we know it, depending on which side is paying her. She charges a fortune—six, seven, eight hundred bucks an hour. Like a big-time lawyer. That's another reason we can't stand flacks—jealousy." He laughed.

"Anything I should watch out for?"

"Get ready for a fight if you disagree. And she and truth—I'd say they're more acquaintances than friends."

I was a block from the Bleecker Street subway station when I passed Ballato's, a timeless old-school Italian restaurant. I was still running early, and the smoked salmon sandwich had ceased to satisfy, so I enjoyed a plate of fried calamari and a fortifying vodka before resuming my journey uptown to meet one of capitalism's soldiers of fortune.

Third Avenue was busy at the end of the workday. Traffic crawled between the lights. Lines queued for the commuter buses to the Bronx and Queens. People walked quickly, hurrying home to their families, eager to get out of the cold. I didn't feel part of it. My workday wasn't over and I had no one to go home to. I'd held myself to a single drink at Ballato's. Maybe, if I was lucky, one of Julia Leitz's all-important deals would blow, she'd stand me up, and I could retreat to another saloon.

Something had been tugging at me in the empty restaurant, something I was overlooking, but I couldn't grab hold of it. Perhaps only that a day spent with a crushed Marianna Leitz, a terminally ill Jenny, and a hamstrung Stern left me unsettled. Never mind Andras's and Irina's bank accounts. I was delving into all kinds of problems that weren't mine and couldn't do a damned thing about. Except make them worse if I discovered one of the Leitzes had conspired to undercut their brother. Julia Leitz didn't promise to break the mold.

It had taken a minute to peg the guy following me when I came out of Ballato's. I'd all but forgotten about the gray Camry until I crossed Houston and saw a balding man sitting in the big window of a pool hall on the far side, looking out. He held a folded tan overcoat in his lap. He probably thought the dim light of the billiard parlor provided the perfect cover. He hadn't counted on the streetlight directly above his head. I couldn't be sure he was the same guy who'd been in Bedford, but I wasn't about to bet against it. His face and clothes said he was American. Nothing about him, starting with competence, said he was working for Nosferatu. Still, he had to be working for someone.

I kept walking, down the stairs of the Bleecker Street station. He followed a minute later. When the train came, I got on, and he did as well, the car behind mine. At Fourteenth Street, I waited until the doors started to close and hopped off. He wasn't fast enough. I was tempted to wave as he passed.

I climbed back to the street and caught a cab uptown. I'm not sure why I bothered—except old habits die hard.

Julia Leitz's building was one of dozens of similar Third Avenue structures, mediocre, knockoff international-style skyscrapers, all equally forgettable. I didn't bother to look for Tan Coat. He would know my destination or not. I showed my driver's license to the lobby guard and took the elevator to the sixteenth floor. Maroon letters announced THE LEITZ GROUP in flowing script. The receptionist had gone home, but a harried-looking young man answered when I buzzed and led me through the halls and cubicle clusters to a corner office with two secretaries' desks outside. The place was still busy with the sounds of keyboards, phones, TVs, printers, and voices. The staff was young—twenties and thirties. Unlike her brother's shop, these kids were fully dressed, some even wore skirts and ties. Most had the same harassed look as the man who'd let me in.

I waited at a respectful distance while the kid stuck his head in his boss's door. He recoiled as Julia Leitz's twang blew out. They could have heard her back in Queens.

"SHIT! I DON'T HAVE FUCKING TIME FOR THIS. WE'RE ALREADY GOING ALL FUCKING NIGHT. I TOLD HIM TO CALL. WHY DIDN'T HE FUCKING CALL, GODDAMMIT? WHY DIDN'T HE CALL?"

I stepped around the young man into the office. He shouldn't have to answer for my sins.

"He didn't call because he forgot," I said quietly. "He apologizes. No harm done, at least not to him. If this is not a good time, he can come back later—or perhaps tomorrow. I'll tell your brother you were busy."

Julia Leitz sat behind a table-desk strewn with papers. A flat screen held down one corner, three more behind her head. The furniture, prints, carpeting, and curtains were all decorator neutral, without personality, conveying nothing. The woman behind the desk was plump, but not overly so, and dressed in a white blouse open at the neck. She was neither attractive nor not. Bags under her eyes indicated she lived the lifestyle she espoused. She took a big swallow from a glass next to a Diet Pepsi can. I don't know whether the mention of her brother changed her mood or temperamental outbursts ran in the family, but she seemed to cool as I stood there.

"That's okay," she said, standing. "It's been a long day. Going to be a long night. Sit down. Later won't be any better."

She came around her desk and took an upholstered chair. She wore a black skirt beneath the white blouse and black shoes without heels. I sat in a matching chair across a glass coffee table.

"I won't waste your time," I said. "I'm here on your brother's behalf. I want to know about some people—perhaps a man and woman, stating they were lawyers—who might have come to see you a few weeks ago."

"Who else have you spoken with?" Her tone was aggressive, she was on the attack. For no reason that I could see.

"Your sister and brother-in-law. And Jenny. I'm seeing Thomas tomorrow."

"Don't believe anything they tell you."

One more manifestation of Leitz family closeness. Remembering my reporter-friend's admonition, I passed on the opportunity to disagree. But I did ask, "Why not?"

"Thomas hates me. Hates Sebastian too. He's jealous. Always has been. He doesn't make a dime, and he spends like a drunken sailor. Probably spends on drunken sailors. Anyone who's successful, anyone with a real job, who does something important, we're a target." She leaned back and crossed her arms, resting her case.

I wanted to ask if she believed teaching was unimportant, but I said, "And Marianna?"

She waved a hand dismissively. "You've seen her, you know."

Sympathy, it appeared, was something else Julia Leitz was only distantly acquainted with.

"You did get a visit? A man and a woman? Lawyers?"

"Yes. About a month ago. I've got a card here somewhere." She went to her desk and dove into the papers.

"SHEILA! HERE NOW!"

A thirty-something woman appeared at the door.

Julia said, "Those lawyers that came here last month, right in the middle of the Asco deal, remember? No notice. Not anything we were working on, something about Sebastian . . ."

"I remember."

"They left a card."

"Got it," the woman said.

She disappeared and came back thirty seconds later. She handed a card to Julia who passed it over to me. Same one I'd received from Marianna.

"Need anything else?" Julia said. "I've got calls . . ."

"Yes, I do," I said. "Just a few minutes. Can you describe them?"

"What do you mean?"

"What did they look like? What did they say?"

114

"Oh. Ordinary. Lawyers. They asked questions about Sebastian. Some kind of background check. Related to the network deal. I told them what they wanted to know. I was in a hurry. Asco was a huge transaction, biggest merger ever in the human resources software space. A game-changer, but not a marquee business, hard to get attention. We landed the front page of the *Journal*."

She leaned back once more, basking.

Marianna, drunk, emotionally devastated, tells them nothing. Julia, one could argue the more sophisticated, at least professionally, pays no attention, buys the cover story because they look the part, they're familiar in her world, and spills the beans—to the extent she had beans to spill.

"What was that—what they wanted to know?"

"Is this really important? They were checking him out. He's trying to buy two TV networks. No one's ever done that before. Due diligence is part of the process. Just came at an inconvenient time, like I said."

"What did they want to know?" I pressed, trying to break through her need to bring everything back to herself.

"They asked questions about our family, our parents, where we came from, that kind of thing."

"They ask about the layout of your brother's trading floor?"

"I don't remember. I don't think so. Why?"

"It didn't occur to you, this was all information they could've gotten elsewhere—or why they needed to know?"

"What are you implying?"

"I'm trying to get a fix on these people. I'm not sure they were who they claimed to be."

"WHAT DO YOU MEAN? DO YOU THINK I'M NAÏVE?"

"I'm just asking questions."

"The law firm was legit. I checked the Web site. Called the office."

"Talk to anyone?"

Pause. Realization dawning. "Yes."

"A receptionist and a recording?"

"WHAT THE HELL ARE YOU SUGGESTING?"

"You were conned, I'm afraid."

"BULLSHIT. I checked the Web site. Here." She went to her desk, typed on the keyboard, and swiveled the flat screen toward me. "Look."

"It's a Web site, all right, hosted somewhere in Eastern Europe."

"HOW THE HELL DO YOU KNOW THAT?"

"I get paid to know. You describe your brother's office to them?"

"NO! I told you. Why would I do that?"

"Because they asked."

Her face turned bright red. The decibels jumped. "GET OUT! I'm calling Sebastian right now."

"Call ahead."

I sat still while she played the bluff as long as she could, all the way through ten digits of the phone number, before she replaced the receiver. She moved papers around the desk, struggling to keep her temper under control. I'd stepped over the line, a couple of lines—I probably shouldn't have stopped for the vodka—but I didn't care. Three head cases and a death sentence in one day was too much.

"What do you want?" she said.

"Have you lent your brother Thomas money?"

"What's that have to do with anything?"

"He spends like a drunken sailor. Your words, not mine. Have you lent him any money?"

"No."

"How about your husband? Would he?"

"No, of course not."

"Would you know?"

"YES, GODDAMMIT, OF COURSE I WOULD KNOW. WHY WOULDN'T I KNOW?"

She shoved more papers. She looked at all four flat screens and clicked her computer mouse. "I've got eighty-five new e-mails . . ."

Once again, the subject of Walter Coryell hit a nervous nerve. This time, with his wife. It might have been her confrontational attitude, it might have been because she was married to the guy, but this time I didn't back off.

"Did the people who came to see you talk to your husband?"

She stopped shoving papers and thought for a moment. The first time she'd taken time to think since I arrived. "Walter's very busy. He's got his own company—highly successful. He's out of town right now. He travels a lot on business."

"That doesn't answer my question."

"I don't know. I doubt it."

"But you don't know for sure."

"Is this really important?"

"Why didn't you attend your brother's wedding?"

"What?"

"Why didn't you and your husband attend your brother's wedding?"

"What's that have to do with this?"

"Just a question."

"I have work to do." She grabbed her computer mouse and shoved it across the desk. The phone rang.

"That's your conference call," Sheila said through the door.

Julia Leitz reached for the phone and stopped and looked at me. I waited while it rang.

"I have to take this call."

"Saved by the bell."

"What the hell does that mean? I have to take this call."

I stood. "I'm sure the whole damned deal depends on it."

Third Avenue was quieter now. The cold air felt good. I was annoyed with myself. Julia Leitz got under my skin. The whole family pissed me off. I felt sympathy for Jonathan Stern, not necessarily a sympathetic guy. How did levelheaded, smiling Jenny Leitz put up with this lot? How would she manage when her illness really took hold? I would have locked them all in a single Lubyanka cell and thrown away the key.

I looked around for Tan Coat, but he was nowhere in sight. Maybe he hadn't guessed my destination—or was learning better technique. I flipped a mental coin. Heads—find a quiet tavern. Tails—skip the tavern, go home, eat a Spartan dinner, and go to bed. Plenty to look into in the morning. In my mind's eye, the coin landed on the sidewalk, rolled along a crease in the concrete and disappeared into a sewer drain. On par with the rest of the day.

Bar and dinner could wait. I walked to Grand Central, rode the Lexington Avenue Express between Fourteenth and Fifty-ninth Streets a few times to give Tan Coat a chance to show himself. When he didn't, I switched at Fifty-ninth to the N to Queens. The first stop across the river put me at Queensboro Plaza. I walked a few minutes to the block of Twenty-second Street between Fortieth and Forty-first avenues, the headquarters of YouGo Here.com, Walter Coryell's company.

★ CHAPTER 15 ★

An empty commercial block in an empty commercial neighborhood. Five-story brick and concrete buildings on one side held warehouses, electricians, cabinet makers, a lighting manufacturer, and more than a few empty spaces for rent. The single- and double-height structures opposite were home to an auto repair shop, a refrigeration company, a metal fabricator, and one small apartment conversion, if the satellite TV dishes outside three of six windows were any indication. No delis, restaurants, or bars, unless you counted the "gentlemen's club" near the subway offering the opportunity of meet one of Tiger Woods's mistresses up close and personal. Hardly a service industry neighborhood. Definitely not a successful dot-com neighborhood.

Number 40-28 stood midblock and won the contest for most peeling paint and FOR RENT signs. Roman numerals on the concrete cornice broadcast the date of construction as MDCCCVII—a few years after the classical era. The door was steel with a small, reinforced glass window. Empty tiled vestibule behind. An intercom by the door had a dozen buzzers with yellowed signs. The only one ending in ".com" was YOUGOHERE. I pushed it and got no response. I pushed again with the same result. The elevator at the far end of the vestibule opened, and a middle-aged black guy with a graying mustache pushed open the front door.

"Hey," I said, "I'm looking for the guy at YouGoHere, supposed to meet him at seven thirty." I guessed at the time.

"Good luck to you, man. Ain't never seen that dude. Go on up and take a look, that's what you want."

I thanked him as he walked into the night.

A slow elevator with a worn-out cab deposited me on the third floor at the head of a short cinderblock corridor with four steel doors. Three had signs. None said YouGoHere. The unlabeled door was sandwiched between the elevator and a space labeled GROARK CUSTOM FRAMERS. I knocked. No answer. I tried the other three with the same result. My watch said 7:55. The hell with it.

Back downstairs, I crossed the street to see if there were lights in any of the windows. None. A wasted trip, but hadn't I expected that?

I remembered a first-rate Italian restaurant, another old-style New York institution, a half-dozen blocks away. I'd been taken there a few years before and thought more than once about returning. The tug of a vodka martini and a good Bolognese sauce was setting up another mental coin toss when headlights turned into the block. Instinct pushed me into a dark doorway. The lights swept the parked cars, and motion caught my eye—a head ducking, a moment too late, behind the windshield of a Chevy sedan. Could have been a trick of the lights, but I stepped farther back into the darkness. No way Tan Coat could have followed me here—and certainly not in a car. A black Cadillac Escalade rolled to a stop outside number 12. The driver kept the engine running. Nobody got out. I didn't move.

Five minutes passed. Then another five.

My muscles started to ache mildly, but waiting is an acquired skill, one I'd learned, along with every other Russian, as a kid. No more movement from the car down the block.

A flash of fire in the SUV as the driver struck a match. The flame illuminated a blood-drained face as it lit a cigarette held by misshapen teeth.

The spectral driver drawing on the smoke was Nosferatu.

The music was coming from my apartment. Only two to the floor, one at each end of the hall, the elevator in the middle. My door was ajar. Loretta Lynn, I was pretty sure, backed by steel guitar, bass and drums, floated in my direction. She was singing about being true to her man while he's gone—if he doesn't overdo it. I like Loretta—but I don't own any of her records. No question, though, she was on my stereo. My first thought was that I'd been followed, but Loretta didn't seem Nosferatu's style.

Almost ten o'clock. Nosferatu had smoked his cigarette, then two more. He'd made two calls on his cell phone. I didn't move a muscle the entire time. No one else came down the block, vehicle or pedestrian. The guy in the other car, if there was a guy in the other car, stayed out of sight. After the third smoke, Nosferatu climbed out and went into the building using a key to open the front door. I watched the windows on the third floor. No light came on. Coryell could have drawn curtains or shades. Nosferatu could be doing his work in the dark. He could be visiting someone else altogether. Still no movement at the car down the block. Ever so slowly, I got out my phone and tapped Coryell's number, not sure what I'd say if anyone answered. No one did. After a handful of rings I got a recording.

Nosferatu was inside exactly twenty-four minutes. When he came out, he walked up and down the block, ten yards in each direction. He stopped about five short of the car where I'd seen movement. Once again, I didn't move a millimeter. Neither did the guy in the Chevy. If he saw either of us, there was nowhere to run. After two minutes that stretched through half the night, Nosferatu got back in his SUV. He smoked another cigarette, made another call, started his engine and drove off. I waited another fifteen minutes before I started breathing normally.

I took a chance and walked to the other end of the block before turning left and back to Queensboro Plaza. A calculated gamble—I had little to lose. If there was a guy in the car, he'd already spotted me going in and out of Coryell's building. If he was Nosferatu's man, I wouldn't be walking around. If it was Tan Coat, he already knew what I looked like. Sure enough, a man in a Chevy Malibu tried hard to look invisible as I strolled past. Definitely not Tan Coat—this guy wore a suit and had a full head of hair. Lots of people appeared to be interested in YouGoHere and Walter Coryell. Forty minutes later, as I got off my elevator, I was still thinking about that. But my immediate concern was who was in my apartment. Nosferatu hadn't spotted me, I was almost certain of that. But what was this?

A pause on the CD and a new song started, Loretta singing about a honky-tonk girl crying out her lonely heart. My heart did a back flip and landed in my throat. I got my breathing under control for the second time in an hour, walked down the hall, and pushed open the door.

Victoria sat on my couch, glass in hand, looking drop-dead gorgeous and staring straight at me.

"Goddamned Russians. It's about time you got home. I've been here since seven, and I'm hot and hungry—or I was when I arrived. When the hell are you going to learn to keep some wine in the house?"

★ CHAPTER 16 ★

We didn't get any dinner. Not much sleep either. But when I awoke at my usual 6:00 A.M., her head on my chest, my arm around her shoulders, her leg across mine, all was right with the world.

I had a thousand questions, of course. She hadn't let me ask one. We went straight to bed and rediscovered each other slowly until heat and passion took over, and we thrashed across the sheets like two teenagers who have just figured it all out. When we came up for air, she still wouldn't let me say a word. The second time was slow, contained passion until the very end, when we both exploded and collapsed in a single mass of sweat and flesh. Just like the first time—even better. Before I fell asleep I told myself this time I'd resort to padlocks and handcuffs before I let her leave again.

She seemed to read my mind.

"Don't worry. I'm not making the same mistake twice," were her only other words that night.

I believed her, but I also thought it would be just my Russian luck to go for my morning run and come back to an empty apartment. I couldn't move without waking her, which I didn't want to do—truth be told, I didn't want to move at all—so I lay there, dozing, thinking about what had brought her back and trying not to let the ghostly image of Nosferatu, smoking his cigarettes, intrude on an otherwise perfect morning.

"Don't you go running or jumping or pumping at an ungodly hour of the morning?" she said, smiling at me, her eyes as big and green and deep as the Nile.

"Pumping perhaps. And I'm not leaving," I said.

"Jesus. I'd almost forgotten the humor. You don't need to worry. I told you that last night."

"You are a woman of your word."

"What's that supposed to mean?"

"Just what it says. You told me you'd leave before, without so much as a kiss good-bye, and that's exactly what you did. I'm staying put."

She laughed. "You're right. I did. But not this time."

"What changed?"

"Not you, I'm willing to bet."

"Guilty. But I can try."

"Uh-huh. We both know how good you are at that. We can discuss it. We can discuss lots of things, which I'm looking forward to, but first, I'm ravenous. I never did get dinner. I couldn't find anything worth eating in your fridge last night, and believe me, I looked. Get out there and hunt or forage or whatever men do, besides pump. I want a real breakfast. Bacon, eggs with Tabasco, remember? Move it!"

She rolled out of my grasp with a playful slap and skipped to the bathroom. She flicked her beautiful behind for my benefit before she closed the door.

I lay there another minute holding on to the image of a present-day Aphrodite frolicking across my bedroom. Victoria de Millenuits, Victoria of a Thousand Nights, was ten years younger and two inches shorter than I am. She had a figure that would make Sophia Loren take a second look and turn green when she did. Long, thick black hair, those Nile-deep green eyes, a big laugh, and a Bardot pout when she was unhappy. She had brains to match her looks and a temper that trumped both. She also had that highly successful legal career, most recently occupying perhaps the top prosecutorial position in the entire country. And a firearm permit. The first time I met her she threatened to have me deported.

What she hadn't had was luck with men, a run I perpetuated when I came close to breaking her heart—after promising twice that I wouldn't put myself, or her, in that position. Compounding matters, I couldn't even provide a good explanation of what had happened without putting Aleksei's life at risk, and I couldn't explain that either. That's when she left.

Something had brought her back, she'd tell me the story in her own time, but it sure looked like love. I was going to keep my promise this time, I told myself again, knowing as I did so, I was being untrue to her and to me. Fate has a way of letting you know when you're making commitments you can't keep.

The hell with fate. Love was stronger than that. I'd fucked up once. I wasn't going to do it again.

She'd just come out of the shower—Aphrodite, like Sophia, would have been green too—when I joined her in the bathroom.

"Yikes," she said when she saw my bruises. "I didn't notice those last night. You look worse than last summer. What happened this time?"

"Someone wanted to send a message, and he selected me as the messenger. They look worse than they feel—now."

"You go looking for trouble or does it just find you?"

"I wasn't looking to get beat up."

"But I'll bet you did something that attracted the beater's attention."

"Indirectly."

"See what I mean? What was it this time?"

"It's Foos's fault. He asked me to help out a friend." I reached for her towel, but she slapped away my hand.

"And the friend beat you up?"

"Nosferatu beat me up. He's a six-foot-seven Belarusian with buckteeth, named after a German vampire. The friend tried to crush my legs under his granite conference table."

"You're teasing me, and you'd better stop." Her temper was still in place—the Bayou twang, I'd learned, was its early warning system. I held up my hands, palms facing her.

"All true. I swear."

"Christ. You need someone to take care of you."

"I'm taking applications." I made another try for the towel. She slapped me away, with a smile.

"Breakfast, remember?"

"There are all kinds of hunger."

I pulled at the towel once more. This time she let it fall away as she came into my arms. She was damp and warm all over and hot and wet where it counted. She gave a little cry and sank teeth into my shoulder as I lifted her behind and planted her against the wall to find my way inside. The cry melted to moan.

"Make me one promise," she said.

Uh-oh. "I won't lie to you again," I said.

"You don't have to lie. Just tell me you won't let me leave, like you did last time."

I laughed and said, "That's the easiest promise I can make."

"You've got me right where you want me—in every possible way. Take me like you mean it."

We ate a long, large, leisurely meal, desire sated for the moment, each of us unsure how to start the conversation we both wanted to have. The departure—breakup—six months before had been abrupt. She'd walked out of my apartment, willing me to do something, anything to try to stop her—and I hadn't moved a muscle. I'd wanted to, I'd been desperate, every part of my body was trying. I do learn from my mistakes. Some wise person once said you get to make three or four big decisions in life—try to get more than half of them right. I'd fucked up my first couple, paid the price for decades, and was still digging myself out of that hole with Aleksei. So as much as I'd wanted to stop her, I'd let her walk. To do otherwise was to send my son to his execution.

Now we were back at the very same kitchen counter, each of us wanting to explain our actions, tell the other how we felt, why we did what we did. We both knew there was no question of incrimination—bygones were already bygones. Forgiveness, to the extent any was necessary, had been granted in an instant last night. The need to explain is one of the most basic human desires. We all want to be loved—we also need to be understood. So the question at the moment, as we chewed bacon, scrambled eggs (with Tabasco), and English muffins, was how to get started.

I said, "Where did you go?"

"Several places. Home to Louisiana. Not much left there for me now, since my mom died. Then my sister in Miami. She's got breast cancer. Double mastectomy. That'll give you some perspective."

"How is she?"

"They think they got it all. She's doing okay, except her husband, who's some kind of oceanic consultant, ran off with a hot Cuban babe from his firm. Apparently she's something in a wet suit. Seems he's been banging her for the last year, including the whole time my sister's been sick. Men can be real bastards."

I didn't disagree. There was no point. Besides, she was right.

"Once Louisa went back to work, I went out to West Texas. Town called Marathon. Spent the last month there, thinking things over. I wanted solitude, and it's pretty damned lonely."

"Beautiful, though," I said. "Gage Hotel?"

"Goddammit! How in the hell do you know everything I do? He told you, didn't he? He and that computer serpent-thing . . ."

"Nobody told me anything. The Gage is the only hotel in Marathon. About the only thing in Marathon, period. You can cut the atmosphere with a knife. Great restaurant."

"*You've been there?*"

"Uh-huh."

"Shit. Momma taught me lots of things. But she never said, 'Don't date a spy.'"

I told her the story of trying to outrun the Basilisk. I'd spent a week at the Gage, where they put a package of earplugs by your bed, as if they're going to be any help against the mile-long freight trains that rumble through town at 3:00 A.M.—fifty yards from your room.

We traded notes about West Texas. Solitude and loneliness don't begin to describe it. Neither do awe-inspiring or beauty. Her favorite spot was the McDonald Observatory outside Fort Davis, where from an altitude of almost seven thousand feet, you can see the stars and planets through high-powered telescopes with virtually no interference from ambient light on the ground. Mine is Donald Judd's Mecca of minimalist art in Marfa, which he built on an old army base he'd bought from the government—where he'd been stationed as a teenager. Not unlike Muhammad's epicenter, visiting requires a pilgrimage—the closest airport is El Paso, three and a half hours away. In a way I think Judd understood, it makes getting there half the fun.

Victoria had visited *Chinati,* as Judd called his desert creation, and not to my surprise, didn't think much of it. "Art my ass. Concrete rectangles. Steel boxes. Neon lights. That's not art."

Minimalism is like my shaved head, people like it or they don't. Victoria was forcefully in the latter camp on the art question. There'd be time enough to argue that later.

"I listened to a lot of Tom Russell while I was out there."

"*Now* you're talking. Bet he doesn't have any more use for those antelope shacks than I do."

Antelope shacks are what the locals, most of whom agree with Victoria, call the concrete structures Judd placed in a field alongside Route 67.

"What did you do, while I was away?" she said.

"Nothing much. Series of one-night stands."

"What?! You son of a . . . !"

The right hand came flying across the counter. I resolved to take my punishment like a man and waited for the sting of the slap. She stopped before she got there.

"You really are a bastard."

127

"Sorry. Couldn't resist. Hard for a virile Russian male in the prime of virile Russian maleness to admit he's been rendered feeble and helpless by a capitalist vixen."

"Spare the socialist horseshit. Did you miss me?"

"I spent most of the time moping, you want to know the truth. Didn't do much of anything. Foos can confirm that. He wouldn't let me use the Basilisk to find you, which made it worse because I knew how easy it would be. I drank too much. That just made me think more about you. Tried to break out of it by going to Moscow. Saw Aleksei. First time I've spent with him since he was a baby."

"How'd that go?"

"Not great, about as well as can be expected, I suppose. Not easy, starting again after almost thirty years. Worse than starting from scratch, really, because there's the baggage. Why'd I leave? Why didn't I let him know where I was? Why did I lie to his mother? Underlying all those questions, of course, is the unspoken premise—why were you only thinking of yourself? And why should I believe you're any different now? Then there's my career with the Cheka, not to mention the family connections, which are a huge issue for him. He's borderline irrational on the subject, not that I blame him. Hard to get past how much damage we did—and the number of people we did it to. Also hard to explain when it all happened in another time, another place, another world really."

"Even harder when you're too scared to tell him the truth, right?"

I looked across, stunned. How the hell could she know about Beria?

"Hey, what's wrong? What did I say?"

I could hear Lavrenty Pavlovich chuckling in the background. I waited for him to appear, but he stayed away. Then I realized she was talking about the story I'd told her of my upbringing—my birthplace, my mother's death, the orphanage, being sent back to the Gulag. She was the first person I'd ever told—she had no reason to judge and condemn a *zek,* she barely knew what one was. She was assuming I'd be scared to tell Aleksei, terrified of what his reaction would be, as indeed I had been. Before a bigger terror reared his head. Beria chuckled again.

"Nothing's wrong, I'm fine, but who's the real bastard now?" I said.

"Hey! I didn't mean it that way. I meant to say, I understand."

"I know that," I said gently. "Truth hurts, as someone once pointed out."

It hurt even more if it involved Lavrenty Pavlovich Beria. I wasn't ready to tell Victoria—or anyone—about that.

"Does he blame you—for his mother?"

"He says he doesn't and I believe him. But he needs time to process everything that happened. I'm glad I went but it was probably too soon to start rebuilding."

"You going back?"

"Maybe in a month or two." Or sooner, if I could figure a way to reestablish Sasha's access to the Cheka archives.

The green eyes stared straight at me. Almost anyone would have asked again what happened that night at JFK. Aleksei had saved my life, but in the process, he'd dispatched Iakov Barsukov and his murdering henchman to reunite with Lenin, Stalin, and, certainly, Beria, south of the last terrestrial border. Since Iakov was second only to Putin in assuring the Cheka's continuing ascension in post-Soviet Russia, Aleksei's life expectancy would be measured in minutes the day the organization found out he was anywhere near the airport that night. I will never breathe a word, not even to her. She recognized that, and the fact that she didn't ask made me think we really did have a chance.

She said, "Did you really spend all that time moping? Over me?"

"Like I said, ask Foos. He got me the job I'm working on because he was tired of my hanging around bothering him."

"I believe you. Mostly, I believed you last night and in the bathroom this morning. But don't think I won't ask. Just to be sure."

"Good to be trusted. They teach you this in law school?"

"I learned trust in reform school, remember?"

I did. She'd done time in a juvenile detention center as a teenager when she stole her stepfather's car—her escape after he tried to rape her.

"Speaking of law school, you going back to work?"

"Never fully left. Telecommuted part time."

"How'd you explain so much time away?" It can't have been that simple telecommuting to a U.S. attorney position.

"Told them I had some female medical issues to deal with. You work mainly with men, nobody wants to ask too many questions. Then my sister had them for real, so I was covered. I'm looking forward to the office. We've got a big case building, that's the other reason I'm back."

"Not just me?"

"Sorry, shug. I love you, I think, and I love my job. Don't ask the order."

I was willing to accept whatever order she stated. We held hands across the counter.

She said, "Do you know why I left?"

"You said you would. You gave me fair warning. That's one reason I didn't try to stop you."

"I wouldn't bring that up—not a point in your favor."

Honesty's not always the best policy, I guess. "You told me if I fooled around with the law, you'd stop fooling around with me—or words to that effect. Your job and career were too important, and I had to respect that. I heard you loud and clear. It's just . . . Fate is hard to explain."

"Don't give me that fate bs. You're pigheaded and there's an adage about old pigs and new tricks. But that's not the reason—or the whole reason."

She was watching me, waiting for the answer she seemed certain I knew. Except I didn't. I'd taken her threat—or promise—at face value. When she followed through I blamed only myself—and fate.

She watched and waited another few moments before she shook her head. "Men are just too obtuse for words. I was scared to death you were going to get hurt—or worse. I still am. That kind of fear was new to me. I couldn't live with it. So I ran away. There—I've said it."

I wasn't sure how to respond. I stroked the back of her fingers.

"What changed?"

"I spent most of the last month thinking. Every day, by the pool at the Gage Hotel. I'd go out there to read, swim, sleep, but mostly I just thought things over. I figured out two things. I love my job and I love you, like I said. I couldn't telecommute forever, so, if I stayed away, I'd be unemployed, lonely, and still in love. That prospect didn't have a lot to recommend it. If I came back, I could get back to the office, see you, and work on trying to overcome the fear. I was hoping against hope that maybe you'd help. Then I saw your recent set of bruises. So much for that idea."

"I told you, I didn't go looking for them."

"But they found you. They're always going to find you. I'm still not a hundred percent sure I can deal with that, but I'm going to give it my best try."

"I couldn't be happier. I mean that. I'll try too. But . . ."

"But what?"

"I've still got to finish this job Foos got me into. And the guy who gave me the bruises is still out there. I saw him last night, in Queens, just before I came home. He's circling around the Leitz family—that's Foos's friend."

"And you can't leave it alone, of course."

"I told Leitz I'd help. He's got more problems than maybe he knows. I'd be leaving him hanging. Foos too. And there's the not insubstantial matter of my fee."

"I told you before, only two things men care about—sex and money. How much fee?"

"Million dollars."

I thought I could surprise her, and I did. "A million dollars?! You're kidding, right?"

"No joke. Plus use of a painting, four months a year. A Malevich."

"Who's Malevich?"

"You're not going to like him. Russian. The guy who got those Marfa steel boxes and neon lights rolling—fifty years earlier."

"You're right about not liking him."

"The painting in question cost Leitz eighty million."

"This guy owns a painting worth eighty million dollars?"

"One of many."

"Jesus. Who is he?"

"Financial rocket scientist. Hedge fund manager."

"And why is he willing to pay you a million dollars?"

"To find the guys who are trying to derail a big deal he's put together, or that's what he thinks. It's worth sixty or seventy billion. My fee gets lost in the rounding."

"Sixty or seventy billion?! Wait a minute—is that the TV deal? It's been all over the papers."

"That's right.

"Well dammit, shug, what are we doing sitting here? Let's get working."

"I thought sex and money only got men's attention."

"Us country girls have a deep-rooted respect for cash."

"What about the trouble? Nosferatu might be downstairs now, for all I know."

"The guy who beat you up?"

I nodded.

"For a million bucks, I'll take the chance. But . . ."

"Having second thoughts?"

"Not on your life. Just you go down first."

★ CHAPTER 17 ★

Nosferatu was nowhere to be seen, and we walked to the office hand in hand. A clear, cold day, with a whipping wind. Halfway there, Victoria shivered and I put my arm around her. She burrowed in close and stayed there until we reached the lobby.

Upstairs, the expanse of the Basilisk engendered a small intake of breath.

"Jesus. Is that all computers?"

"Yep. Servers."

"How many are there?"

"Never counted. Twelve rows, maybe twenty-five racks to a row, ten servers to a rack. That's . . ."

"Is this the Big Dick thing your partner in crime boasts about?"

"A small piece of it. Probably the only noninvasive piece out there."

"It invaded me as I remember."

"Sometimes the end justifies the means."

"That's a matter of opinion. So you really could've found me, if you'd tried."

"In less time than it takes to fly to El Paso."

"Shit. And it's legal?"

"Uh-huh."

"Don't think I'm not going to look into that."

We emerged from the server farm. Pig Pen heard us coming. He looked Victoria up and down, as he does with all newcomers. I was afraid he was going to whistle, a trick his boss taught him, but instead he announced, "Bohemia Bombshell!"

"What did he say?" Victoria said, turning.

"Sounded like 'Bohemia Bombshell.' It's a compliment, I think."

Pig Pen used to greet female visitors, almost always Foos's Eastern European models, with "Cutie! Hot Number!" Apparently he'd been expanding his vocabulary.

"He's a parrot. What's he know about Bohemia? Or bombshells?"

"African gray, to be precise. Don't sell him short. He gets his vocabulary from his boss, the radio, and his own bird brain, in that order. I'm responsible for foreign languages. *C'est vrai,* Pig Pen?"

"Russky."

"See what I mean?"

"Wait a minute! He can . . . converse?"

"Sure. Why not? He's smart, and he thinks he's human. Visitors always pique his curiosity."

"I don't believe this."

Pig Pen was clutching the mesh in his office door. Victoria walked slowly in his direction.

"Bohemia Bombshell," Pig Pen said.

"I'm from the Bayou, parrot. Can you say, 'Bayou Bombshell'?"

He looked her up and down again. 1010 WINS played in the background.

"Guess you're right about bird brain," she said.

"He'll figure it out if he wants to," I said. "Foos says he's up to almost three hundred words. He can provide a complete report on the morning traffic interspersed with commercial appeals for food. How're the bridges and tunnels, Pig Pen?"

"Twenty minutes, Holland. Ten, Lincoln."

"GWB?"

"Ten, upper. Five, lower."

"See what I mean? East River crossings?"

"Usual backups." He fixed on Victoria. "Tiramisu?"

"Tiramisu?"

"His latest infatuation. Used to be pizza. Victoria is an aficionado of Italian food, Pig Pen. I'd keep at it, if I were you. You might get lucky."

He climbed up the mesh to eye level and stared straight at her. "Bayou Babe. Tiramisu?"

"*Now* you're talking," she laughed.

"Bayou Babe."

"Where'd he get his name? Wait a minute. Let me guess." She sniffed the stale marijuana smoke in the air. "Late drummer for the Grateful Dead?"

Foos's boom box rumbled across the space. "Give the lady a cigar."

"Bayou Babe. Cigar," Pig Pen said.

"It's rare that I'm happy to see a member of the prosecutorial profession return to the fray, but in your case, I make an exception," Foos said.

"Owing, I believe, to our mutual friend here," Victoria responded, "who I understand has been somewhat out of sorts."

"Total flow-breaker. I kept telling him not to worry, but . . ." He shrugged.

"I also gather you and your cyber-serpent declined assistance."

"As I told him, only a complete fool would take sides."

"You got that much right." She nodded at the server canyons. "He says that thing's legal, but he's a socialist. You're probably a socialist too, but at least you're an American. How about it?"

"It's entirely legal, and that, Ms. Bayou Babe, is the whole problem, in a nutshell."

He turned and retreated to his office. Victoria looked at me. "Is it me, or is he like this with everyone?"

"Pretty much everyone. He's fanatical on the subject of privacy. You—or more accurately your employer, the U.S. government—is Public Enemy Number One, in his view."

"I know. That foundation of his . . ."

"I'm on the board, remember? So's Pig Pen."

"Christ. Why am I not surprised?"

"The problem, Foos will be quick to tell you, is not the Basilisk. It can retrieve, sort, analyze, and match data faster and more efficiently than anything else, but it can only do that because the data got saved to be searched and analyzed in the first place. The real problem is the Big Dick—and all the information it collects and keeps on you and me and everyone else—all in the name of marketing, public safety, antiterrorism or whatever other excuse the Dickers come up with."

"Now wait just a minute. Who are you to talk? You used to do much worse. Your government spied on everybody."

"True enough. My bosses would have killed for this kind of capability. That's why I'm on STOP's board—I've been where this leads."

"But you have no problem using it for your own ends?"

"Like the man said, it's legal. Why shouldn't I?"

"I can't win."

"Play your cards right and maybe you'll get a demonstration of the beast at work."

135

We went to Foos's door. He was packing his messenger bag.

"Happy now?" he asked.

"Pure state of bliss, no thanks to you. I saw Nosferatu last night, outside Leitz's brother-in-law's building in Queens. The brother-in-law wasn't there. Nosferatu had a key."

He straightened, thinking for a moment. "That can't be good."

"Nope. But there's that issue of perspective."

"Always. Let me know if you need anything. Got a meeting."

"What are you two talking about?" Victoria said.

"He'll explain, I'm late," Foos said and grinned at Victoria. "Going over to the ACLU. We're looking at ways to collaborate."

"Okay if I give her a little demonstration of the beast at work?"

"She's a Fed, Turbo. Strictly limited access."

He lumbered out the door.

"I'm beginning to understand one thing," she said, "why you two get along."

"How's that?"

"You *are* both socialists. Neanderthal socialists."

"Sharing had to start somewhere. C'mon, demo time."

"Cuckoo time, you ask me," she said, but she followed me to my office. Pig Pen took a shot as we crossed the open space.

"Bayou Babe! Tiramisu?"

"It's still breakfast time, parrot. Nobody eats tiramisu for breakfast."

That stumped him, but I guessed not for long.

Victoria took the chair I placed beside mine, and I opened my laptop and worked the keyboard. The Basilisk hissed. It took Walter Coryell's name in its jaws and retreated into the darkness of its cave. A few minutes later it reemerged to spit out its findings.

The Leitzes all had their problems. Marianna and her husband. Julia and her obsession over her work. Thomas and his financial irresponsibility. Coryell was different. Maybe because he was only an in-law. Coryell was a fraud.

He and Julia maintained a joint checking account. She deposited $12,000 every month, he deposited $4,000. No small amount, certainly, but it suggested he was making around $100K annually. Julia said he was very successful. I couldn't find anything that looked like a year-end bonus or dividend payment from his company. She, on the other hand, was bringing home a salary of $300,000 and banked a year-end bonus/profit share of $2.5 mil. Those all-consuming deals paid off—at least financially.

More to the point, Coryell didn't leave any spending trail. I'd partly guessed the Internet entrepreneur story was bull. Now I was looking at the credit card records of a man who supposedly traveled frequently on business—who hadn't paid for a plane ticket, hotel room or rental car in years. Nor were there any lunches, dinners, Broadway shows, operas, baseball or basketball games—none of the things you'd expect a successful businessman to be spending his, or his company's, money on. He had his own car—a two-year-old leased Volvo—garaged near the family's apartment. Gas purchases indicated he didn't drive a lot, other than back and forth to their house in Ancramdale in Columbia County—and he didn't go there much either.

"That's it?" Victoria said.

"All there is," I agreed.

"This thing's a bust."

"You weren't listening. The Basilisk isn't the threat. The Big Dick, the databases—they're what's evil. And the fact that the Dick has so little information on our man Coryell tells us something, quite a lot, actually."

"Like what?"

"Like maybe he isn't who he's supposed to be. Like maybe the existence of another credit card in another name hooked up to another Social Security number, out of reach of preying eyes like mine."

"You mean, Jekyll and Hyde?"

"Jekyll and Hyde with plastic."

"Shit." She got up and walked around the office. "We never thought of that. Why are you interested in this guy?"

"Client's brother-in-law."

"And if he leads a double life . . . ?"

"Somebody bugged Leitz's computers, maybe connected with the TV deal, I don't know. But whoever did it knew the layout. Coryell's the one member of the family I can't get a fix on. It's like he's part of it, but not. Never around, didn't go to Leitz's wedding. No one in the family wants to talk about him. I bring him up, they change the subject. Even his wife."

"That doesn't mean anything necessarily . . ."

"True enough, but I saw the guy who beat me up outside Coryell's office last night. He's almost certainly involved in the bugging, and he had a key to the building."

"But Coryell wasn't there."

"Right."

"Still circumstantial."

"The only reasonable doubt I have to satisfy is my own. And maybe Leitz's."

"You have motive?"

"Still working on that."

"Show me what else this Big Dick can do. Christ, listen to me, I'm talking like you two."

"You heard Foos. Strictly limited access for Feds."

"I'm just kibitzing. Come on."

She smiled, and my heart backflipped again, just as it had last night. I would have looked up anything or anyone she wanted.

"Let's check something."

I went back to work on the keyboard. In less than a minute I had the vehicle identification number for Coryell's Volvo. A few minutes after that, the service records from the Manhattan dealership, appeared on the screen.

"What are we looking for?" Victoria asked.

"Mileage. The Volvo's two years old. Say it gets twenty miles a gallon, average. Coryell's gas purchases total eight hundred gallons, if we figure three bucks each. The car should have sixteen thousand miles on the clock. Service records say thirty-one thousand two-fifty at the last appointment, a month ago. Who's buying fifteen-thousand-miles worth of gas? And who's driving the car?"

"Wife?"

I told the Basilisk to rifle through Julia Leitz's purchases and extract the gas charges. They totaled $1,172—maybe twenty-five tankfuls, one every other month.

"Add eight thousand miles for her, which is generous, and we've still got seven thousand miles, give or take, unaccounted for."

"Someone used cash."

"Maybe. Pattern suggests credit, but I can get the Basilisk to match that up with their ATM withdrawals if you want."

"You can do that?"

"Take a few minutes."

"Jesus, that thing's pure poison."

"Where do you think it got its name?"

"Okay, seven thousand miles. Still not all that much."

"Twenty-two percent of the total on the car."

"Then tell me this, smart guy: Why doesn't his wife notice?"

"She's not paying attention."

"Oh come on! That's just male . . ."

"Uh-uh. She's smart. Tough too. But she's totally focused on her work, family's an afterthought. Her siblings told me that and I've met her. It rings true."

"She got kids?"

"Two."

"What kind of woman—"

"Spy school lesson—value judgments only get in the way."

"You suggesting I butt out?"

"Not at all," I said quickly. "Let's look at phone calls."

I worked the keyboard, and the Basilisk went back to its cave. It returned almost immediately with two lists of numbers—those Coryell called and those calling Coryell. They had one thing in common—they were short.

"Once again, not what you'd expect from a supposedly successful businessman," I said.

"I'll say. Can you tell . . . ?"

"Patience."

I sent the beast in search of the names the numbers belonged to. That took a few minutes longer. While we waited, I put my hand on Victoria's knee and started up her thigh. She knocked it away.

"Stick to business," she said with a smile. "You've got me curious now."

"Curiosity wasn't my goal." I returned the hand to the knee. She let it stay there.

The calls came back up, with names this time, sorted by date, as the numbers had been, the most recent listed first. Most of the recipients of Coryell's outgoing calls didn't mean much to me. Incoming calls were another matter.

Victoria said, "Hey, that's you!"

I was at the top of the list—my call from outside his office last night. Below it was an unlisted, disposable cell phone—Nosferatu's, I was almost sure. I made a note of the number for future reference and told the Basilisk to group the calls by name. Thomas Leitz jumped off the screen. Eight calls over the last few years. I had a hunch about the timing. The Basilisk hissed—you know it, run with it. I went back to the keyboard.

"What are you doing?" Victoria asked.

"Maybe earning that million dollars."

The detail on Thomas Leitz's calls to his brother-in-law appeared. Sure enough, each call over the last four years coincided with the pay down a few days later of his credit card debt. The Basilisk had answered one question— where Thomas was getting the money—but it raised several others. Where was Coryell getting it? And why was he giving it to Thomas? And how much of this did Sebastian Leitz know?

Victoria said, "I'm still here, remember? What'd you find out?"

I told her.

"What is it with this family?" Victoria said.

"They've got more money than most. But once you start to dig into any family, you shouldn't be too surprised by what you find. As I remember, your old man had you arrested for stealing his car. How normal is that?"

"My stepfather. And he was pissed that I wouldn't put out."

"See what I mean?"

She removed my hand, stood and walked around the office again.

"What are the chances," she said from the window, "if I asked nicely and it was really important—stopping some truly evil bastards—your partner in crime would let me do a little research for a case I'm working on, with appropriate supervision, of course."

"He'd rather swallow Pig Pen."

"Yeah, I thought you'd say that."

"You've got the entire United States Department of Justice at your disposal."

"The goddamned Department of Justice is coming up short, if you want to know the truth. Your pal and that serpent of his produce more than a legion of FBI."

"He's aware of that. Hence limited access for Feds."

"You *are* both socialists."

"Guilty, but I can only speak for myself. What's the case?"

She shook her head. "I've got institutional constraints, which is too bad, not least because I think you could offer some insight into the guys we're going after."

"Is that a compliment?"

"I meant it that way. But we might as well face it. We both have misspent youths. And you . . ."

"Haven't rehabilitated myself?"

"You're the one who said it."

"If you're afraid of wolves . . ."

"Don't go into the forest. You told me that once before. One of your proverbs."

She sat on my lap facing me, legs straddling mine, her face a few inches away. "I have to tell you, shug, I'm here in the middle of the forest and I'm happy about it—over the moon, to be honest—although the why of it is still a total mystery."

" 'Love's like the measles. The older you get it, the worse the attack.' "

"Another proverb?"

"Bohemian poet, early twentieth century. Rilke was his name."

"His humor is on a par with yours."

"Don't be too quick to judge. He also said that for one person to love another is the most difficult task there is, the one for which all others are just preparation—or words to that effect."

That got a thoughtful look from the green eyes. "According to Kris Kristofferson, love's the easiest thing there is, if you pick the right woman—or man."

"Dueling poets. Their job is helping us see ourselves. Doesn't mean they always agree."

"Tell me this, you and your Bohemian know-it-all—why is it the things I love about you are the same things that scare me to death?"

"Rilke knew all about that. He said, 'Our fears are like dragons guarding our deepest treasures.'"

"You making this up?"

"Uh-uh. Think about it. You said this morning that you're scared to death something will happen to me. I'm frightened that I won't be able to fix things with Aleksei, and I'm terrified I'll do something to drive you away again. Sound like dragons and treasures to me."

She put her hands around the back of my head and kissed my lips. "I think I like that, but I need to think more about it. Since you just upgraded yourself to treasure, though, you can buy me lunch."

"I'd love to, but I have to meet a screaming queen on Houston Street at noon."

"Excuse me?"

"Leitz's brother. His description, not mine. How about we reconvene at a place I know in Chinatown at two. Best dim sum in New York."

"All right, but what am I supposed to do with my dragons between now and then?"

★ CHAPTER 18 ★

Thomas Leitz didn't exaggerate.

A scattered assortment of people mingled outside P.S. 146. One man stood out. He would have stood out in a circus. About five-ten with a platinum Mohawk that added three inches at its peak. Blue and white silk pants that hugged his skinny frame from hips to ankles. Purple leather ankle-high boots with pointed toes. A bright purple collar flopped over an equally bright orange cashmere sweater. He hadn't bought any of it on a teacher's salary. His face was pointed and could have been okay looking if God hadn't forgotten his chin. His Adam's apple bobbed below his lower lip. Even in New York City, I would have bet the dacha on his having tenure.

I'd left Victoria with a hug and a kiss outside my office building and walked north, mildly annoyed at Leitz and his family for intruding on our reunion. No getting around the fact, though, that Thomas Leitz had something on his brother-in-law and needed interrogating on that and other subjects. I walked at a leisurely pace, thinking about Victoria and dragons and treasures—and attraction. Beauty is only skin deep, or so they say. I'm not so sure, but I'll cede the point. While there was no question her looks worked a kind of black magic on me, it was unlikely that my shaved head and stocky physique had the same enchanting effect on her. We did have several things in common. She was tough and strong minded, with every reason to be so. I can be tough minded too. She was self-made in every respect, as I was. Neither of us had a family life to speak of. We were in the same line of work (sort of, and sometimes on opposite sides), lived alone and didn't mind it, until recently. We were both loners, without intending to be so.

Her childhood, like mine, taught self-reliance at an early age. Her father took off when she was a kid, and her stepfather almost killed her mother in

143

a drunk-driving accident. Mom got hooked on painkillers. Stepdad chased Victoria with lecherous intent whenever he wasn't too drunk. He caught her one night, but she laid him out cold with a cast-iron frying pan and took off, stealing his car to make her getaway, which is what landed her in the juvenile detention center. She was smart enough to realize where her life was headed if she didn't take a different path. Reaching that kind of turning point, and recognizing where you are when you get there, was something else we shared.

She enrolled in junior college, then the University of Miami on ROTC and spent four years in the Air Force. She went to law school at Miami too, on Uncle Sam. She got a job at a Miami firm and thought she was on her way professionally until she found that every man she met, including bosses and clients, were more or less like her stepfather—only interested in one thing.

She got fired for refusing to put out, as she put it, got even, one more thing I admired, and got a new job with the Miami DA. They left her alone, and she built an impressive record jailing the same kind of SOBs who'd made her life miserable. Their lowlife intentions weren't limited to trying to get laid—fraud, embezzlement, perjury, and theft were as common in the business world as the underworld. She wanted to make some money so she moved into private practice with an Atlanta firm, keeping the same scumbags she'd been prosecuting out of jail. She didn't like it, but that didn't cause her to be any less effective. The Atlanta firm got acquired by Hayes & Franklin, a big Wall Street legal outfit, and she put in to move to New York. Wasn't long before she was a partner and running the combined firm's white-collar crime practice—an $80 million business. The first time I asked one of her law partners about her, he called her a piranha. Of course, she'd moved on to the U.S. attorney's office by then and just jailed his biggest client.

Success can be sexy, I suppose, but skin deep too. More often than not, the insecurities that lie beneath the urge to succeed form the foundation of character. I preyed on insecurities in the spy business, they're what makes people tick. (Had I known that in my twenties, I probably would have passed on proposing to Polina and saved us both a world of heartache.)

One dragon guarding the attraction Victoria and I felt for each other was the fear of doing something to screw it up and drive the other away, as I'd told her. I was afraid I'd make another mistake, as I had with Polina and Aleksei—and with her almost six months before. It didn't have to be my fault. Fate could—and probably would, since I was Russian—intervene. I just had to screw up one more time, and I knew how easy that was to do.

Her dragon took a different form. We'd traded life stories the first time we had dinner. Somewhere in the recounting, I recognized beneath the tough-gal veneer a brittleness as fine as my own. Takes one to know one, perhaps. She did her best to cover it, but self-doubt was part of her makeup—doubt about her judgment, doubt about her own attractiveness, doubt about whether she could make something like this work. And fear about how she would feel if she failed. I hadn't had the chance to ask too much during our first round of romance, but I was pretty sure her stepfather and his successors had taken their toll. Despite her looks, smarts, and success, she doubted what she brought to the table of a relationship. As a result, I was willing to wager, she hadn't had many that were serious. Faced with the prospect of one now, she was scared of fucking it up, just like I was. The reasons were different, but that made the fear no less real. And when I went off on my own, or declined to talk about what I was working on, as I had about Aleksei, I put those insecure dragons on high alert.

Rilke nailed fear. I'd have to look into what he had to say about doubt. Beria fell into step.

Excellent, Electrifikady Turbanevich. You've assessed the situation with astute Cheka prescience. And, as usual, totally sidestepped the question of whether you're ready to do anything about it.

I was about to defend myself when my ruminations were stopped in their tracks, as was I, by the improbable sight of a large statue of Vladimir Ilyich Lenin in full stride, arm raised to show the way, atop a Houston Street apartment building. I'd heard about this, but never seen it. The brainchild of the developer who'd put up the otherwise mundane brick complex, which he, of course, named Red Square. The statue, a large clock with misplaced numbers around its face and the clever name were supposed to give the building some Lower East Side hipster chic. No doubt Lenin changed the world. Few would argue for the better, and even they would have a hard time applying concepts like hip or cool to the first Soviet dictator. I wondered idly whether the developer had considered what his neighbors a few blocks to the north—the heart of Ukrainian New York—thought of his vision.

Thomas Leitz saw me and peeled off a small group as I approached.

"Mr. Leitz? I'm Turbo."

I held out a hand, which he ignored while looking me up and down.

"Tough guy. Boyfriend beat you up?"

One more interrogatory chore. The Leitz siblings were consistent in their absence of eagerness to help their big brother.

"He did land a few blows," I said, leaving his question, if there was one, unanswered. "Can I buy you a cup of coffee?"

"We don't have that much to talk about. I don't know anything about my big brother's business and what I do know I'm not sharing. Any more questions?"

Coercion worked with Jonathan Stern. Thomas Leitz looked an easier push-over. "About thirty-five thousand."

A frown on the chinless face. "What's *that* supposed to mean?"

"Four credit cards. Thirty-five thousand dollars. You could be wearing some of it right now. Carried for months, paid off in November. You're already another eight grand in the hole. Where's the money come from?"

"Who are you?"

"A well-informed guy. I know a lot more. Question is, what am I going to do with it?"

"I don't have to talk to you. I don't care what Sebastian says."

"Eight grand says you do. You going back to the same sugar daddy to take care of that? What's he going to want this time?"

"WHAT ARE YOU TALKING ABOUT?"

"Tall guy with buckteeth and bad skin. Know him?"

"NO!"

"I don't believe you. But I'll tell your brother what you said."

I didn't think Thomas Leitz had ever met Nosferatu, but I needed to be sure, before we got on to other matters. I'd taken a step and a half west along Houston Street when he cried, "Wait!"

I took another couple of steps for emphasis before turning back. I don't think he was shaking, but he could have been.

"Let's go somewhere we can talk," I said.

He nodded once and I followed him to a footbridge over the FDR Drive and into a park scattered with baseball fields between the roadway and the river. I've run through it on many mornings. He found a bench and sat at one end, head in hand, elbows on knees, eyes straight ahead, not looking at me. I sat at the other.

"Where'd you get the money?" I said.

He shook his head. "Not from anyone you know."

"The tall guy?"

Another shake. "I don't know any tall guy."

"Some people came to see you. Tell me about them."

He nodded, twice. "A man and a woman. Lawyers, they said."

"Names?"

"Don't remember. I told them I had nothing to say. We didn't talk long."

"What did they want?"

146

"Questions about Sebastian, his business, his family. Some kind of background check, they claimed."

"Describe them."

He was no more revealing than Marianna or Julia, but they had to be the same two people.

As he talked, a lone man crossed the footbridge and turned north away from where we sat. He was of medium height and build and wore a tan overcoat and a flat cap. He followed a path until he was fifty yards away and leaned on the railing, looking out over the river.

"They ask about anything else?" I asked Thomas.

"I don't remember. The rest of the family, I guess. Marianna and her husband. Julia and Walter. I didn't tell them anything, if that's what you want to know."

"They ask about your debts?"

"NO! I told you . . ."

"So where did you get the money?"

"STOP IT!"

"I'm not a nice guy, Thomas, and I need information. Where did you get the money?"

"I . . . I got a loan."

"Who from?"

"I don't have to tell you that."

"Family?"

He nodded slowly.

"Who?"

"I have . . . friends."

Lying, like waiting, is an acquired skill. It takes practice. Thomas Leitz wasn't good at it. The Cheka's approach to interrogation was to use the first lie like a club and beat the subject up and down until he offered up all the other mistruths, half-truths and made-up truths he was harboring. That would've been easy with Thomas—he handed me the club at the first opportunity, and I already knew the answer anyway. The Cheka, however, was always after a confession first, truth was rarely an objective. I was looking for honest answers—and help. Thomas Leitz could supply either or both, though not if I turned myself into a complete enemy. I changed the subject.

"I spent the morning with Marianna. She's in pretty bad shape."

"Her husband's an asshole."

"Maybe. I think she needs help. She's hitting the bottle hard."

"Why are you telling me?"

"You're her brother."

He shook his Mohawk and looked at the ground. "Poor Marianna. I do feel sorry for her. But she shouldn't have married him if she didn't love him."

"That's what happened?"

"What do you think, smart guy?"

He was stepping around something there.

"She told me she lent you money once. Fifteen grand. You hit her again for twenty-five and she turned you down. She said you weren't very nice about it."

He raised his head and laughed out loud—braying long and high. Tan Coat turned to check us out.

"HAH! That's rich. Did she tell you she was smashed, so blitzed that she practically knocked over a waiter with a tray of food? Three brandies while we were there. While *I* was there, who knows what she drank after I left. She was still mixing them with ginger ale then. Ugh."

He looked around in a conspiratorial fashion and lowered his voice. "Did she tell you what she called me? This was before we even talked about money. When she ordered the second drink, I suggested maybe coffee would be good. She told me to mind my own fucking business. Her words, not mine. Then, when I said maybe she should think about help, she said, 'At least I'm not queer.' "

He leaned back and raised his palms upward, as if to ask, *What am I supposed to do?* I now had two sides of another story. I didn't care much where the truth lay this time, but the evidence of Marianna's troubles—and her ability to pretend they didn't exist—was mounting.

"When was the last time you saw her?"

"Christmas. Family rat-fuck. At Sebastian's, of course. I try to avoid them as a rule, but holidays . . ." He shrugged. His voice had taken on a bitter edge.

"The whole family there?"

"Uh-huh, Sebastian, Jenny, the kids. Marianna and her children. Not Stern. Even Julia put in an appearance, mainly so she could tell everyone about all the oh-so-important bullshit she's working on. And Walter was there. Hapless Walter. That's Julia's husband. First time we'd seen him in years. Sebastian sets great store by family acting like family, and Sebastian gets what he wants. Always has. You're so smart, you've figured that out already."

Something there, besides the outsized chip balanced on Thomas Leitz's orange-clad shoulder, was interesting.

"Hapless Walter. Why do you say that?"

"Because he is. You meet him, you'll see."

"He doesn't usually attend family functions?"

Thomas grinned, just a little. "So, something you don't know."

"Tell me about him."

The grin went away. "Nothing to tell," he said quickly. "Poor guy's got loser written all over him—and he has to put up with her. We all dig our own graves."

Maybe spending the holidays alone wasn't so bad after all.

"Why doesn't he attend family functions?" I pressed.

"He just doesn't!" He looked around the playground, eyes sweeping past Tan Coat without comment. "I don't have all day. You were asking about the lawyers."

I let him change the subject, for the moment. "Did they ask you anything about your brother's office? Location, layout, computers, stuff like that?"

He shook his head. "No. Wouldn't have mattered if they had."

"Why's that?"

"I've never been there. No reason to go."

He was telling the truth now, I was all but certain. "So they didn't ask you to do anything?"

"No."

"And they didn't offer you money?"

"NO! I already told you, I have *friends*! This conversation is over. I don't care what you say. Stay away from me. Stay away!" He jumped up from the bench.

"Not so fast, Thomas. We're not finished. I've got more questions about Walter."

He tried to look resolute, but it came across as petulant. "Why should I tell you anything about him—or anyone else?"

"So I don't tell anyone about Walter and you."

A long silence—before he sat back down. "I don't know what you're talking about."

"Sure you do. Walter's the one who's been paying your bills—for years. Every time you borrow too much, max out those credit cards, you call him, he comes through. What've you got on him? None of my business, I'm just curious. Must be pretty good, I figure he's shelled out two hundred grand so far."

"I DON'T HAVE TO TALK TO YOU!"

"Yes, you do, Thomas." I put a hard edge on my voice. "This is called the squeeze. Get used to it. You have to talk any time I ask. What do you have on Walter?"

He sniffled—cold or tears, I couldn't tell which. When he spoke, he was barely audible. "Nothing."

"I don't believe you."

He looked away and looked back. His voice seemed to find some strength. "I don't care what you believe. It's true."

It wasn't true. I was certain of that. But as Victoria had pointed out, my evidence was circumstantial, based on timing. I couldn't trace the cash from Coryell to Thomas. I couldn't even connect Coryell to the cash. I backed off again, a little.

"Why doesn't anyone want to talk about him? Not Marianna, not Julia, not you."

"There's nothing to talk about. Walter's a nonentity. No personality. Nothing for anyone to have a relationship with—that's the best way to put it. He's never around, and when he is, he's just there, but he isn't. Like his body's just a shell. I don't know why Julia married him, except maybe opposites attract. Or he was the only one she could find who'd put up with her bullshit. Point is, you could ask anyone about Walter and you'd get the same answer."

I wanted to ask again, if Walter was such a nonevent, what could Thomas have to blackmail him with.

"What about his business?"

"Julia says he's a big-shot Internet entrepreneur. I wouldn't know."

"You wouldn't? He's getting the money somewhere?"

He turned away and crossed his arms.

"He didn't go to Sebastian's wedding. Why not?"

"You'll have to ask him. Another rat-fuck."

This was getting nowhere. I shifted gears again.

"What's Andras like?"

It took a couple of beats for him to catch up. "Normal, I guess. Average rich kid. No need or want denied. Quieter than most. More . . . introverted."

"That due to the death of his sister?"

"How . . . ?! Oh never mind." Another long pause. "I don't know. He was always on the quiet side. More so after, maybe, I'm not sure."

"He see the body?"

"Everyone saw the body. We were all there. Christmas. We all heard the shot."

"But you got there first."

"What's that have to do with anything?" An edginess in his voice.

"That's what I'm asking you."

"I'm not going to talk about that, I don't care what you do," he said trying again to sound firm. "It's . . . too horrible."

"Okay. What about interests? Andras's, I mean."

"Oh, how about that? Finally something you don't know." He paused again, perhaps relishing the moment. "Computers."

"What about them?"

"He's nuts about them. Number-one thing. Spends all his time online. He's got more gear than I have outfits."

"What about Irina?"

"Who's Irina?"

"Friend? Girlfriend?"

"Don't know her. Sorry."

He didn't sound sorry.

"When was the last time you saw Andras?"

"Christmas, like I said."

"Andras was there?"

"Of course. I told you—we all were." Shrillness on the rise. "Very important to be present and have a good time."

"How did he seem, Andras?"

"About the same as always. I didn't pay much attention." Another silence. "Wait! I do remember one thing."

"Go ahead."

His voice took on the conspiratorial tone. "Christmas lunch. There were some fireworks this year. Andras and Sebastian. I remember thinking, What set that off? Halfway through lunch, Julia got a call and announced she had to leave. Some big fucking deal, of course. She just took off, as she does. A few minutes later, Andras said something to Sebastian. I was at the other end of the table, I couldn't hear what. Sebastian told him to forget it. Andras said no way. Sebastian started to lose his temper. You've seen that display, I'm sure. Andras wasn't having any. He shouted something like, 'I am not staying here with him,' and left. That was it."

"Who was he referring to?"

"Walter, of course."

"Why of course?"

"No other candidates that I know of."

"Why would he say that?"

Smug replaced shrill. "No idea."

"Okay," I said. "What happened then?"

"We went back to lunch, pretended nothing happened."

151

"That normal?"

"For us, it is."

"And Andras didn't come back?"

"Nope."

"And Walter didn't say anything?"

"Walter never says anything. Julia does the talking for both of them."

"Anybody else? Say anything?"

"As you may have found, since you're so fucking smart, we Leitzes are very good at ignoring things, sweeping problems under the rug, where they can fester out of sight, out of mind, where no one has to acknowledge them."

His assessment was colored, as everyone's is, by his own resentments. That didn't mean it was inaccurate.

"One more question."

"Good."

"Since you're all so good at sweeping things under the rug, what have you got on Walter?"

He shook his head once, stood, and started off without looking back.

"THOMAS!"

He stopped about six feet away. He didn't turn back.

I said, "Tell me this much—whatever it is, the tall man I mentioned, could he or anyone else be pulling the same levers?"

He didn't hesitate. Another single shake of the head and he almost ran to the footbridge over the Drive.

I waited on the bench until the last speck of orange disappeared on the other side. The man in the tan overcoat didn't budge. Two things were clear about Thomas. He had something—maybe several somethings—to hide, but whatever it was almost certainly had nothing to do with his brother's computers.

★ CHAPTER 19 ★

I took the rest of the afternoon off.

The dim sum place was a hit. We followed lunch with a movie in the Village, a romantic comedy Victoria chose. I didn't find it particularly romantic or comedic, but my sense of humor is usually out of step with Hollywood's these days. My mind was also on the Leitzes, who were providing a better story, although not much about them was romantic or comedic either.

The wind had died down, and we walked home, stopping at an old-school Village butcher for a couple of veal chops, which I ordered cut thick, and a liquor store for some red wine. The chops, stuffed with prosciutto and mozzarella and sautéed with a sage brown sauce, were as delicious as was the wine, a Pinot Noir from Oregon. Bud Powell played bop piano on the stereo, causing Victoria to wrinkle her too small nose in mock distaste whenever he launched into one of his more angular solos. I think it was mock, she didn't complain out loud. The last of the wine led to holding hands on the sofa and that led to holding everything else in bed. I fell asleep thinking she'd been back a bare twenty-four hours and we were already settling into a routine that was fast becoming one more thing to hold on to.

I left her sleeping at 6:00 A.M., took my usual run through a cold, dark southern Manhattan and stopped at the office on the way back. At 6:55 on Sunday, the space was tomblike. Pig Pen was still asleep—contributing markedly to the silence.

I fired up the Basilisk and fed in Andras Leitz and Walter Coryell. The beast went to its cave.

Andras had called his uncle last night—three times. Uncle Walter hadn't answered.

I sent the Basilisk back for the location of Andras's cell phone.

Newburgh.

Okay, I asked, what's the kid been up to?

It bucked and hissed. *Let me tell you.*

Andras had hopped the 4:30 Delta shuttle to New York yesterday afternoon, while Victoria and I were in the movie house, taken a cab from La-Guardia to the Harlem–125th Street train station, paid with AmEx, where he'd purchased a roundtrip ticket to Beacon, across the Hudson from Newburgh, also with AmEx. The exact location of his calls to his uncle was vague, somewhere south of town. *Not my fault,* the beast said, *cell phone location can be spotty, depending on the service provider. Do your own legwork.*

Nothing else new on Walter Coryell in the vast reaches of the Big Dick, which further supported the supposition of another identity.

I went back to the spending records of Andras and Irina. They were both regular patrons of Crestview Pizza and Mike's Grocery, both on Main Street in Crestview, Massachusetts. Their purchases took place on nights and weekends. Irina bought her gas at Crestview Citgo, filling up every couple of weeks, at night. Except last night. She'd bought almost eleven gallons at 12:24 A.M. at service station on the Massachusetts Turnpike, a mile from the intersection with I-84. Right on the most direct route from Newburgh to Gibbet.

I checked Facebook, looking for a picture of Andras. To my surprise, he didn't have a page. Neither did Irina. Andras supposedly spent all his time online. One more thing that didn't add up.

I walked the two blocks home, stopping for breakfast makings. Victoria was just stirring.

"Where've you been?"

"Run. Research. Breakfast in twenty minutes."

She emerged as I finished frying sausage and whipped the eggs for an omelet. No sleep in her eyes.

"What kind of research, shug?"

"Whereabouts and whatabouts of certain Leitzes."

"You couldn't have done this yesterday?"

"Staying current." But her point had a point.

"Bull. You didn't want prying eyes."

"We each have our own cases."

"That just means you're not sharing. How about some Tabasco in the omelet?"

I did as she asked, and we ate in partly contested, mostly contented, silence, especially when I relented and told her what I'd found and that I had no idea what it meant.

She acknowledged the gesture silently with a nod and a smile.

I said, "Why are you so interested in the Leitz case?"

"Because it's yours. When I was sitting by the pool at the Gage Hotel, one thing I figured out for certain is, we're in this together. If you're absorbed in something that's likely to lead to trouble, then I'm worried. If I'm on the outside trying to peek in at what you're doing, like last time, we aren't going very far. I can't live that way, and I don't think you want to either."

I took her hand and looked into her eyes. "You're right, of course. Want to talk about what you're working on?"

Green flash. "You're a bastard."

"Just making a point. In the spirit of togetherness, however, I'm happy to discuss my case. Want to hear it?"

"Why do I have the feeling I'm being set up?"

"No setup. I've got two teenaged kids, each with eleven mil in the bank. They may be mixed up with an organized crime outfit called the Baltic Enterprise Commission. I know the girl is. Her father, her uncle, and her stepfather are all partners. The Leitz kid's up to something with his uncle, the uncle's being blackmailed by his brother-in-law. The client's sister is a lush who won't give her husband a divorce even though he's sweet-talking any broad he can find into the sack. The client may or may not be carrying on an affair with the ex-wife of one BEC mobster, now married to another. He, by the way, tells me, everything's fine. Welcome in."

At some point during my summary, she'd removed her hand from mine, and now she was winding up to knock me silly. Then she smiled.

"You know, you make it goddamned difficult for a girl to do the right thing. This a national character trait, or did you learn to be a pain in the ass all by yourself?"

"Probably some of both. You read Tolstoy? Dostoevsky? No simple plots."

"Try Faulkner, shug. Or Flannery O'Connor. No normal characters. You'd fit right in. Tell me one thing—would you know any of this without the Basilisk?"

"The problem isn't phones, computers, credit cards, and bank accounts. It's what people do with them."

I almost could hear the Basilisk chuckling two blocks away, if roosterheaded, hawk-bodied serpents can chuckle.

"Including kids?"

"It's all in the Big Dick. Age isn't a factor."

"That ain't right," Victoria said.

"It's your country. Can you keep quiet for moment? I have to call Leitz and he's going to want to lecture me on proper client relations."

"I could give him a pointer or two, but I'll do the dishes instead."

I dialed Leitz's number.

He came on right away.

"You finally surface," he said.

"I've been busy—on your nickel."

"I'm used to having my calls returned."

"Apparatchiks at Lubyanka and Yasenevo used to tell me the same thing. One advantage of working in the field."

Victoria raised an eyebrow as she picked up the plates.

"Lubyanka apparatchiks weren't paying you," Leitz said.

"Neither are you—yet. I need a photograph of your son."

"Andras? Why?"

"The people who bugged your computers have touched every member of your family. I think he's next."

"WHAT?! What the hell do you mean?"

"Just what I said. They've visited your brother and sisters, but you know that by now."

Pause. "He's at school."

"Gibbet School, Gibbet, Massachusetts."

"HOW THE HELL DO YOU KNOW THAT?"

The voice was loud enough that even Victoria heard it. Her eyebrow went up again.

"Big Dick. Point is, if I know, they know."

"You're not saying . . . This has nothing to do with him."

"Tell that to Nosferatu."

"You haven't told me what this is all about."

"Only because I don't know yet. But I do know—from personal experience—these people don't hesitate to use violence. The photo?"

"Jesus. All right. But I don't understand."

"You're up against some bad people. I'm doing the best I can to make sure they don't hurt anyone any more than they already have. E-mail the picture. Soon as you can."

"Tell me this. No business deal is worth my family. Should I back out of the bid?"

"Can't answer that. Like I said, I still don't know what this is all about."

I broke the connection.

Victoria said, "You're a bastard."

"I'm on his side."

"You used fear to get what you want. You have no reason to believe this boy . . ."

"It's for his own good."

"You're still a bastard."

"I've been called worse."

I dialed another number.

Gina answered on the first ring. "Turbo! It's been months. I've been worried. How are you?"

"You mean you were worried about your source of business drying up."

"You can be a real bastard, you know that?"

"A growing consensus around that point of view. You want work?"

"Sure."

I asked how soon she could get up to Beacon.

"It's my last semester, Turbo. I'm on cruise control, just waiting to hear from law schools. And I can use the money."

"I'll send you a picture of a kid. His name is Andras Leitz. He took a train there last night, then went across the river to Newburgh. Probably arrived around nine. Work the cabs at the station, see if you can find one that took him."

"Got it."

"If anyone or anything feels remotely weird, catch the next train out of town."

"You're the boss."

I doubted Nosferatu was in Newburgh, but I wasn't taking any chances. I put down the phone.

"I thought you worked alone," Victoria said.

"I use college students sometimes for jobs like this. Used to use actors, but they're not always reliable. Gina's a senior at NYU, applying to law schools. I'm hoping she gets into one here. She's the best."

"Do I infer correctly that she called you a bastard?"

"Not the first time."

"I think I'd like to meet her."

★ CHAPTER 20 ★

Gina called late that night.

Victoria and I had spent the day on neutral ground—the Museum of Modern Art. We agreed to disagree on the relative merits of Impressionism versus Expressionism. I dragged her in front of Otto Dix, George Grosz, and Max Beckmann, she retreated to Monet and Renoir. We found some common ground in Picasso and Hopper, but lost it again when we got to Kelly and Diebenkorn.

It didn't matter, we held hands and were happy in each other's company. I cooked a chicken in a pot full of garlic for dinner, and she bought another good bottle of wine, a Hermitage from France's Rhône Valley. She said tonight was her turn on the stereo, so we were listening to a medley of Tammy Wynette and George Jones. I was trying to convince her that the fact that Charlie Parker liked country music was a good reason to listen to Charlie Parker—a losing argument, even I realized that going in—when the phone rang.

Gina's voice was full of accusation.

"Turbo, you ever been to Newburgh?"

"Once, I think."

"Then you know what a shit hole it is."

She's never reticent about expressing her opinions.

"You called to give me your impressions?"

"Just noting there oughta be a premium for a burg like this, especially on weekends."

"You said you wanted work."

"What the hell are you listening to? Have you gone redneck?"

"George Jones. I'm told he's more American than John Wayne."

"Whatever. It took the whole day, but I found the cabdriver, and I found the motel where he took the kid. He remembered him because the motel is a total sleaze joint, and he didn't think it was a place a kid like that would go. But now I've missed the last train and I'm stuck in this urban landfill overnight."

"I thought it was a shit hole."

"Don't be a smart-ass."

"Where are you now?"

"Outside the motel—Black Horse Motor Inn. I tried to talk to the manager. He said he hadn't seen the kid. Then he said if he had seen the kid—and he wasn't saying that he had—the kid was long gone. Then he told me to get lost."

"You try money?"

"Turbo, do you hire me because I'm a moron? I offered him a hundred bucks and tried to flirt with him, but I got bubkes. In fact, he kinda threatened me."

Gina has plenty of attributes. She's smart, pretty, engaging—and can flirt with the best of them. If all that, plus a C-note, got her thrown out, then the Black Horse had something to hide. Another kind of approach was in order.

"Get out of there. Find a decent hotel, I'm buying."

"Good luck in this dump."

She told me how to locate the Black Horse, and I assured her the check was in the mail. She muttered something about combat pay and hung up. Of the half-dozen kids who work for me, Gina really is the best. But you do have to listen to a lot of blowback.

The next morning at 7:05, I was doing sixty up the FDR in the Potemkin—alone. I wasn't happy about it—neither was Victoria—but since I didn't know what I'd encounter at the Black Horse, I told her I was better off traveling solo. She said that meant I was looking for trouble. Another argument I wasn't going to win.

The Black Horse was just as Gina billed—a seedy two stories tucked into a row of low-rent strip malls and fast-food joints on the edge of town. Newburgh's had a tough time in recent years, tough enough that a few years ago the mayor offered to host a high-profile terror trial because he thought it might be good for business. Ten cars were parked in front of the Black Horse's two dozen units. Just eight thirty, I sat in the lot, at the far end from the office, and watched. A door to one room opened and a red-faced man looked out, then left and right, before a heavy-set woman walked quickly to her car, head down, and drove off. That scene was repeated a few minutes later, a few doors down, except this time, a fifty-ish man in a suit with no tie held the door for a twenty-ish man in jeans, who made an equally speedy exit. The woman who left the third room, without bothering to check who might be watching, wore a short skirt and sheer blouse beneath her open coat. She looked ten years older than she probably was and had all but certainly spent the previous night working.

Victoria introduced me to a Louisiana songwriter, Mary Gauthier, who has a song about the Camelot Motel and the grace-fallen people who stay there. I had the feeling I was parked in front of the inspiration.

I got out of the car and shivered in the wind. Dust and trash flew around the parking lot, more potholes than pavement. I started toward the office, but something on the ground caught my eye. I knelt for a closer look. A used syringe, its plastic chamber ground into the asphalt, the needle still intact. I strolled the lot and found six more, by which time I was cold and went back to the car. Detroit gets justifiably criticized for its automobiles, but I've never heard a bad word against its heaters. I warmed up while I thought about what I'd found.

The door to the end room on the ground floor opened, directly across from where I sat, and a thin man in his twenties came out, wearing only a flannel shirt and dirty jeans. The cold didn't seem to affect him. He walked toward the fast-food place next door, his right hand scratching his left arm, before he disappeared among the dumpsters that demarcated the two properties. I got out and followed.

The burger joint was doing a good breakfast business and smelled of grease. The average weight of the customers, somewhere north of two-forty, regardless of height or gender, indicated a cause-and-effect relationship at work. The thin man had to wait. He fidgeted and scratched. A sharp face, goatee, long hair tied in a grimy ponytail. I stood in the next line, two back. When his turn came, he ordered egg biscuits with gravy and two coffees light with extra sugar. The guy behind the counter slipped a foil packet into the bag and palmed a fifty in return. Breakfast of champions.

I followed Skinny back to the motel, closing the gap as we approached his room. He took the foil packet from the bag and put it in his pocket. He was still twitchy and didn't notice me until I grabbed his arm as he unlocked the door.

"What the fuck?!"

"Inside."

I shoved him in and closed the door. A woman about his age, also thin, sat on the bed, naked, except for the sheet around her waist. She had gray-blue skin, sunken eyes, fallen breasts, and a needle track running up her left arm. She made no attempt to cover herself. Crumpled foil, a spoon, hose, and syringe on the bedside table.

"Who the fuck are you?" the thin man said.

"Doesn't matter. I'm not here for you. What's your name?"

"None of your fuckin' business."

I took a twenty from my pocket. "Play your cards right, you could earn a couple bucks this morning. Or I can make a shitload of trouble. You choose."

"You wanna fuck Cindy, it's gonna cost ya more than twenty," the man said, leering. I was tempted to hit him, but that wouldn't help things.

"I asked you a question. What's your name?"

"You a cop, mister?" Cindy spoke for the first time, her voice just above a whisper.

I shook my head.

"Talk to the man, Les, we can use the bread."

Les started to tell her to shut up, then thought better of it. I picked up the tinfoil.

"Little short this morning?"

"None of your fucking business."

"True. But maybe I can help you out." I held out two twenties this time.

"Listen to the man, Les," Cindy said.

"Your girlfriend's giving you good advice."

"She ain't my girlfriend. She's my wife."

I was tempted to tell him if she was my wife, I'd wrap her in something for warmth if not decency, but that was none of my fucking business either. I showed them the photograph of Andras.

"I'm looking for this kid. He was here Saturday night. You see him?"

I thought recognition flickered through his eyes, but he shook his head. Cindy raised herself on her knees and looked over his shoulder.

"I remember him. I . . ."

"Shut up, stupid cunt!"

Les spun and slapped her. She fell backward across the bed. Enough for me. I took him by the belt with one hand, the back of the shirt with the other, and ran the skinny body across the room into the wall, headfirst. I dragged him into the bathroom, grabbed the foil packet from his pocket, and dropped him in the tub. He looked up with half-conscious eyes.

I held up the smack. "You make a single sound before I'm through here, this goes down the drain. You hit Cindy again, I will find you, wherever you are, just like I found you today, and pound you until there is nothing left to pound. You understand?"

He didn't move. I stomped on his ankle. He yelped in pain.

"Do you understand?"

"Y . . . yes."

"Don't come out of here until I'm finished."

My threats were meaningless, except to flush his heroin, which he'd realize as soon as I left, but they made me feel like at least I tried. I returned to Cindy, wide-eyed on the bed, still naked. I found some jeans and a shirt on the floor, which I handed over.

"Put these on."

I turned my back, ever gallant Galahad, while she dressed.

"Okay." She was sitting on the edge of the bed.

"If I gave you enough money for a bus or a train, is there somewhere you could go, get yourself cleaned up, start over?"

"You mean . . . leave Les?"

I nodded.

She thought about it but not long enough. She shook her head. "He's all I have."

"He's scum, Cindy. Look at this dump. Is this what you want? He get you hooked?"

"He . . . He's all I have." She started to cry.

I'd tried. Breaking her away from Les would take more than one attempt by one leather-coated Galahad on a cold January morning.

"Tell me about the boy."

She looked away.

I held out the foil packet, making the shift from chivalry to shit. "Tell me about the boy, or I'll throw this into the wind."

"No! Please . . ."

"You saw him. When? Saturday?"

"Yes. I think so."

"What time?"

"I don't know. About nine, I guess. Maybe later. We were going out, get something to eat. He and a girl were a couple doors down. They were yelling, that's how come I noticed."

"A girl?"

"That's right."

"What did they say?"

"I don't know. I don't remember."

"Angry yelling?"

"I think so."

"Angry about what? Please try to remember."

She closed her eyes and scrunched up the hollow face. She was trying or putting on a good act. I waited.

"I know! I remember!" Her eyes popped open, and she smiled, pleased with her accomplishment.

"That's great," I said, clapping my hands in encouragement, feeling like a fool.

"He kept shouting, 'Where is he? Where the fuck is he?' She kept saying, 'How should I know? This was your stupid plan, remember?' "

She looked doubtful for a moment, then her face brightened again.

"At least I think that's how it went. Yes, that's it. I remember the part about 'stupid plan' because she was really angry about that, like he'd done something without telling her, and she was pissed, just like I would have been."

I wondered how often Les left her out of the plan. That was probably unfair, if only because Les didn't seem the type ever to have a plan—beyond securing the next fix.

"Did they say anything else? Anything about this guy they were expecting?"

"No. You don't have it right. *They* weren't expecting anybody, only *him,* he was. And she was pissed because he hadn't told her."

"That's right. I'm sorry." Having remembered her story, she was sticking to it. "What did the girl look like?"

"Tall, blond hair, I think. I didn't get a really good look at her. She was wearing, like, a ski parka. And a wool hat pulled down over her head."

"How old?"

"Same age. As the boy, I mean. Young, twenty, maybe less. I don't know."

"So what happened?"

"Nothing. I mean, they shouted back and forth three or four times, I think. The same thing about where is he, how should I know, then they went inside. We left."

"And when you came back?"

"Didn't see them again."

"Were they still here, you think?"

She shrugged.

"What time did you come back?"

"I don't know. Ten thirty, eleven, maybe."

"And you're sure you didn't see them again?"

"No."

She looked up at me with her sunken eyes. "Can I have my fix now, please. I need it."

I looked over at the bathroom door and made one more stab.

"You sure you don't want to get out of here? I'll take you. You just tell me where."

Her eyes followed mine, stopped on the bathroom door for not long enough, then swung back to me.

"I need it. Please."

★ CHAPTER 21 ★

The motel manager didn't add much to Cindy's story. He didn't want to add anything until I placed a used syringe on the counter and told him my next stop was the Newburgh police if he didn't rearrange his attitude.

A man had rented the room by phone, one night, under the name Brian Murphy, from New York City. The kid had collected the key and paid the bill in cash. The manager didn't see the girl, or if he did, he wasn't saying.

"We get a lot of folks through here, bud. None of them want to be remembered. We do 'em that favor."

If it wasn't the truth, it was a damned good lie.

I returned to the Potemkin's heater and thought about how far I wanted to take this. I'd been hired for one job, and I had the answer to that—at least the pieces. Nosferatu had placed the bug. Coryell was his agent. No doubt in my mind he was the man the cleaners had described. Nosferatu worked for Konychev. Konychev knew Leitz. Leitz wanted a name. That was enough to secure my fee and the Malevich. But I didn't have the connections. What was Nosferatu after? What did he have on Coryell? Why had Coryell sold out his brother-in-law? What did Thomas have on Coryell? And what was Leitz's multimillionaire son up to? The last question was none of my affair, but I've always found it hard to walk away from anomalies like that.

What the hell? Nothing to lose, except maybe my client, and I was all but done with him anyway. I dialed the number of Andras Leitz's cell phone.

"This is Andras." A pleasant-sounding voice, slightly high in pitch, counterbalanced by low volume.

"My name's Turbo. I work with Foos. I'm doing a job for your dad and I have a question for you."

I waited while he processed that. "Dad didn't say anything about you calling."

"I didn't tell him I planned to."

I waited some more.

"What's the name of Foos's parakeet?" he asked.

"Always good to be sure," I said. "It's a parrot, as you know. Pig Pen. He calls me Russky. He flunked charm school, which you also know if you've met him."

He laughed, relaxed. "That's for sure. He calls me Whiz Kid."

"At least that's complimentary."

"It's embarrassing. Especially around Foos. You said you have a question. Sorry to rush. I've got class in a few minutes."

"I'll be quick. The job I'm working on has to do with your dad's office security. I don't know that much about computers, your father's in meetings all day, and Foos isn't around, or I'd ask him. Is your home networked through the Leitz Ahead system?"

"That's right."

"So if someone's online at your house, they're inside the network, inside the firewall."

"Sure. Why?"

"Foos thought he spotted traces of unusual activity. I was trying to think about where it could have originated."

I expected a few moments of silence then a feeble lie. That's what I got.

"I do all my work here at Gibbet, on the school's network."

"Sure." Except during vacations and breaks. I was willing to bet he got straight As in math.

"Tell me one more thing, and I'll let you go." I think I heard him sigh with relief. "When was the last time you talked to your uncle Walter?"

Relief morphed to apprehension, maybe fear. "Why?"

"Nobody's heard from him. You've been trying to reach him."

"How do you know that?" Definitely fear now.

I kept my voice pleasantly conversational and nonthreatening. "I know a lot of things, more than I want to, actually. You were at the Black Horse Motor Inn in Newburgh Saturday night. You tried calling your uncle three times. Was he supposed to meet you there?"

He took a long time before he said, "I don't know what you're talking about. My class . . ." He tried to keep his voice calm and level, but I could feel the stress through the atmosphere.

"Uncle Thomas says you're all good at sweeping stuff under the rug, and

I think each of you has stuff you don't want anyone else to know about. You seem to."

Another silence. I let him simmer.

"If you don't want to talk about it, maybe Irina does. She was there too, right, at the Black Horse?"

When the odds are four to one in your favor, it's no surprise that you win the bet.

"NO!"

"Hey, don't get excited. I was just going to give her a call. She could've heard from your uncle."

"STAY AWAY FROM HER! YOU HEAR ME? STAY AWAY! THIS CONVERSATION IS OVER."

He broke the connection.

I dialed Irina's cell phone. He got there first, or she just didn't answer. I was sent to voicemail. I didn't bother with a message. She'd see I called, discuss it with him (or maybe not), and decide whether to answer when I called again.

The heater blew warm air, too warm. I got out and walked around the windy parking lot. I'd accomplished what I knew I would. Drawing myself in deeper. But I was no closer to the link I was looking for—Andras-Irina-Coryell to Nosferatu. I got back in the Potemkin and pointed the bow south toward the city.

I tried Irina from the Bronx and was mildly surprised when she answered.

"Andras tell you about me?" I asked without introduction.

"You're Russian."

She'd done some homework, quickly. "That's right."

"Where?"

"Moscow mainly, but I've lived all over. New York now."

"Cheka?"

Definitely doing some checking. She had the means and connections.

"That's right, First Chief Directorate, if you're interested."

"Chekists are pigs."

"That what you tell your stepfather?"

She didn't pause—or bite. "I only wanted to hear your voice, so I can avoid it if I hear it again. I have nothing to say."

She had plenty of presence for her age, no question about that, even over the phone.

"Hold on. I don't want anything to do with you or Andras. Your bank accounts are your business."

I meant to freeze her and I did. I could hear soft breathing, the breaths were shorter than a minute ago.

"I only want to know about Andras's uncle Walter. What happened at the Black Horse?"

"What do you know about that?"

The question came fast, accusation wrapped in nerves. I'd pricked the tough-girl veneer. But only slightly, she asked *what* not *how*?

Maintain the ascendancy. They teach you that in Cheka Interrogation 101. They didn't train you specifically to interrogate seventeen-year-olds, but anyone, of any age, could be in the chair. My mother found that out. What had she been asked? What had she answered? Beria chuckled in the background.

"You and Andras were supposed to meet Uncle Walter at the Black Horse. He didn't show. What happened?"

She laughed. "You're not as clever as you think you are. I don't know anything about any Black Horse. Any more questions, Cheka pig?"

She understood ascendancy as well as I did.

"Let's talk about those bank accounts."

"I don't think so."

"Lot of money for a couple of teenagers."

"You don't know what you're talking about."

"Twenty-two million is a lot of money to make up. But like I said, I'm really interested in Uncle Walter."

"Be careful, Chekist pig. You know what happens to Chekists who make mistakes."

She cut me off. The girl was tough and smart—and experienced, much more so than she should have been. Jenny Leitz had picked up on it, but she hadn't grasped the full degree. Irina had played our short interrogation like an expert. Not that surprising, perhaps, her father and stepfather were top oligarchs. She'd been learning at the feet of experts since she was a baby. She and Andras were doubtless comparing notes. I still couldn't see what any of this had to do with the bugging of Leitz's computers.

Not that it mattered. I fully expected to be fired by the time I got back to Manhattan.

★ CHAPTER 22 ★

Suspicion confirmed.

Leitz was waiting at my office. He and Foos were bent over a laptop in the open area, comparing notes on something. Leitz had switched to blue cashmere today. Same corduroys, from the looks of it, same shoes.

"Don't you believe in progress reports?" Leitz said, looking up, trying to be confrontational, but not able to manage it. His eyes were red with bags underneath. He was tired, and for him, decidedly subdued. Looked like Jenny had told him of her diagnosis.

"Didn't see the need. You had your man in the tan coat for that."

He started to say something, stopped and shook his head. "He figured you spotted him—on Houston Street."

"Before that—outside Marianna's."

"How'd you figure he was working for me?"

"Process of elimination. Who else would have someone following me around?"

He nodded. "Serves me right. Foos said I could trust you, but . . ."

"I'm told you like to control things."

He nodded again. "Guilty."

"You want your report now?"

He shrugged. "If you think it's necessary. I actually came down here . . . I want to ask you to stop. The computers, whoever it was, it just doesn't matter that much anymore."

He looked down at the coffee table.

"I'm finished anyway," I said. "I can tell you who and what if you want. But it's likely to cause more pain."

"That's not possible."

171

"I know. I'm sorry."

It took a minute before he raised his head. Tears in his eyes. "You . . . you know?"

"She told me. Only when I asked, although I already knew about the doctors and the tests."

"Jesus." He started a lunge for the laptop. For a moment I thought he was going to hurl it across the room. Foos thought the same thing and was ready to grab it first. But halfway there, Leitz just collapsed and fell back on the sofa. Sorrow overwhelmed temper. Foos was unconvinced. He closed the lid and moved the computer out of range.

"Life ain't fair, man," he said, mainly, I think, to say something.

I went to the kitchen and came back with the vodka bottle. Leitz shook his head when I offered him a glass.

"It'll help, if you don't overdue it."

"You mean, like Marianna?"

I shrugged.

"Just a little," he said.

I poured him a finger. He took a sip and put the glass on the table and wiped his eyes. "I'm sorry. I didn't come here to unload my burdens on you."

"That's all right." His family had already done that.

He picked up the glass, took another swallow, and shook his head when I offered a refill.

"Tell me what you found out," he said quietly, "although I've almost decided to abandon the TV bid. I've got more important things to focus on."

He sounded sincere. I believed him, but I wondered how he'd feel a day or two or ten down the road. *I'm determined we should all lead as normal a life as possible,* Jenny Leitz had said. She'd be encouraging him to keep on.

"We can do this another time if you want," I said.

He shook his head. He was struggling to stay afloat in an emotional tsunami. For the moment, the trader was still in control. "Go ahead."

I double-checked with Foos. He dropped his lopsided visage ever so slightly in assent.

"Your computers were bugged by the Baltic Enterprise Commission—an organized cyber-crime outfit. We told you it was someone like this, and we were right. They specialize in Web hosting for phishers and spammers, but they've expanded into hacking for hire and industrial espionage. Nosferatu, the man who beat me up, is the BEC's enforcer. I established that through contacts in Russia. He got the cleaners to place the bug."

"How did he . . . ?"

"Your brother-in-law, Coryell, was the agent. He was with Nosferatu when they bribed the cleaners. He told them where to put it. The cleaners described him. I've since seen Nosferatu at Coryell's office. He had a key."

I half expected an explosion—*WALTER? WHAT THE HELL DO YOU MEAN? WALTER?! I DON'T BELIEVE IT. HE'D NEVER* . . . What a difference a day and a diagnosis of death make.

All he said, weakly, was, "Walter?"

"Afraid so. I wish there was another explanation, but . . ."

"Why would he . . . ?"

"Coryell's compromised. He's being blackmailed, I assume by Nosferatu and the BEC, but also by someone else. I don't know what the leverage is, but it's powerful. It's already cost him two hundred grand by my count, maybe more."

The money focused his attention. "Two hundred thousand? Blackmail? Who told you this?"

I was trying to get through the story without squealing on Thomas. I didn't give a damn about him, but he wasn't connected to the main event, and adding his troubles to the mix would only make matters worse for Leitz. Maybe I was doing my own under-the-rug sweeping.

"It's in the Dick," I said.

"But . . . Have you talked to Walter? What does he say?"

"I haven't seen Walter. Neither has anyone else—in at least a week."

"What about Julia?"

"She tells me her husband is very busy. I doubt she knows anything about blackmail or Nosferatu, and I haven't enlightened her."

He shook his head. "Okay, but . . . Jesus. Tell me about this Baltic . . . what do you call it?"

"Baltic Enterprise Commission. It's a partnership—three oligarchs—that's suffered some setbacks and internal disagreements in recent months. The founding partner's Efim Konychev. He still runs the show, maybe, but in that world, disagreements often lead to violence. Someone tried to gun him down in Moscow last month."

I was watching for the reaction. He didn't try to hide it. He fell against the back of the couch like a man who'd been slugged. I waited, but he didn't say anything. The eyes, still red, went blank as he stared into the distance of the space. I hesitated a moment before delivering the next blow.

"Konychev's sister is Alyona Lishina."

"CHRIST!"

The old Leitz came back in an instant. He balled his fists, leaned forward, and flailed in the air. Foos picked up the laptop.

"WHAT THE FUCK IS GOING ON?"

He pushed himself to his feet, thought about kicking over the coffee table, thought better, and marched around the room. Pig Pen, who'd been attracted to the door of his office by the commotion, beat a fast retreat to his back perch when Leitz headed in his direction. I glanced at Foos, who shrugged and nodded—*You're doing the right thing*. I wasn't certain I shared his confidence.

Leitz came back and stood close to my chair. "What do you know about Konychev?"

"Sit down and I'll tell you."

He went back to the sofa.

"He's an oligarch—now. He was a high-level propaganda apparatchik in Soviet times. He bought up media properties during transition. He controls most of the nonstate media in Moscow. He also grasped the commercial potential of the Internet early. All the spammers, phishers, and pornographers out there need servers to call home, preferably servers somewhere hard to find, in a jurisdiction with authorities who aren't eager to assist the rest of the world's police. The former Soviet republics have such places in abundance, and as new converts to capitalism, they were keen to attract the business."

He shook his head again. "I had no idea."

At the risk of setting off another explosion, I said, "I find that hard to believe."

"No . . . You don't understand. I really didn't. I didn't know who he was."

I waited, my skepticism evident. Foos shifted in his seat, reached for the vodka bottle, thought better and left it where it was. He wasn't buying either.

Leitz looked from one of us to the other.

"Okay, I know it begs credulity. But . . . here's what happened. I met a woman, back in October, through my son, actually. He's dating—or trying to date—her daughter. They go to the same school. She's wired into the New Russia. Her husband's . . ."

"I know who he is. Taras Batkin. Russian-American Trade Council. It's a front. He's also BEC, by the way, one of the three partners, and Alyona's first husband, the girl's father, is the third."

"Oh my God. I had . . . You have to believe me . . . I had no idea. I've been played for a total fool. If this gets out . . ."

174

Sounded to me like he was already rethinking the TV bid, but I stayed quiet.

"I was working on the network transaction," Leitz went on, "putting together a limited partnership to pursue it. My bankers were having trouble raising money. TV's out of fashion among institutional investors and . . . I was a victim of my own hubris. Nobody wanted to put money with someone who was seen as unpredictable—'mercurial' was the word you used the other day, right?"

"That's right. They worried you might decide to give the money back," I said with a smile.

That got a small grin in return. "Exactly. Anyway, Alyona was all over me in the following weeks. Not the way it sounds, she was all business and she was relentless. She said she could raise hundreds of millions, maybe billions, and I offered her the same commission deal I give my bankers. She organized lunches and dinners and presentations. We went to London and Paris and the South of France. That's when the rumors started. There was nothing ever to them, I promise you that. It was all business. Jenny knew every move I was making. I met all kinds of people I never knew existed, and more than a few did invest. But there was always one big fish out there—the white Russian whale she called him, it was her idea of a joke, but she wouldn't say any more. Meetings kept getting set up and canceled. I offered to go to Moscow, but she said that wasn't a good idea. She wouldn't say why."

I knew why, but let him tell his story.

"Then, in December, she tells me I'll get a call. I do, and a man comes to see me, and he's in a position, through a partnership he controls, to invest three hundred million, maybe more. You have to understand, in this kind of deal, the value of three hundred million is three billion or higher because of the leverage it allows. I was suspicious, of course, but he seemed to know all about her—and me. I was also getting ready for the day when we'd have to raise our bid—and I needed his money. I told him his group and any investment would have to pass scrutiny with U.S. regulators, the SEC. He said that wouldn't be a problem."

"Konychev," I said.

He nodded. "It all fits."

It did fit. "You meet him in your office?"

"Yes."

"He placed the voice bug under your desk. You get his money?"

"We made a handshake deal, and our lawyers have been doing the paperwork, but I haven't heard from him directly again, no."

"You won't. You won't see any money either."

Leitz buried his head in hands. Foos and I exchanged a look that said, *Give him some space.* Foos took the laptop to his office. I returned the vodka bottle to the kitchen, leaving Leitz a wide berth on my way to my office. Even Pig Pen picked up on the tension and kept quiet. I think he turned down his radio.

I felt a large presence at my door a half hour later. Leitz looked worse than when I arrived.

"I didn't mean to add to your troubles," I said.

"Not your fault. You did what we agreed. Give me an account number, I'll have your fee wired tomorrow. I'll tell my lawyers to draw up a loan agreement for the Malevich. Best to document that."

"Thanks."

Even under the pressure he was feeling, the business brain was functioning. I told myself not to be judgmental—I was the beneficiary.

"What are you going to do about Coryell?" I asked.

He shook his head. "Walter . . . Let's just say, this is one more in a long string of issues with Walter."

I nodded. Not my business to press. I thought once more about saying something about Marianna and Thomas, whose problems were no less serious, or potentially threatening. Let them pass. Andras called out from a Siberian corner of my mind—*Hey, what about me and my eleven mil?* I told him to shut up. Don't climb into another man's sleigh, as another of our proverbs goes.

Leitz stepped through the door and stuck out his big hand. I stood and took it. His grip was almost painful.

He said, "I can't say it's been fun working with you, but . . . I guess, I hope we meet again under better circumstances."

"Me too."

He let go and lumbered across the floor until he disappeared among the servers. I stood in my door rubbing my wrist.

Foos appeared, shaking his mane. "Man don't know what hit him."

"I think he's got a pretty good idea. Problem is, he doesn't know what's coming around the curve up ahead. Like that song you play, trouble ahead, trouble behind . . ."

"You'd be better off dead?"

"Let's hope not."

★ CHAPTER 23 ★

I told Foos I needed a straw man, and he set me up with William Ferrer. Foos consults for banks and financial institutions, partly because he enjoys charging usurious fees for jobs that to him are pedestrian, and partly because he wants to keep tabs on what the bastards are up to, as he puts it. He maintains a stable of well-heeled straw men—straw women too—synthetic identities he's created by marrying deceased persons with other people's Social Security numbers. He gives them the financial basics—bank accounts, credit cards, sometimes passports and driver's licenses—and brings one to life when he needs someone to do something anonymously. One of his ways of toying with the Big Dick.

Tomorrow when I received Leitz's money, I'd move a hundred grand into Ferrer's account at Citi, where he was already sitting on $2,748, and send a debit card to Aleksei. Half of me said it was guilt money for having abandoned him as a child, the other half pegged it as down payment on the guilt to come, courtesy of L. P. Beria. The little bit that was left rationalized that Aleksei had provided a key tip about Alyona Lishina, so this was his commission. That part of me walked home happy. Except I kept thinking about smiling, terminally ill Jenny Leitz, who was soon likely to add more pain to her list of ailments. Half of the world's major religions lay claim to a righteous God. I agree with the Bolsheviks on one thing—who'd want Him? He's a mean-assed SOB.

By the time I reached my door, I pushed those ruminations aside. I was a million dollars and a third of a Malevich up. The odds against that were astronomical, some kind of celebration was in order. I told Victoria to wait downstairs while I went to the garage.

I'd trade my apartment for the look on her face when I pulled up in the Potemkin.

"Wow! That's the biggest car I've ever seen. A Cadillac, right?"

"Eldorado. 'Seventy-five."

"'Seventy-five? We were fighting the Cold War in 'seventy-five. How the hell . . . ? You're a socialist. How many socialists drive Cadillacs?"

"Always wanted one," I said. "Ever since I saw a picture in a magazine, the first time I was stationed here. I found this in Florida in 'ninety-three. It's called the Potemkin, after the battleship and Eisenstein's movie."

"What movie? Who's Eisenstein?"

"You have some holes in your education."

"They didn't teach Communist Party propaganda at Thibodeaux High. This thing got a heater that works?"

"It was built in Detroit. You want to put down the top?"

"I may be crazy, but I'm not stupid. I'm also a warm-blooded girl—as you've been rediscovering."

I took the FDR to Fifty-ninth Street and continued uptown on First Avenue. If Victoria guessed our destination, she didn't say anything. I found a parking place on East Eighty-first.

"Giancarlo and I are on a first-name basis," I said.

She smiled broadly, and we walked two blocks to Trastevere.

I held the door and followed her in. Giancarlo knocked two customers and a waiter sideways in his haste to get across the room.

"Signora, I . . ."

He was uncharacteristically confused by proper restaurateur-patron protocol, unsure whether to hug her, kiss her, or just shake hands. She solved the problem by putting her arms around him and kissing both cheeks. He looked at me over her shoulder as if to say, *What did I tell you?*

"It's good to see you Giancarlo," she said. "It's good to be home. Turbo tells me he's become a devotee of your cooking."

"*Si,* Signore Turbo, he comes all the time. But always alone, until tonight." His voice dropped and he leaned forward, whispering, "And I don't think he appreciates the wine."

"He has a lot of holes in *his* education. We're working on that."

Giancarlo gave every indication of owning the world as he led us to a table. He fussed over getting Victoria seated and unfolding her napkin. She said she'd like a martini and I nodded in agreement. He came back with the drinks, recited the specials, and we chose the seafood salad and wild mushroom pasta we'd had the first time we were there together.

178

When the salads came, Giancarlo appeared with a bottle that he held out to Victoria, label up. "A 'ninety-seven Brunello, the Montosoli from Altesino. My gift. Welcome home."

"Thank you, Giancarlo. That's very kind. Turbo thanks you too. In fact, I think I can hear him sighing with relief."

Giancarlo looked at her, beaming, then at me. "To tell you the truth, signora, so can I."

"Just out of curiosity, how much was the wine, do you think?" I asked as we drove downtown.

"On his list? Probably five hundred, maybe six."

It had been completely different from that first Barolo. Different grape, different region, different climate and soil, Victoria said. But it shared a complexity of flavor and structure that was surely intriguing—but not $500 intriguing.

"Another bottle I won't be having again," I said.

"Don't be a cheapskate. I'm not a cheap date."

"Five hundred dollars is more than most Soviet collective farms produced in a year."

"And where is the Soviet economy now?"

We put the Potemkin in the garage and walked through the chilly streets to my apartment.

"That was a lovely evening, thank you," she said, taking my hand in hers.

We made love slowly and luxuriously.

"Mmmmm. It doesn't get any better than this," she said before she fell asleep.

It does get worse. And it would, starting the next morning.

WEEK TWO: THE FLOP

★ CHAPTER 24 ★

Victoria declined my invitation to run with a sleepy, "Are you fucking crazy?"

I did five miles and returned at seven to find her still in bed.

"You're going to have trouble transitioning back to working hours."

"Lawyers start late."

"As I remember, you used to go around the clock."

"That was before my virtuous American work ethic was undermined by the socialist Evil Empire."

We ate eggs and toast and coffee and she said she had to visit the office before going uptown and reclaiming her apartment from the dust covers, the first step toward reentering her normal life. I felt a tug at that. She felt it too, and squeezed my hand. "It's only uptown, you dope. Closer to Trastevere."

"That's what I'm afraid of."

That put an end to the squeeze, and she went to get dressed.

Victoria went to her office and I went to mine. Foos was elsewhere, Pig Pen was absorbed in the morning rush hour, and I spent an hour sipping coffee while I thought about the Leitzes, my newfound liberty and good fortune, and why I didn't feel better about the state of the world than I did. Victoria was back—and gave every indication of intending to stay. The winter of discontent hanging over the House of Turbo had morphed unannounced into spring. I was a million dollars ahead, and didn't have to pay estimated income tax until April. One price of my adopted county. I owned a Repin self-portrait and could look forward to the unrestricted enjoyment of a painting most museums would kill for. How many people hit that kind of trifecta? I still had Beria to deal with, and no good idea of how, but he was just a ghost at this point, despite his periodic appearances, or so I tried to tell myself, a long-dead madman whose madness had died when he did, with no ability to inflict pain or suffering or death any longer—or so I tried to tell myself. I couldn't quite get myself to believe it.

At the moment, however, present tugged harder than past. I was finished with the Leitzes, but I didn't feel done. Too many open questions. What did Thomas Leitz have on his brother-in-law? Why did everyone in the family, except maybe Jenny, get nervous when Coryell's name came up? How did he get tied up with Nosferatu and the BEC? Where was he spending his time, leaving no trail for the Basilisk? And where did seventeen-year-old Andras get $11 million—$22 million, if I added in Irina's take?

If I pushed it, what was really roiling me was what Thomas Leitz said about sweeping things under the rug. The Leitz family made a lifetime habit of it, but didn't I as well? My Gulag past. My fear over Beria. Things had happened to them—I had no idea what—that they didn't want to confront. Was I any different? I'd been running from my upbringing all my life. Now I was running from my prospective parentage. Maybe the fires of Leitz burned a little too close to Turbo's home. Leaving theirs untended left me only my own to contemplate.

Confusion, one step ahead of dejection, was overtaking satisfaction when the phone rang.

"This is Pauline Turner," a woman's voice said. "I'm sorry I didn't get back to you sooner. I've been away and just got your message."

Half a beat before it clicked—Turner, Mrs. Leitz the first.

"Thank you for returning my call, but the matter I called about . . . It's been taken care of."

"Oh." Pause. "Is everyone all right? Your message said Sebastian . . ."

"Everyone's fine," I said, although I wasn't sure that was true. "It concerned your husband's office, we figured out what the problem was."

"Then Andras wasn't involved?"

"No." I wasn't sure that was true either. "Why do you ask?"

Another pause. "Just making sure. Mother's protective instinct, I suppose."

That sounded good, but I didn't believe it. I should have said good-bye and hung up.

"Tell me one thing," I said. "Your son—what's his relationship with his uncle Walter?"

A long silence. When she spoke, her voice was quiet and scared.

"Why did you ask that question?"

"There appears to be some tension between them. I was curious about the cause."

"When . . . They're not supposed . . . When did you see them together?"

She pressed the question like an accusation. I backed off and tried to reassure her.

"I haven't. I haven't met either one, to be honest. It's more what others have told me."

"Who told you? What did they say?"

She fired those questions like shots, the voice just above a whisper. The protective instinct was in high gear.

"Nothing specific. I'm sorry if I upset you."

"*Tell me!* What does any of this have to do with Sebastian's office?"

The whisper was almost a shout. I moved the conversation to neutral territory.

"Have you been visited or called by two people, man and a woman, claiming to be lawyers looking into Sebastian's TV bid? Probably back in December, before Christmas?"

"No. I don't think so. I would've remembered that. Lawyers, you say?"

"That's what they claimed. They questioned your former in-laws. I was curious how far they went."

"Please! What's this all about?"

"Somebody bugged your ex-husband's office. They had help from Walter Coryell."

"What's that have to do with Andras?"

Hang up!! A chorus screamed in my head. *This is no longer your case and it can't go anywhere good.* Stubbornness paired with curiosity is a tough combo to shut down.

Beria materialized by the door. *You're still a Chekist. You always will be.*

I ignored him.

"Andras was trying to reach his uncle over the weekend. I think he set up a meeting with him, but Coryell didn't show. The two have no history of contact. That made me wonder."

"*Andras called Walter?* That's impossible."

"Not according to phone records."

"But . . . Andras would never . . . and Walter . . . he knows . . . Is Sebastian aware of this?" The panic was back in her voice.

"No. We didn't discuss it."

Another long pause.

"You said your business with Sebastian is finished?"

"That's right."

"Then, please, I need to ask a favor."

I waited.

"It's very important—for all of us. Please don't ever tell anyone what you just told me. About Andras and Walter. All right?"

"Why not? What's wrong?"

"You can't possibly understand. No one can understand. Just promise me, you won't ever breathe a word."

"I'm not sure I can do that, Ms. Turner. I'll need more specific—"

She hung up.

I was still holding the receiver in my hand, wondering what else was being swept—swept back?—under the rug, when the "arrrr-oooo-gahhhh" of our door horn sounded. Probably Foos—he likes to hit it on the way in. Pig Pen yelled out "Boss man!" After a minute, no one emerged from the server farm and the horn blew again. I put down the receiver and went out to the lobby. Three men in suits stood in the elevator vestibule. One suit was expensive and elegantly tailored. The other two were cheap and cut large to accommodate the guns carried under their owners' arms. All three looked impatient.

The expensive suit was Taras Batkin, BEC partner and stepfather of Irina Lishina. Leitz and his extended clan weren't letting go that easily. That didn't surprise me nearly so much as the relief I felt at being back in the game.

I remembered what Aleksei said about Batkin and his title as I pushed the button that releases the electronic lock.

"Please come in, Mr. Ambassador. You can call me Turbo."

★ CHAPTER 25 ★

Pig Pen took one look at the queue that marched out of the servers and said, "May Day. Russky parade."

I have no idea where he gets it, but he never misses.

"What the hell?" one of Batkin's bodyguards said, hand under his jacket, turning toward his cage.

"Just a parrot, with a warped sense of humor," I said.

The bodyguard walked toward Pig Pen's office, hand in place. Pig Pen retreated to the back perch.

"Tell him to leave the parrot alone," I said to Batkin. "He's harmless."

Batkin barked an order in Russian, and the bodyguard returned to the parade. Pig Pen stayed where he was.

Batkin was trimly built, about five seven. He wore a navy suit with an electric-blue windowpane check. His shirt was bluish-gray, with a white collar and French cuffs, blue and purple striped tie. His face was comprised of geometric forms—circular head, circular eyes, pyramid nose, square mouth. The eyes were the same color as his shirt. The black hair was applied with glue, unless I missed my guess, although the toupee was a good one. I wondered what he made of my shaved pate. He had a thick gold wedding band and, next door, a diamond encrusted pinkie ring. A short Russian crow, dressed like a peacock—with a hairpiece. He, no doubt, considered himself quite dashing. The Napoleonic complex was a foregone conclusion. I reminded myself not to judge the book before I'd read the first page.

"We can talk in here," I said pointing to a glass-walled conference room.

The other bodyguard stepped toward me. "Arms up," he said in Russian.

I shook my head.

"Up, asshole."

I turned to Batkin. "You came to see me, unannounced. I presume you have business to discuss."

Batkin said, "My men are protective. That should not surprise you."

"I don't appreciate being patted down in my own office. That shouldn't surprise you."

He looked me over calmly, deciding whether to concede a pawn this early. His concern was control, not safety. "You give me your word, you are not armed?"

"Wait here," I said. Always good to establish ground rules with the Cheka.

I went to the kitchen, opened the old safe we keep there, and took out a .50AE Desert Eagle automatic with a six-inch barrel. It's the size of a hand-held bazooka with the firepower to match. I'd taken it away from its unhinged owner a year before and kept it around principally for intimidation purposes. I checked the empty chamber, left the clip in the safe and took the gun back to the open area. The second bodyguard was reaching under his arm when I tossed it to him.

While he fumbled, I said to Batkin, "When I am armed, this is what I carry. They use them for deer hunting here—and to stop the occasional pickup truck. Feel better now?"

He smiled and went into the conference room. I took the Desert Eagle from the bodyguard—he was looking it over with a professional's interest, albeit a professional dimwit—put it on a side table, and followed.

"Let's start over," I said as I closed the door. "To what do I owe the pleasure of your visit?"

"You've been harassing my stepdaughter."

So much for starting over.

"I talked to her yesterday on the phone. I asked her a question. I didn't believe the answer and told her so. I'm more honest than she is. That's the long and short of it."

He nodded, as if that was the answer he expected. "This about the Leitz kid?"

He was up on her affairs, but it wasn't my place to confirm them. "You can ask her that."

"I can see why you annoyed her. Why didn't you believe what she said?"

"She was lying. She's good at it, I'm guessing she's had plenty of experience, but she's not as good as she thinks she is."

He nodded again. "You were in the Cheka." A statement, not a question.

"Twenty years. First Chief Directorate. But you know that. She knew it too. She's not a fan of the organization."

He nodded once more. "Iakov Barsukov's protégé. Until you got cross-wired with Lachko. The details there are a little murky."

"They don't matter." Except maybe to Lachko and me. Iakov didn't care anymore, although he had, intensely, at the time.

"He was a good man, Iakov. A Chekist's Chekist. The organization came first. He never let outside considerations get in the way. Lachko . . . Lachko is a different story. So's his fucking brother."

A bitter edge to his voice. He didn't have much use for the Barsukov brothers. That was to his credit. Although he was wrong about Iakov—I'd found out the hard way and almost died in the process—at his hand. But that was the story I could never tell.

"You've read my file," I said.

"I was actually more interested in the earlier part of the file—what happened before the Cheka."

I didn't answer. Alarm bells were ringing too loudly in my head. The early part of my file was totally bland and uninformative—Iakov had made sure of that. It was called a clean passport, my Gulag past had been expunged from the record. A former *zek* was a *zek* no more and could hold his head high without fear of shame or spurning or repulsion. Or that was the intention. But somehow Nosferatu had learned the truth. Now Batkin was making a similar implication. Or was I just paranoid?

"I'm not sure I follow," I said as flatly as I could.

"Of course you do. My file reads the same, almost exactly the same, word for word."

He took off his jacket and hung it carefully over the back of a chair. He undid a cufflink and rolled up the blue-gray sleeve. The arm was covered in tattoos in Cyrillic script.

"Vyatlag."

He let that sleeve go and undid the other. More tattoos, different images and words.

"Gorlag. We were all in the same boat. Where were you, not that it makes any real difference?"

★ CHAPTER 26 ★

I felt like I'd been punched—knocked flat. Gobsmacked, as the Brits say, a term that doesn't translate, but somehow does. Batkin watched as I tried to clear my head. He'd thrown a calculated blow and hit—maybe harder than he knew. The surprise wasn't his background, but the ease with which he admitted it. I don't have the tattoos to record my time, but I could no more have owned up to Dalstroi and Vorkuta in the way he did than I could have put myself back into those state-sponsored hells-on-earth that formed my childhood.

"Surprised to meet a fellow traveler?" he said.

I nodded. The best I could do.

"There's thousands of us. You know that."

"But . . ."

"None of us talk about it? Of course. But what are we really afraid of? My Gulag upbringing is marked all over my body. No denying it. I don't advertise it, but I don't try to hide it either. You, on the other hand . . ."

I nodded again, as forcefully as I could. Probably looked feeble to him.

"None of us can move forward until we understand where we came from. When I read your file, I assumed you understood that. Your career here."

The mention of my career here snapped me back to the present. He'd done a lot of research. He was using past and present to work me over. To what end?

He redid his cuffs. "You haven't answered. Which camp?"

"Dalstroi . . . Then Vorkuta," I said, defeated.

"Languages, that's what Iakov saw?"

"That's right."

"He had an eye for talent. Mine's organization. I organized the *zeks* at Gorlag, there were thousands more of us than the guards, who by that time were totally demoralized. We—the *zeks,* I mean—were about the only thing working in the Soviet economy. We deserved a little better than nothing. I made people think about their worth. We organized. We struck. We shut down the camp more than once. It wasn't easy. Some died. They would have died anyway." He shrugged. "But we got noticed. We got results."

I was starting to think clearly enough to replace "we" with "I" in his recounting.

"So Iakov . . ."

"He found me, like he found you. He launched a successful career." He lifted his jacket off the chair, put it on, sat down and shot a gold-linked cuff to underscore the point. He'd also finished bonding.

"Tell me about Irina. What did you want from her?"

I answered, it was the easiest thing to do. "My interest was her boyfriend's uncle. If you want an apology, I'm sorry."

I wasn't sorry in the slightest, she could more than take care of herself, but it seemed the diplomatic thing to say, and I was looking to reestablish equilibrium in the conversation.

"I'm sure you said nothing untoward," he said, also the diplomat. "Irina can be a difficult girl. She's had a difficult childhood. Her father is a difficult man. She bore the brunt of that, while she was growing up. One reason she lives here now, with her mother and me."

I didn't point out she wasn't exactly living with her mother and him, and I was having a difficult time with the repeated use of the word "difficult." Too easy. It conveyed trouble without telling anything of its nature. Unsure of where to go next, I waited.

"I came here to ask for your help," he said after a moment.

That couldn't be good, but . . . maybe . . .

"Irina is up to something, involved in something, I don't know which or what. It may involve this boy, again, I don't know. Her mother is worried. So am I."

Buy time. "Have you asked her—if anything is wrong, I mean?"

"Of course. Both her mother and I talked to her over the Christmas holiday, before she went to Moscow to see her father. She kept us at arm's length. As you pointed out, she's learned the art of prevarication. She may not be as good at it as she thinks—you're right about that too—but she's practicing."

I almost said, *Every chance she gets and maybe for good reason.* Instead I waited some more.

He waited too.

Then he said, "I'm very fond of the girl. If I had a daughter, I'd like her to be . . . I'm more than fond of her mother. But what you say is true. She's gone off the road somewhere, and we are both worried—her mother and I—that she could be going to a dangerous place. You know who her father is?"

I nodded. He sounded every inch the concerned parent, but the calculated assault of the last few minutes undermined that.

"You want me to find out what she's involved in?"

"That's right."

Buy more time.

"Suppose I already have a client?"

"Does his interest conflict with mine—or hers?"

"It could."

"You have obligations. On the day that your first client's interests come into conflict with mine, I release you. Will that do?"

Ever the diplomat. Except that wasn't where he came from. His tattoos said he was Gulag *urki*—the criminal class. He was also a Chekist. If—or when—his interests and Leitz's, or anyone else's, came into conflict, another solution would be found. But that would happen regardless of what I said. And, I was coming to realize, he was in a position to help me in a way perhaps no other person could.

"Let's talk compensation," I said.

"I am a wealthy man. I will pay what you require, within reason."

"I don't want money. I want information. Or, more accurately, unfettered access to information."

"I'm not sure I understand."

I told him what I had in mind.

When I finished, he walked around the conference room looking at the view, looking back into the office, looking at me.

"I understand what Iakov saw," he said. "That is a most finely tuned proposal. What, I must ask, makes you think I'm in a position to deliver—or that I won't cross you?"

"You can deliver. I haven't lived in Moscow for twenty years, but the way things work hasn't changed that much. We're both Chekists. We understand each other. I won't give you reason to cross me. I know what will happen if I do. If you cross me, you can count on my tracking you down, carrying that Desert Eagle."

He smiled broadly, for the first time since he arrived, and extended a hand.

"I believe you," he said.

I took the hand. I didn't believe him. Not about anything he said.

Beria appeared by the window, smiling.

★ CHAPTER 27 ★

Victoria said, "You have no idea how difficult this is for me."

Actually, I could make a pretty good guess, but I wasn't about to say so. I leaned in and tried to look sympathetic.

"You're a fraud. Don't pretend you're not enjoying this. I can see it all over your face." She shoved me away, but smiled as she did so.

We were on my couch, enjoying a predinner drink, red wine for her, vodka for me. I had a pork roast in the oven, coated with rosemary, sage, garlic, and olive oil. Victoria licked her lips as soon as she walked in the door, but the rest of her body language indicated she'd had a bad day.

The rest of mine hadn't been overly productive either. After Batkin left, I'd replayed mentally the conversation with Andras's mother. I couldn't see anything that caused her panic or fear, both of which came out of nowhere. I went back over the Basilisk's records, and they showed nothing more than a wealthy divorced woman teaching at a small Minnesota college, enjoying regular visits from her son and periodic vacations at health spas and ski resorts, one of which she'd just returned from. I worked the data on Andras and Irina without any more success. Despite what his mother said, Andras was still trying to reach his uncle. He'd called twice yesterday and once this morning without connecting. Walter Coryell gave every indication of having gone incommunicado. Irina, however, was still buying pizza at Crestview Pizza and soda at Mike's Grocery. I called Gina and got her voicemail. She called back just after Victoria walked in.

"Sorry, Turbo! Back to back seminars. What's up? Not Newburgh again, I hope."

"Maybe worse, from your point of view. Crestview, Massachusetts—Hicksville to you. Probably a four-hour drive from New York. How soon can you get up there?"

"You paying? Tonight."

"Tomorrow will be fine. Get the Valdez out of the lot. I'll set it up."

"This another hot-sheets joint?"

"Crestview Pizza and Mike's Grocery, both on Main Street."

"What about them?"

"They're favorite spots of the kid you tracked in Newburgh, Andras Leitz. Also his girlfriend, a tall, blond Russian named Irina Lishina. Sorry I can't be more specific on the description. Watch your step with her, she's a tough customer."

"Sure. What's the deal?"

"Andras and the girl are students at a fancy private school in the next town, Gibbet. I think they're up to something in Crestview. They hit that pizza joint several nights a week—when they should be studying or in bed. Pick them up there, follow them, let me know where they go."

"Okay, but . . ."

"What?"

"Do I have to drive the Valdez? That car's the most uncool thing on the road."

"Ford—bedrock of the American economy."

"You're showing your age, Turbo. Google's the bedrock of the American economy these days."

"Try taking a date to a drive-in in a search engine."

"Drive-in? Turbo, there hasn't been a drive-in . . . You're crazy."

"Did I tell you I'm leaving you that car in my will?"

"Just my luck. A car I hate to drive and won't be able to sell."

I hung up.

"I'm glad to see you treat all your lady friends with the same gentle and affectionate touch," Victoria said.

I fixed our drinks and asked Victoria about her day, and that's when she said, "I wouldn't ask if I had any choice, but I don't. I need help."

"*Socialist* help?"

"Don't start."

I couldn't resist. "Assistance from a one-time foot soldier in the army of the Evil Empire?"

"I'm warning you, goddammit . . ."

"Or are you looking for some old-fashioned KGB tradecraft?"

"If you don't . . . Shit. I knew this wouldn't be easy. And before your ego inhales any more of its own manure, I only need *you* to get *him* to let me use the Basilisk."

"Ahhh, the painful truth will out. Here I am, ready to rush to the aid of the beautiful damsel in distress, capitalist temptress though she may be, and I discover, in the nick of time, that I'm only being used, in typical vixen fashion, as a poor means to an ignoble end. I think I'll go fall on my carving knife."

"Did anyone ever tell you, without a doubt, you are the biggest pain in the ass ever to come out of Mother Russia?"

"It was a favorite theme of my ex-wife, although she was a lot more histrionic about it."

"And how long did that marriage last?"

"Eight years, but it seemed longer."

"An eternity to her, I'll bet. Look, I'm prepared to pay. Sexual favors. Dinner at Trastevere. A case of that rotgut vodka you drink. Name your price."

"Who says I can be bought?"

"You're going to make me beg, aren't you?"

"The thought crossed my mind, but I'm really just trying to find out what I'm signing on for."

"You can be a real bastard."

"Probably not your best sales pitch."

I took her glass to the kitchen and refilled it along with my own. "We've got half an hour until the pork's ready. Tell me your troubles."

I think she started to call me another name, then thought better of it.

"It's this case I came back for. Not mine—I didn't start it—but I inherited it, and if it goes south, it's on my watch."

"It's headed south?"

"Yes, dammit. That's what I'm trying to tell you. I thought we were headed for indictment. The reason I came back when I did."

"*I* thought it was *me*."

"Sorry. Don't play games. I told you that."

"You did," I admitted. "What then?"

"DoJ's like any other big organization. Nobody wants to give the boss bad news. So all the e-mails I got while I was away . . ."

"Overstated the case?"

"One way of putting it. Blew smoke up my skirt is another."

"Sounds just like the Cheka."

"Don't start that. You can't compare—"

"You just said, like any other big organization. What's so different?"

"Never mind. You want to hear my story or not?"

"I'm all ears."

She didn't look like she believed me, but she said, "All right. We've been working with a handful of big city police departments—New York, L.A., Chicago, Houston, Atlanta. They have technology that allows them to monitor file-sharing sites on the Internet—in this case, child pornography. We got search warrants and taps on the guys swapping the porn so we could see who they were doing business with. That led us to a credit-card payment processing company. Same process we followed six or seven years ago, which led to the bust of a pretty big ring. But we didn't have this kind of technology then, so this time, we're swimming in a much bigger pond."

"How many people we talking?"

"Not sure yet. Last time it was ninety thousand."

"How much money?"

"Not sure about that either. Some of these guys spend ten, twelve thousand a year online—or more."

"Ninety thousand at ten grand is pushing a billion."

"Right and that billion, if that's what it is, is disappearing—right here. The trick for these guys is getting the money out of the country and into their accounts overseas. In this case, Belarus, we think. It gets pretty murky over there."

"Baltic Enterprise Commission?"

Green flash. "How do you know that?"

"BEC's the market leader for that kind of service. I could've told you that two days ago, when I asked about the case."

"I have institutional constraints, remember?"

"I remember. As someone on the outside looking in . . ."

"You are the biggest goddamned son of a bitch . . ."

"Just making a point—in the only son of a bitch fashion I know."

"I never should have started."

"I'm still listening."

"You're enjoying yourself way too much is what you're doing."

"I'm ready to help."

She took a sip of wine. "I may have to switch to that kerosene you drink, just to get through this. So . . . we follow the money trails, and they all lead to a big payment processing firm here—in Queens—ConnectPay. We think it's the one moving the money overseas. Firms like that, they operate under the radar. They can act like banks—take in money, move it around—but they're not banks so they're not subject to the same regulations, especially reporting regulations. This one only exists online. We go to the address in Queens—it's not there. I mean, the building is, but not ConnectPay. We go looking for the guy who runs it—Franklin Druce is his name, with some partners who are partnerships owned by partnerships who take you on a tour of the entire Caribbean before they send you to Eastern Europe. The real bitch is, we can't find a damned thing on this guy, Druce. Someone running a business like that, there should be something. Maybe not a criminal record, but an arrest record, some mention in the file, something. He's not even in the goddamned phone book. That's why I need the Basilisk."

"The other day at the office, when I said Walter Coryell could have another identity, Mr. Hyde with plastic, you said, 'We never thought of that.' You were talking about Druce, right?"

"Right."

"What's the address in Queens?"

"Twenty-second street, number forty twenty-eight."

"You've got a man watching the place."

Another flash. "I give up. How . . ."

"I saw him. Last Friday night, right before I came home. The same night I saw Nosferatu there. It's Walter Coryell's address too, Leitz's brother-in-law. We may be able to help each other out. But, since you said you're willing to pay, there is a price."

"Somehow I knew there would be. What price?"

"What do you know about Efim Konychev, like how come Homeland Security suddenly let him into the country?"

I could feel her tense up beside me. "Where do you get all these questions?"

"DoJ and State kept him out because he's an organized crime figure. Homeland Security overruled. What happened?"

"How do you . . . ?" One more flash of anger.

"Spies have lots of sources."

"Don't try to be funny. This is important. What source?"

"Very high placed . . ."

"If you . . ."

She was getting ready to belt me.

"Okay, okay. Russian blog. Ibansk.com."

"*Blog?!*"

"That's right. Written by a guy known as Ivanov. Ivan Ivanovich Ivanov.

Everyman. He does have highly placed sources—the best in Russia. Ibansk means 'Fucktown,' by the way."

"Nice."

"Apt. So what happened, with Homeland Security?"

"Don't ask."

"I thought you were looking for help."

"I am. I want to see this blog. I need to know what it says—exactly."

"Sure. But it's in Russian."

"You can translate."

"Maybe—if you ask with appropriate affection, deference and respect."

"Okay. You're right." She took my hand. "You either translate this Ivanhoe . . ."

"Ivanov."

"Or one of us is sleeping on the couch."

After dinner, Victoria pronouncing the pork a success, I got the computer and logged on to Ibansk.com. Ivanov had a new posting on Konychev. I skimmed it quickly.

"Seems Konychev's still in New York."

"What?!"

I translated.

High Noon in New York City?

The world is a big place, but perhaps not if one travels in the seemingly small circles of the Ibanskian oligarchy.

Exhibit A—Efim Konychev and Taras Batkin, brothers-in-law, sometime partners, mortal enemies, personal proponents of Ibanskian revenge, especially on each other, faced off this week, everything but guns drawn, across the floor of a Manhattan café.

Ivanov will set the table. Maison sur Madison was the venue—a New York see-and-be-scene known for elegant if tasteless meals, left mostly uneaten by emaciated models and their testosterone-laden peacock patrons. Did Ivanov mention stratospheric prices? They go without saying. Little surprise then that it appeals to a clientele from all corners of the Ibanskian empire who share great wealth and minimal taste. "Eurotrash" is the American term of art, and as much as Ivanov hates to admit defeat when it comes to a matter of words, he can't come up with a topper.

"He's got style," Victoria said.

"Zinoviev's turning in his grave."

"Who's Zinoviev?"

"Russian novelist. Inventor of the original Ibansk." I went back to reading.

Everyone knows the bad-blooded background between Konychev and Batkin. The Kremlin-enforced partnership. Konychev's failed attempts to torpedo his sister's romance and marriage. Attempted assassination. Assassination tried the other way. Yet here they were, two old comrades seeking overpriced sustenance. And certainly unwilling to remain in the other's company.

Konychev's party was seated when Batkin and his entourage arrived. Words were exchanged. Hands reached under overcoats. The owner intervened, at risk of his own scalp, and convinced Batkin and Co. to take their leave. A bad day for him—he'll never see Batkin or his kopeks again.

Lunch was served—Konychev and Co. dined on sautéed scaloppini, risotto Milanese, and roasted artichokes. Most un-Ibanskian fare. Washed down by Mouton-Rothschild '82. Total tab? A very Ibanskian $5,100.

"Christ! What the hell does he think he's doing?" Victoria muttered at the sink.

"You talking to yourself?"

"Just wondering if all you Russians are ignorant peasants. Artichokes are an absolute Cabernet killer. They didn't taste a drop of that wine, and it probably cost them most of that fifty-one hundred dollars."

I had a feeling she was talking about more than the menu, but I said, "I'll be sure to tell Konychev next time I see him. One more paragraph."

Ivanov can add a related tidbit. One person missing from Konychev's party was the feared enforcer of the Baltic Enterprise Commission—a shadowy figure of unknown name and uncommon strength—who has been spotted in New York of late. Lunch might have been someone's last supper had he decided to attend.

"That's the guy who beat you up, right?"

"Right."

"Read me the earlier article, the one about Konychev and Homeland Security."

I scrolled back and read it aloud.

Her only comment was, "Shit."

"Need any more translation services?"

"Who is this guy, Ivanov? Where does he get his information?"

"Nobody knows—on either score."

"How widely followed is he?"

"Very."

"Damn it."

"What's wrong?"

"Just about everything. I really need the Basilisk now. How 'bout it?"

"I'll try but whether he agrees is anybody's guess."

"What time can we start?"

"You go running with me at six, we can stop at the office on the way back."

"I'm not *that* desperate. Let's say breakfast at eight."

★ CHAPTER 28 ★

"Bayou Babe! Tiramisu?"

Pig Pen was on the case the moment we walked out of the server aisles.

"Get a wall clock, parrot," Victoria said. "Nine thirty, breakfast, remember?"

I think he muttered, "Prospect Parkway—lane closed," as he paced the floor of his office. He'd met his match in Victoria.

Foos came to his door to check the commotion. "To what do we owe the pleasure?"

"It appears that Leitz's brother-in-law, Walter Coryell, may have a hidden identity, Franklin Druce. Victoria thinks Druce is behind a payment processor for kiddie porn sites. We want to check him out."

"Which one's asking?" Foos said with a grin, planning to enjoy the moment.

Victoria looked at me.

"We both are," I said. "I still want to know what Nosferatu and the BEC have on Coryell. There's also my new client, Taras Batkin, stepfather of Andras Leitz's girlfriend, Irina."

"You're working for Batkin?!" Victoria cried. "You didn't say anything about him."

Foos's grin broadened. Pig Pen climbed the mesh in his door, attracted by his nemesis's distress.

"That a problem?" I asked.

"He's . . . He's . . . Shit. You know what he is. What the hell are you doing for Batkin?"

"That's between us. But I might be persuaded to tell tales out of school if you do the same about Efim Konychev."

"You can't be serious."

"Why not? Batkin can be very useful to me. He thinks his stepdaughter's up to some kind of trouble and wants to know what. We made a deal."

"What kind of deal?"

"Like I said . . ."

Pig Pen picked the wrong moment to take another shot. "Bayou Babe . . ."

"Quiet, parrot!"

He shook his feathers and went back to his radio.

Foos said, "You think this trouble could involve the Leitz kid?"

"Their bank accounts say it does."

"What bank accounts?" Victoria said.

"Remember I told you about the two kids with eleven mil each in the bank—back when we were sharing? What about Konychev?"

"Dammit, I . . ."

"And how is Coryell connected?" Foos asked.

"Andras and Irina were supposed to meet him at the Black Horse. He didn't show. Andras has been trying to contact him ever since. The guy's gone underground—maybe as Franklin Druce."

Foos nodded. "Your lucky day, Bayou Babe. We'll make an exception to the no-Fed rule, just for you. But . . ." He looked at me. "Stay on the reservation."

Foos went back in his office. Victoria said, "What did I ever do to him?"

"Nothing," I said. "Be glad he likes you."

"He likes me?"

"He would have reset all the passwords if he didn't. Come on—before he changes his mind."

Pig Pen thought about trying again as we passed his cage, but when Victoria shot him a look, all he said was, "Route Three, fuel spill."

It took less than ten minutes for the Basilisk to confirm Walter Coryell and Franklin Druce were indeed Jekyll and Hyde with plastic. In addition to the address, which Druce listed as both home and office, their driver's license photos showed two poor images of the same ordinary-looking, brown-haired man. Druce was CEO of ConnectPay, and the company deposited forty-four grand a month into a checking account at B of A. He spent a big chunk of it online, mostly with ConnectPay, at a long list of what looked to be child porn sites. A consistent three to five K a month. Bricks-and-mortar charges were at gas stations and restaurants all over the Northeast—Connecticut, New Jersey, Vermont, New York, sometimes Massachusetts, Pennsylvania, or Delaware.

I told the Basilisk to line up the food and gas purchases. The beast whined and hissed—*You already know the answer to that*—but did as instructed.

"One-night stands from the looks of it. He buys gas and food in the same town. No hotel or motel charges, though. Must pay cash for those. Thinks he's clever."

I could almost hear the Basilisk snort with contempt.

"What do you mean?" Victoria said.

"Druce is a pedophile. He's using the money he makes from ConnectPay to support his own habit. Every few months, when he gets bored just watching kids online, he sets off around the countryside to hook up with one. That explains the extra mileage on his car, remember?"

"Christ."

"In fact, looks like he's been on the prowl this week. Bought gas last Wednesday in Rockville, Connecticut. No meals though."

I asked the computer for the phone number for Coryell's garage. A Hispanic voice answered. "*Sí. ¿Hola?*"

I went with Spanish too. "*Hola.* This is José at Manhattan Volvo. We're supposed to pick up Walter Coryell's car Monday for service. Have it ready at eight, okay?"

"Wait a minute."

I could hear him talking to someone else in Spanish in the background.

He said to me, "*Sí,* that's okay, but it's not here now. Hasn't been since Wednesday."

"Oh. Maybe there's a mistake. I'll check with the customer and call you back."

"What was that all about?" Victoria asked.

"Coryell took his car out of the garage Wednesday and hasn't come back. Julia told me Friday her husband was traveling on business. I wonder if maybe . . ."

I sent the beast back to its cave. It returned in an instant, blowing fire, triumphant.

"There's your answer," I said, pointing to the screen. "No one could find Coryell because he's been cooling his heels, as Martin Druce, in the Tolland County slammer in Rockville. He was busted on Wednesday. Take a look."

"Goddamn," Victoria said. "That explains a lot." She leaned in to read the screen. "Attempted rape, solicitation of a minor, indecent exposure, the list goes on and on. At least we got him."

"Don't count your Coryells too quickly." I sent the Basilisk after his bank records. "I'd move fast if I were you. He wrote a check for five hundred thousand yesterday. Looks like he bailed himself out."

"No!"

She pulled out her phone, found a number, and was soon giving orders to someone on the other end.

While she talked, I went back to Druce's bank information. A handful of withdrawals, all cash, all five figures. The dates went back four years. A quick check confirmed they corresponded with Thomas Leitz paying off his shopaholic debts.

"GODDAMMMIT!" Victoria cried. "How the hell . . . ? Never mind, I already know. . . . Get a man back on Fourteenth Street. . . . Yeah, I won't hold my breath."

She put the phone back in her bag. "Sometimes I think FBI stands for 'Forever Behind It.'"

"Flew the coop?"

"Yesterday. Had a kid in his car when he got nabbed, but the kid got smart and ran. Cops found condoms, K-Y Jelly, all the usual paraphernalia. Only good thing is no one was hurt. Could be a tough case though, parents are already backing away—don't want the attention and publicity."

"He have any ID other than Franklin Druce?"

"Apparently not."

"What's your next move?"

"Hope he shows up back in Long Island City. I'm betting he's halfway to Shanghai." She banged her hand on the desk. "Dammit!"

"Don't be too quick. He's been doing this for a while. If he's smart, and the record so far shows that he is, then he's planned for this. He's probably got another identity lined up, ready to go. He sheds Franklin Druce like an old snakeskin, reemerges as Walter Coryell, and goes back underground as John Q. Sleazeball. He's out half a mil, and fingerprints are a problem, but no one has Coryell's prints on file, and his won't match Sleazeball's in the event someone has them. He's still at liberty."

She looked at me with skepticism. "Why is it that you always know every scumbag's next move?"

"Misspent youth, as we've discussed."

"Don't discount the rest of your life experience."

"There is a risk Coryell/Druce takes on a new identity and disappears entirely, but somehow I doubt that. Too much money tied up in ConnectPay for one thing. And he's got his partners to worry about. They don't like surprises. That fact might give us some leverage."

"Don't think I haven't thought of that. No us, though, shug. You stay away from Coryell. He's Federal property now."

"This is the gratitude I get?"

"So long as you're working for Taras Batkin, it is."

"Suppose what I'm doing for Batkin is purely personal?"

"Only thing personal about Batkin is the fact that I'm gonna nail his ass to the jailhouse wall."

Something clicked. "You're working with Aleksei again, aren't you?"

"Don't ask questions."

"Konychev—he's part of your case, right?"

"I said . . ."

"You're having a hard time keeping Efim Ilyich on the leash, aren't you? He's not supposed to be going out to lunch at Maison sur Madison or any-where else."

"If you don't . . . Oh, never mind. Dragons and treasures, that's my new mantra when it comes to dealing with you."

"I'm trying to help."

"You have helped, and I'm grateful." She gave me a squeeze and a kiss.

"Tell me this much—why all the secrecy surrounding Konychev?" I said.

"Who's asking—you or your new client?"

"Point taken. I'll do my own legwork."

"You would anyway, no matter what I said."

She did have me pegged.

"Make me one promise, though," she said. "Whatever you're doing for Batkin—it is personal, right?"

"Like I said, he's worried about his stepdaughter. He thinks she's up to something and wants to know what." No need to remind her that whatever it was almost certainly involved the BEC. "And no money's changing hands, if that makes a difference to you."

She frowned. "No money? You are getting paid, right?"

I nodded. "Information. Or access to information. He's the only guy I know who can provide it."

Another frown. "What kind of information?"

"Family history. Gulag history. I'll tell you all about it once I know what *it* is. Could amount to nothing." Hope springs eternal.

She was looking me up and down, but the frown had turned into a smile. "This on the level—or you cooking up another one of your screwball Rus-sian plots?"

"On the level."

"Good. Remember, I don't like surprises either. I gotta get to the office. Right after I thank that lion tamer you work with for the assist. And stay away from Coryell."

I did as instructed, for the most part, because I figured the next surprise was right around the corner. I was right, and it was a doozy. But only the first in a hell of a string.

★ CHAPTER 29 ★

Two days is a long time when nothing's happening. I told myself to be patient—when I was in the Cheka, two days was nothing. I used to spend weeks, months, sometimes years, working an agent until he or she paid off. But I was playing a long game then—the Cold War stretched for decades. Victories were few, at least on our side, so the time they took faded once they were recorded. This was twenty-first-century America—waiting was for losers and wimps—you were expected to produce something every day.

Victoria was antsy too—and patience, as a song goes, was not a virtue she possessed.

"Goddamned judge. How long does it take to grant a search warrant?"

"We used to get 'em in hours. On the infrequent occasions when we needed one."

"Don't start."

"Just pointing out the relative merits of different systems."

"Horse-you-know-what. You're just pulling my chain—and enjoying it."

I was enjoying her company—and that contributed to my feeling frisky. She appeared to be enjoying mine as well—at least she was making no haste to return to her apartment uptown. We spent most of our time together talking about things other than the business at hand—everyday things like books and music and movies. The first phase of our romance had ended before we had that chance. Now, we found that, as with art, we had little in common on any of them. Her tastes ran to Hemingway, honky-tonk, and comedy. Mine took in hardboiled noir, bop, and the filmed version of hardboiled noir. The disparities led to spirited arguments that inevitably (and happily) led to equally spirited reconciliation.

Her presence was keeping Beria at bay—as if she locked some door, and he could no longer get in, or maybe she just filled all the available emotional space with love and good cheer (interspersed with the occasional threat), and there was no room for his malevolence. It had been days since his specter last appeared. I made the assumption that this bode well for the future, in all kinds of ways.

Occasionally, we circled in on the subject at hand or one of its multiple manifestations—Batkin, Konychev, the BEC, Coryell/Druce—and if we reached a point of contention, we circled out again. We felt tension and not, we both understood the situation. Get used to it, I told myself more than once, this could be what it would be like going forward. I remembered the feeling I'd had with my ex-wife—I couldn't talk about my work with her—and I knew where that led. This was different—and better.

While Victoria was at the office, I worked the Basilisk. Thursday, it produced a few tidbits. Coryell/Druce had returned two calls Tuesday when he got back to town. One to Andras. One to the nameless cell phone I'd matched with Nosferatu. Nothing after that. And nothing from Gina. I started to call her more than once but no news meant nothing to report. She'd get in touch when she was ready.

Disobeying orders temporarily, I made a surreptitious trip to Long Island City for a look-see. Victoria's FBI man was watching the building. Other than that, not much going on.

Batkin called Thursday late to keep the pressure on. He wanted a progress report, he said. I had none. He wasn't pleased.

"I can close the archive doors as easily I opened them."

"I can walk away from a teenaged girl and her overbearing stepfather too. Neither of us benefits either way."

We were both bluffing.

Friday morning, I realized I'd made a mistake. Ibansk.com was the catalyst, with the news that the BEC had dropped offline. Ivanov was uncharacteristically brief. He'd been taken by surprise too.

Bye, Bye, BEC?

Has hell frozen over? Pigs learned to levitate? The fat lady finally bellowed?

Even Ivanov is shocked. Word reaches his humble abode that the Baltic Enterprise Commission is kaput, as in no longer functioning. The Internet is suddenly a safer place, or so we're informed.

Ivanov is skeptical. But a survey of some of the less savory sites on the World Wide Web appears to support the news. They are indeed defunct—as in no response, nothing, *nada, nichts, nichto.*

Has the heavily armored scourge of the Web finally been felled by some silver cyber-bullet? Or has it only gone into hibernation?

Check back soon. Ivanov's intrigued.

It occurred to me that I'd been looking at everything from the wrong perspective—just like I'd told Leitz. I'd borrowed his point of view, understandable in the circumstances, he was the one who'd hired me, but a mistake nonetheless. Konychev—or whoever was behind the bugging of Leitz's computers, and my money was still on Konychev—didn't give a damn about TV networks. He was looking for something else.

I scrolled back through Ibansk.com, noting the dates of Ivanov's posts that mentioned trouble in the BEC. One in August, two in September, two more each in October and November, three in December, including the news of the Tverskaya attack, and two in January. The most recent, before today, was last week, the day after I'd been beaten up by Nosferatu.

Ivanov hears the premier hoster of hackers has itself been hacked— although whether this was simple vandalism or invaders with more insidious purposes is thus far unclear.

Next to that list, I put down the sequence of events involving Leitz as I knew them. The computer activity Foos had spotted in the Leitz system had occurred in August, the same time when the BEC's troubles began and the first three million showed up in accounts belonging to Andras and Irina. The brute force attack on Leitz Ahead came shortly after. Alyona Lishina approached Leitz in October. More Leitz computer activity around Thanksgiving. Another transfer of funds to the kids' accounts. The fake lawyers followed, dispatched to question the Leitz family. They pretended to ask about Leitz to support the background-check story, but they were more interested in everyone else. Every Leitz sibling—Marianna, Thomas, and Julia—told me as much. They'd all been asked about *the other members* of the family, not just Big Brother Sebastian. Konychev was attacked in December, around the time Nosferatu and Coryell placed the bug. Konychev and Nosferatu and the BEC had Coryell in their pocket. They were in business together. Konychev and Nosferatu weren't looking for information on Leitz's firm or TV deal. They were looking for the guy who was interfering with the BEC's network.

Andras Leitz, computer whiz.

That's where his budding fortune came from—or at least part of it. He and Irina were ripping off the family business, her family business. The timing fit. So did the bank, in a circumstantial way. The million-dollar transfers came in August and December, from a bank in Estonia. More than probable the BEC would do business in Tallinn.

I called Victoria.

"Search warrant come through yet?"

"Don't get me started. I'm ready to start taking scalps around here as it is."

"When it does, check the bank records."

"Turbo, America won the Cold War, remember?"

"We can argue history later. I'm betting you're going to find four transfers out of ConnectPay's account at B of A, two each of one-point-five million in August and two each of two-point-five mil in November. If you can follow them, I bet they lead to accounts owned by Andras Leitz and Irina Lishina. Might be tough, though. I think the money gets washed and dried on the way. It ends up in Estonia before coming back here."

"What have you been up to now?"

"Just thinking." I told her about my misassumptions.

"Huh," she said. "That actually makes sense. I'll look into it and let you know. *If*—I ever get my goddamned search warrant."

She hung up. I went to Foos's office.

"What are the chances Andras Leitz could get inside the BEC network?"

He thought for a moment. "Without knowing any particulars, I'd say not good. They're well protected, better than most. Andras is smart, but . . ."

"Someone's been causing the BEC technical problems for months. According to Ivanov, they've knocked it offline altogether."

"No shit? Give me a minute."

I went back to my office and fed Andras's name into the Basilisk. He was on the move again. Wednesday noontime, he flew to LaGuardia on AmEx. Late Wednesday afternoon, he withdrew $2,900 from a half-dozen ATMs—all in Queens. When I mapped them, they formed a parade down Queens Boulevard. Then the trail stopped. Not a single electronic transaction since. He'd stocked up on cash and gone underground. Why? I had the feeling the answer had to do with Walter Coryell.

Foos appeared at my door.

"You're right. I tried several known BEC IP addresses. They're all non-responsive. But I still don't think Andras . . ."

"Suppose he got inside some U.S. servers connected to the BEC, like his uncle Walter's. Could he access the network, make mischief?"

"That's possible. But . . ."

"Why?"

"Yeah, why do it?"

"If I'm right, he ripped off eight mil for openers."

"This can't be about the money."

"True. I don't have a good answer for why. But he was in Queens Wednesday. Withdrew three grand then dropped offline."

"Huh. You gonna tell Leitz?"

"My client's Taras Batkin now—and his stepdaughter is right in the middle of this."

"So?"

"So I'm going to think about it."

I didn't get a chance to think long. Gina called a few minutes later.

"Those kids are up to something, but I can't tell what. It's a nighttime operation, though. Last two nights, I didn't get to bed until after three. I figured you didn't want to hear from me then."

"You figured right. What's up?"

"I found the kids' place. And they're definitely doing something strange. It's on the second floor and they got all the windows covered over, like they don't want anyone to see in."

"Where?"

"Crestview Main Street. There's a liquor store across from the pizza joint, in the next block. This place is over that. Looks like they got the whole floor. Two-story building, one entrance and a fire escape."

"How'd you find it?"

"Two kids showed up for pizza Wednesday night. Ten to ten. Not the Leitz kid and the girl, but two others. They looked like Gibbet School kids, I know a couple at NYU who went to that place, and they're a type, you know? I took a drive by when I got up here. That campus has more money than most country clubs. Looks like everybody should be wearing blue blazers or white dresses and be waited on by—"

"I get the point."

"Anyway, these kids were driving a BMW, New York plates, BDK one-three-five-eight. They bought a pie to go and went across the street. The entrance is around back. I circled the whole building. Every window's covered, no lights anywhere, except one over the door outside. All you can see inside is stairs going up into the dark. They stayed until after two. I didn't call you yesterday because I didn't know who they were. Last night the Russian chick shows up. I'm pretty sure it's her—tall, blond, real looker. She hits the pizza joint and goes in the same entrance as the others. I thought about going up the fire escape, but you told me to lay back, so I did."

The BMW was Irina's car. The ghostly image of Nosferatu, all six-feet-seven inches of him, fingernails as long as knives, materialized in my imagination. He could make me come to miss Beria.

"You did right. How late did she stay?"

"Two thirty-eight. I tailed her back toward the school, but she turned off on a side road just short of campus. Martin Lane. No way I could follow without getting spotted. What kind of high school lets kids go and come at all hours?"

"The kind that believes their students don't use the same toilets as the rest of us. You didn't see the Leitz kid?"

"Nope. But he could be inside the place above the liquor store, for all I know."

"You've done your job. Pack up and head for Logan. I'll catch a late afternoon shuttle. Meet me at the gate with the car keys."

I called Victoria, and told her she was her own for at least one night. She asked where I was going, in a tone that indicated she didn't expect an answer.

"Batkin business," I said, which was true.

"Shit."

That she didn't precede "shit" with "bull" said she believed me, and she wasn't happy about it.

"I'm running down the connection between the Leitz kid, the Lishina girl, and Coryell/Druce. Could be fruitful for you too."

"There's laws about what kind of evidence we can use, you know."

"How's that search warrant coming?"

Silence.

I started to say good-bye, but she'd already hung up.

★ CHAPTER 30 ★

Gibbet, Massachusetts, settled in 1635 according to the marker announcing the town line, still had all the signs of a prosperous New England colonial township. Why they named it after the gallowslike structure from which convicted corpses were hung as deterrents to those who might follow their misguided path was a question, but four centuries ago someone apparently thought it was good idea. Town founder was a hangman, perhaps. In the intervening years, the Gibbet folk had built lots of white and gray wood-sided houses with green and black shutters. A brick town hall, stone library, and Doric-columned historical society lined Main Street, interspersed with Federal, Greek Revival, and Georgian homes. The supermarket, gas station, and convenience store all looked out of place. The police station, fire station, and post office had been moved to the edge of town, their former Main Street facilities now occupied by an Italian restaurant, health food store and Pilates center. Gibbet had made a seamless transition from the seventeenth to the twenty-first century.

Hayfields Drive ran south out of town, a big leafy road, or would be come spring, with a wide double yellow stripe. The houses here were bigger and whiter and grayer. The owners weren't mowing their own lawns. A tall wrought-iron fence demarcated the border of the school's property and paralleled Hayfields Drive for the better part of a mile until I came to the entrance. No sign, but two square stone columns supporting iron gates with medieval coats of arms left little doubt this was an institution that took its importance seriously.

The Duke of Wellington supposedly said the Battle of Waterloo was won on the playing fields of Eton. Gibbet School had taken the Duke at his word and was doing everything it could to apply the principle in the land that won a revolution against his countrymen. Gibbet's playing fields stretched in all directions—soccer, football, baseball, track and field—snow-covered now, but ready as soon as spring arrived to prepare this generation of aristocratic kids for the next nineteenth-century war. Scattered among the fields were copies of eighteenth-century Georgian buildings and a late Gothic chapel. The Valdez was decidedly out of place.

I parked the car and strolled the plowed pathways through the fields and buildings. No one else was out, which meant no one questioned my presence, but there was no one for me to question either. Sunday night, the buildings were all locked, dorm and nondorm alike. The chapel, administration building, gym and performing arts center were dark. Lights in the dorms, built to look like houses, as well as in the Russell Wilcox Stu-Fac Center, which all required an electronic pass to get into. The place exuded as much welcome as the Gulag camps I grew up in.

I found Martin Lane, the side road Gina had described, a quarter-mile cul-de-sac with three houses and a barn. Parked in the driveways were a Ford Explorer, a Saab, two Subarus and a Dodge Ram pickup. No BMW, but it could have been in the barn.

Four and a half miles away, Main Street, Crestview, was a study in contrasts. A hardscrabble, working-class town, whose best days were a century behind it. The houses were side-by-sides and double-deckers, many with peeling paint. At 8:30 P.M., the sidewalks were all but rolled up. Downtown was next to a rail yard and handsome enough in a way that evoked its blue-collar roots. The business district stretched four blocks. About a quarter of the store fronts were empty. The pizza place anchored one corner. The grocery was two doors down. Both looked exactly like they should. A half-dozen chrome-legged tables and fake leather chairs filled the former, racks of the supposed staples of modern life—chips, soda, cereal, toilet paper, and laundry soap—the latter.

I pulled into a parking spot across the street from the liquor store at the other end of the block. The lights were still on there as they were at the pizza place and the grocery. The rest of the street was dark. Enough parked cars to give me cover. It had been snowing heavily when I left LaGuardia, but the storm hadn't moved this far north yet, a good thing for me. A chilly, dark night, cloud covered sky, no moon. Also all to the good for my purposes. The snow was coming, though. I could feel it.

I sat in the dark for fifteen minutes. Two cars and a police cruiser passed. None paid me any attention. No pedestrians. I could see the guy behind the counter in the liquor store reading the paper, marking time until closing.

No light or sign of life from the second floor. At 8:55, he stood and folded the paper. A few minutes later the lights went off. A minute after that, he came out, and turned to lock the door behind him. He walked down the block until he came to a Honda showing more than a few years of age, unlocked the door, climbed in and drove away. The grocery store closed a few minutes later. The pizza joint was the only life left, maybe still hoping to sell a pie or two to the kids from Gibbet School. Or it didn't know it was done for the night but was holding true to its hours.

Gina said Irina came last night at 9:50, the others around the same time the night before. After dinner, after study hall, after they were supposed to be tucked in for the night. No way of telling whether anyone would show up tonight, but if they did, I doubted they'd come any earlier. I made sure the dome light was off, checked the rearview mirror, and pushed open the door. A gust of damp wind cut through my flannel pants. I locked the door quickly in case the guy in the pizza joint—or anyone else—was paying attention, trotted across the street, and took shelter in the shadows. I walked down the block, sticking close to the dark building, all but invisible, I figured, turned the corner and went around back. A parking lot of mostly broken pavement. A couple of Dumpsters backed up on train tracks that hadn't been used in years. Like Gina said, a single bulb shone over a doorway at one end of the building. An iron fire escape dropped from the second floor at the other. The windows were all dark. A rat scrambled across the lot, coming straight at me, until it veered off and found protection under one of the Dumpsters. Supper time.

I returned to the Valdez and its heater, mildly regretting not buying a pint of vodka before the liquor store closed. Never a good idea to drink on duty, but who knew how long I had to wait. The Boston public radio station played a recording of Shostakovich's preludes and fugues. I knew the record—the pianist, Tatiana Nikolayeva, supposedly had inspired the pieces. You don't hear it often. I sat in the dark, marveling at Shostakovich's ability to write a series of works in which not one, but two, beautiful songs played off each other, point and counterpoint, with absolute harmonic perfection in every note. Bach had done it three hundred years earlier, of course, but for my money, Shostakovich had raised the bar. Bach would argue that Shostakovich cheated—he employed dissonance.

Shostakovich had morphed to Mozart just after 10:00 when a pair of headlights turned into Main Street from the direction I faced. I slid down behind the wheel as a dark colored 3 Series BMW came straight toward me until it swung off into the parking lot behind the liquor store. I waited until the lights were out of sight and ran to the alley at the other end of the building, not worrying this time about who might see me. I reached the back in time to see a young woman, tall and blond, unlock the door below the lightbulb and go inside.

I walked back to the train tracks, looking up, waiting for a light to go on. Nothing.

No light on the Main Street side either. I returned to the parking lot. Still dark. As Gina said, they had the windows blacked out.

I was heading back to move the Valdez when more headlights swung into the lot. They belonged to a black Cadillac Escalade, which looked a lot like the black Cadillac Escalade I'd last seen in Long Island City. I followed the rat to the Dumpsters, ducking behind before the SUV's lights swept across. Then they were gone. I peeked out to see the taillights turn left onto Main Street. I stayed where I was.

Two minutes . . . Three . . . Four . . .

Fifteen before the headlights announced the Escalade's return. I didn't move.

This time, the driver did one revolution of the parking lot, pulled up next to a rundown concrete structure that had once been part of the rail yard and maybe still was. The same spot I'd been thinking to park the Valdez. I couldn't see the driver but any doubt was erased by the New York plates.

I waited a cold half hour, checking my watch while I shivered, to see if Nosferatu would get out of the car. Three brief flashes of light from the cab indicated he hadn't kicked his smoking habit. When I was convinced that he was waiting, as I was, I crossed the tracks, bent low until I was shielded by buildings on the other side. I took a circuitous route back to the Valdez. Gambling, I moved it, lights off, to the rail yard behind the parking lot, next to a building where it was all but hidden but still had a distant view of the Escalade and the lighted door beyond.

That's where I spent the night.

★ CHAPTER 31 ★

Dawn would've just been lighting the sky, had there been any sky to light, when they came out. Snow had fallen hard all night, starting about the time I moved the car. Six inches or more now on the ground. I'd been dozing on and off, but you learn to keep one eye half awake. Foos had called a little after 2:00 A.M.

"Weird shit. BEC's back online."

"You sure?"

"I'm calling at two a.m."

"What's going on?"

"Could be anything. Technical difficulties. Somebody—maybe Andras, like you suggest—screwing around inside, but they fixed the problem."

"Could Andras do this?"

"Technically feasible. There's still the question of why."

"I'll tell you this. I'm sitting outside some kind of crash pad he's got in the next town to his school. I'm pretty sure he's inside. I know the Russian girl is. Guess who else is watching the place?"

"He suck blood?"

"Not mine, I hope."

"You got a plan?"

"Not beyond figuring out what's going on. And keeping Nosferatu away from the kids, if I have to."

"I'll hang here. Let me know if you need anything."

When the door opened, Irina and Andras stopped under the naked bulb just long enough for me to get a look, before they hustled through the snow to her car. Neither looked around nor looked worried. Neither appeared sleepy either. Irina took the driver's seat, and the BMW backed out and pulled away. I waited for the Escalade to follow, but it didn't. The BMW pulled into Main Street and disappeared. I couldn't follow. I couldn't move without being spotted.

Wait . . . and wait some more. Five minutes before the Escalade's doors opened, and the tall man's head rose above the car. He wore a broad-brimmed hat and the same overcoat I remembered from Second Avenue. He removed something from the back of the SUV and walked toward the building. A short man got out of the passenger side and followed. He wore an overcoat, no hat, and had a large messenger bag strung over his shoulder. With a quick glance around, Nosferatu used a crowbar to pull down the fire escape ladder. He and Shorty climbed to the second floor, and Nosferatu spent a quick minute fiddling at the window. Then he pushed it up, and they climbed inside.

I flipped another mental coin. On the assumption Nosferatu's attention was now focused inside the building, I put the Valdez in gear and drove as fast as I dared toward Gibbet. The road was a mess. The plows hadn't reached it yet, and the Valdez made its own free-form progress. No other cars, the only reason I didn't hit any, but we came close to the ditch three times. When not pumping the breaks and spinning the wheel, I told myself Andras and Irina couldn't be going much faster, but they had a big head start. The single set of tire tracks ahead of me made generally straight progress, an indication they were taking it easy or the Bimmer had all-wheel drive. The tire tracks turned into Martin Lane. They stopped at the door of the barn.

I left the Valdez by the main road and followed footprints. At the back of the barn, I was just able to reach the sill of a high window. I pulled myself up. The glass was dirty, the interior dark, but parked inside was a 3 Series BMW.

I dropped to the ground and ran along a well-traveled path through earlier snows across the corner of a field toward the woods. The footing got more treacherous in the trees but I kept up a good pace until I emerged, a quarter mile later, at one end of a Gibbet School soccer field. The footprints led around the goal toward the school's buildings. A hundred yards in the distance, through the screen of falling snow, I could make out Andras and Irina walking quickly, heads down. Just a couple of prep school kids returning to campus at the crack of dawn.

I retreated to the woods and ran for the Valdez.

The Escalade was still in the parking lot. I parked in the same spot and slid down in the seat.

I'd been gone a half hour and sat another forty-seven minutes before Nosferatu and the short man came out the front door. They walked straight to the SUV without looking around. Nosferatu carried a backpack by one strap. Shorty still had his messenger bag. They climbed in and drove off. When he got to Main Street, Nosferatu turned right, away from the road to Gibbet, but that didn't mean anything.

Daylight was still trying to gain traction, the snow fell thickly. A good time not to be seen. I got a screwdriver, flashlight, and crowbar from the trunk—the same tools Nosferatu had used. I hooked the fire escape ladder with the crowbar, as he had done. The ungreased iron creaked, but the snow muffled the noise. I didn't wait or look around but climbed the rungs to the platform and took the stairs above two at a time. An old-fashioned wood-framed, double-hung window with a half-moon lock and plenty of give. I slipped the screwdriver through the crease and pushed the lock around. The lower window opened easily. A blanket inside hung from ceiling to floor. I stepped in, closed the window, and listened.

Silence. I waited a minute to be sure. The place felt empty. I pulled the hanging blanket aside.

Pitch black. My flashlight fought darkness down a long hall that ran the length of the building. Eight or ten doors on either side. I stayed where I was for another minute before I tried the door on my left. It opened with the squeak of old hinges. A small, empty room. Cobwebs and dust illuminated by the flashlight beam. Another blanket hung from the ceiling against the far wall, a window behind it. I closed the door and tried the next one. Empty room, the same size, blanket over the window. Same story in the two rooms across and the two on each side after that. Sixteen rooms in all. Two bathrooms faced each other mid-hall. One had two grimy toilets, two dirty sinks and a shower that hadn't been used in years. The fixtures in the other were new and relatively clean.

The place had been a flophouse, cheap rooms for rent by the night, week, or month. At some point, business had dried up or the town fathers decided this wasn't the kind of operation they wanted on Main Street. Probably vacant for years before the kids took it over.

The room near the new bathroom had been converted into an outsized closet. A half-dozen hanging racks on wheels, holding vintage costumes for men and women with an emphasis on undergarments and nightclothes. Across the hall was a dressing room. Three tables with mirrors, two full-length mirrors on the wall, lots of makeup and wigs. The drawers of two bureaus held a selection of sex toys as well as handcuffs, riding crops, chains, boots, chaps, ropes, masks, and nylons. The room next to that was furnished to look like a bedroom, but it was more a bedroom set, with a video camera on a tripod in the corner. The Sheetrock walls were scratched and marked, roughly used. A double bed against one wall, unmade. A beat up wing chair against another. A desk in front of the third, next to a blanketed window. Laptop on the desk, cable running to the camera in the corner. The camera was positioned to take in both the chair and the bed.

Three more rooms were set up in similar fashion—bed, chair, desk, computer, camera. Two of the beds were four-posters. A studio for multiple productions, all going on at the same time. At the end of the hall was an open area with a counter and three doors. One door was closet-size. A hanging blanket covered the second with stairs behind, descending to the outside. A rack of hooks by the third, labeled 1 to 16, confirmed this was indeed an old flophouse. Inside, an office with a desk, sofa, table and chairs, a computer on the desk next to a rack of servers. One more blanket over the window. I pulled it back to check the parking lot. Empty except for falling snow.

The table was littered with a pizza box, beer and soda cans, and a full ashtray. Stale smoke hung in the air. I pushed the butts around with the tip of my screwdriver. Tobacco and marijuana.

The computer was asleep. I hit a key and it came to life. A Web browser contained the home page of WildeTimePlayers.com. Oscar Wilde himself stared out from the screen with long hair and Victorian frock coat, his arms outstretched, holding a collage of photographs showing bodies, no faces, in various stages of undress. None were outright naked, none were overtly pornographic. None looked to be over eighteen either.

A menu bar gave me multiple options—SIGN IN, REGISTER, PERFORMANCE SCHEDULE, MEET THE PLAYERS, PAST PRODUCTIONS, MY ACCOUNT. Just like Amazon or Netflix. I clicked on MEET THE PLAYERS and a dialogue window popped up—PLEASE SIGN IN. I clicked on SIGN IN and was asked for a user name and password. I clicked on REGISTER and was asked to designate a user name and password and pay a fee of five hundred dollars. To do that I had to establish an account at ConnectPay.

I tried the HISTORY bar. Someone had been working the pages. The clock in the corner said 8:06 A.M. I called the office on my cell phone, hoping Foos was true to his word. Six rings before he answered. His voice was grumpy.

"This better be good."

"It's not. Bad, getting worse. I need a keyboarding bug—pronto. I'm sending you an e-mail."

"That it?"

"We need to check out a Web site. We're going to want zombies and a straw man."

"That bad?"

"Worse, like I say."

"Give me a minute to hook up a zombie. I'll send the e-mail back through that."

I opened the e-mail program and sent a blank message to pigpensboss@ pigpensplace.com. A minute later, I got a reply. I clicked on the attachment, which launched itself, installed itself and disappeared. A second later my e-mail and the reply self-evaporated as well.

"Done," I said. "Straw man?"

"How much we need?"

"Five hundred to open. Don't know after that. Figure a couple grand."

"Hold on. I'm sending you a parallel screen app. Click on the attachment and you'll see what I'm doing."

"Great. Get rid of it when we're finished."

"Why is it you constantly assume you're dealing with Homer Simpson?"

I ignored the rebuff—not undeserved—and clicked on his e-mail.

The financial history of one Malcolm Carver appeared on the screen. He had checking and savings accounts at Citibank with balances of $2,315 and $3,356, respectively. He also had a Citi Visa debit card and an American Express gold card. His address was in Bethpage, New York.

"He'll do," I said.

"I've got zombies lined up in Hungary, Italy, and Indonesia. That enough?"

"Should be sufficient. Address is WildeTimePlayers.com. Wilde with an 'e', as in Oscar."

The zombies were an extra precaution. I doubted the Crestview cops had the technology to monitor online activity, but Victoria and the FBI could be monitoring ConnectPay. I don't know much about the laws governing child pornography, but I assumed we were about to break a few.

Foos typed in the address. The home page of WildeTimePlayers appeared on the parallel screen I was watching.

"I see," he said.

"It'll get worse. Malcolm has to register. That triggers the five bills."

He did as instructed, creating a username, MalMalware@yahoo.com, and opening an account for Malcolm Carver at ConnectPay tied to his Citi debit card. By this afternoon, his account would be five hundred dollars lighter.

"Now what?" he asked.

"Try MEET THE PLAYERS."

A new screen appeared with photos of Andras Leitz, Irina Lishina, and three others, dressed—or more accurately, mostly undressed—in the vintage costumes I'd seen down the hall. There was no attempt to hide the essentials here. Andras wore pantaloons dropped around his knees and a codpiece pulled up to his stomach, exposing his genitals. His penis was partly erect. Irina's breasts showed clearly through a sheer camisole, the hem well above her shaved crotch. The other kids were similarly exposed. Below each was a name—Salomé, Dorian, Algernon, Basil, and Sybil.

I could almost see Foos shaking his gray-black mane. "Shit, that's Andras."

"Afraid so."

"You know the others?"

"The girl in the see-through is the Russian. I'm guessing the others are kids at Gibbet School."

He grunted. "The names are all Oscar Wilde characters, right? Not that it matters."

"They're not Dostoevsky."

"You want to see more?"

"No. But we need to know how bad this is."

"We do?"

"I do. Sorry you're along for the ride."

He grunted again.

"Click on one of the other kids. Keep it as anonymous as possible."

"Oh, that makes it much better."

Fifteen minutes later we had a complete picture of the Web site and the WildeTimePlayers' operation—or as complete as we wanted to get. The Players offered an à la carte menu of content, charging different rates for photos, videos, and "private auditions." The photos and videos, which set Malcolm Carver back another three hundred dollars for a quick and perfunctory survey, came in solo, duo—boy-girl, boy-boy, girl-girl—and three-way packages. Not much, as in nothing, was left to the imagination. No private auditions available at the moment—they were strictly live and priced accordingly.

Foos said, "I need coffee. Back in a few."

I got up from the computer and checked the window. Still snowing, no action in the parking lot. Growing up in the Gulag, I saw more than my share of depravity. Starvation. Murder. Exploitation. Rape. The worst was babies turning on their mothers, pounding their chest with fists too tiny to hurt, because the mothers were too emaciated to feed them. Forty years later, they still haunt the occasional nightmare. As a spy, I was taught to prey on human weakness—psychological, emotional, sexual, professional, financial.

I don't harbor many illusions, the world is an ugly place, and I can't say I felt any particular shock or outrage at what we'd seen. But in a place I didn't want to be, couldn't wait to get out of, in the middle of a northeast blizzard, I tried to fight off a profound depression. It wasn't just the sleaze. Porn by definition involves exploitation. These kids, who had everything, were exploiting themselves, or each other, or both. They wrapped their brand with an ersatz Victorian theatrical veneer and convinced themselves that somehow this made it all okay—a good or productive or funny way to spend their time. For what? The money? That explanation still didn't work, and I couldn't see one that did. I'd dealt with lots of twisted people with fucked-up motives, but it was beyond my ability to imagine where and how these kids had gone so far off the rails. I don't know how much depravity Foos encountered as a California-raised child genius, but he's one levelheaded dude, as they say these days. Even across the ether, I could feel the Web site sucking his energy.

I returned to the computer.

"You back?"

"Yeah."

He said, "You think Leitz has any idea?"

"Nope."

"You gonna tell him?"

"That's one of many questions I can't deal with right now. I gotta get out of here."

"I'll clean up the electronic trail."

"Check something first—recent activity on these servers, between seven and eight this morning."

"Hang on."

The screen in front of me filled with lines of computer code, which scrolled, flashed, disappeared, flashed and scrolled again.

Foos said, "Somebody spent the better part of an hour looking for outgoing activity. They found it and copied it."

"Can you tell what it is?"

"It'll take a while."

"Do it. I'll call once I get out of here."

"On it."

I put the computer to sleep, wiped off any surfaces I'd touched, pulled the hanging blanket in the reception area aside, took a final look around and started down the stairs.

If I'd come in the front door, I would have missed it. A strand of monofilament stretched across the stairwell, third step from the bottom, ankle level. It shone with the dancing dust against the light outside the door. Coming in the other way, no light behind . . .

My flashlight beam tracked the strand through a staple in the wall back up the stairs.

Scanning each step, I reclimbed the stairs. Another strand of monofilament across the second from the top, in case whoever came in missed the first one. I'd chanced to step over it on the way down. I stepped over it again back to the lobby and followed both strands to the closet. They ran under the door. I reached for the knob and stopped.

Options. I was looking at an obvious booby-trap, Nosferatu the trapper. He could have rigged the closet door as well. But he expected whoever came up the stairs to trip the string. Still . . .

I took out my phone and called Foos.

"Update. Activate the zombies and download everything you can from the WildeTime servers."

"You okay?"

"Yeah, but Nosferatu's wired this place to blow. I'm now a one-man bomb squad, so if I don't call back . . ."

"Pig Pen will mourn."

"He's in my will. How long you need for the downloading?"

"Wait a minute."

"Waiting may not be a good idea here."

"Right. Lots of data. Terabytes. Few hours minimum."

"I'll buy you as much time as possible."

"Keep me posted."

"If I can."

I went back through the space, carefully this time, opening every door, looking in every corner. Every hair on my back stood straight up—all telling me to get out while I could. I tried not to listen.

I found four wastebaskets in four bedroom closets, all filled with gasoline. The fifth closet held the kind of five-gallon can you get at any gas station. It was half full.

Nosferatu had improvised. He'd set the trap to kill the next person who entered, presumably one of the kids, then burn the place to the ground. Why? Time enough to worry about that later—or so I hoped.

I moved the five-gallon can to the working bathroom. I filled it from one of the trash cans and carried it out to the Valdez, careful to avoid both tripwires, and poured the contents into the tank. A messy operation, environmentally

226

incorrect, but nobody would die. Two more can-fulls, two more trips to the car. One more survey of the space. No more improvised Molotov cocktails. Still the closet door to deal with.

I called Foos.

"How much more time you need?"

"Lotta dense shit. Three hours, maybe four."

"I've got one more thing to do here. Might be the last thing. If you don't hear from me there's a reason."

"Pig Pen . . ."

"I know . . ."

I went back to the closet door, the tripwires running underneath. Inside, almost certainly, was another container of gas connected to some kid of trigger. Question was, had Nosferatu triggered the door as well. I put the odds at eighty–twenty against. One in five. Not as good as Russian roulette, one in six. On the plus side, there was no reason for it. On the down side, he'd gone to a lot of trouble to make sure that he set off an inferno.

Foos needed three hours plus. If I called the cops, he wouldn't get them. If I opened the door, and bet wrong, he wouldn't get them either.

I grabbed the knob and pulled.

Nothing.

I leaned against the jam and exhaled.

Inside was another wastebasket. Next to it a mousetrap, the monofilament tied to the spring. Tin foil wrapping both ends and a cable running to a plug in the wall. Someone coming in trips the wire on the stairs, flips the trap, closes the circuit and . . .

Boom.

Nice guy, Nosferatu.

I pulled the plug. Breathing normally for the first time in an hour, I carried the last can of gas to the Valdez and dumped it in.

I called Foos again.

"I still need time," he said.

"Take it. I've cleaned out the bombs. I'm going to get the kids. Call Leitz. Tell him I want Andras in the headmaster's office—now. I need his okay to take him with me. If he argues, tell him I don't want his blood on my hands."

"Should I tell him about Crestview?"

"Only if you have to. This is life and death for his kid—thanks to his kid—and his best chance for life is with me."

"Lucky you."

"Remember who got me into this?"

★ CHAPTER 32 ★

It was still snowing as I drove back to Gibbet School, but the road had been plowed and sanded. I stopped in the driveway outside the administration building and called Batkin.

"I was wondering when I would hear from you," he said.

"You're not going to be happy that you did. I have no time to explain what's going on, but none of it's good for your stepdaughter. That's her fault, I'm afraid. Seems she's been pursuing the Internet's oldest profession."

"What the hell is that supposed to mean?"

"She and some friends have been running an online pornography ring— with themselves as producers, directors and, I'm afraid, stars."

I waited for the intake of breath, and I got it.

"Are you certain Irina's involved?"

"Let's just say I've seen a lot more of her than I was looking for."

A pause while he processed what I said. I was pretty sure where he'd go, and I was right.

"Do you know . . . ? Who's responsible? Who got her into this?"

"Don't know if anyone did. I think she and some pals were doing this on their own."

"Is the Leitz kid involved?"

"I'm not saying who was involved. She's got worse problems. I just left their production studio. It's in the town next to Gibbet. It was booby-trapped to blow sky high. Irina could easily have been the one to set off the explosion."

"What the hell? Who . . . ?"

"How about a tall, ugly man, Belarusian, six-seven, pockmarked face, buckteeth, superhuman strength?"

Another intake of breath.

"Karp is here?"

"If that's his name, yes."

"I may have underestimated my old friend Efim Ilyich. You've met Karp, I take it?"

"Once."

"I'm impressed. Not many survive the experience."

"It was touch and go. He have a full name?"

"Karp is the only one I know. Konychev's muscle. A man without a heart."

"I can attest to that."

"What did he want with you?"

"Tell me to mind my own business."

"Were you interfering in his?"

"Not intentionally."

"That wouldn't make any difference to Karp. He was a *zek* who became a guard who became the right hand of the camp commander. Gorlag, after my time. They say he likes young boys and blood, not necessarily in that order. He has quite a track record on both counts. You should watch your step."

I didn't point out the irony of his advice. "I intend to. I need to get your stepdaughter out of town. When he finds out his trap didn't blow, I don't know his next move."

"What do you want from me?"

"Help with the school. I need them to release the girl to me."

"I understand. Where are you?'

"On the campus."

"I'll call the headmaster. You'll bring Irina home?"

"If that's what you want."

"As soon as you can."

I presented myself to the headmaster's secretary—a sharp-faced woman of a certain age and dress, who looked me all over and didn't hide the distaste at what she saw. Not entirely her fault—a night in the car and a morning spent transferring petroleum products out of a flop house porn den didn't leave me presenting my best.

"I'm afraid Dr. Paine is extremely busy, booked all day. Perhaps tomorrow . . ."

"Tell Dr. Paine to squeeze me in. He has my name from two of your parents, Sebastian Leitz and Taras Batkin."

She frowned at the tone and the name-dropping. No way, in her universe, I should know such people.

"As I said . . ."

"Tell him I'm waiting. Now, please." I put my best Cheka authority, meant to convey inevitability, into my voice. "If you don't, I will."

She managed to get up and go into the office behind without spitting.

She came back a half minute later.

"Dr. Paine will—"

A man with shoe-polish brown hair that looked dyed, four to five inches shorter than my six feet, bustled out the door right behind her.

"Mr. Vlost, Philip Paine, pleased to meet you. My apologies if you've been delayed. This is all . . . very irregular. Please, come in."

He extended a hand and gave me a limp handshake. He wore round tortoiseshell glasses, a Harris Tweed jacket, striped tie, gray flannel trousers, and penny loafers—with pennies. I followed him into his office. The dragon secretary retreated to her perch, still looking for a spittoon.

Paine circled his outsize mahogany desk and pointed me to a seat across.

"How can I help?"

I stayed standing.

"I'm here for Andras Leitz and Irina Lishina."

"Yes. Dr. Leitz and Ambassador Batkin called. But, as I'm sure you can appreciate, we have rules, procedures, responsibilities. Not to mention classes to teach. I can't just release . . . I need to know . . ."

"What do you need to know?"

"I need . . . Why do Andras and Irina have to leave school? Clearly there's some sort of issue. Dr. Leitz and Ambassador Batkin were vague as to its nature. There may be other students involved. There may be issues that affect the school. We need to make sure . . . Perhaps you could . . ."

Philip Paine gave every indication of being an insecure man, hiding behind the stature he presumed his office held. A midlevel private school apparatchik who had somehow risen to Politburo power and understood he'd climbed above his station. He was past uncomfortable, not yet panicked, but headed that way. On a better day, I might have worked him with more subtlety.

Today I said, "The issue is this: I'm here to pick up Andras and Irina. They're in danger. Their parents have told you to expect me. What are we waiting for?"

Paine wrung his hands and tried once more. "I'm sorry. But here at Gibbet, we don't just release our students into the care of people . . . when we don't know. . . . We have responsibilities. In loco parentis . . ."

No matter what the system, there's always some bureaucrat trying to protect his turf. The Communist Party member responsible for overseeing his part of a five-year plan somewhere in the Urals. Philip Paine at Gibbet School. The motivations were the same. Behind them was fear of making a mistake and the loss of position and the privileges that could follow. Paine was frozen in inaction.

I took out my phone and hit redial. Batkin answered on the first ring.

"Turbo. I'm encountering resistance."

"What kind of resistance?"

"Headmaster."

"I'll take care of it."

Paine looked pained. The dragon put her head through the door. She wanted to breathe fire, but none would come.

"Ambassador Batkin on line one."

Paine gulped and picked up the phone. While they talked, I dialed Leitz.

"Foos called," he said. "What the hell is going on?"

"No time for that. I'm at Gibbet. Nosferatu's here. I'm trying to get Andras out of town. I'm getting a hard time from the headmaster."

"His name says everything you need to know about him. I'll call right now."

"He's waiting to hear from you."

I pocketed the phone and took the offered seat.

Paine hung up from Batkin, looking like the apparatchik who's just been told he's won a one-way trip to the Gulag.

Dragon-lady opened the door. "Dr. Leitz on line two."

I crossed my legs and nodded at Paine.

"Looks like I'm holding two kings. You?"

It took eight hours to get back to New York. Snow fell for most of the trip. Cars spun out left and right. I kept a steady pace around thirty and tried to maintain as much distance as I could from other vehicles.

The kids were quiet in the backseat. They'd come to Paine's office, when finally summoned, sullen and nervous. At least Andras was. Irina was impossible to read. Andras wore a sweater over corduroys, like his father. Irina had a turtleneck under her ski jacket and dark jeans. The presence I'd noted in our phone conversation was evident in person. Some Russian women have it, even at a young age, as if she had the world exactly where she wanted it, in the palm of her hand—current circumstances not withstanding. Neither kid's demeanor improved when informed they were riding back to New York with me.

I introduced myself without explanation and let them stew across Massachusetts until we got on I-84 into Connecticut.

"I've been in the playhouse," I said.

That got no response. I watched through the rearview mirror, and I think they glanced at each other, but they said nothing.

"I'm not going to ask what you thought you were doing, but I am curious about one thing. When you left this morning, a tall man, ugly SOB, spent an hour in there. He'd been watching the place all night. He left behind enough gasoline to blow your little studio to Timbuktu, and he rigged it so the next visitor—maybe one of you—would set it off. Boom, good-bye. How come?"

That got their attention. Andras went wide-eyed and looked at Irina, who slid down in her seat and tried to disappear—not so much from me, I thought, but from him.

"You said—"

She cut him off. "Shut up. Not now."

"Karp," I said. "That's the tall man's name, I'm told. You know him, Irina?"

Her eyes shot fire into the rearview mirror.

"Who's Karp?" Andras asked.

"SHUT UP!" Irina shouted.

Andras turned away, chastened.

The dynamics of their relationship became clearer. More Cheka training—when an opening presents itself, drive a wedge through it.

"Karp's a professional assassin, Andras. A man who enjoys hurting people. I know that from personal experience. He works for Irina's uncle."

Burn one bridge to build another. Irina had the same look my ex-wife used to get before she flew into a rage in the last days of our disintegrating marriage. Andras's eyes got wider.

"Assassin?!"

"Shut up!"

"What'd you guys do to piss Karp off?" I said.

"We didn't do . . ." Andras whispered.

"Andras, if you say one more fucking word, I'll never speak to you again."

He looked away.

"Karp's still after both of you," I said. "Think about that. We have a long drive home."

I took another shot on the stretch between Hartford and Waterbury. I'd stopped at an exit that featured an array of fast-food options, chose Burger King for no reason other than it was open and empty, waited for the kids to use the bathrooms, passed up the opportunity to do so myself, for fear I'd be solo when I came out, and asked if they wanted anything to eat. They bought Whoppers and fries and Cokes. I passed on that opportunity too. Fast food is one American invention that holds little appeal, and hunger is one more thing Russians learn to deal with from an early age, especially in the Gulag. Standing behind them at the counter, in the bright fluorescent light, I noticed a rough, red, scar peeking out the top of Irina's turtleneck, marring the otherwise fine skin. I hadn't seen that before, I was pretty sure, and I'd seen a lot of Irina last night.

"So, who'd you guys clip for that eight mil?" I asked as we pulled back on the highway and they unwrapped their meals.

"We have nothing to say, Chekist Pig," Irina responded before biting into her Whopper. Andras looked at her, clearly uncomfortable, then caught my eye in the rearview mirror. He held his burger in his lap and said nothing.

"The way I figure it," I went on, as if discussing a movie or last night's ball game, "the seven mil each of you guys has—all those transfers from State Street—are your WildeTime profits. Nice work if you want to do it. But the three mil in November and five in December, that puzzled me—for a while. You might have gotten away with it if you'd only hit them once. But the second time—Thanksgiving vacation, right?—you got their attention. Karp put a tap on your old man's system, Andras. They had a good look around. You didn't cover your tracks quite well enough and now you've got Karp on your tail. He got Uncle Walter to help, by the way, with your father's computers. Which reminds me, did you see him on Wednesday?"

His eyes grew wider than ever. "I didn't . . . ," he started to whisper.

"ANDRAS! Remember what we promised."

He gulped, took a bite of his burger, and studied his knees.

"You didn't what? See him?"

He kept his face down. Irina watched him and watched me. She was on high alert.

"I think you saw him. He tell you he was in jail? Child rape, Andras. Your uncle has a serious problem. But maybe you already knew that."

He started to shake, head still down. Irina put a hand on his shoulder while she kept her eyes on me in the mirror.

"Haven't you said enough, Cheka Pig?"

I ignored her. "That why you wanted to disappear so bad, Andras. You hit half the ATMs in Queens after you left your uncle."

He was still shaking. Irina had acquired a more thoughtful look, and it occurred to me I'd just told her more than I should have. It was also clear I wasn't going to break her hold without a sharper weapon, and probably not so long as she was present to protect her interests. With nothing better to do for another three hours, I kept at it anyway.

"You know who you've gone up against, don't you, Andras? I'm sure Irina's told you all about them. They run in her family. All the way through it. Baltic Enterprise Commission—same outfit that probably hosted your WildeTime Web site. Same people that have Uncle Walter by the you-know-whats. They own him and they own ConnectPay. You do know that, right?"

"Shut up, Pig!"

"Maybe Irina was a little short on the details. I can understand that. Her uncle started the BEC. Her father's a partner. Her stepfather's another. Maybe she has her hand in the honey pot too. How 'bout it, Irina?"

"Fuck you."

"Thing is, Andras, you screw around with people like that, they don't care who you are, who you know, who you're sleeping with. You rip them off, they want restitution—and blood. Not necessarily in that order. They need blood to tell the next guy not to try. That's why Karp is here. That's why he's after you. Both of you. You put up a good act, Irina, but he'll break your neck as easily as he breaks your boyfriend's."

It could have been my imagination, but Irina chewed more thoughtfully. Maybe I'd really penetrated her tough-girl Russian veneer this time. Andras wasn't chewing at all. He just stared straight ahead, out the windshield, alone in his thoughts. I had the idea that, as troubling as those were, they were probably safer than anywhere else he could be.

Around Danbury, it stopped snowing. The kids slept, Andras leaning against the door, Irina's head on his shoulder. Foos called to announce he'd finished the transfer.

"Worse than we thought," he said. "Kid's in this deep."

"How deep?"

"Wrong people catch him, they'll bury him alive."

I kept one eye on the rearview mirror. No movement. "You mean the same people as this morning?"

"Uh-huh."

"They know what you know?"

"Yep. Where are you?"

"Danbury. Slow going."

"I'll be here."

I pushed up the speed to forty-five and called Victoria.

"You okay?" she asked.

"That's a relative question, but yes, I'm alive and functioning."

"Don't be cute. Where are you?"

"I-Eighty-four, an hour from New York on a good day, probably two tonight."

"I-Eighty-four? What the hell are you doing on the road?"

"Snow's stopped."

"You know what I mean. Pull off, find a motel."

A car ahead of me went into a skid. The phone fell to my lap as I braked gently and moved lanes. The sliding vehicle swiped the snow covered guardrail as I passed.

"Turbo?! You there?!" Victoria called.

"Sorry. Car ahead just spun out."

"Can you hear yourself talking? You're no good to anyone dead, least of all me."

"The sweetness of your sentiment is all I need to bear me back to town."

"Christ! You are the most stubborn—"

"National trait. Only foreign invaders are defeated by snow. Have I told you how snow and Russian stubbornness turned the tide of the Great Patriotic War?"

"Save the propaganda and focus on the road. What happened in Crestview? Foos said you'd encountered difficulties, but everything's okay now."

"Foos exaggerated—about okay. I've got the Leitz kid and the Russian girl in the backseat. We've got Nosferatu on our tail, maybe. They've got him on their tail, certainly. Neither of them will tell me what's going on, I was up all night last night, and this is a long trip. So I'm in a bad mood. But I'll be back in your arms in a few hours."

"There's something you need to know."

"I'm listening."

"I'm breaking rules telling you."

"I understand."

"Alexander Lishin."

Uh-oh. "The backseat, remember."

"That's why you need to know. He's dead."

I checked the mirror. All still.

"Where? When?"

"He was found in the Moscova River fifty miles outside Moscow. Apparently there was a thaw and he bubbled up through some thin ice. The CPS got there first. They've got a tight lid on. He's been dead several weeks."

I looked in the mirror again. Irina hadn't moved, still sleeping soundly or giving a good performance of same. Did she know?

"Cause?"

"Run through with a fireplace poker and the body dumped. The poker broke through the ice. He'd been tortured about eight different ways before he hit the water."

"Thanks. I understand everything you mean. We'll talk about it when I get there."

"You coming home?"

"I've got to drop off the kids. Then a stop to make. Then probably the office."

"A stop? What kind of stop?"

"I'll tell you when I see you."

"How'd I know that's what you were going to say? I'll be waiting."

I spent the last ninety minutes of the drive thinking about Victoria's news and whether Irina had any idea and what it meant. I came up empty on all fronts. I would've given a bottle of vodka for a laptop and the ability to read what Ivanov had to say. Victoria said the CPS put a lid on. I was willing to bet the Valdez—and the Potemkin—that Ivanov had the story.

The kids came to life as we crossed the Willis Avenue Bridge into Manhattan. The streets were quiet and empty. We got to Irina's house first, which would give me a few minutes with Andras. She anticipated that and whispered something about "remembering our promise" before she kissed him on the cheek and got out of the car. Her stepfather opened the door when I rang. He tried to greet her, but she brushed past without a word. He looked at me, the blue-gray eyes cold but sad.

"Would you like to come in? Drink? You've had a long drive."

I could see he had a hundred questions. What parent wouldn't? I wanted out of there before he started asking.

"No, thanks. I've got another delivery to make."

He hesitated, ever so slightly. He wasn't used to being turned down, but he sensed it was better not to push. "We'll talk tomorrow. I'll call in the morning."

No question about it being first thing. That would be enough time for me.

Andras avoided mirror eye contact as I drove slowly down Park Avenue. We had the street to ourselves, a good thing since it was slushy and slippery.

"So what's the deal between you two," I asked in my best friendly, conversational tone. "She your girlfriend? You going out?"

He didn't answer, didn't even look up. I wanted to tell him that I knew girls like her, that I'd married one of them and been where this led, and he didn't want any part of it. He wasn't going to listen.

"What I said back there on the highway, about the Baltic Enterprise Commission? That's all true. If you've ripped them off, they will not rest until they catch you. I've seen Karp—the tall man, the assassin—at your father's office, at your uncle Walter's building, and at your place in Crestview. He knows who you are, Andras. He knows who she is too. Her stepfather may be able to pull some strings on her behalf, but I very much doubt he'll pull any for you. And that doesn't mean they still won't use her—hurt her—to get to you. Seventeen's pretty young to start living underground. If you tell me what's going on, maybe I can help figure a way out. That's what I'm going to tell your dad, but I'm making you the offer first. I don't want anything in return, but you do have to tell me the truth."

He didn't respond, he just looked around the car, as if examining for the first time where he'd spent the last eight hours. I caught his eye in the mirror and held it. He leaned forward, and I slowed to a crawl, ready to stop altogether. There was a moment when I thought he might open up, but it passed. He fell back in the seat and buried his head in his hands.

He was honoring his promise to Irina. It occurred to me that he just might be more scared of her than Karp.

Leitz himself came to the door, like Batkin. The greeting here was warmer. He hugged his son, and Andras hugged back—with what appeared to be obvious affection. Maybe he was just glad to be rid of me. The kid went inside and Leitz shook my hand.

"It seems I am continually in your debt."

"You might not think so when you hear the whole story."

"How bad is it?"

"I don't know it all yet, but I'm not exaggerating when I say life and death. I think he's used his computer skills to rip off the people who bugged your network—the Baltic Enterprise Commission. That's why they did it, by the way, they were after him, they were never interested in your TV deal. The fake lawyers interviewing your brother and sisters, maybe even Alyona's involvement—they were all part of the effort to find out who was stealing from them."

"Andras? Stealing? Baltic Enterprise Commission? He's a boy, a school kid!"

"I don't know how to tell you this. He's a school kid with eleven million dollars in a dozen different bank accounts. He and Irina and a couple of others are running their own criminal enterprise. A pornography operation—in which they produce, direct, and star. This isn't conjecture. I've seen the whole thing. I can document the bank transfers."

Leitz shook his head back and forth, eyes wide, mouth suspended in a circle. I'd hit him hard, perhaps harder than I should have, but I was feeling the impact of the last twenty-four hours. He tried a couple of times to collect his wits and speak but the wits weren't cooperating.

"There's more," I said. I told him about Nosferatu and the explosives. "Talk to your son. Maybe he'll open up to you. I tried a few times. No luck. Something has a strong hold on the boy. Probably Irina, but it could be something else."

"All right. But . . ."

"He isn't safe here. You can hire security, but I wouldn't give most rent-a-cops much chance against these guys. If I were you, I'd get him into hiding—a hotel somewhere busy where no one will notice or care about one more person. Take away his cell phone. Don't tell anyone where he is. Especially not Irina. I've got a couple of leads to follow, but if he decides to talk about what he's been doing, maybe we can figure a way out of this. That's his best chance."

"And if he doesn't?"

"He won't have to worry about college admissions."

★ CHAPTER 33 ★

Twenty-second Street in Queens was dead quiet at 8:00 P.M. and filled with snow. The plows had made one pass, but that had been hours earlier. I parked the Valdez against a snowbank, partly blocking the street, but there was just enough room for a car to pass, if any came by, which seemed unlikely. I walked the block, looking for signs of life and finding none, including no sign of the FBI. They probably figured nobody would be out. Or maybe they took snow days. I'd have to ask Victoria.

I stopped by a van with AAA-ACE-ACME LOCKSMITHS on the side, parked across the street, engine running, and knocked twice on the window. A small, wiry man got out.

I'd made one more call from the road, while the kids were sleeping. Fyodor, proprietor of AAA-ACE-ACME, whom I pay well for the occasional B&E job, told me I was out of my fucking mind. I told him I'd add two bills to his normal fee. He agreed to meet me in Long Island City.

In four minutes, we were through the front door and on the elevator. Fyodor wrinkled his nose when we got off on the third floor. The stench was intense in the closed hallway. It got stronger near the door to YouGoHere .com. Fyodor knelt at the lock and did his work quickly, taking seven, maybe eight minutes. When the last click clicked, he pushed the door open and doubled over, retching. I gagged when the wave of stench hit me. I pulled Fyodor up by his shirt and yanked him back toward the elevator.

"You were never here."

"I never wanted to be."

I gave him seven hundred dollars, and he left without a word. I stopped in the hall, letting the stink dissipate, not wanting to go in, knowing I had no choice.

I didn't have anything to cover my face. I took the deepest breath I could, and moved fast through the door, pulling it closed behind me. The room was dark, I tripped over something immovable, cried out and lost the air in my lungs. I inhaled, stifled the urge to vomit, and kept going, feeling for the window. I found a metal blind and glass and a crank and cranked it. I yanked up the blind and put my head through the opening, sucking cold air, trying not to throw up.

When my insides settled down, I dropped the blind, leaving the window open. I flicked a light switch by the door.

They say flies find a body within hours of death. They'd found Walter Coryell—the source of the smell had to be Walter Coryell—and invited all their friends over for a feast. I'd set several clouds abuzz. A prehistoric mass of maggots seethed around the ears, nose, and eyes. The body slumped over the desk that had tripped me, bloated with bacteria, head at an impossible angle, the no-longer-recognizable remains of eyes in rotting sockets turned to the ceiling. The fresh air diluted the stink, but not enough.

The headquarters of YouGoHere.com was a one-room office. Three file cabinets, drawers closed. Same with the desk. The room itself was plain as plain could be. Desk, chair, two other chairs on the other side. All cheap metal and plastic construction. No signs of search or violence other than the body with the broken neck. I went back to the fresh air of the window while I looked around again.

Something was wrong, aside from the body. A printer and a copy machine against one wall. A cheap table against another. No computer. No servers, a staple for any Internet firm, but also no desktop machine, no laptop, no nothing. YouGoHere might be a rundown sham of a business, but even a sham needs the basics, if only to put up a credible front.

Holding my breath, I made a quick circumnavigation. Next to the copier, against the wall across from the window, I found a patch of floor, two feet by four, where the color was darker than the surrounding linoleum. The size of two server racks placed side by side. They would have shielded the floor from the sun. I eased the copier away from the wall. A half-dozen cable connectors stuck out of a plastic plate in the Sheetrock. The servers had been here.

Coryell's corpse wore a white shirt and khaki pants, both stretched tight by bloated skin. Running shoes on the feet. A navy blue ski jacket hung on the back of the chair. A bulge in his rear pocket. I reached for it. I don't know why it felt creepy—there was nothing he could do now, except stink and breed more flies—but it did. I worked the wallet out and went back to the window.

Eight twenties in the billfold, a New York driver's license, two credit cards, Visa and American Express, and a B of A bank card, all in the name of Franklin Druce. I found an identical wallet in the desk drawer with a license and bank and credit cards issued to Walter Coryell.

The other drawers yielded nothing. Neither did the file cabinets. I replaced the wallet, eased the copier back against the wall, took off my jacket, and wiped everything I'd touched. Holding my breath again, I put down the blinds and shut the window. The stench closed around me in an instant. I let myself out and took the stairs two at a time down to the street. The cold, wet air outside was about the sweetest smell ever.

★ CHAPTER 34 ★

"Russky!" Pig Pen called when I emerged from the server farm. "Tiramisu! No gigolo."

He was grinning, if parrots can grin, custard hanging from his beak.

Victoria and Foos sat opposite each other over a chessboard on the coffee table. She jumped up and ran to me. She was wearing jeans that had been sewn on, boots, and a black T-shirt advertising Tootsie's Orchid Lounge in Nashville. Tootsie had made it to fit her. We hugged tight, and some of the misery of the last thirty-six hours fell away, until she pushed me back.

"Phew! You stink, if you don't mind my saying so."

I didn't mind. I'm sure she was right.

"Bayou Babe. Tiramisu! Russky gigolo," Pig Pen said.

"Pig Pen and I are bonding," Victoria said.

"I'm not so sure I'm going to like this."

"You jealous?"

"Now that you've demonstrated yourself to be a soft touch, he's not going to let go easily."

"Bayou Babe," Pig Pen said.

She turned to face him. "Quiet, parrot, or you'll be eating rice pudding before you know it." To me, she said, "You smell like death, not warmed over."

"There's a reason for that."

It wasn't what I said but how I said it—more hard-edged than I intended.

"Uh-oh. This that stop you mentioned?"

" 'Fraid so."

"Careful, Turbo, she's a much better chess player than you are," Foos said, coming in our direction.

"I never claimed to be any good at chess."

"Neither does she."

"Hey! All I said was . . ."

"That you were only a beginner?"

"Did you beat him?" I asked. If she had, she was seriously good. Foos wasn't grand master material, he didn't have the discipline, but he wasn't too many levels below.

"We drew twice," Victoria said. "We were just starting the rubber match."

"Go back and finish. I've still got stuff to do."

"Uh-uh. I want to hear what you've been up to—and how many laws you broke."

"To be continued," Foos said. "I got all that material you asked for, Turbo. How's Andras?"

"Okay, physically. In a shitload of trouble otherwise."

"Maybe more than he's aware," he said. "Let me know when you want to take a look at those servers."

"First things first. Drink."

"What servers? And what about a shower?" Victoria said.

"Has to wait, I'm afraid."

"Always thinking of yourself," she muttered.

Foos grinned and headed for his office. I went to the kitchen and poured a large glass. Victoria raised an eyebrow but didn't comment.

"Food next," I said as I went rummaging through the mostly empty fridge.

"Want to talk about it?" she said.

I was leaning over the vegetable drawer. I stopped. Being asked to talk about it was new to me. I've lived a lonely life in those terms. No parents, and as a kid, my friends were usually looking for a way to climb up my back, as I was theirs. I could talk to Iakov, until I found out I couldn't, but his sons were worse than the kids in the Gulag. When I was married to Polina, I didn't discuss my work. The Cheka demanded secrecy and loyalty. Foos and I discuss work-related matters but he's not long on discussion generally and about as sympathetic as a cinder block.

On the other hand, as soon as I started talking, I'd be headed down a street with no way out at the other end. Too many crimes had been committed—not just by me—for her to ignore. The kids were in it up to their necks, and she'd rightly demand they go to the cops. I'd already sent one into hiding, and the other's stepfather—my client—was unlikely to look kindly on a request to serve her up to the law. I could tell her what happened, but I was in no position to do what she'd want done—although I doubted she'd see it that way. I told myself to stop rationalizing and play the hand. I closed the drawer and unbent myself.

"Coryell's dead. That's the smell. Just spent enough time with the corpse to confirm he's your man Druce."

She didn't blink or act surprised. "Where?"

"His office. No sign of FBI outside."

"We pulled him. You had to go there tonight?"

I nodded. "Those kids are in life and death danger, and he's the link—or was. I didn't know he was dead. Correction—I expected he could be but wasn't sure. His neck's broken. Several days ago, judging from the stink and the flies."

"I already know the answer to this, but I'll ask anyway—you call the police?"

"Believe it or not, I did. From a pay phone."

"You leave a name?"

My turn to raise an eyebrow.

"Never mind. Take what you can get. Hang on."

She took a cell phone from her pocket and gave someone a short list of orders about the NYPD, Coryell, and his office.

"Want to hear about the computers?" I said when she finished.

"What computers?"

"ConnectPay's. The ones that probably have every transaction the company ever made recorded on their hard drives. Not to mention customer files, money flow, BEC data . . ."

She'd been pacing the kitchen while she made her call. She stopped and faced me. "What about them?"

"They're missing. Not in Coryell's office. They used to be, I saw where they were. Somebody took them. Maybe the same somebody who killed him."

"Goddammit. You got any good news?" She paced some more.

"I'm alive. And you know a lot more than you did two days ago."

That stopped her again. She came back toward me.

"How the hell did I get myself shacked up with a serial felon?"

"Felonious sex appeal?"

"Don't start with the humor—and don't give yourself airs, especially not tonight. How'd you get into Coryell's office?"

"You don't really expect me to answer that."

She shook her head. "No, I don't. You touch anything, take anything?"

"No one will find fingerprints."

"I'm sure that's true. Answer the question."

"I opened the window. I moved the photocopier away from the wall and put it back. I checked Coryell's wallet. It's in his hip pocket, where I found it. I interrupted several hundred musca meals."

That got me a look.

"Flies—there's lots of them."

"Ugh." She resumed her pacing. "You know, shug, aside from your own criminal intent, which I'm trying hard to overlook, all this information you serve up, I don't know if we can even use it. We've got laws, conventions, rules of evidence."

"You're a prosecutor. I'm an ex-spy. If what Foos just said about your chess acumen is true, I'm guessing you'll find a way."

"You're an ex-spy bullshit artist."

She put out her arms. I stepped into her embrace.

"No! My mistake. I think that smell's growing. You need a bath, maybe disinfectant. If that doesn't work, one of us is definitely sleeping on the couch."

I shook my head. "I've got one more job to do. It's why I came back here. It's ugly and unpleasant and probably involves your man Konychev. I'm also going to need your help with something."

"Do I anticipate more laws being broken?"

"Can't say no. But law or no law, there's no good way out of this particular swamp."

"Remember I grew up in a swamp."

"Doesn't mean you want to return."

She put a hand on each cheek and planted her lips on mine—briefly.

"You're not the only who can take a selective approach to truth telling. Let's go—that is, if he'll let a Fed sit in."

"If you really drew him in chess twice, he's too devastated to say no."

I grabbed the bottle and two glasses in addition to my own, and we went to Foos's office.

"Showtime," I said.

"I was afraid of that," he said.

He moved his desk chair aside to make room for the two I brought around. He made no comment on Victoria's presence. Pig Pen wasn't the only one she'd been bonding with.

I put the glasses and the bottle on the desk. Foos poured a drink. Victoria shook her head, no.

"First stop, see if WildeTime.com is still online."

"No need. Whole BEC network is down."

"Again? That's not good for the kids."

"The kids—or kid—are the ones who took it down. That's what I meant when I called."

"Andras really took down the BEC?"

"Uh-huh. He's been toying with ConnectPay for months, starting last summer. He spent weeks looking around, figuring out what's what. He tried a few minor data-corruption programs, nothing too serious, more experiments than anything else. Then he found his way through the BEC firewall. A few more data-corruption forays, reconnaissance missions, enough to cause some glitches. Then he clipped them for that three mil in August and the five at Thanksgiving. Like he was ramping up. A couple weeks ago, he planted a real worm, nest of worms actually. Data corruption big time—designed to make a total mash of everything. The first time it twists a few files—as a warning. That was the little hiccup a few days ago. The second, if it isn't disabled, the worms bore their way through everything, eat it all from the inside out, leaving a long trail of cyber-shit in its wake."

"Let me guess. The second launch was today."

"Correctomundo," Foos said. "They may have backup systems unconnected with their main servers, but if not, the BEC is well and truly cooked. And even if they do, they've got a big job getting back in business. Could take weeks, probably months."

"That's a lot of income."

"Billions."

"Did he cover his tracks?"

"He did inside the ConnectPay servers, but all the activity is clear as day on his own system. Didn't reckon anyone would be looking at it, I guess."

"Naïve."

"He's a kid, a smart kid, but a kid."

"And the guy this morning could see it?"

"If he's remotely competent, he saw everything I did."

"You're right about buried alive. If they don't dismember him first."

Victoria was watching silently, a mix of surprise and thoughtfulness on her face. I reached for the phone and called Leitz.

"You get your son somewhere safe, like we discussed?"

"Working on it right now."

"Don't delay. It's worse than I thought. And don't tell anybody—not your wife, your family, anybody where he is. Anybody who knows is in the same kind of danger."

"Why? What's happened?"

"I'll explain when I see you."

Victoria said, "That kid's a suspect. You're aiding and abetting."

"That kid's dead—as soon as they finish torturing him—the moment anyone in the BEC knows where to find him."

"You can't keep him in hiding forever."

"I know." Problem was, that's exactly how long Karp and Konychev—Batkin too?—were going to keep looking. She was giving me her best prosecutorial glare.

"Suppose I need to talk to him?"

"We can discuss that."

"Uh-uh. You get no special dispensation from me. Not when it comes to doing my job."

"I understand. I'm not expecting any. But there may be other answers." I did my best to sound confident. I could see she didn't believe me any more than I believed myself. I turned to Foos.

"If the ConnectPay servers were disconnected before the data destruction program launched itself, there's a chance they weren't infected, right?"

"If they were offline, and Andras didn't trash them too, they're probably okay."

"Looks like you still have your case, if we can find those servers," I said to Victoria. "Although we may need them to bargain for the kid."

"Hold on, shug. You can't . . ."

"We'll cross that bridge when we come to it," I said quickly. "We have to find them first. And if Nosferatu killed Coryell, it's a moot point—he's already got them."

"You still can't . . ."

Time to change the subject, even if it was only a temporary reprieve. I said, "Let's take a look at the WildeTime data. Start with e-mail. Search on Newburgh."

I could feel Victoria's glare as I watched the computer. Foos was cool as a cucumber—once again declining to take sides, at least overtly. It took a minute to find an exchange between someone named frankyfun and Salomé—a half-dozen messages arranging a five-thousand-dollar private "in-person audition" at the Black Horse Motel for the night of January 15.

"Who's that?" Victoria asked.

"Frankyfun is Walter Coryell."

"You sure?"

"Dead certain, actually."

"Doesn't your sense of humor ever take a night off?"

"Carpe diem."

"Carpe my ass. Who's Salomé?"

I resisted the temptation to carpe the obvious comeback. "Salomé is Andras's girlfriend, Irina. What else is there on franky?"

Foos worked the keys. Franky was a regular. He'd paid for "private auditions," mostly with Salomé, about once a week for the last six months. All recorded.

One of the worst things about this kind of investigation, it makes you question your own motives. Are they based on prurience? How much do I need to see? We all have tendencies, I'm told, but most of us keep them buried. For those who don't, and have the funds, here was a menu, just like a diner. Cute underaged Russian blowjobs in column A. Sweet-faced American boy pulling his pud in column B. For kiddie doggy, choose column C. Got a thing for teenaged lesbians . . .

Victoria muttered, "Jesus, I can't believe this. You weren't kidding about the swamp. I'll take that drink now."

She reached for the bottle.

"Pick one at random," I said to Foos.

Foos pointed and clicked. We got Irina/Salomé doing a solo masturbation act, at the direction of frankyfun, who'd paid $699 for the privilege. It took a short minute to figure out how it worked. Irina was on the bed in one of the rooms I'd seen that morning. She stared out at the camera, clothed in a vintage velvet dress with lace collar, made up to look like an even younger girl, pigtails and all. She shed velvet to reveal underwear that was decidedly twenty-first century, then she removed that piece by piece and went into her self-pleasuring act. She received direction from franky via e-mail, which someone was reading at the computer on the desk and relaying to her. One of her fellow players, no doubt. Andras? Boyfriend as virtual pimp? That was more depressing than I wanted to contemplate.

"I've had enough," Foos said.

"So have I," Victoria echoed.

"One more thing," I said. "What's the date on the scene we just watched?"

"Last May," Foos said.

"See any sign of a scar on Irina's neck?"

"Nope."

"Neither do I. Pick a more current one."

He found another private audition, ordered up by frankyfun just two weeks ago. She used a lot of pancake, but the rough skin was difficult to hide. The scar was there.

"Enough," I said.

"What's that about?" Victoria asked.

"I don't know. Noticed it on the drive from Gibbet. I'm going to check it out."

"How're you going to do that?"

"Spy sources."

That got me a look, but she didn't press it. "How many clients you think these kids have?" she asked.

A quick survey indicated almost three hundred, with an average monthly tab of two grand.

"They've been pulling down north of seven mil a year, minus Connect-Pay's cut."

"This can't be about money," Victoria said. "These are rich kids, right? They have money. They have futures."

"Another question we still don't have an answer for. Go back to that frankyfun e-mail," I said to Foos.

He scrolled through the full exchange—four messages, franky arranging a tryst with Salomé at the Black Horse.

"I'm betting that's not Salomé. It's Andras using her account."

"Can't check that, if he logged on with her user name."

"No need to. Only way it fits. The junkies said he was shouting, 'Where is he?' and she said, 'This was your plan.'"

"Junkies?" Victoria asked.

"Witnesses," I said. "They weren't stoned. I caught them just before their morning fix."

"Great!"

"The guy in the playhouse this morning? He try to hide his tracks?"

"Uh-uh," Foos said.

"He knew Nosferatu was going to blow the joint."

"What?!" Victoria shouted.

I told her about the playhouse and the explosives.

"Jesus Christ! You're a one-man wrecking crew. You didn't call the . . . Shit, never mind, why am I asking?"

"I removed the gas. Put it in my car. Nobody got hurt."

"Oh great. You could have been . . . What makes you think . . . ?"

"Once a Fed . . . ," Foos said. I guess he couldn't resist.

Victoria got ready to belt him. He grinned. They hadn't bonded as much as I thought.

252

"Do either of you realize how many laws . . . Of course you do. And you're happy about it."

She stood, knocking her chair over backward.

"Nobody's any worse off than they were before," I said. "We haven't changed the dynamics here one bit. The kids were in danger, they're still in danger—all of their own making. Coryell's dead. He was already dead—also his fault. You know more than you did four nights ago, when you were ready to trade anything for help. I'm out a night's sleep, but I picked up some free gas in the deal. And—even though we can't take credit for it—it appears one of the truly nasty players on the Internet has been knocked offline. This is where I need your help."

"That's not the point, and you know it." She stomped her feet and walked around the office. Foos watched, stifling a chuckle. She stopped in front of me. "What help?"

"I need the FBI or somebody trustworthy—not the local cops—to go to Crestview tonight and retrieve the WildeTime servers, before Konychev or Batkin or someone else gets them. Even though those kids are already all over the Internet, let's not make it worse by having all that content fall into the wrong hands. They may be useful to you too."

She took another walk around the office and came back and looked me straight in the eyes. Annoyance, concern, fear, and love were duking it out in hers.

"This is what it's going to be like, isn't it?"

"Welcome to the inside."

"I should've stayed in Marathon—maybe even that reform school. I'll make the call. Then let's go home."

Foos winked.

★ CHAPTER 35 ★

"That kid has to be a suspect in his uncle's murder."

"I don't think he did it."

"What you think isn't relevant. What you know—about him, about the uncle—that's material."

"It's all there for the cops to find, if they look."

"That's not the point either. And one thing isn't there, and that's the kid, thanks to you."

"He won't do you any good dead."

We sat across from each other at my kitchen counter, eating a late meal of bread and cheese and vodka and wine. I'd washed off most of Coryell's corpse's stench, to her approval, but I was resisting her admonishments to tell my tale to the police, which had her increasingly pissed off.

We'd checked Ibansk.com before leaving the office. As expected, Ivanov was already on the Lishin story.

Gone Lishin?

I provided a rough translation.

"I take it back. He's worse than you are," Victoria said.

Terminal troubles at the Baltic Enterprise Commission, Ivanov can report, of both the technical and personal persuasion.

The service is offline again, as dead as one of its founding partners, Alexander Lishin, found yesterday, his decomposing corpse adding its own peculiar pollution to the Moscova.

Not much is known about Lishin's demise—yet. The body was

clearly dumped, and the cause of death is a well-protected secret—for the moment. Ivanov has learned that the stiff has been stiff for several weeks.

As for the BEC, it appears the glitch a few days ago was only a harbinger of things to come. A mysterious cyber-attack has blown through the vaunted defenses and torched everything it could reach— which is to say, everything. Restoration, if even possible, is expected to take months.

Retribution, however, is another matter. But against whom? And who's calling the shots? Lishin sleeps with the fishes. Efim Konychev remains in hiding, except to venture out for sustenance, in New York. Taras Batkin has played no active management role in recent years. He's employing his considerable talents feathering his nest—and those of his Cheka colleagues—also in New York. Maybe Ivanov should plan a trip to that trans-Atlantic Ibanskian playground.

One more question (well, two) occupies Ivanov above all others. Who has it in for the BEC—and why?

"I've got the same question, shug. Why'd he do it? Andras."

"The girl put him up to it."

"Typical. Blame the woman. Why?"

"Don't know. But after eight hours with them, I can tell you she's running the show."

"Merle Haggard said the same thing about Bonnie and Clyde. History's on your side for once. What's her motivation?"

"That I don't know. I wonder whether it has to do with the death of her father, but the timing doesn't line up. She and Andras started in on the BEC back last year—months before Lishin got run through."

"I need my people to talk to her."

"I'll ask Batkin, but I won't cross him."

"You cannot hide behind your client."

"I'm not hiding. Nosferatu doesn't care about laws or rules of evidence, neither do his bosses. You heard Foos—the guy I saw this morning spent enough time on the WildeTime servers to finger Andras for the BEC worm. Maybe Irina too. That's why Nosferatu wired that place to blow, taking everyone inside with it—including, as it turns out, me. He'll know by now he failed—and he'll be looking for the kids. He won't be reading them their Miranda rights."

"That's not the goddamned point. It's the cops' job—my job—now. Can't you get that through your hairless head?"

The green eyes were afire. For my part, exhaustion and vodka were overcoming good sense.

"I'm beat. Let's go to bed. Nothing's going to change in the next few hours. We can pick up the argument in the morning."

The fire ebbed. "Good idea. Tomorrow is another day."

"It certainly is."

It certainly was.

Starting first thing in the morning when, while we were warming up the argument over breakfast, someone tried to assassinate Taras Batkin.

★ CHAPTER 36 ★

They didn't get him. And in the confusion, Irina did a runner.

Batkin had his own armored Mercedes. This was New York, not Moscow, but Ibansk knows no formal borders, as Ivanov often points out. Despite the snow that had buried the city, Batkin and Irina emerged early Friday morning. He told me later they were going to church, St. Nicholas, the Russian Orthodox cathedral on East Ninety-seventh Street. That sounded an unlikely destination for either of them, but I didn't argue the point.

At 7:30, two bodyguards checked the street. It had been plowed twice in the last thirty-six hours, but the asphalt was still covered with a layer of slush and ice, on top of which was two inches of snow. That didn't stop the guards from calling the driver to bring the car. Usually, the parking space in front of the house was kept clear by the city, and one of the guards would hold the door while two more escorted Batkin from the house across twelve feet of sidewalk into the rolling fortress.

This morning, four feet of packed snow occupied the limousine's parking spot, deposited there by the Department of Sanitation's snow plow garbage trucks. Batkin's bodyguards had hacked a narrow, slush-filled channel from sidewalk to street, not unlike the Gulag laborers who dug Stalin's canals in the 1930s with exactly the same tools. When the guards checked the street, all they saw were neighbors shoveling the sidewalk. The armored limo pulled up at the end of the snowbank canal. One guard opened the door. Two others brought Batkin and the girl out. As they picked their way toward the car, one "neighbor" to the east and another across the street opened up with mini–Uzi machine pistols hidden beneath their overcoats. The guns fire nine-hundred-fifty rounds a minute, although each magazine

259

holds only thirty-two. It looked like the shooters got off a couple of clips each when I surveyed the damage a few hours later. Two bodyguards died in an instant. Batkin was lucky. He pushed Irina to the ground and his leather-soled Italian loafers slipped on the ice. He ended up on top of her in the slush, bullets pummeling the packed snow all around. One more bodyguard was wounded, and another hit the eastern "neighbor" square in the chest with four nine-millimeter slugs. The other shooter ran for it, the Mercedes in hot pursuit, but the car was as useless as the Potemkin on the slippery pavement. The driver lost control and piled into a row of parked vehicles, totaling two Range Rovers. The man disappeared down Madison Avenue. When Batkin pulled Irina up, she bolted in the other direction. He tried to chase her, but she was hightailing it down Fifth before he got halfway to the corner.

I know how it happened from the news reports—four TV crews, with helicopters, were on the scene in minutes—and from Batkin himself. Once he'd recovered, he called me.

I wasn't aware of any of this until Foos phoned at 8:50 and said in his usual succinct style, "Better turn on your TV."

Victoria was explaining the finer points of obstructing justice. To be fair, her concern for me and the law she was sworn to uphold was equally genuine. That didn't stop it from grating. I hadn't had near enough sleep to make up for the night spent watching the playhouse, the events of the day and last night's vodka, which left a dull thudding at the back of my head. I'd hoped the combination of exercise and cold air would clear it away, but the downtown streets were too slippery to run without risking broken bones. I'd settled for a chilly walk around southern Manhattan that cleared nothing. I was in no mood to argue my case over breakfast—aware I didn't have much of a case to argue. I tried to hide behind the position that I couldn't do much of anything until I knew more about what was going on, even though I didn't have any immediate idea how I was going to find that out.

Victoria wasn't buying any of it, which had her on the subject of obstruction when Foos called.

"Somebody took a shot at your ambassador buddy."

"He's not a buddy. You mean shot, like murder shot?"

"I mean a hundred of them. He's lucky to be alive."

I turned on the TV and was treated to an aerial view of East Ninety-second Street. Both ends of the block were jammed with police cars. I could see what looked like a limo piled into parked cars on one side. A breathless voice-over announcer recounted sketchy details of the assassination attempt.

"He wants you up there, ASAP," Foos said.

"Who?"

"The ambassador. Who else?"

"He called?"

"Couple minutes ago. Said your cell phone's off and to get you a message to meet him at his house as soon as possible."

"How'd he sound?"

"How do you think? Somebody just tried to kill him. Bad way to start the day."

Victoria had gone to the bedroom when the phone rang and reappeared wearing one of my black turtlenecks, the core of my winter wardrobe. It was almost big enough to fall off.

"You need some color in your closet. Everything you own is black, gray, or beige."

"I think you made that point once before."

"Didn't take. Like everything else I say. Something besides turtlenecks and T-shirts would be nice too."

"Cuts down on decisions. Think of all the time I save."

"So you can get into more trouble. What's going on?" She pointed at the TV.

"Somebody tried to assassinate Taras Batkin."

"Jesus! Here?"

"Uh-huh. That's East Ninety-second Street."

She approached the TV and stood fixated as the announcer repeated the few facts they had. I poured some coffee and gave her a cup. She barely noticed it was in her hand. When the newscast cut to a commercial, she shook her head and said, "That's impossible. This is New York."

"Happens in Moscow all the time."

"That's different. That's . . . We have rule of law here, goddammit."

She was angry. This was an attack on her country, and on her, as well as Batkin.

Having no answer, I shook my head. "He wants me to come up there."

"Who?"

"Batkin."

"What?! He wants to see you?"

"Foos says he called a few minutes ago."

"You can't go up there."

"Why not?"

"After everything we talked about? He's a criminal! He's . . ."

"That doesn't mean I am."

"Don't you understand anything? After yesterday? And last night? You just keep . . . I can't deal with this. I gotta get going. I've gotta get out of here."

She started for the bedroom, stumbled and fell against the couch. I was there in an instant, helping her up, making sure she wasn't hurt. I tried to hold her but her fists pummeled my chest.

"Vika! Stop! I'm just going to talk to the man."

"I want that girl in my office before noon!"

She pulled away from my embrace and holding up the turtleneck all but ran to the bedroom, the door slamming behind her.

I stood in the middle of the floor, arms suspended in the air, the TV news announcer prattling away behind me. I had no idea what he was saying. I was still there when she reemerged, fully dressed, and walked out the door without saying good-bye.

This time, I did follow, as far as the elevator.

"Vika, I'll do what I can about Irina. But tell me what's wrong."

She shook her head.

"Is that no? Why not?"

She looked up, eyes full of tears. "If you think about it just a little, you'll figure it out. Just bring the girl. I have to go."

The elevator arrived with a chime, and she got on, keeping her back to me. She didn't start to turn around until the door was closing and the cab dropped from sight.

★ CHAPTER 37 ★

Controlled bedlam at Madison and East Ninety-second. The cops had the block sealed. News crews, reporters, and onlookers jostled for position. A major catastrophe and everyone wanted a piece of the action. The police were edgy, as was the crowd, even though at 10:40 A.M., three hours after the attack, there wasn't much left to see. The bodies and the limo had been removed. All that remained was a snow-covered street filled with cops and emergency workers milling around.

The snow slowed everything. I'd walked from the Ninety-sixth Street subway station, thinking about Victoria and Batkin, Irina and Andras and Leitz, trying to put the pieces together. I had assumed Victoria's case was against Konychev, hence her unwillingness to talk about him. Now, it appeared it could be Batkin—or both of them. Konychev had to be Suspect Number One for this morning's attack. One or the other or both would be going after Coryell's missing computers. But if Nosferatu had killed Coryell, presumably he had them. Konychev was after Andras and Irina. Batkin appeared unaware of his stepdaughter's involvement in the destruction of his business. Alexander Lishin had been murdered, presumably by one partner or the other. The disintegration of the BEC ownership structure, as well as the business itself, had to be total. One thing was clear—Irina stood at the center of it all. Maybe that's what Victoria meant when she said I'd figure it out. That seemed too easy, but it was certainly why she told me to bring her in. Still, I felt like I needed a scorecard.

In New York, everyone is responsible for clearing the front of his or her own building, which means the city's sidewalks get shoveled in patchwork fashion. Park Avenue is lined with big apartment buildings, and they have staff, and the staff have shovels, snowblowers, and salt. The side streets, lined with town houses, were uneven going—clear in front of several houses, then a foot of snow for half a block. The temperature had risen overnight then dropped back into the low twenties at daybreak, adding a crust of ice— and another layer of shoveling difficulty. One blessing was lack of wind. The late morning was clear and dry—the exact antithesis of the way I felt. My brain resembled the sidewalk—a slushy, opaque, half-frozen patchwork of a few clear facts and a lot of buried connections waiting to be shoveled out. Beria joined me briefly as I walked, the first time I'd seen him in days.

Don't forget about me. I'm still part of this.

I told him to beat it.

The police wouldn't let me into Batkin's block until I phoned, and he sent one of his remaining battalion of bodyguards to fetch me. A chorus of "Hey! Who's he?!" rose from behind as the police moved the barrier to let me through. A broad-backed man, whose forebearers probably shepherded my fellow *zeks* to work in the forests of the Kolyma camps, led me silently down the icy block. I noted the crumpled sides of the parked cars and the bloodstained snow bank riddled with bullet holes. I had the memory of another ice- and snow-crusted time and place—a prison camp covered in the blood of its unfortunate inhabitants. I was one of them, I'd been lucky enough to escape, and now I was walking back in under my own power, drawn by a fellow sufferer whose motive matched the bloody snow in its opacity. Beria watched from Batkin's door, grin in place. Victoria's admonition to figure it out knocked hard at my brain.

The transition from crime-scene street to Batkin's neoclassical living room jarred. He sat in a maroon velvet armchair, surrounded by royal greens and golds and reds. The room was smaller than Leitz's, but the high ceiling gave it grandeur, as did the paint, wallpaper, and fabrics, none of which came from Home Depot. He was wearing a dark purple silk robe, ankle-length, with what was almost certainly a mink collar. Russian funeral suit in a czar's palace. His hairpiece was in place. Had it remained intact during the shooting? A half-full brandy snifter sat by his chair. He looked up as I entered, gray-blue eyes difficult to read—sad, certainly, but still hard.

"Thank you for coming on short notice. Drink?"

"I'll join you." If that collar was mink, the brandy was probably good. No point in not being sociable, and it might help melt the ice upstairs—or so I told myself. He pushed his robed body to its feet and went to a large, heavy sideboard holding decanters and glasses. He was moving all right, but perhaps not with the full confidence of purpose he'd had Wednesday at my office. Dark blood clotted on the half-moon forehead and plump left cheek.

The side of the pyramid nose was scratched as well. Minor injuries, under the circumstances. He brought me a snifter and indicated I should sit.

"Irina's gone," he said.

I stifled a curse. If anyone acted foolishly, I half expected it to be Leitz, not an experienced hood like Batkin.

"What happened?"

He told me about the attack.

"Did you argue?"

He shook his head. "We probably would have, but I couldn't get her to talk. Her mother's away—in Moscow—and Irina went to her room as soon as she got here. Refused to come out. I tried to talk to her through the door, but . . ."

He sipped his brandy while I considered the irony of a Chekist unable to interrogate his own family.

"And this morning?"

"We were going to church. I thought maybe it would help her . . ."

He trailed off as if unsure what kind of help was being sought.

"What can you tell me about this . . . this group she was involved with?"

I noted his use of past tense and thought to correct him. He mistook my hesitation.

"Remember my tattoos. I doubt you can shock me."

Having no idea what was going on, or whose side anyone was on, or even what sides were available to join, half of me decided this was an instance where evasion, rather than honesty, was the best policy. The other half, thinking about Victoria, said the best way out of this mess was to put my cards on the table, as I knew them to be, and look for an opportunity to walk away. As that half climbed to 60 percent, I told him about the Players, minus names and addresses. I also omitted, for the moment, the Walter Coryell–ConnectPay connection and Andras Leitz.

As I moved deeper into the story, Batkin stood and walked around the room, glass in hand. I couldn't see what he was thinking, he kept his back to me for the most part. I could only imagine the impact, even on a Gulag- and Cheka-hardened psyche. I'd warned Leitz about how the last case had ended badly for everyone involved. This one was going places I could never have contemplated.

When I finished, Batkin shook his head, his back to me still, and said, "She's always been a troubled child. I blame her father."

He would. "Why do you say that?" I asked, mainly to keep the conversation moving.

"Alexander Petrovich was the antithesis of a family man. He never should have married. He treated Alyona like a doormat, running around on her with a new woman every week. He didn't care if she found out, he didn't give a damn how much he hurt her. It was even worse for Irina. He ignored her, as if she was someone else's child. When she tried to get his attention, he threatened Alyona, screaming at her to get the girl away from him before he beat her."

Again, he was using the past tense. He could have been referring to the marriage. He could have been talking about the late Alexander Lishin. He could have played a role in his death. He could have read Ibansk, as I had last night. I kept silent.

He took a swallow of brandy. I sipped while I waited. Wherever it was from—Cognac, Armagnac, somewhere else—it was a far cry from Marianna's Presidente. He swallowed some more and put the glass on the mantel.

"Who has the group's computers?"

Time to evade, if not outright lie. "I assume they're still in the building in Crestview."

"Address."

A command, not a question. I shrugged, only a little uncomfortable at pointing out the viral nature of the Internet to a man who'd built a business based on it.

"Any number of clients have downloaded any number of pictures and videos. I haven't searched the Web, but . . ."

His hand cut me off, the voice testy. "Yes, I know all that. I want the address."

"Main Street, above the liquor store. Fire escape is the best way in," I added helpfully.

"Who else was involved in these . . . Players?"

I shook my head.

"What's that supposed to mean?"

"You asked me to find out what she was up to. That was the deal. No reason to drag anyone else into it."

"They're already in."

"They're kids. Fucked-up kids, but kids. They have parents and stepparents too."

He nodded slowly. He didn't like my answer but he wasn't going to budge me off it.

"Who was behind the attack this morning?" I asked, only partially to change the subject.

Batkin watched me carefully. The eyes were still clear—they showed no fear, nor effects of the brandy.

"The obvious candidate is Konychev. But as much as I hate him, I have a hard time believing he would be that stupid. Even if he had been successful . . . he knows the price as well as I do."

"Revenge for Tverskaya?"

"I had nothing to do with that!" He spoke too quickly and realized it. "It's also not his style."

"If you say so."

"How much do you know about my esteemed friend, Efim Ilyich?" Batkin asked.

"What I read on Ibansk.com. You and he don't get along."

"Don't put too much faith in that son of a Cossack whore. Ivanov makes up half of what he writes. One day he'll pay for the lies he tells."

Usual Cheka knee-jerk response. He managed to get deep under the organization's skin. One reason I did have faith in Ibansk.

"So you and Konychev are actually pals?" I said, perhaps more provocatively than I meant.

"I loathe the stinking *pedik*. But we made a deal. Neither of us wanted to make it—we both would have preferred to finish the other off. However, we had . . . encouragement. The kind only a complete fool would disregard. I've upheld my end. But now . . . Enough of that. Find Irina."

I had to find her anyway, but I wanted out from under any obligation, if only to straighten things out with Victoria. Besides, I'd done what he asked.

I said, "That's not part of our deal. I've done what we agreed on."

He picked up his glass and returned to his chair. He sipped slowly, looked at me for what must have been two or three minutes before he said, "I have the information you want."

I sat back, stunned by the claim, but also by how he, or anyone, could have discovered anything this fast. I'd heard nothing from Sasha.

"How?"

"Your man was slow. He was also . . . diverted. While he was down a blind alley, I had my own people searching. Some things aren't that hard to locate if you know where to look."

"And?"

"Find Irina."

"We had an agreement."

"I'm making a new deal."

I shook my head. "Why should I go along with that?"

"Because you will recognize that you have no choice."

What I recognized was the nasty feeling I get when I've stayed in a card game too long, miscalculating my opponent's hand, and was about to pay for my mistake. I took a sip of brandy and played for time.

"I don't follow," I said.

"I think you do. Find Irina, and I give you the results of my search. Walk away and I give them to your son. I'm sure he will be most interested to learn of his ancestry."

How the hell did he know my every fear and insecurity? Beria appeared by the fireplace, fingering the king of spades, his message all too clear.

Never underestimate the Cheka.

Perhaps I had been living away from home too long. Batkin was watching me across the top of his glass, enjoying himself in some perverse way, if that was possible on such a morning.

"Only Irina?" I said.

"I don't need help with Konychev, if that's what you're asking."

"What about Karp?"

"If I were in your shoes, I'd kill him before he killed me."

★ CHAPTER 38 ★

I stepped into the street, not sure what to think. The refection of sun on still-clean snow blinded. In Moscow, a layer of black soot would already be settling. The snow here would get dirty soon enough, but for now it was bright white everywhere.

I walked east toward the subway, squinting. I'd spent another half hour probing Batkin about the BEC and the extent of his knowledge about its demise. No question he was one tough SOB—as well as an unreliable witness and an accomplished liar. He was a Chekist after all. On balance, however, I was inclined to believe him. At least until I checked out his account.

He confirmed the essential facts about the Baltic Enterprise Commission and the split between its leaders. Konychev, the media mogul, and Lishin, the technology expert, had built the business. Web hosting for spammers to start, in the Internet's early days. They'd been successful—so successful they attracted the Kremlin's attention. An enterprise with mastery of this mysterious new medium—ultra-mysterious to the dinosaurs who rarely ventured outside the fortress walls—was frightening. They injected Batkin into the partnership, ordered him to get his arms around the BEC and its activities and report back. He did that. He also recognized that Konychev and Lishin had only begun to tap their creation's potential. For three men, each of whom wanted the other two dead, they made a toxic and formidable team. The business grew and expanded and spun Internet gold. Batkin kept his Kremlin bosses far enough at bay that the partners were allowed to enjoy the fruits of their labors.

The trouble started over the summer. Long-simmering animosities bubbled to the surface, and disagreements over business issues turned up the heat. Then the technical problems hit. Annoyances at first, just as Foos had described. Minor hackings, data corruption, cyber-vandalism. Things like that had happened once or twice before, not often, but they had a big Internet footprint, they would be a target for any fool who wanted to boast about hacking the BEC. The partners were concerned, but not overly so—until three mil vanished in August. That got their attention. Their technical people worked the data. Karp flew to New York.

Karp reported some progress. He'd identified the source of the theft attack. Konychev boasted they'd have the culprit soon. Batkin and Lishin were losing patience, fast.

Another five million went out the cyber-door in November. Karp leaned on Coryell. Elizabeth Rogers started making the rounds. The BEC leadership was apoplectic. It wasn't just the money. They weren't used to this kind of treatment—and the inability to do a damned thing about it. Lishin told Batkin it had to be an inside job—their defenses were too strong to be so easily breached. Lishin ordered Konychev whacked. Batkin didn't put it that way, but we were Chekists, we understood each other. The killers missed, Konychev went into hiding.

Batkin didn't say anything about the most recent cyber-attack that felled the BEC or about Lishin's death. I didn't ask. I wouldn't have believed him on either of those questions. It was possible that he had been playing me for a sucker since that first visit to my office. I could have delivered Irina into the hands of her jailer, maybe executioner, last night, which was why she ran the first chance she got. Even money, though, that neither Konychev nor Lishin had confided in him. No reason for them to have done so.

As I picked my way through the snow-packed sidewalks, I tried to handicap whether his concern for Irina was based on her safety or a desire to reunite her with her dead father or some idea that she, or Andras, could lead him to the missing ConnectPay servers, now more valuable than ever. Perhaps even the foundation the BEC needed to rebuild. A man like him would already be thinking about that.

First things first. I called Victoria. She was in a meeting. I left a message that Irina had taken off. I didn't say anything about Batkin. I'd call again as soon as I had more information. Then I found a payphone and dialed Moscow—Aleksei's apartment.

"Coffee?" I said.

"When?"

"Sooner the better."

"Do you know what time it is? Never mind. Ten minutes."

I walked a few more blocks, until I found another pay phone and dialed Aleksei's disposable.

"You hear about Taras Batkin?" he asked.

"Just left him."

"What?!" Then, "Why am I surprised?"

"It's not what you think."

"How do you know what I think?"

A fair question.

"I can tell you all about it—it's his stepdaughter. She's playing some dangerous games, and she's run away. You know the BEC's offline?"

"Old news."

"How about the late, unlamented Alexander Lishin?"

"Ivanov broke that story."

I listened for anger or frustration but didn't hear any.

"Here's something else, the real reason I called. I'm assuming you'll be able to pinpoint the date of Lishin's demise. Check whether his daughter, Irina, was treated around that time for a wound to the neck, right side, just below the ear. A cut, maybe a burn, bad enough to leave an ugly scar."

"That's not going to be easy."

"I'm assuming you have hospital contacts. You can do it quietly. It might be the bulldozer you need to push the roadblocks aside—if you want to. You have a suspect yet?"

"Don't ask. What's your interest in the girl?"

I started to give the same reply—*Don't ask*—until I heard Beria chuckling. I spotted him across Lexington Avenue, shaking his head with a smile.

You don't get it, he mouthed. *You never will.*

"I think she's the one who took down the BEC," I said to Aleksei.

Sharp intake of breath. "How . . . ?"

"She had help. Her boyfriend's a computer geek. His uncle was a key cog in the empire."

"Was?"

"He checked out last week."

"Connection?"

"Maybe. Probably. Not sure. Konychev's enforcer is after the kids. Name's Karp by the way. You can pass that on if you like. I need to keep the girl's role under wraps."

"You trusted me. I can return the favor. I'll let you know if I find out anything."

271

I hung up. Maybe that was the start of something. I looked around for Beria. He was gone. I continued down Lexington and stopped at the window of a coffee shop. Cheka and BEC troubles were sidelined by the immediate prospect of a club sandwich and fries—not my usual lunch diet, but comforting in the prospect that they might soak up the brandy. My hand was on the door when my cell phone buzzed.

Thomas Leitz's voice was high, shrill and hysterical.

"YOU HAVE TO HELP ME! YOU HAVE TO!"

★ CHAPTER 39 ★

"What's wrong?" I said.

"EVERYTHING! IT'S YOUR FAULT! He's out there. I can't move. I can't do anything!"

"Who, Thomas? Who's out there?"

"The tall man. HE'S STALKING ME!"

I dropped my hand from the coffee shop door. The fear coming through the phone was real. People brushed past, bumping me from either side on the snow-narrowed sidewalk. I pushed on down the block until I found a doorway providing shelter from the pedestrian traffic.

"Okay, calm down. Tell me what's going on."

"He's out there. HE'S WATCHING ME!"

"Describe him."

"The man you told me about. You told him where to find me, didn't you? DIDN'T YOU?"

"Cool down. I didn't tell anybody anything."

"I DON'T BELIEVE YOU. HE'S OUT THERE!"

"Thomas! Stop! You called me. I want to help. You have to tell me calmly and specifically what you are seeing. Understand? Where are you?"

"He's out there."

The hysteria receded, a little, the borderline panic remained.

"Where are you?" I repeated.

"My apartment."

"Okay. What's going on? What do you see?"

"He's across the street. He's watching me!"

"How long has he been there?"

"I don't know. I was going out. To . . . He came towards me. STRAIGHT

AT ME! I ran back inside. I've been watching. He hasn't moved. He's waiting for me!"

"How long ago? How long ago were you going out?"

"I don't know. Ten minutes."

"Okay. Good. What does he look like?"

"The man you told me about. Tall. Ugly. Bad hair, bad teeth."

"You have a doorman?"

"Yes . . . Part-time."

"There now?"

"Until four."

I looked at my watch—2:30 P.M. The doorman would be no match for Nosferatu, but the fact that he was still across the street said he didn't want the complication of getting past someone. Question was, what did he want?

"How many entrances to your building?"

"How should I know? I . . ."

"Thomas! I'm trying to help. Answer my questions. This is important. How many entrances?"

"The front door?"

"Good. Fire escape?"

"From the rear window. Down to a well in the back."

"Then what?"

"Back out to the street."

"Next to the front door?"

"Yes."

"That's it?"

"I think so."

No way for Nosferatu to get in without the doorman seeing him. Or so I hoped.

"Listen to me," I said. "I'm going to hang up for a minute. I'll call you right back. I want you to watch the tall man. Tell me what he does. Okay?"

"I need help!"

Cheka training, any training, if it's done right, is hard to shake. I had Thomas Leitz in the palm of my hand. I could help him, I could also get something in the process. The process wouldn't be pretty.

"You shouldn't have blackmailed Coryell all these years," I said, making my voice hard, almost cruel. "That's what this is about. The tall man knows what I know. You want my help, there's a price."

"WHAT?! What are you saying? I didn't . . ."

He was crying. I ignored that and pushed. "You did. You hit him up. You used him every time you needed money. Now the tall man wants to know what you had on Walter. So do I. That's where we are today. You can deal with him or you can deal with me."

"That's not fair. You're a bastard. I didn't."

"Him or me, Thomas. I'm hanging up. I can call back or not. Tell me which way you want this to go."

Tears, choking, sniveling. Maybe I should have felt sorry, but Thomas Leitz was a user whose string of using had run out. No remorse on my part.

"Good-bye, Thomas."

"WAIT!"

"Wait for what?"

"I'll do what you say."

"What I say is this: When I call you back, you are going to tell me what you had on Walter Coryell. That's the deal."

"But . . ."

"No but."

A long wait. Longer than it should have been. Thomas Leitz was terrified, but not terrified enough.

I broke the connection and started to count. I got to seven when the phone buzzed in my hand.

"Next time I turn it off," I said.

"You're a bastard."

"Tell it to the tall man. If he lets you. He likes breaking necks. He'll break yours in a second."

I cut the connection again. This time I got to four.

"OKAY! Whatever you say."

"What did you have on Walter?"

"Make him go away first."

"If you don't tell me, I'll make him come back. And I'll be right behind in case he fucks up."

"Make him go away. PLEASE!"

"Watch your window."

I walked down the block until I found a pay phone. I punched in the number the Basilisk had identified calling Coryell's office last week.

A Belarusian voice said, "What?"

"You and I have a lot to discuss, Karp." I spoke Belarusian.

"Who the fuck is this?"

"Someone who knows who you are. Someone who knows where you are. Someone who has what you want."

I could almost hear him spit in the snow.

"Fucking *zek*. I know you, asshole."

"Fuck your mother. You want to do business or trade insults?"

"I don't trade with *zeks*."

"Kiss the computers good-bye then. I've got other buyers."

I hung up and started counting again. When I reached twenty-five, I called Thomas on my cell phone.

"What's he doing?"

"Throwing a total hissy fit. He just punched the wall, I think."

"Good. I'll call you back."

"Wait . . ."

I called Nosferatu on the pay phone.

"Reconsider?"

"You're a dead man."

"We all are. Are we dealing before we die?"

"What do you want?"

"Leave the fairy alone. He has nothing you need. Get out of his neighborhood and we'll talk. That's the deal for now."

I felt mildly guilty about the "fairy" part. But us tough guys have to bond like everyone else.

"Maybe I'll just kill him now."

"Then you won't hear from me again. And I'll let your boss know how you fucked up."

I hung up before he could respond.

Thomas Leitz said, "He's leaving! He's walking down the block and . . . he's gone! How . . . ?"

"I called in some debts. Your turn now. What about Coryell?"

"It's not . . . I didn't . . ."

"If I don't make a call, he's back in five minutes."

Another long wait. It was taking time for Thomas Leitz to realize his luck had run out.

"Good-bye, Thomas. What time does the doorman get off?"

"WAIT! Okay. Go to the school, my locker. I'll give you the combination. You'll find what you want taped under the top shelf. No fucking good to me anymore."

"Why do you say that?" I asked, although I knew the answer.

"You haven't heard, smart guy? Walter's dead. They found his body yesterday. You and Sebastian and Julia can all have a great time remembering what a wonderful human being that shit was. You can read the note at his funeral. I won't be there."

WEEK THREE: ALL IN

★ CHAPTER 40 ★

Never underestimate the impact of boredom on a teenager. I didn't experience any. My daily concern was getting through the day. The cold, the work, the guards, the whole system, even many of my fellow *zeks*—they all had it in for me. I wasn't unique, they had it in for *everybody*. That was life, if you can call it that, in the camps. Whatever energy you managed was focused on making it to tomorrow. Looking back, I've often wondered why we bothered—tomorrow would only replay today.

Andras Leitz could not have come from a more different time and place, and holed up, as I came to find out, in a suite at the Regency Hotel, with only a TV for company—no one to talk to, no one to friend or tweet or text—he was bored. So, only somewhat to my surprise when I called him from the lobby, he told me to come up to his room. Of course, the news that Irina was on the run might have had something to do with it too.

I got lucky at Thomas Leitz's school. A construction crew was collecting weekend overtime while they drank coffee and laid a new floor in the main hallway. They didn't give me a second look when I told them I'd forgotten some lesson plans. I went from the school to the office and made a copy of the note Thomas had hidden for the last four years. It answered one set of questions and opened another. I put the copy in my wallet and the original in the safe. I walked home hoping I wouldn't encounter the emptiness that was there. No more empty than I was used to, but all the more so because of what I'd hoped to find.

I could have called her. What would I say? I'm still working for your man,

Batkin, because he has a hold on me I can't explain? Ever hear of Beria? My father, Beria? She probably blamed me for Irina being on the loose as well.

I got the vodka from the freezer and spent a lonely evening thinking about Leitz and his family. I'd wandered into the middle of it, eyes wide shut, and had them opened to the horrors of the kind that can only be delivered by those closest to us. I'd grown up with a different set of horrors until I got the opportunity to join the enemy I couldn't beat. But even today, I was still victimized—by my past and by Taras Batkin because he knew how much he could hurt. Stop, I told myself. You're still a victim only because you allow Batkin to make you one. I could have called his bluff this morning. I still could. But I didn't—and wouldn't. I was afraid. I had the chance to right a thirty-year wrong, but not if Batkin blew it up before I even got started. Maybe Aleksei wouldn't care. Hard to know, but I was scared to take that bet. So I'd sold a piece of my soul to Batkin—at least for the time being. I had the sense that the Leitzes had made a similar deal some years ago.

Beria put in a brief appearance, across the room, chuckling.

I know all about selling souls. You'll get used to it after a while. We all do.

He didn't leave when I told him to go away, but he didn't say any more either.

As I sipped my vodka, I kept thinking that some event had set off the horrors of the Leitz family. The obvious candidate was the suicide of Sebastian's daughter, Daria. Everything from Pauline's breakdown to Marianna's drinking to Thomas's blackmail dated to four years ago. But I was guessing there was something else, something earlier, something that had been, in Thomas Leitz's words, swept under the rug—an open wound growing more infected with each passing year. At some point, nothing short of amputation would cure it. Perhaps Sebastian and his siblings believed that the early death of their parents was sufficient tragedy for one lifetime, that they were entitled to bury any others. They were justified in doing whatever was necessary to avoid the heartbreaks that inevitably came later, as they do to all families.

My deliberations were punctuated with refills of my glass and checks of my watch and the hope that the next sound would be the chime of the elevator and the scrape of Victoria's key in the lock. Beria shook his head.

No key by 9:30, and the Leitzes were growing foggy in a vodka haze, so I took myself and Lavrenty Pavlovich over to a brew pub at the Seaport that makes a passable burger and pretty good beer. Neither shed further light. When I got home, the apartment was still empty and I had the first unhappy premonition of what that emptiness could feel like if it lasted beyond the next day or two.

I went to the office early and worked the Basilisk. Irina had hit eight ATMs after she took off, withdrawing a thousand dollars from each as she made her way downtown. I'd spelled out the game plan for her, two nights ago in the car. The last withdrawal was on Canal Street—Chinatown. Not where I'd expect her to run. Unless . . .

In the last few years, low-priced bus service between New York and Boston has become a booming business. The Fung Wah Bus company was the pioneer, running hourly coaches from Chinatown to Chinatown. Irina wanted her car. That would give her freedom. I reached for the phone to call Gina and stopped. Too much time to get to Gibbet. There had to be a faster way.

Feeling a touch of the same satisfaction I used to get when I fed some Yasenevo desk jockey the kind of bullshit that would make his life miserable for a week or two, I called Philip Paine. Dragon Lady had been tamed, she put me straight through. He didn't sound happy to hear from me.

"I need a favor, on behalf of Leitz and Batkin."

"We're not in a position to—"

"There's a barn near your campus, on Martin Lane, right off Hayfields Drive. I want to know if there's a car in it, a BMW Three Series with New York plates."

"This is a very irregular request."

"It's important."

"Do Ambassador Batkin and Dr. Leitz know you're calling?"

His reliance on titles grated—if only because they slowed everything down. I ignored that and put down my bluff.

"Call them if you wish. I'll hang on."

An easy bet, and I won.

"What does this have to do with . . ."

I raised just to make sure. "It has to do with a group of students at your school who've been running a porn ring right under your nose. The Feds are aware of it, and I'm trying to make sure it doesn't blow up in everybody's face."

A very long silence.

"*Pornography?*"

"*Child* pornography. A crime—good tabloid copy too."

"Oh, my God . . ."

283

"You'll get someone to check the barn?"

"Please . . . Don't do anything. I'll call right back."

The car was gone, as I suspected. Paine peppered me with panicked questions, which I evaded. He grew increasingly excited until I hung up. I felt more guilty pleasure—akin to what the Germans call schadenfreude, delight in someone else's difficulties. Paine should have kept better tabs on his students. In loco parentis, as he said.

With the cash and her car, Irina was going to be tough to track. My one link was Andras. I called Leitz.

"I need to talk to your son."

"Not a good idea."

"I'm not concerned with good or bad. I need to talk to him."

"He's in a safe place. Like you suggested."

"I'm not going to give him up. He's in a world of trouble—of his own making. I'm his best chance to get out of it, maybe in one piece."

"The answer is still no."

"He may feel differently."

"You've been paid. You've gone to extra trouble, I'm aware of that. Tell me what you consider fair compensation, and I'll consider it."

Did he think I was shaking him down? Or was he trying to buy me off?

"How do I get in touch with your pal Konychev?"

He paused. "Why?"

"It could help your son."

"I . . . I don't know."

"You have investors you don't know how to contact? I find that hard to believe."

"I know where to find his lawyers. I only met the man once."

I wasn't sure whether he was telling the truth, just being cagey, or outright lying. I didn't have time to think about it.

"Talk to your brother recently?"

"Thomas? Why?"

"He had Nosferatu outside his apartment yesterday, he's looking for your brother-in-law's computers."

"What would Thomas know about those?"

"He's been blackmailing Coryell for the last four years."

"WHAT? Thomas? Walter? Blackmail? What the hell are you talking about?"

284

"One of the things this is about. One of the reasons I need to talk to your son."

"What blackmail?"

"I suspect it has to do with the death of your daughter."

A long silence. Then a whisper. "Daria?"

"That's right."

Another silence. "Your services are finished. Don't call again."

I started to respond. But I was talking to a dead line.

★ CHAPTER 41 ★

I'd told Leitz to take it away, but I asked the Basilisk if Andras was using his cell phone.

No deal, it responded.

Okay, what's Sebastian Leitz been up to?

Ah-ha, the beast said, *you're not as dumb as you look.*

But Leitz was. For a supposed genius, he was rock-fucking stupid. He'd used his American Express black card to guarantee a suite at the Regency for a guest named Robert Klein.

I left a note for Foos to be on call before I caught the subway uptown. I spent most of the train ride cursing Leitz. Not just for his overprotective stubbornness, but his idiocy. The Regency was a well-known luxury hotel and exactly the kind of place a rich Wall Streeter would park his son. Worse, at Park and East Sixty-first, it was right around the corner from his mansion. Leitz probably figured—again foolishly—he could look in on the kid on his way to and from power breakfasts with his Wall Street advisers over fifty-dollar eggs in the Regency restaurant.

I called "Robert Klein" from the lobby. He shouldn't have answered but he did.

"It's Turbo—your chauffeur, remember? We need to talk, about Irina. I'm downstairs."

"What about Irina?"

"She's gone. On the run. What room?"

"My dad said . . ."

"I know what he said. I told him to say it. Things have changed."

Silence.

"She's in trouble Andras. Big trouble. You can help her. You may be the only one who can. I'm Foos's friend, remember? Call him if you want."

More silence.

Then, "Room eight-oh-one."

He answered the door wearing jeans and a plaid shirt. He was tall in a way that I hadn't noticed over the weekend, in my haste to get out of Gibbet. Almost six one, with blue eyes and a soft-featured baby face. His hair was curly, like his father's, more brown than red, and cut neatly around his head. His eyes looked past me and darted up and down the hall, before he stood aside. I wasn't sure who he was looking for, but I would have bet his bank account on his old man. We shook hands. His grip was firm enough, but uncertain, quick to let go.

A suite at the Regency was not the way I'd treat my son if I'd just found out he'd been running a porn ring, but Aleksei would say I had my own fatherly shortcomings. The living room reflected someone's idea of what wealth should look like. Expensive wallpaper, striped fabrics, chintz pillows, solid, anonymous furniture. Three doors leading elsewhere, two bedrooms and a bathroom, I guessed. The kid standing in the middle of it looked out of place.

"Thanks for letting me come up," I said, starting easy. "How're you doing?"

"Okay, I guess." He plopped on a striped couch. "To tell you the truth, I have no idea."

"You're going through a rough patch."

"Yeah. What about Irina?"

"She's run away, like I said. You heard about her stepfather, yesterday?"

He nodded. "It's my fault."

"I don't know that. I want to hear your story."

His hand sliced through the air. Tough kid. Or kid trying to play tough. "What else do you know about Irina?"

I settled in on an upholstered chair across from the sofa. "She took off right after the shooting, like she was waiting for a chance to run. She withdrew eight thousand dollars, went to Gibbet, and picked up her car. I think she had a destination in mind. I think you might know where it is. She doesn't believe this—she thinks she's smarter than he is—but if Karp, the assassin, finds her before I do, he'll snap her in half like a little bird. I like his chances a lot better than hers. Any idea where she went?"

He put his head in his hands and said nothing.

"Andras—you can help her."

"It's all my fault."

I had no patience for that self-pitying refrain, but I backed off to give him a chance to think.

"Tell me about the Players? Your idea?"

He shook his head. "It just happened, you know?"

"No. I don't know."

He shook his head again. "I can't explain. It just kind of happened."

I'd thought, perhaps, the events of the last few days would have been traumatic enough to make him want to talk. He wasn't ready. Part me, the Cheka part, said sweat him, punish him, the kid was guilty, a child-criminal, criminal first. Would've worked, more than likely. Maybe he deserved it. Maybe we'd get to that. But not yet.

"How long ago? When did it start?"

He shrugged. "Few years."

"Why? How? Who rented the place above the liquor store?"

He shrugged again. "We all did."

"We?"

"Yeah. We."

"Who's we?"

"You already know that. If you don't, then . . ."

The kid was thinking.

"Why?"

"Why what?"

"Why'd you do it?"

"We had our reasons."

"Had or have?"

"What's that supposed to mean?"

"Just asking if the reasons are past or present? You want to tell me about them?"

He shook his head.

"You know we're going to get there sooner or later, don't you?"

"I'm not sure I should be talking to you. I think I should call my dad."

"Go ahead."

He didn't move. Neither did I.

"You ever think you'd end up here?" I asked. "A spot like this, looking at options, or absence of options? In a box?"

He took a minute before he shook his head, no. The first positive sign since I arrived.

"Life works like that. You think you control it, to the extent you think about it at all, then fate intervenes, shit happens, shit multiplies, and here you are. I'm not sure you know half your own story. Want to hear it?"

He paused, then nodded. He didn't look happy. I wouldn't have either.

I took him through the whole tale. The bug on his father's computers. The interviews with his aunts and uncles. The junkies at the Black Horse. I skimmed over uncles Walter and Thomas for the moment, we'd come back to them. It took maybe half an hour.

"You tricked your uncle. You used Irina's—Salomé's—e-mail to set up the date at the Black Horse. She found out and followed you there. You weren't expecting her, you were waiting for him. He didn't show. You didn't know he'd been busted with a kid in his car a hundred miles away."

"That's what you were talking about Saturday? When you said rape?"

"Rockville, Connecticut, is where it happened."

"How do you . . . ?"

"Know what I know? I have lots of sources. Your friend Foos helped."

I retraced the ground we'd covered in the car—I wasn't sure how much had sunk in—I figured the repetition wouldn't hurt. He didn't interrupt. He stayed head down, then stood and walked around the room, looking here and there, but seeing little. He returned to the couch where he curled up in a fetal position. He made me feel worse than a Cheka interrogator. Every piece of information I flung inflicted pain.

I wound down the story. He was in tears. Tough kid evaporated. This was a family matter, except the failings of the family had let others in, to take advantage. Thousands of kids victimized in the pictures and videos Walter Coryell and the BEC enabled. I couldn't rectify that, but I couldn't let it go on either.

"You know where this is going, don't you?" I asked.

He shook his head, still crying.

"Sure you do—Uncle Walter."

"What about him?"

I took out the note from Thomas Leitz's locker and put it on the coffee table in front of him.

"I'm sorry, Andras, you have to believe that. This is from your sister."

He unwound himself slowly. It took a minute or two for curiosity to win out over self-pity. At least that was my unkind perspective.

He unfolded the paper and read it. He crushed the note and dropped it as if it burned his fingers. He cried loud, hard enough to shake the walls of the hotel.

"OH, NO, JESUS GOD. I DIDN'T . . . I COULDN'T . . ."

"Walter was the bad guy. He caused this. Do you understand that?"

He curled up again, shaking his head.

"Andras?"

"Leave me alone."

"This isn't your fault."

He shook his head.

"It's his. He's the reason you've done everything you've done. The reason you all have. You've got to acknowledge that."

No response.

"Andras?"

"I need . . . I need some time . . . alone." The voice was below a whisper.

I didn't like that idea, but I didn't see any way around it, if I wanted to stay on his side.

"Okay."

He got to his feet and wandered aimlessly off toward one of the bedrooms. I started to follow, to see where he was going. He closed the door in my face.

I went back to my chair. The family had delivered nothing but trouble since I'd met them, each member finding a deeper mine to dig. The note on the table looked up at me. The key, I'd told Andras, not sure I was right, until he reacted. None of us can make excuses for abuse, especially of a child. But all too often we seem able to find an excuse for covering it up. For all the right reasons, we tell ourselves, oblivious to the magnification of the crime.

My cell phone buzzed.

Victoria said, "Turbo, where are you?"

"Can't say."

"Can you talk?"

"A little."

"I'm outside your office. I'm sorry about yesterday. I'm . . . I'm having a hard time reconciling all the conflicting things that are going on."

"And I don't make it any easier."

"I wasn't going to say that. But . . ."

"I know. I'm sorry too."

"Will you be back?"

"Not sure when. I'm trying to find the girl before Nosferatu does."

"That what Batkin wanted?"

"Yes. But I'd be doing it anyway."

"He still your client?"

"Not voluntarily. I tried to walk away."

"I don't understand."

Beria was sitting in a chintz-covered chair.

How are you going to explain that, smart guy?

"I'll tell you all about it when I see you. If you're asking whether I still feel any obligation to him, the answer is no."

Beria frowned at that.

Victoria hesitated a moment. "I thought about what you said. There are things you should know."

"About Konychev?"

"Among other things, yes."

"Tell me."

"I can't, on the phone."

"I can't leave here now. I'll be back as soon as I can."

"Your stubbornness is going to be the death of one of us."

She hung up. More in frustration than anger this time, or so I hoped. She was trying, I wasn't helping. That's the way fate works. Beria smiled.

I picked up the note and pulled apart the crushed-up ball. I flattened it on the table. Daria Leitz's tidy script reached through the years, grasping for vengeance.

If you want to know how this happened, ask Uncle Walter.

★ CHAPTER 42 ★

The first crash was a thudding bang, behind the bedroom door. The second was accompanied by breaking glass. The third, more glass.

Door locked. Another crash. More shattering glass.

I kicked the door. Once. Twice. Some give on the third try. The wood cracked on the fourth, and I hit it with my shoulder. It crashed open. Andras was climbing through the shattered window across the room. A blast of cold air blew through my clothes.

"ANDRAS!" I shouted.

He turned, just for a moment, enough for me to grab the leg that dangled inside the sill. I hung tight while I gathered my feet under me.

"ANDRAS!"

"LET ME GO!"

"NO! THAT'S NO ANSWER."

He pulled hard, twisting and squirming. My grip slipped. I reached around his knee.

"LET ME GO!"

"NO!"

I got my legs underneath and pulled.

He wasn't giving up. He grabbed the window frame for leverage. Blood splattered from his slashed hands.

Fuck this.

I locked my left hand on his knee and reached for his belt with my right. It closed around leather and denim. I braced my feet against the wall and yanked with everything I had. He fell back into the room on top of me.

"NO!" He was up in a flash clawing back for the window.

I caught the belt again and pulled him back. He fell to the floor. I rolled on top. He kept fighting. I rolled him over and struck him across the face.

"NO! LET ME GO. I DESERVE TO DIE."

He kept squirming, but I was forty pounds heavier and spent more time in the gym. I got his arms to his sides and pinned them with my knees. His legs kept kicking but to little effect. The carpet was stained with blood. His hands looked badly cut. Not long before someone came to investigate. Robert Klein's cover, flimsy to begin with, was blown.

The thrashing slowed. He was breathing heavily, strength spent. "You should . . . you should have let me jump."

"No way."

"Why?"

He was still thinking, and his thinking was still focused on him. What makes kids—adolescents—so goddamned confident the whole world revolves around them?

"I've already seen a lifetime of pointless deaths. We've got Irina to worry about, remember? I still need your help, for her."

He stared up for a moment, some sense returning.

"Listen to me. We're going to wash your hands. You've got glass in those cuts. Then we're going to get help. You try one wrong move, you do one more stupid thing, I will knock you cold and leave you there, wherever there is. And that'll be last call for Irina. You understand?"

He nodded. He was scared and in pain.

"Let's go."

The sink ran red as we flushed blood and glass. The palms were shredded. He was lucky not to have severed fingers. I wrapped his hands in towels and grabbed a couple extra for the road.

"Get your coat. We can't stay here."

"But . . ."

"Do as I say. You need medical attention. Move."

He got a wool coat from the closet.

"Put your hands in the sleeves so they don't show. We're going downstairs, outside, turn right and right again on Sixty-first."

A man in a black suit with a silver name tag came off the elevator as we got on.

"You hear anything unusual up here?" he asked. "Disturbance? Breaking glass?"

"Nope." I pushed the button for the lobby.

"What room are you in?"

"Eight-fourteen."

"Thanks."

The man hurried down the hall. The door closed. We made it through the lobby. An empty cab cruised East Sixty-first Street, and I hailed it. There was no time to check for Nosferatu or anyone else. I gave the driver an address on East Seventh Street and worked my cell phone as we sped downtown. Andras slumped against the door and didn't say a word.

"Lucky kid. He's lost more blood than's good for him, he's got a dozen stitches in each hand, and he's fortunate he's still got hands to stitch. Looks like he crushed a beer bottle in each one and refused to let go."

"Something like that," I said.

Petro Lutsenko, M.D., said, "I know. Don't ask. Don't ever ask."

He walked around his desk and sat across from me. A good looking fortysomething man of Ukrainian descent with a large nose and smiling eyes, the looks a bit marred by a pair of unusually hairy ears. His father had been on the Cheka's payroll for the occasional discreet medical repair when I was stationed here in the eighties. Petro had joined the old man's practice, with his newly minted M.D. from NYU, and kept up the family tradition. For which he was well compensated. I'd been waiting a long hour while he treated Andras.

"All built into the fee," I said.

"Speaking of which . . ."

"On its way here."

"He's resting and should keep resting for a day or two. I've given him a light painkiller and a sedative. I'm going to prescribe some antibiotics. What name . . . ?"

"Warren Brandeis."

He looked up from his pad. "Very funny."

I shrugged. "Not my joke. It's a real name."

"If you say so."

It was. One of Foos's straw men. The actual Warren Brandeis must have had left-leaning lawyer parents, which hadn't mattered much when he dropped dead of a heart attack at age fifty-two. Foos had loaded a couple of bank accounts with twelve grand and given him three credit cards and a driver's license, all of which were on the way to Lutsenko's office along with a checkbook so I could pay the good doctor off. My picture was on the license. An SUV was waiting for Brandeis at Avis on East Eleventh Street. We were burning one of our better identities on Andras.

Foos arrived and exchanged small talk with Lutsenko, whom he likes well enough to use as his own internist, while I wrote out a thousand-dollar check on Brandeis's account. Foos agreed to wait while I picked up the car. I trotted through the cold streets, checking my rear periodically, but saw nothing. To be sure, I took a subway to Grand Central, the shuttle across town, the Seventh Avenue IRT back downtown and a cab to East Eleventh Street. If Nosferatu was following, he'd need help not to have lost me. On the other hand, he could be waiting back at Lutsenko's office.

I double-parked the Ford Explorer outside. The block was empty. Lutsenko brought Andras outside. His hands were wrapped in white gauze. He looked tired and unhappy. I got out and helped him into the car.

"You're going to have to deal with Leitz," I said to Foos.

He nodded. "Figured that."

"He's gonna be pissed. Tell him it's for the kid's own good. Putting him at the Regency was asking for trouble."

"Figured that too. What do I say when he asks where he is now?"

"You don't have any idea."

"Has the benefit of being true. He might go to the police."

"If he does, tell him the *Post* will be digging into Walter Coryell and Franklin Druce by morning."

"He won't like that."

"Tell him I'll be in touch."

"That'll make him feel much better."

We got snarled in rush hour traffic. I kept an eye on the hundred cars behind me as they pushed and jostled for position on the way into the Holland Tunnel, where we'd all sit in place as the snake worked its way though its underground skin. If there was a tail, I had no way of spotting it, but I kept watch anyway. Andras leaned against his door, eyes closed. Traffic remained heavy along the turnpike extension until we reached the tolls at the junction of I-78. I took the interstate west thirty miles into New Jersey and switched for I-287 south. Another twenty miles and I exited with the neon sign for the Doubletree Hotel in sight. The hotel was close to the highway, surrounded by a few office parks and not much else. I bought a suite for the night, certainly less luxurious than the Regency, using my own name. We'd be gone before daybreak.

We went up to the room. Inexpensive, functional, well used, and all the atmosphere of the office park next door. No chintz here, but plenty of poly-ester. Andras took off his coat and dropped himself on the sofa.

"Now what?" he said.

"Something to eat?"

"Okay."

I called room service and ordered two steaks with fries, a Coke for him, and beer for me. I kept watch at the window, which overlooked the parking lot. A few cars pulled in, but their occupants appeared harmless. I found myself musing on what we all did for luggage before the invention of the wheeled suitcase. Andras kept his thoughts to himself. Time enough to let those loose.

The food came and we ate in silence. The steak was tough and tasteless, but I was hungry. I took heart in the fact that he ate hungrily as well.

When he finished, he fell back against the sofa and said, "All right, you brought me to the middle of fucking nowhere. What do you want?"

★ CHAPTER 43 ★

"Start with Uncle Walter."

"Asshole. I don't want to talk about him."

"You're going to have to. Sooner or later. To me or the police."

He shook his head.

"You kill him?"

"NO! He was . . ."

He turned away.

"He was what?"

"I'm not going to talk about that."

"He was what, Andras? Dead when you got there?"

He turned further until I was looking at the back of his head. The kid had spent his whole life overprotected by a rich father. The idea of vulnerability hadn't sunk in.

"Listen carefully." I put the telephone on speaker and punched in Nosferatu's number.

"What the fuck now, dead man?" he said in English.

Andras faced the phone.

"Fuck your mother," I said. "What are the ConnectPay servers worth to you, Karp?"

"Your life—maybe."

"The kind of stupid answer I'd expect from a *pidar gnoinyj*. Try again."

The slang translates literally as "rotten faggot," but as with so many Russian expressions (this one actually originates in the Ukraine), the meaning is much stronger. I was accusing him of being a passive homosexual fuck-bag with an acute case of the clap. No reason he should have a monopoly on the insults.

"You pathetic *pizda*"—cunt—"I will make sure you swallow your own balls before I break your neck."

"That what happened to Druce? You kill him on purpose, or did you fuck that up too?"

"I didn't kill that *petuh*"—male jailhouse whore—"I didn't need to. *Oy'ebis'l!*"—Fuck off!—"Why the fuck am I talking to you?"

"The servers," I reminded him.

"I want them. And the kid."

"What kid?"

"Don't waste my time. You're a *zek,* too stupid to live. The Leitz kid. Thinks he's clever. Thinks he can fuck the girl and steal the money. He's going to pay."

The voice was like ice. Just above a whisper. Andras sat frozen on the couch. I looked at him and put my finger to my lips.

"Who do you want more, Karp—the kid or the girl? Maybe we can make a deal."

"No deal, *zek.* I'm going to take care of everyone—you too—in my own time."

"Guess I was wrong, then."

"You've been wrong your whole life, *zek.* Fortunately for you, it's almost over."

A click and the line went dead.

Andras stared at the phone then back at me. "Who . . . Who is that guy?"

"The assassin. The one I told you about in the car. He means what he says. He's been told to get rid of you and Irina both. He's headed here—probably an hour or two away."

"Here?!"

"Don't worry. We'll be long gone. Feel like talking about Uncle Walter now?"

Andras walked around the room, animated, not stopping. Karp had gotten his attention, maybe even more than sister Daria's note. Up until now, it had been some sort of game for him. All played out long distance, anonymously, through computers and the Internet. He could stay removed, in his own world, protected by his technical expertise and his rich dad. After he made three or four perambulations, I had the feeling the shell of protectiveness was crumbling.

He was at the window when he turned back to face me.

"Why didn't you let me jump?"

Cracking, not crumbling. He was still thinking about himself.

"I grew up in a tough place. Too many people died. For no reason. Kids, parents too. Other parents fought to keep themselves and their kids alive. Most failed. Kids were left to fend for themselves. Man eat man. Man eat woman. Most of us ate whatever we could. That was the deal, every day. You learn the hard way about the value of life."

Blank stare.

"You study history at Gibbet School?"

"Sure."

"World War Two?"

"Yeah."

"Concentration camps?"

"Yes."

"Russia? Soviet Union?"

He shook his head.

Another strike against American education.

"I grew up in a concentration camp, Soviet version. They were different, they weren't about murdering Jews, but no less brutal. They were about murdering everyone. I saw more kids die than you have classmates. I'm one of the lucky ones. I made it."

It struck me I was using the same technique Batkin had on me—to the same end. We were both Chekists. Whatever works.

"You were in a concentration camp?"

I had his attention—finally.

"That's right. Labor camp. Gulag camp."

"Irina said her stepfather . . ."

"Was too. Same deal."

"But he's . . ."

"He's what?"

"HE'S A PIG!"

Maybe my history lesson was a mistake. He resumed his walk.

"Andras, tell me about Irina. She's a beautiful young woman. What's the deal between the two of you?"

He arrived back at the couch and fell backward on it, face held in bandaged hands. "She . . . We . . . Shit, you'll never understand."

"Try me. You have to know by now I'm trying to help."

He shook his head. "No. You can't."

"I think I can. Uncle Walter—he abused your sister. That's what the note meant, right?"

He looked up, pain penetrating every part of his face.

301

"Where'd you get that note?"

"It's going to hurt worse if I tell you."

"Can't hurt any worse."

I didn't want to do this, but I needed him to trust me and open up. More pain, for him, was the price.

"Uncle Thomas was the first to get there, right? First to find the body?"

He snuffled. "I came in right after. It was . . ."

"Horrible. I'm sure. Daria wrote the note before she . . . she used the gun. Thomas took it. And used it for years to blackmail Walter."

"Uncle Thomas? Blackmailed Uncle Walter? I don't get it. What for?"

"Thomas needed money. He spent . . . He spends more than he has. It's an addiction, like any other. People do bad things, even in families. Maybe especially in families."

He shook his head violently. "I always thought Uncle Walter . . . I always thought . . . It was supposed to be . . ."

"Thought what? What was supposed to be?"

He shook his head again and buried it in the cushions.

I took a deep breath. I didn't want to say it, but no avoiding it now. I told myself it was for the best and hoped I wasn't rationalizing.

"He abused you too, didn't he?"

I'd hit home. He sobbed into the sofa. I let him cry. There was no comfort I could offer.

After a while, I said, "It's not your fault, you know."

He raised his head and looked at me, face red and stained with tears.

"IT IS MY FAULT! I didn't do anything to stop him."

"You can't blame yourself for that. Nobody else will."

"You don't get it. You can't. He made me feel like I was special, you know. I realize it sounds sick now, but that's how it works. It was our special thing. I knew it was wrong, but I didn't want it to stop, because then I wouldn't be special anymore. I didn't know about Daria. I didn't."

"It wasn't your fault Andras. He manipulated you. The same way he manipulated your sister. And lots of others. It was his disease. Not yours."

"NO! That's not it. That's not what I mean. You don't know. YOU DON'T!"

I had a bad feeling. "Okay. I'm listening."

His voice dropped to a whisper, as if he feared he'd be overheard.

"Everybody knew. Mom and Dad. Aunt Julia. Everybody. Nobody did anything about it."

"That's still not your fault."

"Yes it is—I didn't make them."

★ CHAPTER 44 ★

We sat in the rented SUV, heater running, while Andras finished his story. He'd got most of it out upstairs before I announced it was time to move. Two reasons. We had a destination now—back to Massachusetts—and we'd have visitors shortly. I'd made it easy for Karp to trace us. I didn't have a plan, just the gamble that if he was focused on me, I could stay a step ahead and protect Andras while we kept moving, and he'd have a harder time hurting anyone else, like the girl.

As with many people who have held a secret for as long as he had— especially as painful as this one—it all came tumbling out once he started. The abuse, which had gone on for several years. The Christmas party when Julia had barged in, Walter's hands in Andras's underwear. The whispered arguments that followed, among his parents, his father and Julia, everyone but Walter. Andras was twelve years old. He understood they were talking about him, about him and Walter. What he didn't understand was why nothing happened. Everything went back to the way it was before. Except he was no longer special to Walter. He hadn't understood why, although he put it down to getting caught—and that was somehow his fault in his mind. He figured out some years later that Walter had been effectively exiled. He didn't show up at holidays or family functions anymore, some excuse was made about how busy he was. That was how the Leitzes dealt with it. What Andras didn't know, what no one apparently knew, according to him, was that Uncle Walter had already started on Daria and somehow managed to keep it up even after being banned. Andras suspected as much when Daria committed suicide, but there was no proof, and he kept his fears and accusations to himself.

The suicide led to his mother's breakdown and his parents' divorce. She never said so, but it was clear to Andras that she blamed Leitz for everything that had happened. Andras was confused and frightened—his own experience and his family's response, or nonresponse—still weighed on his young mind, as did his guilt over Daria. He was glad to seek refuge in boarding school, far away from the whole scene.

It was a boy named Kevin, three years ahead of him at Gibbet, who introduced Andras to the world of online porn for a fee. Somehow he knew to seek him out. He'd been there too. In Kevin's case, it was his next-door neighbor, a doctor, who initiated secret touches and more—and then a whole, huge world of men who were only too happy to buy computer gear, pay apartment rentals, and shower gifts and cash on kids like Kevin and Andras if they were willing to strip, jerk off, and do things with their friends in front of a Web cam. Turned out there were several kids at Gibbet with similar experiences. That didn't make the school unusual, maybe just par for the course. One came up with the idea of the Oscar Wilde theme. Andras was the computer expert. He wired and equipped an earlier, two-room apartment in Crestview, before doing the same in the expanded playhouse above the liquor store. The clients paid for it all, then the kids started charging on a fee-for-service basis. No client complained. None of the kids took it that seriously. It was kind of a lark, a joke. They felt more pity than anything for these sad perverts who shelled out thousands to watch them prance and preen in costume before jerking off or jumping into the sack. Hooking up with monetary benefits. Andras hadn't even focused that seriously on the money. He didn't need it, but he kept opening new bank accounts to hold the growing stash of cash.

"So you were all abused kids?" I asked, just to be sure. "That was the common bond?"

"Yeah."

"Usually family members?"

He thought for a moment. "Usually, not always . . . like Kevin."

"What about Irina?" I asked as gently as I could.

"What about her?" he snapped, immediately on the defensive.

He shook his head violently from side to side. I got ready to grab him, in case he tried to run. But he only swiveled in his seat and looked out the window. Not the time to push it.

"Okay," I said. "What happened next?"

What happened next was that he started to have feelings for Irina. She held him at bay, but relented with time, and they began going out as well as hooking up for the benefit of their growing Internet audience. He found nothing odd about this progression of events—I understand it's the way it often works with kids today (minus the online show-and-tell)—but it still seemed odd to me. On the other hand, everything about his story was bizarre. He began to feel protective and wanted her to stop performing. She told him to mind his own business. I could hear her, and I guessed her language was more colorful. He couldn't let it go. He began to monitor her online activities, especially her "private auditions." He grew increasingly jealous of "frankyfun" as franky took up more of her time. He hacked into franky's account at ConnectPay and was horrified—but not necessarily shocked—to find it belonged to a guy with the same address as Uncle Walter. It didn't take him any longer than it had me to make the connection.

Andras started toying with franky electronically—inserting minor malware programs into ConnectPay's servers, causing modest data corruption and periodic operating glitches. He confronted Irina again. She told him to back off, she could manage her own affairs. So he sent a message to franky, from Oscar, telling him bad things would happen if he continued to pursue Salomé. Franky didn't believe him. Salomé kept performing. Andras hacked into ConnectPay's servers, accessed the company's bank information and moved three million dollars through several accounts into his own and Irina's. He figured that was enough to get franky's attention. Oscar sent franky another e-mail informing him of the "fine" for not obeying the rules and warning him the next one would be double. When franky continued to pursue Salomé, Andras hit ConnectPay for five million in November.

He told the tale calmly and precisely, without emotion. Except when I asked about Irina. Somewhere along the story line, we moved from fact to fiction. I let him keep talking. We'd go through it again, maybe more than once, and the inconsistencies would begin to show themselves.

Things stayed quiet through December, but franky was all over Salomé as soon as they got back to school. So Andras, using her e-mail address, made the date at the Black Horse. Only franky didn't show. Irina did, and she was royally pissed off.

I felt no sympathy for the late Walter Coryell. I did wonder if there were any members of the Leitz family who weren't putting the squeeze on another.

Andras figured the only way out of Irina's doghouse was to resolve things with franky once and for all. As soon as his uncle got sprung from the Tolland County jail, Andras arranged to meet him on Wednesday in New York. But when he arrived at Coryell's office, nobody answered the buzzer. Uncle Walter didn't answer his cell phone either. He went looking for Coryell at home. He wasn't there, neither was Julia, of course, but the kids let him in. He hung with them until they got reabsorbed in their videogames, then he tossed his uncle's bedroom, taking every key he could find.

Two of the keys got him into YouGoHere's offices—and another world of trouble. Coryell was dead at his desk. The body wasn't yet bloated, and it didn't stink. If Andras was telling the truth, Coryell had been killed sometime Tuesday night or Wednesday morning.

Andras had been clever—not smart, but clever. Smart would've walked away—or called the police. As it was, he'd acted with coolness well beyond his years and done the job he decided to do, leaving the slimmest of trails. But he didn't know that he was going to have someone like Karp looking for him.

He locked the door to YouGoHere and toured Long Island City on foot, withdrawing a few hundred dollars at the ATMs he passed along the way (he hadn't counted on the Basilisk either, but who does) until he found a motel where no one would notice one more person coming and going. He rented a room for two nights, cash. He returned to Coryell's office, stopping at a UPS store to buy cardboard boxes. He dismantled the servers and the server rack, packed them up and transported the lot by gypsy cab to the motel. Leaving everything there, he took the subway to Manhattan and the Fung Wah Bus to Boston, got to Gibbet, picked up Irina's car, and returned to Queens. He loaded up the servers and went back to Massachusetts, one step ahead of the snowstorm. He stored everything in the barn and went into hiding at the playhouse while he figured out what to do next. He'd confessed the whole thing to Irina, of course, and she persuaded him to go back to school, as if nothing had happened. Then I showed up.

It was a good story, especially for a seventeen-year-old. I wondered how much was his and how much hers. I knew one thing—only about half was true.

"What were you planning to do—with the servers?"

"Don't know. I just thought . . . I couldn't just leave them there, you know?"

I was about to tell him I didn't believe that when a black Escalade swung into the hotel drive and stopped just past the lighted entrance. New York plates. No way the occupants could see us thirty yards away, but I pushed Andras down in his seat and slid lower in mine. Two men climbed out awkwardly, as if something under their long overcoats inhibited their movement. They went inside. A third descended and followed more slowly. His head just cleared the hotel door.

Nosferatu.

The boxes holding the servers were still in the barn, covered with a blue plastic tarpaulin. We loaded them into the Explorer and started back toward New York. When we got off the Mass Pike onto I-84, I called Foos.

"I'm traveling with the kid and ConnectPay's servers. Don't want to bring them into town."

He grunted. "Where you feel like stopping?"

"How about Stamford?"

"I'll call back."

Ten minutes later, he said, "Super Eight Motel, I-Ninety-Five, exit six. I've booked three adjoining rooms. Brandeis. I'll take the first train out, gets in at six forty-four."

"Call Victoria before you leave. Tell her I'm on the move and will call when I can."

"She gonna appreciate a five a.m. wake-up call?"

"Doubt it."

He grunted again and hung up.

I set the cruise control at sixty-eight. It occurred to me, as I crossed Connecticut for the second time in three days, this was better support than I ever had when I was with the Cheka.

★ CHAPTER 45 ★

The Super 8 was clean, functional, and anonymous. In other words, perfect. Or almost—too close to the highway and train station for my purposes, but I would have taken us to the center of Siberia if we didn't have business to conduct.

We rolled in at 5:22 A.M. Andras hadn't said much during the drive, leaving me to my ruminations. I couldn't tell whether he was sleeping as he slumped in his seat, or ruminating as well. Moody, Aunt Marianna said. Introspective, Jenny Leitz corrected. He certainly had enough material to occupy his thoughts, starting with how he was going to stay out of jail—assuming he stayed alive.

I went back over his story a couple of times. I believed the abuse and his desire to keep his uncle away from Irina. I didn't believe he'd ripped off ConnectPay—or the BEC—as a means to that end. I certainly didn't believe he'd taken the servers—going to all the trouble to cover any trail—with no idea of what he planned to do with them. I also wasn't convinced Coryell was dead when Andras got to his office. Hard to see a seventeen-year-old murdering his uncle—never mind by breaking his neck—but no less difficult than seeing him running a child pornography operation. I could check part of Andras's story with Victoria, if the FBI had reestablished its stakeout in time—and if she was still talking to me. That gave me something else to ponder as I drove through the night.

I saw her face, more than once, floating in the night air, just outside the windshield, smiling one time, pouting the next, intruding when she decided to, just as she'd done in the months she'd been gone. She faded and was replaced by Beria, his all-knowing grin mocking from beyond reach. *Fuck your mother,* I told him. He frowned and disappeared. Victoria came back. *Call me,* she said. *I have things you should know.*

Not now, was my response. What was that? Leitz's dangerous arrogance? Partly. My own hubris? Certainly. Doing things my own way for too long. More certainly. Worse, was I unwilling to let her into a part of my life I was determined to wall off as my own? In that territory, maybe I really did want to fly solo. Beria reappeared, nodding vigorously. Good thing Andras was with me. Otherwise I might have stopped at the first hotel with an open bar.

I made Andras wait upstairs while I carried the servers up to the motel's second floor. He was all but sleepwalking, exhausted, emotionally drained, and functioning at about one-third capacity. I suggested a shower before we went to the train station and stood guard outside the bathroom. I skipped mine, I didn't trust him not to run. He perked up when I said we were going to pick up Foos.

"Really?! He's coming here?"

"You weren't listening last night."

He shook his head. "Sorry, I was caught up in my own space, you know?"

This kid had been through more than most boys his age. Still, his self-centeredness grated, but maybe I was just tired.

Not much activity around the Stamford station. The train pulled in right on time. A few people got off, Foos among them, carrying a duffel bag with a backpack over his shoulder. Andras took off like a shot. He was still trying to wrap his arms around the big man as I caught up.

"I can't believe you're here," Andras said to Foos. "I think it's going to be okay."

"Don't count on it," he said. "You fucked up, big time."

The skinny arms fell away as Andras recoiled.

"I thought you . . . ," he said.

"I know what you thought," Foos said. "Don't make assumptions. About me or anyone else. You're in a shitload of trouble and you've put me on the hook with your old man, who's my friend. Turbo too. This is not how I was planning to spend my day."

Andras turned away. Foos nodded at me. I nodded back. The psychology was honest and perfect. Setting himself up as the bad cop made Andras's only option to rely on me. I'd have to reconsider my views on mathematicians.

Foos said, "I'm hungry. Let's get breakfast. You hungry, Andras?"

Andras nodded meekly.

"Turbo, we're in your care. Find us a diner, preferably one with superior pancakes."

Andras smiled faintly, and I went with the program, meaning I stopped at the first place I spotted on the way back to the motel.

We ordered, and I sat back chewing my bacon, eggs, hash browns, and toast, sipping coffee while Foos devoured a platter-size plate of pancakes and worked Andras over in his own huggy bear merged with porcupine style. He extracted the same story. All the weak points sounded weaker the second time through. When it was finished, he asked the same question.

"What were you planning to do with the servers?"

Andras shook his head and looked at his plate.

"Don't know," he whispered. He was having a harder time lying to Foos than he had to me.

"Bullshit, man!" Foos said. "I get up at five a.m., travel all the way up here for this kind of crap?"

He said it with a smile, but the voice was bordering on hard. Tears formed in the kid's eyes. He was between a rock and a hard place—and the hard place's name was Irina.

Andras shook his head. "I'm sorry. It's true. I . . ."

"Don't make it worse," Foos said. He looked at me. "Let's blow. We got work to do."

I used some of Warren Brandeis's cash to pay the bill, and we drove back to the motel. Upstairs, Foos eyed the servers and took out a laptop and a handful of cables from the duffel bag.

"Set 'em up, let's see what we got."

"I can help," Andras said eagerly.

Foos turned to him, the usually sparkling eyes dark and hard. "Uh-uh. I'll explain a few facts of life. Turbo here has put his ass on the line for you. There's guys out there willing to kill for these things. You and I are friends, but I'm on his side, and you're not playing straight. That means we can't trust you. So, no, you can't help. Go get some sleep." He turned his back, shutting him out.

Andras teared again as he stood there, hoping Foos would relent. When he didn't, the boy walked slowly to the connecting door to his room, shoulders slumped.

"Leave it ajar," I said.

He did as he was told.

"That's some hold that girl has," I said softly.

"You sure it's her?"

"Can't see who else."

"Thought I could crack the shell, but it's tough, as you say. I'll take another shot later."

I don't normally bet against him, but in this case I wasn't ready to give his chances better than even money.

We stacked up the servers, sixteen in all, and connected the cables. Foos plugged in his laptop, sat at the small motel desk, and went to work. I checked on Andras, who was curled up, asleep, still clothed, on top of the bedspread. I felt sorry for him, but he didn't make it easy.

I thought about calling Victoria, but decided to wait and see what Foos found. I took the shower I'd passed up earlier. Hot, hard spray massaged tired muscles. I stretched out on the bed in the third room and went under immediately. I was dreaming about Victoria and video cameras when I heard him call.

"Turbo! You better check this out."

The bedside clock radio said 8:15. I felt the stiffness and lethargy you get with too little sleep after too long without any. I stretched, rinsed my cotton mouth in the bathroom and went next door.

Foos's laptop screen was filled with rows of data—names, numbers, amounts. A digital carpet of information.

"Remember that case I told you about, the one the Feds busted? Based in Belarus, ninety thousand customers?"

"Yeah."

"Double it. They're close to two hundred thousand accounts here, averaging ten K a year each, maybe more. I need more time with the data. But we're talking two billion a year, minimum. Say ConnectPay took five percent, that's a hundred mil."

"Real money."

"Uh-huh. Before the scamming."

"What scamming?"

"Looks as though someone's expanding the revenue stream by keyboarding the client base. Once they get bank and credit card access, they've got an app that starts adding small charges or making small withdrawals. Money moves through a series of banks, bogus accounts no doubt, then overseas. Guess where?"

"Belarus?"

"Very good. Looks like they're still testing the waters. Started a few months ago. They've only hacked a few thousand, netted about twenty mil so far. Tip of the iceberg. They've got endless material to work with."

In my exhaustion, I had another vision, this time, a lineup of old-fashioned western wanted posters across the wall, Konychev, Batkin, Lishin, Coryell, Nosferatu. At the end of the row, looking out of place, but maybe not, were Andras and Irina.

I shook my head and the image vanished. "I never met the guy, but this sounds a little too advanced for our late friend Walter Coryell."

"Actually, you can buy apps like this online if you know where to go. But you're right. The scamming's being run remotely. Some other computer, some other place working through zombies, hacking in. That and the money trail that heads for your old 'hood suggests other involvement."

"Like BEC involvement?"

"Good place to start."

"BEC ripping off the BEC?"

"Technically, no. BEC ripping off BEC's customers."

I had a thought. "Or the reason Alexander Lishin is no longer among the living. He had the expertise. He tried a solo venture, figuring what Konychev and Batkin didn't know wouldn't hurt them. Probably would still be getting away with it too, except Konychev had someone searching for whoever was ripping them off, and that guy found Lishin's trail."

"Works for me."

I lowered my voice. "Where do the kids fit in?"

He shook his head. "It's not the scamming. Timing doesn't line up, for one thing. For another, I can see where someone hacked into the frankyfun account months ago, and it's a whole different picture. Does leave hanging the question of what Andras was going to do with the servers."

"I'm guessing it was her idea—and that's why he's so close-lipped. He's told us all about himself, but every time the story gets close to her, he veers off in another direction."

"Protecting her?"

"Could be what he thinks."

"Then what's she up to?"

"No good, I'm all but certain, but beyond that . . ." I shrugged. "She's also gone underground with eight grand in cash."

"She'll fuck up. Everyone does."

"Maybe. Time's not on her side—or ours." I told him about Nosferatu.

"Think he really wants the kid?"

"Yeah, I do. Get the Basilisk to recheck Coryell's calls on Tuesday, after he got out of the slammer."

He worked the keyboard and the ConnectPay data field was replaced by the familiar Q&A screen. A short list of numbers, then names, came up. Andras. Nosferatu. Sebastian Leitz.

"Leitz call Coryell or the other way around?"

"Leitz placed the call."

"And got through on the first try?"

"Right."

"How'd he know Coryell was out? Anybody call Leitz right before?"

"Hold on . . . Guy named Patrick Burns."

That name didn't mean anything, unless . . . "Burns call Leitz two Tuesdays ago, from Bedford?"

The key board clattered. "Called from Bedford twice that morning, then from Midtown that afternoon."

Tan Coat. I had a bad feeling.

I told Foos what I was thinking, and he grunted, which is what he does when he doesn't have anything constructive to add.

I called Leitz. "We need to talk. Meet me at your house in an hour."

"Where the hell's my son?"

"Safe."

"I could have you arrested for kidnapping."

"I saved his life last night."

"What the hell happened? The hotel said broken window . . ."

"I'll tell you when I see you."

"Where are you?"

"I'll be there in an hour."

"Can you baby-sit?" I asked Foos.

"No problem. Maybe I can convince our young friend to be more forth-coming when he wakes up."

I called Victoria from the road.

"Where are you this time?" she asked without preamble, her voice flat and neutral. I listened for anger or concern or hostility. Nothing there—yet.

"Just leaving Stamford."

"And what's in Stamford?"

"The Leitz kid. Foos. Me. ConnectPay servers. Which I came by without breaking any laws that I know of."

She didn't say anything for a minute.

Then, "It's a good thing for you—I think—that you arranged that wake-up call from Foos this morning. Not that I was getting much sleep. I was worried sick."

"I'm sorry. I haven't been in a place where I could call."

"You have time to explain?"

"I'll tell you all about it. Can we meet at your place? Noon?"

"Why my place?" Her voice was suspicious.

"I've got business uptown. Then I'm probably on the move again."

"On top of everything else, you've turned into a gypsy. Okay. Noon."

Beria appeared, shaking his head.

★ CHAPTER 46 ★

I caught the tail end of the rush hour and reached East Sixty-second Street at 10:45 A.M. The sky was dark gray and presaged more bad weather. 1010 WINS confirmed the forecast—another storm on the way, possible accumulations of eight to twelve inches. With only two days to recover from the last one, everyone was back on blizzard alert.

Snowbanks packed the side streets, parked cars crusted in place, covered in dirty white. I found a vacated spot on Leitz's block, full of shoveled snow, and forced the Explorer in. The same Filipina maid answered the door, and I climbed the two flights to his office. Impossible to pass through the Rothko chamber without pausing for one revolution of mystical color. I've never taken psychedelic drugs, but I had the idea that this was what it could be like. I pushed on.

Leitz was at his desk, under the Kline. The Malevich was in its place, and I felt two tinges of regret. One for Leitz. His life was probably over, at least as he'd known it. The other for the painting, which was unlikely now ever to grace my wall. Fate having its fun once again.

"Where's Andras?" Leitz said, angry.

"Still safe."

"I thought you were bringing him."

"You don't want him here, for all kinds of reasons."

"What the hell's that supposed to mean?"

I took the copy of Daria's note from my pocket, unfolded it and placed it on his desk, smoothing the crinkled paper. Then I stood back, out of range.

He read it, looked away and reread it. He turned the paper over and back again and read it one more time. When he looked up, he had tears in his big eyes.

"Where'd you get this?"

"Your brother, Thomas. Daria left it when she . . . Thomas was the first to get there and he took it. He's been holding it over Coryell ever since. I know for a fact Coryell's been paying Thomas's bills whenever they got out of hand."

He dropped his head and shook it. "Jesus. I thought . . . I thought we had that worked out years ago."

"Hard for some to kick their addictions."

He shook his head again. "Thomas, Marianna, Julia, and Walter—I've made a hash of all of it."

He didn't include Andras in the list. I waited.

He held up the note. "Does Andras . . . ?"

I nodded. "He tried jumping from the Regency last night. That's the broken glass. He blames himself."

"Blames himself?" Leitz looked confused, and I had to assume the confusion was sincere. Memory can do that, rearrange history, along with responsibility, if you let it. The Soviets were masters of this kind of manipulation—they twisted the collective memory of an entire nation. The current crowd plays the same games.

"He blames himself for what happened to Daria," I said, taking another step back. "For not doing anything about Coryell."

"But it wasn't . . ." Leitz pounded the desk with both fists. "IT WASN'T HIS FAULT!"

He looked around for something to throw, but the desktop was clean, except for a pad and some pencils. He swept those away. His face reddened and he started to rise, fists still balled. I got ready to powder.

He made it halfway up before he collapsed in his chair. His head fell on his arms. I stayed where I was, unsure what he'd do next.

He sobbed—and sobbed some more. A long time, maybe ten minutes. I hoped it was catharsis. When he finally looked up, he said, "It wasn't his fault. Don't you understand that? You have to understand. It wasn't his fault. It was . . . *It was mine.*"

I'm not sure who he thought he was talking to. He seemed to be appealing directly to his son. Maybe, in grief and confusion, he transferred Andras onto me. Not so odd—I'd spent the last several weeks talking to a man who's been dead since 1953. I nodded slightly, to show I did understand, and said nothing.

"What . . . ? What should I do?" he whispered.

"Tell me what happened two weeks ago. Tuesday. You went to Queens, right? To see Coryell?"

He looked confused again at the change of subject. Then the eyes clarified. "Yes."

"You talk to him?"

"Yes."

His voice was still at whisper level. He knew where we were headed, alarms were sounding in his head, but we were beyond his ability to do anything about them.

"He tell you he'd just bailed himself out of jail?"

"That's right."

"After he was caught with a kid in his car?"

Leitz nodded.

"That when you killed him?"

He looked around as if help might be coming from somewhere. He didn't really expect it. When it didn't show, he looked down at the desk.

Another long wait. But when he looked back up, he whispered, "Yes."

I took the chance of coming into range, taking the chair across the desk. Eye level seemed important. I brought my own voice down.

"Tell me."

He looked around again. Still no help coming.

"I . . . I don't know where to start."

"Start anywhere, as someone once said."

"Walter . . . Walter had a problem, but you know that. He called it 'the Urge.' He thought he could control it. But . . ."

"It ended up controlling him," I said.

"That's right. I didn't know that back then. The first thing was Andras, obviously. We got him help, child psychologists who specialize in this kind of thing. That seemed to work. But . . ."

He stopped and looked around again. Help still didn't arrive.

"I guess I was wrong about that too. The question I kept asking myself, after that day Julia walked in and we all came to realize what we were dealing with, is how am I supposed to analyze this? It's not the kind of question you ever expect to face. What am I supposed to do? How do I stop the pain? It's not long before you get to the question of who don't I want to hurt? Or hurt least? It's hard to come to grips with the idea that pain is inevitable for someone, and you're the one who decides who hurts and who walks away. That's where I found myself. I won't tell you I made the right decisions, I don't know. Everything appeared in shades of gray, and I just don't know."

I knew the feeling.

"I made a calculation. We did what we could for Andras. That was the first thing, as I said. The question was, did we turn Walter over to the authorities? Julia was just getting her business off the ground. She's a pain in the ass, but she's so good at what she does, and for better or worse, she loves the guy. Scandal would have killed her. I was raising money. My second fund. Scandal would have killed me too. I'm not afraid to say it. I didn't want to inflict pain on myself. So we made sure Walter got therapy—far away and out of sight. You can say it, if you want, but, yes, we swept it under the rug."

I wasn't going to say it. And I wasn't going to point out that Thomas Leitz already had.

"The therapy seemed to work. So Julia claimed. Things returned to normal. Pauline was the most adamant but she calmed down after a while. We kept Walter at arm's length. Julia knew he wasn't welcome, of course. We did family gatherings without him. There was always some excuse and after a while, it became . . . normal, I guess. If Pauline or I mentioned him, it was never by name. Of course, we had no idea until . . ."

The fists balled again. But his temper was spent, overwhelmed perhaps by years of denial and deception. Perhaps that was unfair—I'd never been through this particular kind of hell.

"When Daria . . . We all jumped to the same conclusion, of course. But there was no evidence. Walter denied everything. Julia said he was never around. We didn't focus on the question of whether Julia, with her twenty-four–seven schedule, would know. Maybe we didn't want to. I'm not sure now. It's all a blur. Pauline broke down. She blamed me, blamed the whole family, and I don't fault her for that. Especially since . . ."

She was right, of course, but I didn't say it.

"I truly didn't know about Andras. He seemed a normal kid. Maybe too much involved with his computers, but I took that as a positive. He was applying himself to something, he was good at it. His grades were good. He was talking about Stanford or Cal Tech. I had dreams of . . . I had dreams . . ."

He got ready to weep again. Hard not to feel for him, but he was avoiding the point.

"Go back to Tuesday," I said.

He took a minute to shift gears.

"I had the man who was following you watch Walter's building. He called me when Walter arrived. I went over. You told me how he'd helped the tall man bug my system. I was furious. I confronted him in that . . . hovel. I'd never been there before. It underscored everything about him, the fraud, the deception. He tried to evade, obfuscate . . . He did everything he could to say it wasn't him. I wouldn't let him get away with it. When we got to where he'd been for the last week, I lost it. Just went berserk, I guess. We fought. The next thing I knew, he was slumped over the desk, not moving. If you ask me now how it happened, I couldn't tell you. It was . . . It was just one of those things."

Murder. Just one of those things. Andras had used almost the same language, talking about the Players.

I got up and walked. Kline and Motherwell and Malevich fired truth, albeit abstract truth, from the walls. Easy for you, I thought. You just had to get it onto canvas. Of course, they had to live it before they could paint it.

Leitz sat motionless at his desk.

"What now?" he asked, pained but resigned.

He was asking me to face the same question he'd wrestled with. Who do you hurt least?

Leitz was a murderer. On the other hand, the world was better off without his victim. Victoria would tell me that didn't matter, and she'd be right. Also hard to ignore that Leitz's actions had set off the chain of events that brought us here today. There were plenty of victims, including his own son and the kids at the Crestview playhouse.

I'm used to making my own decisions, but I'm no good at being a judge. The ones we had in the Soviet Union were corrupt—they had no concept of justice, they did what they were told. Victoria put her faith in the rule of law, which intentionally took decisions like this out of the hands of individuals like me. I could see the purpose of that, but I wasn't quite ready to abdicate.

"The first thing now—is Andras," I said. "I need to get back to him."

"Wait! You haven't told me where . . ."

"Don't intend to. I'll take care of the kid for the next few days. You're in no shape to protect him. If you want to do something, think about coming clean with your family, then the cops. You've all got a ton of healing to do, assuming we get through this. It'll also go a lot easier if you go to the police before they come to you."

"But . . . What about . . . ?"

"Jail?"

He tried to nod, but couldn't manage.

I left him waiting for the help that wouldn't arrive.

★ CHAPTER 47 ★

The snow was already sticking as I walked to Victoria's place at Third and Sixty-fifth. She welcomed me with a big hug and a long kiss and a wrinkled nose.

"You don't stink this time, but I can feel it—you're exhausted."

"Won't lie."

"Want something to eat?"

"Sure." Breakfast seemed a long time ago.

She led me through the living room to her dining area. I hadn't been in her apartment before. I was struck by its temporary feel. Neutral everything— furniture, fabrics, decorations, not unlike the Regency Hotel or Julia Leitz's office. Here, they all but announced, *I'll be moving on*. Question was, where— and when?

"I got sandwiches from the deli. Something to drink?"

"Beer?"

"Is that a good idea? Never mind, I thought you'd ask, so I got that too."

She brought a bottle of Heineken, a tasteless brew, but I wasn't about to say so.

"Perfect," I lied.

She smiled, and I reached for her hand.

"I'm trying," she said. "But, as you pointed out, you don't make it easy."

"I'm trying too," I said, biting back doubt. "I'm not very good at it."

"You can say that again."

"Want to hear about Stamford?" Get the sincerity ball rolling.

I took a long swallow of Heineken. It tasted better than I remembered.

"Go easy, shug. If I know you, you're not done for the day."

She didn't know the half of it. I put down the beer and picked up a sand-wich. In between bites, I told her about Batkin, what he'd said about the BEC, Irina taking off, Thomas Leitz and Nosferatu, and Andras—the note and the overnight odyssey from the Regency to the Doubletree to the Super 8.

"Did you really have to call Nosferatu and rile him up?"

"I wanted the kid to hear what he's up against and I wanted Nosferatu chasing me."

"Exactly my point."

"He doesn't know where we are now."

"He knew where to find you that night he beat you up."

She was right. Arrogance . . . I chewed another bite of sandwich.

"What are you going to do about Leitz?"

"Don't know."

"He should be prosecuted. He could maybe plead it down to manslaugh-ter, but he's looking at prison time for sure."

"I figured that."

"And?"

"I told him to go to the police. But he's got a terminally ill wife and a seriously screwed-up kid. Not going to do anyone any good if he's in the slammer."

"That's not the point, and you know it."

"It is the circumstance."

"Circumstances get considered at sentencing time. The law says you can't go around breaking people's necks."

She staked out the position I expected her to, and I couldn't argue against it. But coming from a system where the law could be made up on the spot by anyone carrying a card that said ChK, GPU, NKVD, KGB or FSB, I had a hard time seeing it with such absolute clarity.

"I can tell we're gonna keep having this argument," she said.

"That's a good thing, from my point of view."

She smiled. "At least you've answered one question."

"What's that?"

"Why they did it—the kids. Some kind of power trip."

"I don't follow."

"You said they were all abused—that was the common bond—usually by a family member or someone close to them. The abuse wasn't just physical—it takes its psychological and emotional toll too. This was their way of getting back at their abusers. They owned these guys, their customers, psychologi-cally speaking. They told them when to tune in, made them shell out thousands—tens of thousands—to watch. They were the performers, but that didn't bother them. It was all about control, psychological control. Power trip, like I said."

"Huh. I hadn't thought about it quite that way. I wonder . . . Remember the other day, we talked about how Irina's the one calling the shots but I couldn't see her motivations? I think you just put your finger on it."

"Power trip?"

"Control. Power. And in this particular instance, revenge." I called Foos on the cell phone that came with Warren Brandeis. "How's the kid?"

"Just woke up. We're starting to talk. How's his old man?"

"Not so good. He admitted killing Coryell."

Foos was silent, something else he does when he doesn't have anything constructive to contribute.

I said, "I'll tell you the rest when I see you. Right now, I need to know if Irina still has her phone offline."

"Hang on, I'll check. . . . Still offline."

"Keep an eye on it. I have a feeling it'll be back on shortly."

"You'll be the first to know."

"What are you thinking?" Victoria asked.

"Business first. You want the ConnectPay servers?"

"You serious?"

"It's either you or Nosferatu. You're a lot prettier. Nicer too, most of the time."

That got me a whack across the back of the head, but it was playful—I think.

"I suppose there's a price," she said.

"Of course. This is a capitalist country, as you keep reminding me."

"Why is it now you've decided to listen? What do you want?"

"Couple weeks at the Gage Hotel?"

That got me another hug and kiss. "When can we leave?"

"You've got your case, remember?"

"All too well. That's what I wanted to talk about."

"I'm all ears."

"I'm guessin' your mouth will be involved before too long."

I smiled and kept silent to show I was trying. The Brandeis cell phone buzzed.

Foos said, "You hung up too fast. Someone's trying to reach the Russian chick. Six calls since four o'clock yesterday. Just a number, no name, must be a disposable."

He read off the number. Didn't mean anything to me.

I broke the connection and dialed the number. A man answered, speaking Russian. "Who the hell is this?"

I recognized the voice from the night on Tverskaya and ended the call. Konychev had Brandeis's number now but that didn't change anything.

"Konychev's been trying to reach Irina since yesterday afternoon," I said to Victoria. "They're playing some kind of cat-and-mouse game, those two, although mongoose-cobra might be a better description."

"Dammit. Remember the question about why Homeland Security let Konychev into the country after DoJ and State were keeping him out?"

"Sure."

"I'm gonna break the rules. This could cost me my job so bear that in mind when you go off to do whatever you decide to go off to do."

"Okay."

"It wasn't DHS, it was us, DoJ, my office. We got DHS to front it so we wouldn't be seen suddenly reversing ourselves"

"Very tricky. Foos will be impressed."

"You're not telling Foos, remember? You're not telling anyone."

"Right."

"Konychev came to us, last month, through umpteen lawyers and intermediaries. He offered a deal. Everything he knew about the Baltic Enterprise Commission and its U.S. affiliates, including everything he knew about one Taras Batkin, in return for immunity, freedom of entry, and cessation of our investigation into his affairs."

She had my full attention.

"When last month, the first approach?"

"December fifth."

"Right after the Tverskaya attack. He was asking a steep price."

"It was a tough call. I wasn't remotely happy about it. But we were nowhere on the case, we needed a kick-start, and it's not my job to prosecute Russian hoods unless they're carrying out their hoodlumming here. Which we believe Batkin is. I made sure we weren't prohibited from turning what we knew about Konychev over to the Russian authorities. We went to the CPS, by the way. They're the only ones over there I even partly trust."

"I'll tell Aleksei next time I talk to him."

"I already did."

I could hear her.

"So?"

"So, we had Konychev, secluded, while we debriefed him. He's evasive to say the least."

"Surprised?"

"Don't start. It's been difficult, a real pain in the ass, not to tell tales out of school. Then he starts wandering off the reservation. That visit to Leitz was the first. The lunch on Madison Avenue that your pal Ivanhoe latched on to was the second."

"Now he's flown the coop?"

"How the hell do you know that?"

"Lucky guess. Rooted in the assumption that it's the reason you're telling me all this. And it's Ivanov, not Ivanhoe."

"It's a good thing you were a spy, because you'd make a lousy diplomat."

"At the risk of making another diplomatic faux pas, you're not the first with that observation. Where were you keeping Konychev?"

"Don't ask too many details. Hotel suite in Midtown."

"Security?"

"Couple of FBI. But their orders were to keep others out, not necessarily hold him in. We relied on his own sense of self-protection."

"Self-interest might have been a better premise. When'd he blow?"

"Yesterday, not long before I called you."

"He's been playing you."

"Tell me something I don't goddamned know."

The temper was in countdown mode.

"How about some coffee?"

She went to the kitchen to get it.

"There's something else. We had the suite wired, in case he got talkative."

"He would have checked for that."

"No doubt. But the FBI does what the FBI is trained to do."

Like the Cheka.

"He didn't talk much, mostly football and crude jokes—almost as bad as yours—and mostly in Russian. But there was one thing. He got a call, Sunday morning. His cell phone, we could only hear his side, but whoever it was had clearly called about Batkin. Konychev said something like, 'Shit, we won't get another shot at him now. Not like that.'"

I drank my coffee. "Doesn't add up."

"Why not?"

"Batkin told me he made a deal with Konychev. Not voluntarily, they had guns to their heads—Kremlin guns. You don't renege on that—at least not overtly—unless you want to spend twenty years in Siberia. Konychev was playing a more subtle game. He was going to give you enough to hang Batkin in a U.S. court—ice him in a way that couldn't be traced."

"You Russians play too much chess. I'm a simple country girl. Konychev tried to kill Batkin and missed. He said he wouldn't get another shot. I've got the tape."

"Hang on. He was speaking Russian."

"Sure. His English stinks."

"So what you have is a translation?"

"Of course. My Russian's no better than his English."

"Where's the recording?"

"At the office. Why?"

"Can I listen to it? Your translator might have got it wrong."

"I don't know, shug . . . I'm already out on a pretty long limb."

"I wouldn't ask unless I thought I could help. It might make a big difference."

She eyed me long and straight.

"What the hell? It's only another couple years in the hoosegow."

She dialed a number and spoke briefly before she handed me the receiver.

"They're teeing it up. That section."

A faint but angry voice came over the line, speaking rapid-fire Russian full of slang and expletives. Hardly surprising the translation got screwed up. I handed back the phone.

"Well?" she said.

"Konychev used an expression—*pizda lasaya*. Means 'cocky cunt,' more or less. '*We won't get another shot at that cocky cunt.*' Your translator assumed he was referring to Batkin. He got it wrong. Irina was the target."

★ CHAPTER 48 ★

Foos called again.

"New data in the Dick. That cell phone called Leitz an hour ago."

"Shit."

I dialed Leitz's number. No answer.

Victoria said, "What's wrong? You look like you just saw that guy, Nosferatu."

"I did. I gotta get back to Leitz's. Konychev's headed there—or Nosferatu is."

"You sure?"

"Board lock."

"Wait! If you're right, it's dangerous. Let my people handle it."

"No time."

"Nine-one-one. Cops can be there in minutes."

I was halfway to the door.

"Konychev's after the kids and the computers. He thinks Leitz knows where Andras is, and he's the link to Irina. So yes, call nine-one-one. I can use the help."

"Turbo, please! Don't go. I'm scared."

She had tears in her eyes to prove it. I came back and took her hands in mine.

"You're right back where you didn't want to be. I'm sorry. But neither of us is going to think much of me tomorrow if I stay here."

"Okay, I'll go with you."

Before I could respond, she said, "I know. Bad idea. Dammit."

"I'll be back before your dragons can get warmed up. Promise," I said.

She looked deep into my eyes before she swallowed and nodded. I took that for permission and kissed her.

"Make that call to the cops."

It was snowing hard when I reached the street, already an inch or more on the ground. I ran, cursing myself for giving Konychev and Nosferatu too much time.

Leitz's door was ajar. No one leaves a door open in New York. Nothing to do but keep going, even if someone was on the other side.

I kicked the door wide and backed away in case the someone had a gun.

Nobody fired. I peeked around the frame. The entrance hall looked just like it had ninety minutes before. Plus blood.

A wet trail across the stone floor. I stepped in and listened. Not a sound, but I could feel people in the house. I followed the trail to an open door at the back. It led down a hall to an enormous kitchen. The Filipina maid lay next to the center island, her dress and apron soaked in red. No pulse from her neck.

I grabbed a kitchen knife, found a back staircase and climbed as quickly as I dared. The staircase bisected a narrow hallway on the second floor before it climbed another flight. A large, airy office to my right. Jenny Leitz sat with her back to me, wearing black, bent over a desk, her head turned to one side. I stifled a cry and put my hand to her neck. I knew the answer before I felt the cooling skin. With luck she'd never heard him coming. I took my hand away and made a promise—he'd know I was there, right before he followed her out of this world.

Anger stomping caution, I ran the corridor to the front of the house. I came out at the center hall staircase. Cold air cut through my clothes. The drawing room was untouched but one French door banged in the wind. I leaned out in time to see a long overcoat turn right up Madison, worn by a tall man with a pulled-forward face.

I took the stairs two at a time, caution forgotten now, and barreled through the Rothko chamber. Leitz slumped behind his desk at an awkward angle.

"LEITZ!"

No answer.

He was fastened to his chair with a hundred yards of duct tape. The sleeves of his cashmere sweater were shredded from elbow to wrist, long red slashes ran down his forearms. The carpet was soaked in blood. I slapped his face. No response. I cut the tape. The arms fell away and kept running red.

I don't know much about bleeding. I called 911 and held his arms above his head, hoping somehow he'd bleed to death more slowly, or maybe the ambulance would arrive in time. I fought to hold down lunch as my shoes squished in the red-soaked rug.

Movement from Leitz. He opened his eyes, ever so slowly, as if the effort was almost more than he could manage. Probably was. He struggled to focus. I think he recognized me because he tried to speak.

"Rest easy," I said. "Help's on the way."

The lips fought to work themselves around a word.

"Just hold on," I said.

"An . . . Andras?"

"He's okay. I still have him. Don't worry."

"Tha . . . That's who . . ."

"That's who they were after, right? Is that what you mean?"

I think he nodded before he slipped into unconsciousness.

Victoria said the cops would get there quickly. She was wrong. But the ambulance was fast, and a second one arrived a minute after the first. I heard the EMS guys shouting downstairs. I yelled, and a man and a woman rushed in and took over. I found the other team and took them to Jenny's office in the back and the kitchen below.

I went through the rest of the house, still carrying the kitchen knife, but found nothing. While I searched, I called Victoria to tell her I was okay, then Foos.

"What should I say to Andras?" he asked.

"He's going to blame himself, and he won't be all wrong this time. But don't spare the details. He's got to face up to some ugly realities, one of which is Irina's been playing him like a well-stocked hand. Tell him another thing—she's out of cards now. She's a dead woman unless he wants to try to save her."

★ CHAPTER 49 ★

I made the Super 8 just before 3:00. Four inches of snow on the ground, gusty wind whipping the blanket of flakes in the air. The radio promised five inches more. "Local accumulations could be higher," the announcer added for good measure. Traffic moved at the pace of a cold snail. I was feeling the lack of sleep, but adrenalin was keeping exhaustion at bay, at least for the moment. I told it to keep pumping.

"How's my dad?" Andras was in my face as soon as I opened the door. His eyes were red, his face full of fear and worry.

"I don't know—that's the truth," I said. "They were taking him to the hospital. He was still hanging on and I'm sure the docs will do the best they can."

"Which hospital? I've got to get there."

"I understand how you feel, but no go. The one thing your dad was able to ask was about your safety. I told him you were okay. We're going to keep it that way."

"Turbo's right," Foos said. "Nothing you could do. We got other things to worry about. Tell him what you told me."

He looked from Foos to me and back again. He had to be struggling with a hundred conflicting emotions.

"Let's sit down," I said.

I took the corner of the bed, and he sat on the desk chair.

"You can't change what's happened," I said with a gentleness I hardly felt. "You can change what's going to happen. That's what your dad would want you to do. Think about that before you answer the questions I'm going to ask."

He looked away.

"PAY ATTENTION, MAN!"

I'm not sure I'd ever heard Foos yell before. Andras jumped like a cornered fox.

"It's Irina, isn't it? She got you to hack into ConnectPay, right?"

"NO!" he shouted. The force of his own voice took him aback.

"Okay," I said. "She didn't. I believe you. Tell me what happened."

"I hacked ConnectPay. That was my idea. But . . ."

I waited for him to continue. When he didn't, I looked at Foos, who nodded.

"It was Irina's idea to steal the money?"

I took the absence of protest as assent.

"And again in November?"

He dipped his head slightly.

"She got you to place the worm that corrupted the BEC's data?"

"Yes," he whispered.

"And when you found Uncle Walter in his office, you called her? She said, 'Take the servers'?"

"Yes."

I could have asked, what was he thinking? His uncle was dead, he'd stolen eight million dollars from organized crime. Did he really think he could just go back to Gibbet School and pretend nothing had happened? No point—he hadn't thought. He hadn't thought at all. He'd just done as she told him. Maybe it was youth and naïveté, maybe it was first love or blind love, maybe it was just plain stupidity. Two kids, each for their own reasons, had taken down one of the Internet's top criminal enterprises. In some eyes, they might have been heroes, but in the ones that counted now, they were just targets to be eliminated, the sooner, the better.

"Okay, I understand what you were doing," I lied. "What about Irina? What was she up to?"

Silence.

I wanted to slap him, then drown his head in the sink. Jenny killed, his father hanging by a thread—because of him. I managed to stifle all that.

"Listen to me. This isn't about you and your promises anymore. They killed Jenny. They tried to kill your father. They tried to kill Irina Sunday morning. She was the target, not her stepfather. Do you understand that?"

He looked at the ground.

"Do—you—know—where—she—is?"

He looked up. "We . . . we always agreed if there was a problem . . . if something happened, we'd meet at my dad's house in Millbrook. No one ever goes there anymore."

"Where in Millbrook?"

"White Horse Lane. Only house on the road. It's more like . . . a farm. We used to have horses. But not since . . ."

Daria died, unless I missed my guess.

Foos was already at the computer, pulling up a map. I looked over his shoulder. White Horse Lane was a mile-long cul-de-sac that ran southeast off Route 44, several miles north of town. Foos switched to a satellite image. Rolling fields interspersed with patches of forest the fields had been carved out of. New York horse country. Few roads. He zoomed in on a large farmhouse with an equally large barn, garage, smaller house, pool, and tennis court. The main house, guesthouse, and garage were arranged like a backward "7" with woods north and west. The barn was a hundred yards to the east. The driveway, an extension of the road, split into a "Y," one prong leading to the barn and the other hooking in front of the main house at the top of the "7," the guesthouse, set back from the corner, and the garage at the bottom of the long side. The closest road to White Horse Lane, other than Route 44, was Caldecott Lane, another dead end, about a half mile south.

"Where exactly is she?" I asked Andras.

"Guesthouse. She has a key."

"And you?"

He nodded.

"Hand it over."

He hesitated.

I thought Foos was going to whack him. Andras must've thought so too. He reached into his pocket and took a key off a ring.

"Alarms?"

More reluctance.

Foos said, "Turbo's on your side, man. But you're losing me fast."

"I'll write down the code."

"Somebody plow your driveway?" I asked.

"Dad has a caretaker."

"And if he encounters Irina?"

"She has a letter to show him," he said quietly.

With a forged signature. Not my concern.

"You set up a communications protocol—a means of contact, cell phone, a way she knows it's you?"

His eyes bored through the cheap carpeting. If they were lasers, he'd be down to the Super 8's basement by now.

"Goddammit! You're wasting time, man," Foos said.

"I call her three times. First time, four rings. Second time, two. Third time, she answers."

"Phone has to be on for that."

Foos banged at the keyboard.

"Back on."

"Calls?"

"One incoming. Guess who?"

"She answer?"

"Uh-huh. Talked three and a half minutes."

"Outgoing?"

"Two. One to the old country."

"Russia?"

"You got it." He read off a number.

"That's Moscow. The other?"

"Seven-one-eight number . . . cell phone . . . in Brooklyn—Brighton Beach."

"She's setting up something—or someone."

"Wait!" Andras cried.

"No time," I said. "Foos, check the Yellow Pages—outdoor equipment or sporting goods."

I was lucky—there was a store a mile away.

"See if there's a Kinko's nearby."

"You're on a roll. Looks like there's one in the same strip mall."

"E-mail a few pages from ConnectPay's database for printing. They could come in handy."

"On it."

Andras shifted back and forth nervously.

"What are you going to do?" he finally blurted.

"First step, convince Irina we're on her side," I said.

"I can help," he said. "I'll call her right now."

How do you tell a kid that not only has he been played for a sucker by his supposed girlfriend, but having got what she wanted, she no longer has any use for him?

You don't. At least, not now.

"Let me get up there first, get the lay of the land. Then we'll see."

"But . . ."

"Turbo knows what he's doing," Foos said, shutting the door on discussion. "He calls the shots."

I was calling the shots. Whether the first statement had merit was anybody's guess.

★ CHAPTER 50 ★

Slow going. Only good thing—Konychev couldn't be moving any faster.

Snow kept falling, wind kept whipping, plows and sanders fought the highway to a standoff. Rush hour traffic inched along. Inevitably, some idiot trying to make time ended up impacted on a guard rail or the back of another car. The Explorer's four-wheel drive held its own, but that was no protection against the impatient fools around me. One of their miscalculations, and I was done.

Konychev and I started out equidistant from Millbrook, I figured, and we had the same traffic to contend with. I needed to get there first, and I wasn't planning on the direct route up the driveway. That put me at least an hour behind. I'd stopped at the outdoor equipment store and lucked into a pair of boots that fit. Better yet, snowshoes. Watching one more idiot in an Explorer like mine lose control and take a Honda Accord to the side made me tap the brake and wonder whether Konychev's Escalade had any better four-wheel drive than my Ford's.

I turned off I-287 and followed a back road route to the Taconic Parkway. The roads were in worse shape than the interstate, but I had them to myself. As I reached the parkway, 1010 WINS reported a four-car pileup where I-287 and the Taconic met, five miles behind. All lanes blocked. With a little luck, Konychev was caught in the backup and I had the head start I needed.

I checked messages at the office. One, from Aleksei, a few hours before. Call ASAP.

No time for coffee protocol. I used Brandeis's phone and called his disposable number.

"Thought you'd want to know right away," he said. "Irina Lishina was treated at a Moscow hospital for a bad wound and infection on December twenty-eighth. She told the doctor she'd fallen on a metal staircase, but he said she'd also been burned. He put her down as a tough kid. She had to be in severe pain the entire time. We're checking DNA now but I'm betting what we found on the murder weapon matches hers."

"You got a date of death for her father?"

"Guess. Good tip. I'm grateful."

He sounded sincere—maybe even a little contrite. Time for that later, I hoped. "You're welcome."

"Think she killed him?" he asked.

"Don't know, but I wouldn't put much of anything past her."

"Konychev's nieces have a penchant for trouble."

"Meaning?"

"See Ivanov yesterday?"

"No time."

"He finally ran down the identity of the girl in Konychev's car on Tverskaya. Tamara Konycheva, daughter of Oleg Konychev. Big wheel in the Barsukov syndicate. And Efim's stepbrother."

"Ivanov have any theories on what she was doing in the car, dressed for a night on the town?"

"He says Uncle Efim likes the girls young and younger and isn't inhibited by family connections."

I thought about that for a minute. Things continued to clarify. "Can you check a Moscow phone number for me?"

"Now?"

"Yeah. Time's running out here for someone." I read off the number Irina called.

"Hang on, this may take a minute."

It took several. "You'll never guess."

"The aforementioned Oleg Konychev?"

"If you knew, what did you need me for?"

"Making sure what I'm getting myself into."

"And?"

"I have a feeling I'll meet up with Uncle Efim and his axman later tonight."

"Be careful."

"I plan to. But I've got another feeling that those two may be the least of my worries."

I broke the connection and called Victoria. Voicemail. I did the right thing. I told her where I was and where I was headed and that I believed Konychev was headed there too. She'd send the cavalry—but in this weather they wouldn't make it before I finished my business with Nosferatu.

The snow narrowed the Taconic to one lane, but the traffic thinned too. Impatient commuters turned off as they neared home. Eventually, a sparse parade of well-spaced cars marched north at a steady thirty miles per hour through Westchester, Putnam, and Dutchess counties. I kept two hands on the wheel, two eyes and half my attention on the road. The rest of me pondered how a seventeen-year-old girl could so successfully confound organized crime. I thought I understood why she'd want to, but not why she thought she could get away with it. Maybe she didn't expect to.

A chicken's hardly a bird, a woman's hardly a person—one of our less appealing, but no less illuminating, sayings. It speaks more to the insecurity of Russian men than the tough-mindedness of our female counterparts. Still, I was unlikely to cite it to Victoria.

The women I knew in the camps were the strongest people there. They had to defend themselves, not only against the elements, the guards and the system—they had to keep other *zeks* at bay too. It wasn't uncommon to wake up to a corpse on the *sploshnye nary*—communal sleeping boards— with a knife wound in the chest or neck, next to where the object of his unwanted attention had spent the night.

In later years, I discovered that in a nation whose history is replete with irony, the position of women was irony amplified. They had no rights under the czars, yet five became czars themselves, including Catherine. History awarded her the same sobriquet as Peter. The Bolsheviks made a big deal of neutralizing gender, but like so many other Communist constructions it was founded on quicksand. Not one woman served in the Politburo under Lenin or Stalin. Khrushchev appointed the first—as (surprise!) minister of culture. She bore the same name as the empress, and with our sense of irony, became known as the second Catherine the Great. After Stalin's wife committed suicide, he had the wives of his Politburo cronies rounded up and shipped off to jail or the camps. Little wonder that wives of future leaders stayed deep in the background, rarely appearing in public with their sour-faced husbands. The first "first lady" to take a high profile was Raisa Gorbachev— with the predictable result of undermining public confidence in her husband and his reforms because people thought she was calling the shots.

As Russia moved from Party control through glastnost and perestroika to democratic chaos to pseudodemocracy run by the Cheka, women came out of the back room. Some flaunted their sex and control over the oligarchs who rivaled the Politburo bosses in coarseness but showered their newfound ornaments with gifts and wore them like prizes—often two, three, four at a time—on their arms. Tamara Konycheva's predecessors.

Others excelled in sports and culture. Still others made their mark in business and professions such as journalism. Many of the crusaders who have been cut down for carrying the flame of truth close enough to scorch the powers that be were female. Still others, if Irina Lishina was any indication, had a talent for crime.

Given the history and the lawless, dog-eat-dog society in which she grew up, it wasn't all that astonishing that Irina thought she could single-handedly one-up the BEC. Her father had helped start it, maybe died because of his role. She'd almost certainly witnessed his murder. Her uncle and stepfather were successful crooks. One of them likely killed her old man. One of them screwed teenaged girls. This was her world. Her actions began to appear totally consistent—an eye for an eye, a wound for a wound, a corpse for a corpse. She'd show she could dish out as much pain as she received.

She'd found a willing agent in Andras. I was betting she had others. I was hoping I wasn't acting as one more. I couldn't swear that I wasn't.

A good time to watch my back—just like I told myself two weeks ago at Trastevere.

★ CHAPTER 51 ★

Nothing was stirring on Route 44, the main road through Millbrook, at 8:00 P.M. Snow kept falling. I stopped and put down the window a mile north of town. As dark and still as I remembered Siberia to be—no houses, no cars, no lights, no sound. No sky either, just falling snow.

Caldecott Lane was two miles farther on. It hadn't been plowed, but I made it far enough in for the darkness to hide the Explorer from cars passing on the main road. My new boots sank six inches into fresh snow. Not for the first time, I bemoaned the fact that the sporting goods store hadn't sold firearms. There are supposed to be more gun dealers in the United States than McDonald's in the entire world, but Stamford was an empty room in the armory. I'd made do with a large hunting knife in a plastic scabbard and an aluminum baseball bat. The thought of either embedded in Nosferatu's bucktoothed face wasn't displeasing.

I climbed a fence and strapped on my new snowshoes. I tucked the hunting knife into the waistband at the small of my back. Standing atop the accumulation of two storms, the top of the fence barely reached my knees. I set off at a clip that surprised me in ease and speed, at a thirty degree angle from Route 44. No moon, no stars, no lights. Just more snow. Even in the middle of an open field, I was invisible.

I was fifty yards from Leitz's place, climbing another fence, when the barn appeared. The drive in front had been plowed during this storm, but hours ago. It showed no tire tracks or footprints. I pressed on, veering north, around the back of the main house, until I reached the pool. I recognized it from the satellite map and the large rectangle of fence top peeking out of the snow. The guesthouse was on the other side, thirty yards away. Beyond that was the garage. The stately main house stood to my left, woods fifty yards to my right. My watch said 8:55.

I waited a good ten minutes, watching, listening. Not a sound. Not a sight. Not a light. I could have assumed wrong and Irina didn't have Uncle Oleg's muscle here after all. More likely, the man—men?—were good and well hidden by the garage.

I moved to the back door of the guesthouse and pressed myself to the building while I removed the snowshoes. The alarm panel showed green. I worked the key in the lock. It turned easily, and the door opened without a creak. I closed it softly and stood in the dark. The heat was on. The house was warm.

I was in a small kitchen. I could make out a counter, stove and sink to my left. Table to my right. Fridge against the opposite wall. Door, cracked open, next to the fridge. More darkness beyond.

Clutching my aluminum bat, I crossed the room in two steps and nudged open the door. Dining room—table and four chairs, fireplace in the left wall, and open French doors at the far end. Still no sound.

I skirted the table to the French doors. A large L-shaped living room wrapped the front of the house. Two windows and a door opposite. The edge of the mantel on another fireplace, backing up on the one in the dining room to my left. Leather armchairs, a leather couch, lots of blankets and throws.

I stood still, sensing someone there I couldn't see on the other side of the "L." I listened for breathing, a rustle of clothing, something. If she felt my presence, she was doing the same thing. The silence was broken only by the mild whip of the wind outside. Stalemate. Three to one she was just around the corner. Same odds she was armed. But I wasn't the one she planned to kill. Or so I hoped. A bad bet. I took a breath and stepped into the room.

She was sitting in the farthest corner, where I expected her to be. Her eyes were wide open and focused on me. Her face showed no surprise. A shotgun rested in her lap, the raised barrel pointed at my chest.

"This is a twelve-gauge pump. I know how to use it. My father taught me. One more step and I will."

"Put down the bat."

I did.

"He couldn't keep it shut, could he?"

"Who?" I asked.

"I'm not stupid, Cheka Pig. Don't treat me like I am."

"He's trying to help."

She laughed. More of a bray—full of meanness, void of humor.

"He's always trying to help. A fool, but he's served his purpose."

"What was that?"

"You're so smart, what do you think?"

"Hacking the BEC?"

She grinned.

"Stealing the eight million?"

The grin widened.

"Placing the worm?"

"That's the best of all. That's what really got . . ." The grin disappeared and she shifted in her chair. The shotgun didn't move.

"Enough, Cheka Pig. I don't have to talk to you."

"No, you don't. But I'm curious. That's what really got—what?"

She didn't answer.

She'd chosen her location with care. Tucked in the corner, she was out of the line of sight—and fire—from every window, unless someone leaned far in the big bay to her left, in which case she had him. She had a clear view of the front door. Anyone using the back would end up entering the room as I did—an easy target. She was wearing black jeans and a turtleneck. The gun in her hand didn't shake or waver. She had a box of shells in her lap.

"Waiting for your uncle?"

Her eyes stayed fixed on me.

"Who then?"

Nothing.

"He give you your scar?"

She seemed to jump in her chair, then settled back down. The impassive mask returned. "What scar?" A touch of something new in her voice—surprise? Fear?

"On your neck. I noticed it the other night, when we stopped at Burger King. I saw it on your WildeTime videos too—but only the recent ones."

"*You've seen my videos?!*" A possibility she hadn't considered—and didn't like.

"Not voluntarily."

"Pervert."

"You don't believe that. What about the scar?"

"You're not just a Cheka pig, you're a Cheka pervert."

"Want to know what I think?"

"NO! I don't care what a Cheka pervert thinks."

Her voice said she did. But continuing this while she pointed a shotgun at my chest was foolish.

"Why don't you put the gun aside? I'll sit right here. We can talk about it. I'm on your side, even if you don't think so."

I eased myself onto an ottoman by the fireplace. It brought me a few feet closer, not that a few feet in the face of a twelve-gauge made much difference.

"I told you, don't treat me like I'm stupid. You are *not* on my side."

I kept an eye on the trigger finger. So long as it stayed outside the guard, I was okay. Maybe.

"When did you last talk to your father?" I asked quietly.

"What's that supposed to mean?"

"Just a question."

She didn't respond. The eyes clouded or seemed to. The light was bad, hard to tell for sure.

"You and Andras riled up that nest of vipers—the BEC, I mean. Was that your intention—set father against stepfather against uncle? Or did you have a particular target in mind?"

She shook her head again. She was smiling this time though.

"Come on, enlighten me. You've got the gun. I'd like to understand. We've got time, nobody's here yet."

"I've got nothing to say to a Cheka pervert."

"You're going to have to say something to someone, sooner or later."

That got me a quizzical look. "What's that supposed to mean?"

"We all have to answer, even if it's only to ourselves in a mirror. That's the way life works."

"Don't give me any heaven and hell bullshit. They tried that at Gibbet. Chapel every morning. I'm way past that."

"I'm talking about right here, right now."

"It's over for me."

"Why's that?"

"It's over."

She said it like she meant it. The finger stayed where it was.

"You sound like Andras."

"He doesn't have a clue."

"Don't sell him short, Irina. He's confused, but he's not stupid. Or evil. Bad breaks, sure. Like you've had."

"What the fuck is that supposed to mean?"

"You know as well as I do. Things happen, not your fault, but they send you down a whole different road. It's not too late to turn off. It never is."

"What the fuck do you know about it?"

"I know because before I was a Chekist, I was a *zek*."

She put a pitchfork through that admission. "Big fucking deal. So was my stepfather—Vyatlag, Gorlag, wherever. He's still a pig. So are you."

So much for the conversational approach. Time was working against me. Two could play the pitchfork game.

"How old were you when he put his hand up your skirt?"

"WHAT THE FUCK?"

"Don't play innocent, Irina. Uncle Efim. Thirteen, twelve?"

"NO! YOU DON'T GET IT! YOU DON'T UNDERSTAND!"

The finger wrapped the trigger. That, I did understand. But I kept at it.

"The Players. Andras and his uncle. Kevin. Andras told me about him, the others. That was the bond, right?"

"NO! It's between me and him. You have no . . . I don't even know what you're doing here!"

I let that go and looked out the window—with one eye. After a minute or two, her eyes followed mine and the trigger finger loosened. I let my breathing come back to normal.

"How many men outside?"

That made her start—and the finger move.

"What the fuck are you talking about now?"

I put an edge of anger in my voice. Not that she'd care, but she was still a kid, twelve-gauge or no twelve-gauge. "Christ, Irina. You're not stupid, as you keep telling me. I'm not either. You're waiting for Uncle Efim. He called right after you turned your phone on. You told him where to find you, told him you'd be waiting. Then you called Uncle Oleg in Moscow. He gave you the number for a man in Brooklyn. He's got men outside now."

"SHUT UP! I DON'T HAVE TO TALK TO YOU."

She was shouting but the finger stayed in place. I pressed on.

"Your cousin—Tamara Konycheva. She's been seen a lot with Uncle Efim. Even I know that."

I was looking for a button, and I'd pressed it. She closed her eyes. I got ready to lunge for the gun. She opened here eyes again. Even in the dark, they were filled with fire.

"How long has he been sleeping with her?" I asked.

"NO! NOTHING YOU SAY IS TRUE!"

The denial came fast and angry.

"Was he still sleeping with you when he started screwing her? Is that why you decided to go after the BEC?"

She switched to Russian. "You fucking son of a whore and a diseased dog . . ."

I went with Russian too. I wouldn't get another chance at this interrogation. I put my best Cheka steel in my voice.

"Here's what I think happened. If I'm wrong on anything, say so. I think your uncle dumped you for your cousin. Last summer sometime. You were too old, used up. He decided to move on to prettier hunting grounds."

"Fuck your mother, you rotten bastard . . ."

"You were pissed. You're used to getting your own way. You and Andras and the other kids had been running the playhouse for a year or two. You knew about his computer skills. You also knew he had a crush on you. You were already bent on revenge when he told you about ConnectPay. So much the better. Frankyfun had been all over you since last spring. Did you know he was his uncle Walter or did that come later?"

She'd leaned forward, pushing the gun in my direction at the start, but she backed off, resuming the impassive state, finger relaxed on the trigger guard, off-kilter grin on her face. She didn't react to my question. The answer wasn't important—to her or to me.

I went back to English. "You strung Andras along while he worked his way through ConnectPay's system and into the BEC. You got him to steal the three million in August. Had him make it look like Uncle Efim was cheating his partners, right?"

The off-kilter grin widened.

"You waited to see what happened. Nothing did. So you hit them again for five mil at Thanksgiving. Still nothing. You were frustrated. You were setting your uncle, dad, and stepdad against each other, but they weren't biting, or so you thought. You were impatient. Plenty was happening, behind the scenes, you just couldn't see it. Your uncle traced the hack—to Andras's dad. They started digging into his company, his family. Karp came over to New York. He already knew Uncle Walter, of course, and he got him to put a bug on the computers at the Leitz office.

"Something else you didn't know—your father was running his own scam. He'd figured a way to rip off BEC clients, starting with ConnectPay, in a way they wouldn't notice—and couldn't do much if they did. Only he wasn't cutting in his partners. He was going solo. Uncle Efim discovered that scam when he was looking for your thievery. I'll ask again—when was the last time you talked to your father?"

She shook her head.

"You can't hide, Irina. A week ago, two? At Christmas? You were in Moscow at Christmas. You must have seen him."

She nodded hesitantly. I had her attention now

"I hope you said an affectionate good-bye. They pulled his body from under Moscova ice three days ago. He had a fireplace poker through his chest."

"NO! YOU LIE! CHEKA PIG!" She flipped onto her knees, leaning forward, pushing the barrel toward me. No more than six feet away.

CRACK!

She jumped.

I dove.

CRACK! CRACK! CRACK!

BOOM! BOOM! BOOM! BOOM!

Two handguns, two shotguns. More shots. Then silence.

I looked up from the floor. Irina knelt in the chair, swinging the twelve-gauge wildly, her finger on the trigger, wrapped tight. She fought the urge to go the window. I kept my mouth shut and body still, hoping she'd forget all about me.

Quiet outside, except for the whistling wind. A minute passed, then three, then five. Irina was fixated on the front door. I thought again about making a lunge for the gun, but I wouldn't get halfway there.

Another five minutes passed. She unbent her knees and flopped back into her chair. The shotgun stayed steady. When she got settled, I worked myself ever so slowly back up to the ottoman. She watched me from the corner of her eye. When I got seated, she swung the gun over to let me know not to move again.

Voices outside, stamping feet. The front door swung open and Efim Konychev walked in. He flicked a switch, and I blinked in the light. He was wearing an overcoat and carried a large automatic in his right hand. His left shoulder was soaked in blood, but he wasn't showing any pain. Irina swung the shotgun halfway between us.

"Hello, Irina," he said. "Not a very welcoming reception. Those men are dead, by the way. What's the matter? You don't love me anymore?"

Behind Konychev stood Karp, holding a shotgun of his own. He closed the door as his eyes swept the room, taking in the layout, the girl, the gun, and coming to rest on me.

He grinned.

★ CHAPTER 52 ★

Konychev did his own survey of the room.

"I've seen you before." He spoke Russian.

No benefit in bringing up where.

"I remember," he said. "Tverskaya. You were passing by. You have a talent for being in the wrong place."

"A lying, fucking *zek*," Karp said. "I told you about him."

"He's that one?"

Karp nodded.

"You'll take care of it," Konychev said.

"He's dead." Another grin.

Foos listens to a bluegrass song about dealing cards with death—the joker's wild, the ace is high. Irina was the joker in this game, maybe my ace in the hole and my one hope for coming out alive, if I played her right.

"Where's your boyfriend?" Konychev asked.

"He's *not* my boyfriend."

I felt a twinge for Andras.

"Think I give a shit? Where is he?"

"Ask him."

He stayed with her. "Call him."

"You can't tell me what to do."

"You and he have caused a great deal of trouble with your stupid games."

"You had it coming."

Most kids would have sounded petulant, not to mention terrified. She didn't. She sounded vengeful—and mean.

"Get her phone," Konychev said to Karp.

349

Irina raised the twelve gauge. "Don't."

Karp and his boss stayed where they were.

"Don't bother," I said. "Kid doesn't have a phone. Have a good trip to Jersey, Fish Face?"

Karp glared. Konychev contemplated. I think Irina almost smiled. She didn't like Karp any more than I did.

Konychev took another look around the room. "Where are the servers?"

Irina shrugged. "Not anywhere you'll find them."

"They're no use to you," he said.

"You want them, I have them."

"Irina, what are you so angry about? What have I done?" His voice was all saccharine now. Irina wasn't buying any of it.

"I WILL NOT BE TREATED LIKE A STUPID GIRL!"

"Irina . . ."

"I know exactly what you've been doing. And with whom!"

The joker was taking the shape of a jealous queen.

"Enough! Where are the servers?" Konychev said.

"She doesn't have them," I said. "You fucked that up too, Fish Face. Stupid *pizda.*"

Karp's eyes told me I didn't have long to live.

"What's that supposed to mean?" Konychev said.

"What I said. You need better help."

"You have them?"

"That's right."

"I don't know your game, but you're bluffing."

"No bluff. I'm going to reach very slowly into my jacket for some papers."

Karp raised his shotgun until it was pointed squarely at my head. Hope filled his face.

I pulled my jacket open in slow motion while I extracted the Kinko print-out. I tossed the folded pages across the room. They landed at Konychev's feet. Shotgun steady, Karp knelt and picked them up.

Konychev grabbed them. His face darkened.

"What do you want?"

"Take Fish Face and beat it. I'll be in touch."

"I don't think so. I credit your industriousness. But you're compromised like everyone else. You tell me where to find the servers. I make sure no harm comes to your lady friend."

"Lady friend?"

"The charming U.S. attorney who has been my hostess these last few weeks. You can't protect her. Not if you're dead. Karp will take care of her as soon as he's done with you."

No time now to think about how he came to have that information. I could only hope there would be later. Or that it wouldn't be necessary.

"Maybe he'd like to watch," Karp said.

"Maybe he would," Konychev said.

"Suppose she already has them?" I said.

"That would be unfortunate."

I sat on my hand.

"We seem to have arrived at a temporary stalemate," he said. "But we have two guns, she has one, you have none. You have no friends here. Any way this plays out you lose."

I did have that joker. Time to put it into play.

"Let's go back to Sunday. Batkin's house. Who were your men shooting at?"

"I have no idea what you're talking about."

"Sure you do. So does Irina. You weren't trying to kill *him,* were you?"

He caught it. So did she. She straightened in her chair.

"You wouldn't murder Batkin, however much you might want to. He told me the same about you. The Kremlin won't allow it. You two have a deal—Kremlin enforced. You're not dumb enough—or angry enough—to buck that. Your men were shooting at Irina. You're on tape cursing them for missing her. Fuck that up too, Karp? You're building quite a track record."

I glared at him to make the point. He glared back with an intensity that told me I was on the right track.

"I heard the tape, just this afternoon. You don't mince words, Efim Ilyich. *'We won't get another shot at that used-up cunt. I should have finished her when I did her old man. She's just an old whore anyway. I've had more fun in a brothel.'*"

Irina said, "Efim?" Her voice was barely audible. Beneath the word was a tone of steel.

Konychev said quickly, "Irina, you have no idea . . . Don't listen to him. He's only . . ."

"STOP!"

"Has Uncle Efim told you about what happened that night on Tverskaya?" I asked.

"What?"

"The girl in the car. Tamara Konycheva, your cousin. I was there, like he said. I saw her. Three bullet holes in her back." I looked at Konychev. "You were having a good time in the back of that Mercedes. She get you off before she bought it?"

"He's lying, Irina! He doesn't know anything."

The shotgun swung in his direction.

"She was dressed for a night on the town, Irina. Dress, makeup, plenty of cleavage. How old was she, Konychev? Fourteen? Thirteen? What's too old for you, by the way?"

"You bastard . . . You told me . . ."

"Nothing's too young for Uncle Efim," I pressed. "You know that, Irina. This isn't the first time he's cheated on you? He keeps saying you're the only one, but he keeps sticking it in younger girls, doesn't he? How many times has he lied to you?

"You bastard. You fucking bastard."

She said it to me, but she meant it for him. I kept my eye on her trigger finger.

"Irina don't listen. He's manipulating you. You know I love you."

"SHUT UP!"

The shotgun wavered. Karp moved.

"DON'T!" I yelled.

The gun steadied—on Karp. "Back off, fucker," she said.

Karp took a step back.

"Is . . . Is it true?" she said. "Was Tamara in the car?"

"Irina, he's only trying . . ."

"IS IT TRUE?"

"It's on Ibansk.com," I said. "You follow that, don't you, Irina? Posted yesterday. Ivanov says Tamara was the girl in the car."

"IS IT TRUE, YOU BASTARD?"

"Irina, listen, I can explain. That's not what this is about."

"Tell me she wasn't there."

"Irina . . ."

"NO! Tell me she wasn't there. TELL ME!"

"She wasn't there."

He wasn't convincing. She wasn't buying.

"Bastard! Lying bastard!"

"If you don't want to talk about Tamara, how about her father?" I said.

Two heads swung toward me. Karp didn't budge. He was looking for an opening.

"I told Irina how his body was pulled from the Moscova three days ago. Fireplace poker through the chest. By the time that happened, he was happy to die. He'd been tortured, Irina, until he begged for it to end. Uncle Efim pulled your dad's fingernails out one by one. No more of those, he went on to his teeth.

He enjoyed it, your uncle did. So did Karp here. He did the dirty work. By the time they finally ran him through, there wasn't much of a man left."

"Irina . . . ," Konychev said.

"Is it true?"

"I said, don't listen."

"BULLSHIT!"

I'd finally broken her shell. She wasn't just angry anymore. Horror, real horror, terror mixed with fear, twisted her pretty face. The tough-girl façade fell away for good, leaving a broken, terrified teenager in its place.

I pressed on.

"You were there, weren't you, Irina? There was some kind of fight. You got swiped with that poker. Hurt like hell, didn't it? You were trying to protect your father, and Uncle Efim didn't care who he hurt. You were already an over-the-hill, trash-heap tart to him anyway."

"You said . . . You said it would be okay. You said nothing would happen. You said you needed to talk to him, business to clear up. YOU SAID YOU WEREN'T ANGRY ANYMORE!"

"Right before he pushed you out the door and started in on the fingers," I said.

"Irina, he's lying. He wasn't there. He doesn't know. He's making it all up. He wants to use you against me."

"IS IT TRUE?"

It's hard to watch anyone's world collapse in on itself, harder still if the person crushed is still in her teens. I shoved those thoughts aside and detonated another explosion.

"You shot your credibility on Tamara," I said to Konychev. "She was probably waiting for you back at your place."

"IS IT TRUE, GODDAMMIT?"

The shotgun slipped. Karp moved. Konychev too. Not fast enough. The gun came back up. The blast caught him square in the chest.

I lunged for Karp. I heard the pump and a second boom. My shoulder exploded in fiery pain.

Konychev fell against me and we went to the floor. Karp was on me in an instant. I tried to roll away, but he had me pinned. No chance against his strength. He pulled my lame arm. I flipped on my back. Pain clawed everywhere. I reached for the knife at my waist. Karp, sensing something, pulled in the other direction. I couldn't quite get there. Another crack of the pump, another boom. Karp's grasp loosened. I thought she'd shot him, but grabbed the knife anyway. He yanked my bad arm again as I got hold of the handle.

My shoulder popped. I fought the wave of pain, rolled and swung wildly. The knife buried itself in something. Karp howled and let go. I got my head up. Irina, fumbling with the box of shells in her lap, tried to reload. Karp was standing, knife shaft deep in his thigh. But he had his shotgun. I was looking into the barrel of eternity.

Joker's wild, ace high. He held the twelve-gauge ace.

"Die, *zek*."

In that instant they say you have, I saw Aleksei and Victoria and my own dangerous arrogance and the inevitability of the game. I'd been lucky before, but . . .

BOOM! BOOM!

Two more blasts. The first—half of Karp's chest exploded over me. He was still standing, still holding the shotgun, still grinning. The second blew out his remaining guts. The body weaved, blood spewing, until it keeled over, dead eyes filled with hatred.

I rolled left, out from under. Pain burned everywhere. Irina fumbled with her gun. I had to get to her . . . A cold wind blew through the room.

"NOBODY MOVE!" a voice shouted.

I wondered who he was yelling at and kept crawling.

"STOP!" the voice yelled.

"TURBO, STOP!"

A different voice. Victoria's. What was she doing here?

I kept crawling.

Irina rotated the shotgun, barrel up. Beria appeared behind her.

"No!" I tried to croak.

"TURBO!" Victoria called.

Irina worked the barrel around.

"Irina! No!" I cried. It came out a whisper.

She had the stock on the floor, between her feet, the barrel under her chin.

I pulled myself up. It seemed to take an hour. I used everything I had and lunged.

"TURBO, STOP!"

I grabbed at the gun stock as the room exploded. Beria vanished, along with Irina. I fell where her feet had been, thinking in one more blind instant whether it was worth it to still be in the game.

★ CHAPTER 53 ★

"You gonna open that package or not?"

Victoria's temperature was rising. Foos shook his head and moved a bishop.

Victoria turned back at the board. Foos grinned.

"Dammit! I should've seen . . . You are making it impossible. He's going to beat me, and it's your fault!"

The three of us sat around the chessboard in the open area of the office. Pig Pen's radio played quietly in the background. Foos and Victoria were settling into a pattern of Saturday afternoon matches, best three out of five. So far as I could tell, neither had yet to beat the other outright. Victoria was still figuring out offense, but she was an instinctive defensive player, and she regularly thwarted his attacks. I had the feeling she'd made a serious blunder, which as she said, was all my fault.

I stood and went to look again at the Malevich, still resting in its open shipping crate, outside Pig Pen's office. My shoulder tugged, but the pain was almost nothing now, two weeks later. My arm was in a sling, which made certain activities somewhere between awkward and difficult, to Victoria's alternating amusement and frustration. My injuries—dislocated shoulder and thirteen twelve-gauge pellets from Irina's shotgun, also my fault, of course—had delayed her reclaiming her apartment, so they were serving a purpose. I was rehabbing the dislocation, and the therapist said I was a quick healer. The wounds from the shotgun were healing according to their own schedule.

"It's a goddamned good thing we came by helicopter," Victoria had said as we flew south to a hospital. I hadn't counted on that, but the snow had moved out southwest to northeast. They'd found two Russians dead by the garage before her men dispatched Karp to an eternal fiery Gulag. I was grateful for their timely arrival but pissed, however irrationally, that they'd cheated me of the privilege. I kept that thought to myself.

I'd spent a tortured twenty-four hours, drugged to the gills, visited by a headless Irina, chestless Karp and Konychev, a paler-than-death Leitz, and a smiling Jenny Leitz who kept trying to tell me it was all okay. I found out later that the smiling woman was actually Victoria, who'd spent the entire time at my bedside trying to calm me as I twisted and screamed. Taras Batkin even put in a cameo, wearing Beria's rimless spectacles. *We know everything,* he said. *How could you ever doubt that?*

Sanity returned as the painkillers receded, but the images themselves were hard to shake. Especially Irina's, at that last moment when everything exploded.

"What about the package?" Victoria again.

The second delivery of the afternoon. A gray plastic shipping bag, Moscow return address—"Foreign Ministry, Russian Federation."

I opened the plastic to find a nine by twelve envelope inside. Addressed to me with a note.

In future, should you live so long, you might want to be careful what you ask for. TB.

"From Taras Batkin," I said.

"What's that bastard want?" she asked.

Batkin had flown the coop the day after the Millbrook Massacre, as the tabloids were calling it. I'd tried phoning him. I'd gone up to East Ninety-second Street once I was able to move again. The town house was shuttered. Ivanov reported, tongue planted firmly in cheek, that he'd been recalled by the Kremlin over a trade dispute.

"He's sending what he owed me," I said.

"He's lucky he got out of town," Victoria said. "What is it?"

"Answer to a question. I'm not sure I'm interested anymore, though."

She shook her head and went back to the game.

Leitz lived. Foos brought Andras into town where he stayed with his father in the hospital until the old man was released. Victoria said the authorities were undecided as to prosecuting either of them. They didn't have all the pieces—she blamed that on me as well—but she didn't push it. Everyone involved had suffered, and no one—including her—had much stomach for causing more pain. Her case against Batkin and BEC was dead, but the BEC was crippled and the ConnectPay database gave her two hundred thousand pedophiles to chase. She wasn't happy, but it was like chess with Foos. She didn't win, but she could declare some sort of moral victory and move on.

Batkin's envelope sat on the coffee table next to the chessboard. Inside was the answer to my parentage. Beria or not. Batkin's note suggested it was, in fact, Comrade Lavrenty Pavlovich, but he could be toying with me, one *zek* to another. I walked around the office thinking about whether and how much it mattered.

Malevich's luminous Suprematist rectangles, floating impossibly on their sea of incandescent white, erased the memory of Irina and Karp and Konychev, at least for the time being. The packing case had taken twice as long as the Repin's to get into. One useful arm didn't speed the process. Victoria arrived for her chess game shortly after Foos and I got it open.

"What's that?" she asked.

"Malevich. Remember?"

"Son of a bitch. *That's* eighty million dollars?"

"On the day Leitz bought it, yes."

"It's rectangles."

"That's right."

"You Russians are all fucking crazy."

"Eldo," Pig Pen said, watching from his office.

"Pig Pen's not Russian," I said.

"Last time I checked, Pig Pen was a parrot. What does he know?"

"Bayou Babe. Eldo," he said. He sounded as though his feelings were hurt.

"You going to argue?"

"I can't win. What are you going to do with it?"

"I'm not sure. Maybe hang it. Maybe send it back."

"Send it back?! You earned it. It's part of your fee."

"Leitz and I made a bet, although he doesn't like the word. He lost. But I'm not sure I won."

"You paid a hell of a price, however you account for it," she said and went to play her chess match.

I thought about losing and price. I hadn't lost, I told myself, and I more or less believed it. I hadn't been forced to fold my hand, even at the very end. My price seemed benign compared with those paid by others. Especially Jenny. And benign compared with the price yet to come—in Batkin's envelope on the coffee table.

Did I want to know the truth? And what would I do once I did?

357

The Leitzes kept sweeping truth under the rug—until there was no more time and no more room. If I left the envelope sealed, wasn't I committing the same sin?

If I was, I asked myself, wasn't I the only victim? What Aleksei didn't know at this point certainly wasn't going to hurt him.

Or was that just more Turbostian rationalization?

I finished unwrapping the Malevich with my good arm and carried it carefully to my office along with Batkin's envelope. I found some hooks and a hammer in the utility drawer in the kitchen. I sank two hooks at one end of the wall next to my desk and hung the painting. I sank another hook near the opposite corner, punched a hole in the envelope and hung it too. I could sense Beria trying to push his way into the room, he couldn't quite manage. Maybe he'd met his match in Malevich.

Victoria appeared at my side.

"Another draw?" I asked.

"Yes, one more." She looked from the painting to the envelope and back again. "What are you up to now?"

"Bookends."

"Bookends?"

She took my hand.

"Life bookends. For purposes of contemplation."

She snuggled under my good arm, hers around my waist.

"Where do I fit in?"

"We're working on that."

She smiled and I gave her a squeeze as I made another promise. This time, I swore I would keep it. On the day her picture went up—not too far in the future, I hoped—I'd take the envelope down and open it and confront the specter, real or imagined, of Lavrenty Pavlovich Beria.

★ ACKNOWLEDGMENTS ★

My thanks to Brendan Deneen, my editor at Thomas Dunne Books, as well as to Joan Higgins. I am grateful to Gwendolyn Bounds, Michael Bounds, Steve Heymann, and Bill Hicks, who read an early draft of this story, pointed out problems and suggested needed improvements.

Special thanks to Peggy Healy, Jonathan Rinehart, and Beverley Zabriskie for their generosity and hospitality. Thanks to my sister, Priscilla, and to Gerri Bowman and Katherine Page, two more generous individuals.

Once again, my love and gratitude to my wife, Marcelline, who so cheerfully puts up with me.